PRECIOUS PORCELAIN

by

NEIL BELL

" The precious porcelain of human clay "

BYRON

LYTHWAY PRESS
BATH

First published 1931
by
Victor Gollancz Ltd
This edition published by
Lythway Press Ltd
Combe Park, Bath
by arrangement with the copyright holder
1974

ISBN 0 85046 555 9

Printed in Great Britain by
Redwood Press Ltd, Trowbridge, Wiltshire
Bound by Cedric Chivers Ltd, Bath

To
BILL AND MARTIN
with love

CONTENTS

CHAPTER I

REGENERATION OF
TOM BLANEY

I

About eight o'clock on a misty October morning in the year of Victoria's jubilee the small fishing-boat *Janet* slipped over the sandbar that runs three miles north and south of the little east-coast fishing town of Blymouth.

Sam Blowers, kneeling in the bows, looked back over his shoulder to the crouched figure baling in the stern. " Your mother's on the cliff, Tom," he said.

In the lee of the cliffs the sail flapped feebly, the *Janet* lost way, a breaker lifted her, and with a grinding crunch she slid softly over the pebbles of the shallows till her bows were clear of the water. A second breaker slewed her stern half-round as the two men jumped out and began to hoist her up the beach over the greased iron of the runners or " ways " to the immemorial long-drawn call :

" E-e-e-e-e-e-yoh ! e-e-e-e-e-yoh ! "

During a pause Tom Blaney looked up and waved a hand to the shawl-wrapped figure on the cliff. The figure gesticulated with outspread explanatory fingers.

Blaney grunted and, with bent head, stared at the fish rolling from side to side in the wash of the bilge-water. The *Janet* was now on to the level. The two men quickened their steps as they ran her the last few yards. " That'll do, Sam," said Blaney. He straightened himself, kicked a " stool " under the boat's side, and leaning over, began to count the catch into a basket.

" Thirty-one, thirty-two, thirty-three, Jesus, what a catch ! and another mouth to feed, eh, Sam ? "

Blowers nodded. " So it's all right, huh ? What's it, a boy ? "

Blaney grinned. " Ay, unless she forgot which arm to wave," he replied.

" It's another mouth to feed, as you say, Tom," went on Blowers slowly, " but it's God's will, as the saying is, and He'll provide."

" God's will my foot ! " smiled Blaney sourly, " none of that ; *my* will if you like, or my damned luck. And I'll have to do the providing. But not just yet. The wife'll do that for a bit ; she knows her job. Pity they can't suck till they're grown-up—he'll be eating more'n I do before he's six."

" They say," observed Sam slowly, as they trudged up the cliff-path with the basket swinging between them, " they say a woman 'on't catch again while she's suckling."

" Oh, they do, do they," replied Blaney sarcastically, " well, they're liars. There's only a year between my first two—how's that ? "

" Lots of the women up round Norwich way," went on Sam, " keep their kids at the breast till they're nine or ten year. When I was butchering up by Boughton thirty years back my landlady was still breasting her boy. He was a fat, tall, strong kid of ten, and to see him come running in from school, and set-to his mother, used to fair make me sick."

" Your stomach's too soft," grinned Blaney, " you ought t'ave married and had a few kids and you'd not retch at anything then. We'll so long. Be in the *Gluepot* to-night and we'll wet his head."

Sam Blowers, shouldering the fish, set off slowly down the street, his crutch-boots thumping the paving, and the basket dripping a trail behind him. Blaney watched him out of sight, and then turning up the alley he opened the back-gate of his cottage and walked into the kitchen.

His heavy boots thudded on the red tiles. He threw half-a-dozen gutted herring into the sink. His sister, a thin, greying woman of fifty, hushed him with a raised hand.

" You saw mother ? " she asked.

Blaney nodded. " Ay," he replied, " how's Alice ? It *is* a boy ? "

" She's bad," said his sister, her eyes watching his face with an air of contemptuous hostility which the man ignored. " Yes, a boy. Born with a caul. That's lucky," she jeered.

Her brother looked at her unmoved. He smiled derisively. " You're right, Jane ; it'll fetch a bottle of whisky any night in the *Gluepot*. Where is it ? Can I see Alice ? "

" She's asleep," replied his sister. " After breakfast, perhaps. What do you want ? "

Blaney stretched his arms above his head and yawned. " My God," he said, " I could do with a couple of pints. For Christ's sake pour me out some tea. And I'll have a couple of the herring. Think Alice'd like one ? "

" Don't be a fool ! " snapped his sister ; " it's only God's providence Alice is here at all."

" Oh, dry up ! " growled Blaney, pouring himself out a cup of tea, and slopping the milk clumsily over the cloth. " I've heard enough about God this morning from Sam. God's will and God's providence and God knows what else."

" You'd be better employed down on your knees now than blaspheming," said his sister. " The babe needs God's help if you don't."

" What's the matter with it ? " asked Blaney, cutting four thick slices off the loaf, and looking round for the dripping-bowl.

" Dr. Venning is afraid there's little chance for it,"
replied his sister. " It was only six pounds. He had to use
instruments."

" He would," commented Blaney morosely, " he likes
'em. He's a damned old fool. So you think I ought to pray,
eh ? What for ? "

" You didn't need to ask what for when you were a boy,"
replied his sister, her voice softening. She went over to him
and put a hand on his arm. " Tom," she said, and waited.

He washed down the mouthful he was chewing with a
gulp of tea. " What ? " he said indifferently, not looking at
her.

" Tom, they think the babe'll not live. Tom . . . may I ? "

" May you what ? why the hell——" and then he laughed
harshly and thumped the table. " Oh, that's it. Bring Father
Dixon, eh ? That's the caper. No. Blast Father Dixon.
What d'ye think Alice'd make of that. That's been your
game ever since we were married. Alice 's chapel and always
has been, and so are the kids. Dammit, you know that well
enough, don't you ! "

" And what are you ? " asked his sister.

" Nothing," sneered Blaney. " To hell with it all."

" You're a Catholic, Tom, as you were brought up, and
you still are ; you can't help it. Tom," pleadingly, " let
me bring Father Dixon."

Blaney pushed back his chair. As he rose hurriedly he
rocked the table violently, upsetting his half-empty cup,
and sending the bread-platter crashing to the floor. He
wiped his mouth with the back of his hand and turned to his
sister. " Shut it ! shut it ! " he said thickly : " that's enough
of it. Now listen. Blast Father Dixon and damn all Catholics. Got that ? Now if there's another bloody word about
any of it you'll not cross my doorstep again."

" You needn't swear," replied his sister tonelessly. She

turned away. "You'd better cook your own breakfast; I've too much to do." She opened the door of the back-stairs, stepped through, and closing the door softly behind her, mounted to the room above. As the door shut the sickly scent of an anæsthetic drifted into the kitchen.

Blaney slammed the frying-pan over the fire, scooped into it some lumps of dripping, and dropping two of the gutted herring into the pan, leaned against the low mantel-piece and stared into the fire.

But Limbus was cheated of a soul, and despite the handicaps both medical and natural with which the new babe began life, it clung tenaciously to existence with its wizened claws, weathered the mauling of the instruments, and within a month had sucked its way to a triumphant seven pounds ten ounces.

It was christened Richard at the little methodist chapel on Blymouth Green, and the same evening Tom Blaney exchanged the caul in the *Gluepot* for a bottle of whisky, six pints of porter, and a packet of shag. He took the porter part of the way home with him, the packet of shag was seized and hurriedly discarded by a prowling gull just after dawn the following morning, and Coastguard Jackson swept up the pieces of a broken whisky bottle from the steps of the Coastguard station when he went on duty at six o'clock; he stared with gloomily appraising eye at the stain which ran down the steps and was lost in the dust at the foot.

2

By the time little Richard was five years old his father had drunk himself out of his part-ownership of the *Janet*. Several promising posts, forced on him by exasperated relatives, he had thrown up or lost; and his last venture, as secretary and treasurer of the local fishermen's benevolent society, had brought him to the gates of Yardley gaol—a last-minute relenting upon the part of the family and a loosening of meagre pursestrings alone saved him from entering that refuge of mistaken endeavour.

A family council now sat upon Tom Blaney's misdoings. Alice's mother, a wise and much-travelled old woman, whose kindness of heart had survived the death of illusion, came hurriedly from London to preside at the meeting.

The family council sat in crowded discomfort in the small parlour of the Blaneys' cottage. There were present Tom and Alice, his sister Jane, his mother, his elder brother Fred, his father's brother Robert and Mrs. Benson, Alice's mother.

Tom sat in the window half-facing his judges. Without moving his head he could look out over the tiny garden to the sea. He had been born and reared in the cottage, and it was a view he had known all his life.

Fred Blaney, who kept the thriving grocer's shop in the little market-place, stood up, cleared his throat nervously, and began to speak. At his first words Tom shifted slightly in his chair, and with a truculently upthrust chin turned his head away and stared at the sea. A little disconcerted, Fred halted and stumbled for a moment, but quickly recovering himself, he resumed his task.

" I am only saying, I am sure," he went on, " what we all think. I am not going to blame anyone ; it is too late for that now. What we have to do, and I am sure we are all agreed——"

" Shut up ! " cried Tom, turning suddenly from the window. " I'll take nothing from you, you smug swine. How much did you give to keep me out of gaol ? How much——"

" I gave it freely," interrupted Fred, his face white, and

his fingers tapping on the table. " I do not want you to——"

" Sit down, damn you ! " Tom shouted, getting slowly to his feet. " I'll have my say first. I'll hear what you've got to say afterwards ; it's all cut and dried, I'm sure. You found me jobs, eh ? half-a-dozen of them. Well thank you very much for nothing. What were they, eh ? Starvation jobs—about a quid a week, which I gave to Alice. I've not had a drink for six months, and the only smoke I've had was some counter-sweepings that dear Fred sent along to Alice for me. And then I found a better job for myself——"

" I don't see how you can call it a better job, my boy," said his uncle Robert gravely, " when you had to take money that didn't belong to you to make the books balance."

" All right, Uncle Bob," said Tom. " I've no quarrel with you ; I've told you, all of you, dozens of times, that I'd advanced money here and there and never got it back."

" But you'd nothing to prove it," observed Mrs. Benson ; " and they all denied it."

" Ay," sneered Tom, " they let me down. Oh, I know you don't believe it. Well, I don't care. Damn the lot of you. You saved me from prison, eh? What for ? Did I ask you to. To save the good name of the family, that was it. Good name my foot. You can——"

" We never pretended it was for your sake," broke in Jane. " And, if you'd like to know, I was against it. A dose of prison would have done you a world of good. But——"

" Oh, dry up, Jane," jeered Tom. " Well, it seems to me we're quits : You all saved me from prison, and I saved your good name. Quits."

" Sit down, Tom," said Mrs. Benson quietly ; " and let's have no more of your nonsense. I'll tell you what we've settled, and I'll tell you also that bluster won't help you. It was the worst day's work Alice ever did to marry you ;

but it's too late to help that now. I thought you a bit of a waster then, but I deceived myself into thinking, God help me for an old fool, that marriage might make a man of you. As if I didn't know it never did for any man and never will do. But I went on being an old fool, and hoped the children would bring you to your senses. You've four now. And you're a bigger waster than ever. I don't know if you've got any good in you, any manhood at all. It's a hard thing to say, but I can't see any. Well, enough of that. There's a job going for you at Barham in the dockyard. It's a good job, and if you like to stick to it, a permanent one. You've served your apprenticeship to boat-building, and you're a clever workman, I'll say that for you. Well, it's in the boat-building shop. To-day's the 25th, and you can begin on the first of July. We'll pay your fare and give you enough for a fortnight's lodging. The wages are thirty-five shillings a week, and out of that you'll send fifteen to me in London. This will help towards the support of Alice and the four children, who are coming to live with me. If at the end of a year you are still in work, have given up the drink, and are prepared to make a home for your wife and children, why, then, we're all prepared to let bygones be bygones. We don't want or expect you to give an answer at once. Think it over, and try to believe we're not your enemies."

Tom sat with his back to them looking out over the sea. He forgot the family council behind him. His mind went drifting back in a sort of desperate longing, a stabbing nostalgia, over the whole course of his life in Blymouth. He could not think clearly. His mind only worked in spasmodic leaps, as he visualised one scene after another. How could he leave Blymouth ? Was that what they wanted him to do ? Did his mother want it ? And Alice ? His truculence had drained from him. He was now a child, cornered, and about to be beaten. An immense self-pity flooded him. His face worked. He put up one hand to his mouth and sat very still.

There was the sound of a chair scraping softly over the drugget. " Well, now ; I think," Uncle Robert was beginning, when Tom turned round and faced them. He looked from Mrs. Benson to his mother, and from his mother to Alice. He licked his lips. His glance wandered from his uncle's good-natured disturbed face to the pale righteousness of his brother's. He flung out a hand toward Fred. " Snot ! " he cried, beside himself, " you snot ! By Christ—" he broke off suddenly and turned to his mother. " You want me to go, mother, eh ? "

" I don't *want* you to go, Tom," she replied briskly, " but you *ought* to go ; you know it. It's a good job, and you know we can't——"

He put up his hands to his ears. Then he looked over to his wife. " Are you in this ? " he asked huskily.

" You needn't ask Alice," interrupted Mrs. Benson, " she's willing, more than willing. And if——"

" I'm asking her, not you," shouted Tom. " She's my wife, isn't she. And they're my kids." His voice trailed away. " Alice, are you on their side ? "

" I'm not on anyone's side," his wife replied listlessly ; " but, Tom, something must be done. We can't go on as we've been doing. We *must*——"

Tom turned away and sat back in his chair. " That's enough ; stow it," he said. " Well, you've had your say, you bloody monkeys, and here's mine. I'm not leaving Blymouth. Alice is not leaving Blymouth, nor are the kids. She's my wife, and they're my kids, and where I am they're going to be. That's the law. Your jobs ? Shall I tell you what you can do with your jobs ? " He made an obscene gesture. " Ay, *that* to you and your jobs. Now what are you going to do about it ? "

Bp

" I am going back to London to-morrow," said Mrs. Benson quietly, " and Alice and the children are going with me. What are *you* going to do about it ? "

" You can't do it," said Tom desperately ; " it's against the law ; by God, you try it, that's all ! "

" Can you support your wife and family ? " went on Mrs. Benson. " You know you can't. Are they going into the Union ? For all you care, I suppose. Well, your wife is my daughter, and *I* care, if you don't. She comes with me to London, and as she won't be happy without the children, why, they come too."

" It doesn't matter about my happiness," muttered Tom.

" It doesn't, at present," rejoined Mrs. Benson. " Make a home for your wife and children, you've a good chance now, and then you can talk about your happiness. Now then."

And suddenly Tom Blaney was grovelling on his knees by his wife's chair, snatching at her hands, sobbing pitifully, horribly, disgustingly. " Don't leave me, Alice," he cried. " Christ, don't leave me ; I can't bear it. Alice, don't do it. I'll work for you. I'll go to Barham, if you'll come with me." He pulled at her hands, holding them to his mouth. She sat quite still, saying nothing. He held her hands away and stared up at her despairingly. " You'll come with me, Alice," he pleaded, his mouth working. She shook her head slowly, and he began to cry out like a whipped child, rocking backward and forward upon his knees.

Mrs. Benson put out a hand and shook him roughly. " Get up, Tom, do," she said not unkindly ; " aren't you ashamed ; get up. You're only upsetting yourself and Alice. She can't come with you to Barham ; you know that as well as I do. Go and make a home for her and at the end of the year——"

" Six months," cried Tom miserably ; " say six months

and I'll do it." Beside himself he turned his face from one to another. " Six months," he said, over and over again. " Mother, say six months. Alice, will that do ? Isn't that enough ? Alice, mother, I'll do anything you ask."

Mrs. Benson looked at Alice, then at Tom's mother, at Uncle Robert and again at Alice. " Very well, Tom," she said, " six months, then, and please God we're not making a mistake."

3

Despite the improbability of the feat, despite Mrs. Benson's doubts, and his brother's incredulity, Tom Blaney stuck to his job at Barham, reduced his drinking to a mere Saturday evening pint, worked for fourteen years in the dockyard boat-building shop, and brought up his family of four within, if but just within, the pale of decency and respectability. There was one period of five months during which that pale narrowed until the family balanced precariously on the last foothold overhanging the deep of destitution. It was during the winter of 1894-5. The naval estimates for the year had been cut down, and new building was postponed indefinitely. At the end of October twelve hundred men, Tom among them, were discharged from the dockyard, and for the five months of that bitter winter Hunger, flat-bellied, gaunt and wolfish, haunted a thousand homes in Barham and Bellingham.

Richard, then a pallid shrimp of seven, remembered all his days the Saturday when his father came home from the dockyard with the news of his discharge. It was just after half-past twelve. The four children, Agnes aged thirteen, Jane twelve, George ten, and Richard, sat at the table, which was laid for dinner. Alice stood at the fireplace, ready to take the suet-pudding out of the saucepan as soon as Tom's knock came at the door. The dockyard was two miles from Bellingham, the small town where the Blaneys lived, and Tom prided himself on doing the distance under the half hour. Richard always went to the door on Saturdays to let his father in, and he looked upon it as a black day when he could not wheedle a penny from his father's limited store.

Richard sat on the edge of his chair, his toes reaching down toward the floor, his hands grasping the chair at each side ready for a spring. The familiar knock sounded, and he sprang from his chair, and ran along the passage to the front door. He turned the stiff milled brass knob and pulled the door toward him. He smiled at his father, and held up his face to be kissed.

His father did not seem to notice him, but pushing by, strode heavily along the passage, leaving Richard to close the door before he trotted in pursuit.

But when Richard reached the kitchen his father was already sluicing himself noisily at the scullery sink, and his mother was placing the pudding on the table, and handing the gravy-boat to Agnes to serve.

They heard their father pulling roughly at the squeaking roller-towel. That was the signal mother was waiting for. She served the suet-pudding, and Agnes ladled the gravy over each portion. Presently Tom came in washed and brushed, with his shirt-sleeves still rolled up. He took his seat, picked up his spoon and fork, and the meal began.

As long back as Richard could remember, for the Blymouth days were already the dimmest of memories less real than any of his dreams, this had been the Saturday dinner routine, and any variation did not occur to him as a possibility. It was like school and bed and the church-bells on Sunday—things not subject to whim or desire but as inevitable as the sunrise and as steadfast as the house.

He bent over his plate, gobbling down the pudding, which he assisted on to his spoon with his fingers when no one was looking. He always left the gravy till he had finished the pudding. He was thinking what a mingy piece mother had given him, not half as big as George's, when his father made a horrible grunting noise. Richard looked up and laughed. And then he stopped laughing. His father was making the ugliest faces, was holding his spoon and fork stiffly away from him, and was staring at the ceiling.

Richard heard his two sisters cry out, saw his brother trying to push back his chair, saw a dreadful look which he did not understand pass over his mother's face.

He screamed " Father ! father ! " Tom Blaney grunted again, and then, rising from his chair, staggered against the table, stretched out his hands toward Alice, and crumpling suddenly, fell on the hearth rug and lay still.

It seemed a long while before his father opened his eyes and presently, helped by Alice, made his way to the sofa. The children watched from the table in a sort of scared and foreboding horror. Richard saw his father shake his head, heard him say, " I've got it," watched his mother's thin, white face grow more drawn, and then, for the first time in his life, he saw and heard in appalled disgust his father cry.

He was to see his father faint many times during the next five months, and often enough in the years that followed. A dozen times afterward he was to see him cry. But no other scene in his life so cut itself into his memory as that emotional surrender. The tears rolling down the great unshaven cheeks, the working mouth, the grotesquely distorted speech, built up a thing of such unnatural abomination that it remained with him for many years as some loathsome obscenity outside the decencies of ordinary human ways. It was not until the war that he had an experience that matched its intensity of disgustful outrage.

Richard was the last of the family to be at school. By

the time he was twelve, his elder sister, Agnes, had gone to London into a commercial college, Jane had begun as a teacher, and George had entered the printing establishment of the *Bellingham Observer*.

During his last two years at school he was taught by a hard-working schoolmaster named Elman, who combined strong disciplinary views with sadistic tendencies of extreme lusciousness. Elman, an elderly bachelor, an abstainer and a non-smoker, had but two joys in life, eating and thrashing ; but these two joys he savoured with the palate of a gourmet.

Round the schoolroom in which Elman taught ran a wooden wainscoting about three feet in height. Many knots at varying heights from the ground were scattered over the wood. Elman would call out an erring boy, measure him with an appraising and voluptuous eye, point to a knot, and say in a soft purring voice, " Put your head to that." The boy having placed his head down, Elman would advance upon him softly, and with a delicate touch lift back the jacket from his posterior. He would then stand back, swish his cane, lick his lips and begin to hum. Suddenly he would stride forward swiftly, and smite with unerring precision. Sometimes he would repeat the dose, and at times, when lust had him at its mercy, he would strike again and again, his eyes shining, his mouth agape, and the sweat running down his face. At times a boy would faint or pass water. The class watched these orgies in a state of sick dismay which held a suspicion of some nastiness beyond its understanding.

The first time that Richard received this punishment, the unexpected pain of the stroke made him leap into the air with so quaint a cry of torment that the class burst into quickly stifled laughter. This saved Richard, for Elman, who at another time would have given him two more for buffoonery, spotted a very plump boy grinning broadly, and sated the rest of his desire upon a more attractive anatomy.

At fourteen Richard entered the Barham dockyard as an apprentice. He stayed there four months, was several times in trouble with the authorities, and as the result of a stabbing affray in which he defended himself from a disgusting practical joke common among apprentices, he left the dockyard and became a pupil teacher in the first Board School built in Bellingham.

At eighteen he entered a metropolitan training college for schoolmasters, and after two years there he obtained his diploma, and was appointed to a school in a suburb of North London.

By this time Tom Blaney was dead and the family had removed to Woodgate, a suburb a few miles within the Essex border. George now held a fairly responsible post in the art department of Fawcett and Green, the publishers in Ave Maria Lane. Agnes was a civil-service clerk in the General Post Office Savings Bank Department, and Jane was a teacher in a slum school down at the east end docks.

The family lived in a small villa. It was a crowded nest. Alice, now somewhat enfeebled from her long struggle with life, occupied a bedroom on the ground floor. Agnes and Jane shared the front bedroom, George had the only other bedroom of any size, while Richard had to content himself with a box-room some ten feet by eight, with no fireplace and but one small window.

This family life in the small villa at Woodgate was an uneasy association, an affair of bickering, of frayed tempers, of unwarrantable interferences, of sullen compromises that brooded on fancied wrongs for weeks, until some uncontrollable outburst brought a measure of short-lived relief.

Edgham, where Richard taught in an elementary school, was eight miles from Woodgate, and he cycled every day in all weathers. He brought to the task of teaching a youthful enthusiasm, a real liking for children, an unusual ability as a draughtsman, and an equally unusual command of English. These two valuable gifts were a heritage from Tom Blaney, but they were counterbalanced by paternal gifts, less admirable and certainly less useful—prodigality, physical laziness, and a disinclination to face reality which is often coupled with cowardice and invariably with lying. But these dubious legacies from Tom Blaney were restrained by a leaven from his mother of caution, doggedness, pluck and integrity. He was nevertheless Tom Blaney's child rather than Alice's.

The result of the coming together of Tom Blaney and Alice was indeed a sardonic commentary upon the pseudo-scientific claims of the eugenists. Had Tom lived a hundred years later he would probably have been sterilised before he was allowed to marry, if, indeed, he were allowed to exist. He was plainly a shiftless, lazy, drunken voluptuary, a liar, a false friend, capable of any cozenage. That he was clever with his hands did not outweigh these disabilities, for manual cleverness is no more than the dexterity of monkeydom.

Alice was a truthful, diligent, essentially clean and honest person. She was emotionally cold and sexually indifferent.

And Tom Blaney married her, and certainly loved her all his days. For nothing else but love could have forced his shiftlessness into the fourteen years hard labour which he performed more or less cheerfully at Barham.

The four children of these two sharply contrasted beings were undoubtedly finer products than they should have been, according to all the hypotheses. The mark of Alice lay upon the offspring more deeply, more indelibly, than the mark of Tom. Agnes was all her mother ; Jane had merely a tendency to her father's laziness ; and George bore but the merest touch of his father's hand. Only upon Richard could the eugenists have gazed with satisfaction—a very mild and tempered satisfaction.

The war came and passed. George served four years in the H.A.C., and Richard a similar period in the R.A.M.C. Both came back physically unscathed, but marked and changed as all the men who took part in that struggle were marked and changed.

George returned to Fawcett and Greens as head of the Art department. Richard went back to his old school.

Agnes was now a Principal Clerk in the Post Office Savings Bank Department and Jane was the head-mistress of her slum school. Alice, now seventy, although physically much impaired, was extraordinarily alert mentally, and was enjoying to the full the comforts she was for the first time in her life able to command.

Richard had made no advance at schoolmastering. He still taught a congested class of eight-year-old boys in a stuffy class-room. He had, however, obtained some repute as a poet. The year before the war he began to contribute verse to *The Saxon Review* under the famous editorship of Harold Austin. It was at the time when Masefield's *Widow in a Bye Street* and *The Everlasting Mercy* had shaken Fleet Street into attention, and verse and verse-making had had a brief popularity, even rising to the dignity of a place in the news. During the war Blaney continued to write verse for Austin's Review and some others, and was numbered among that bright band of gallant ephemera, the war poets. After his return he wrote verse and prose for a few of the staider monthlies, contributed occasional light verse to *Punch*, and wrote controversial articles on war, politics, and education for the more intelligent of the Sunday papers.

It was a poem of his in *The New World* which had brought him a letter from John Arthur Sayers, the playwright ;

and had led to his friendship with Rachel Chesson, the dramatist's very efficient private secretary.

By the summer of 1924 Richard was sick of his job, disillusioned, on bad terms with his headmaster, and his habits and opinions were so barely tolerated at home that only by refraining from comment upon matters under discussion did he avoid an open breach with his family. He had that Easter become engaged to Rachel.

He was at this time thirty-seven years of age, slim, of medium height, pale, grey-eyed, with a shag of long black hair, and clean-shaven except for the short side whiskers affected by the literary group to which he gave a perfunctory allegiance. Although he did not drink heavily the amount he took, little as it was, was beyond his capacity. Drinking was for him a dangerous habit as it exhilarated him, moved his emotions profoundly, inspired him, and endowed him with a facile, fiery and whirlwind vocabulary unknown to him in his sober hours.

Such was Richard Blaney, and such were the elements that had gone to his making, when on a dull, cold, wet morning toward the end of October he opened a door, literally and figuratively, that was to lead him beyond the bounds of human comprehension.

CHAPTER II

HOW RICHARD CAME TO WELLING

I

The actual door that Richard opened on the morning of October 27 was the entrance door to the hall of Banton Lane Council School, at Edgham, North London.

Banton Lane was one of those huge, barrack-like buildings that were erected in thousands in England between the years 1900 and 1914. " Free education for the people," wrote Richard in a pseudonymous article in *Progress*, " was no new thing ; it had been growing slowly and steadily for a generation before the new century dawned ; but following the Boer War, and the awakening of the English to the fact that all was not too well, there had been a sudden passionate rush for intellectual, spiritual and social betterment.

" It was a fruitful and happy time for the crank, the prophet, the uplifter and the pedagogue in all his manifestations. The notion that any improvement must begin with the child soon became the one sure popular appeal in public speeches, in articles in the Press, and in political propaganda.

" There was a phase when the educational systems of other civilised countries were scrutinised and compared with our own. Wonderful statistics were compiled, amazing deductions drawn, and a final verdict given which completely damned the English method root and branch. The French was more intensive and more catholic, the German more thorough and more in touch with modern conditions, the

American more scientific, and the Dutch more cultural. The crown went, however, to Scotland with such a fanfare of trumpets that the bewildered Scots were themselves deluded into a renewal of faith in a system they had begun to despise.

" The first definite concrete result of this morbid dissatisfaction of England with itself was the gigantic crop of elementary schools. They were to be our first line of attack upon (or our outworks of defence against, it was never made quite clear which) the superiority of the rest of the world.

" And so all over the country those barracks sprang into being. Pleasant old gentlemen called them the first rung of the educational ladder. ' We will put the feet of the poorest child securely upon that rung,' they declaimed, ' and thence he may mount steadily up ! up ! up ! ' The speaker usually gesticulated with his hand to show the ascent, ending, without humorous intent, with the hand waving in the air. It was not, however, that the educational ladder ended in the air that was its chief drawback, but that the step from the first rung to the second was beyond the stride of most of the children who filled the elementary schools. Some of the brightest and cleverest might reach a secondary school, and here and there a few brilliant ones get to Oxford or Cambridge, but the public school was out of their reach. And, when all is said and done, four years at an English public school is, at its best, a fruitful human experience, lacking which a man is, in the present state of human society, incomplete."

Banton Lane was typical of its kind. It sheltered eleven hundred and fifty children—boys, girls and infants. It was, in fact, three separate buildings, each with its own staff, head, and organisation.

Edgham was what is called a working-class district.

This quaint and excessively English compound-word embraces the destitute, the unemployed, the criminal, the unemployable, the casual labourer, the mechanic, the skilled craftsman, the small tradesman and the clerk. But where the working-class ended and the professional class began no man knew. The tramp by the roadside and the judge upon the bench might both claim membership without loss of dignity—elsewhere between these two extremes there was but troubled water for the social fisherman, as writer, orator, or political opportunist.

What " working-class district " meant, in so far as it affected Banton Lane School, and in consequence Richard, was a less complex affair. It meant that of the fifty boys in his class the fathers of six would be permanently out-of-work, the fathers of ten only casually employed, and most of the others earning about forty to fifty shillings a week. More, it meant that at least ten boys belonged to a family that lived in one room, and another ten in two rooms. The fifty boys would include five boys whose fathers had run away, three love-children, a tradesman's by-blow, a number of congenital syphilitics, and probably an incestuous child. This last was usually the offspring of a brother and sister belonging to families occupying but one room, rarely the child of a father and daughter.

Such was Richard's class of eight-year-olds at Banton Lane Council School, and such were the other classes. Roughly speaking, it meant that about a quarter of the boys were well-fed, warmly-clad and dry-shod ; a quarter were sufficiently fed, clad and shod ; and the other half included all the stages from thin and shabby down to starved and verminous raggedness.

The morning was cold, foggy, and wet. Richard was fifteen minutes late. The boys, assembled in the hall, had finished prayers, and as he walked along the corridor a

piano began to play " Land of Hope and Glory," the doors
of the hall were flung upon, and the boys began to march
out class by class to their rooms.

Richard stood aside to watch them pass. He watched
their feet. He stared fascinated. Never before had he
realised the fantastic and mercilessly revealing nature of
boots and shoes. Here were a hundred grotesque caricatures,
the litter of lumber cupboards, the harvest of dumps and
dust-heaps. There were sound boots, whole boots, broken
boots, wrecks of boots ; boots patched and sewn hopefully,
boots abandoned despairingly ; boots with half a sole, boots
with no sole, boots tied with string, boots laceless and
gaping. There were men's boots shuffling clumsily, women's
boots trodden over and shapeless, button boots, elastic-
sided boots, and raffish ruins of patent leather ; and there
were cloth slippers, decayed dancing-pumps, and sand-
shoes.

Richard looked up. His own class was passing him. They
grinned at him in friendly fashion and he smiled back,
frowning in mock fierceness at a garrulous youngster out of
step. They were the last out of the hall. He followed them
into the classroom, waited a few moments until they had
settled down more or less quietly, and then, admonishing
them not to talk, he returned to the now vacant hall.

He walked along the corridor and opened the hall-door.

He stared at the floor of the hall. Except for a dry space
about two feet wide all round the hall the boards were
soaked and muddy. He walked over toward the piano,
treading cat-like as if he could feel the water. The music
was still open on the rest. He looked at it and smiled wryly.

He heard a step behind him and turned to find Dale,
another of the staff, a small sandy pallid man in the early
fifties, standing behind him.

" Want to borrow it ? " asked Dale, touching the book.

Richard shook his head, "Land of Hope and Glory," he said, "My God!"

"It's a damned good march," said Dale. "What d'you mean, my God?"

Richard pointed to the soaked flooring. "Look at that," he said, "why half the poor little —— must have been on their socks, if they'd got any. And it's a damned fine morning. Land of Hope and Glory."

Dale laughed. "Come off it, Blaney," he said; "they must march to something. What do you want? 'The Red Flag?' They'd still have wet feet. And they don't feel it. It does 'em good to rough it. If it hurts you so much why don't you buy 'em all nice strong boots. You've a bee in your bonnet about kids. Half-baked socialism. Mostly tripe. It's like that stuff of yours in this month's *New Era*. What do you think you're driving at? I wonder you don't chuck it, if you think like that about your job."

"Like what?" asked Richard.

"Why, that gibberish of yours which you've nerve enough to call *The Schoolmaster*. How you get it published, God only knows. Who's the editor, a Chink?"

"Have you read it?" asked Richard, smiling.

"I've done my best," chuckled Dale; "the old man showed it to me; he's got a copy down in his room. He calls it 'selling the pass.' He'll sock it into you my lad before long. You know his little ways."

Richard smiled. "Look here, Dale," he was beginning when a bell rang.

"Damn!" said Richard, "and I've not marked my registers." He moved away to the door, leaving Dale turning over the leaves of the music-book. Richard had his hand upon the hall-door, when Dale sang out, "Ever read Samuel Butler?"

Richard looked over his shoulder. "Bits," he said.

" Well, read some more," replied Dale ; " he'd discarded all your sort of flapdoodle before he began to write. Now he *was* a man. He made Shaw and——" But Richard had slammed the door behind him.

Twenty minutes later Webb, the headmaster, entered Richard's classroom. Webb was a short, stiffly-built man of fifty-five, with a bushy brown moustache, bushy eyebrows, and bright blue eyes. He was rather taciturn, mumbling through his moustache when he did speak. He always wore a cut-away coat of a by-gone fashion, striped trousers, a high double collar and a black tie. The tie usually drooped so as to show the brass stud fastening his collar, and the collar itself often had the flap outside instead of inside the turnover. He always wore his bowler hat in school, never removing it in any circumstances other than a visit from His Majesty's Inspector. He walked with a rather bird-like strut.

He did not dislike Richard, but considered him conceited, lazy, and a poor disciplinarian. Richard thought him a pompous ass, a time-server and a hypocrite. Webb's evaluation was nearer the truth than Richard's.

" Good-morning, Mr. Blaney," mumbled Webb ; " cycle break down ? "

Richard smiled. " Not this time," he replied, " it was raining so fast at Woodgate that I came by train, and the train was delayed by fog."

" Very unfortunate," jocosely, " cane the boys for being late, and then their teacher comes late. Very tiresome. Shall have to cane you one morning, Mr. Blaney, eh ? "

Richard smiled uneasily. " Why cane them for coming late ? " he said.

Webb raised his eyebrows, but did not reply. He sat down in the chair at the table, placed the cane he was carrying in front of him, clapped his hands and said, " Pens down, 'ands be'ind."

The forty-eight little boys obeyed quickly, and sat staring owlishly at the headmaster. A few looked at Richard, who was standing behind Webb. He frowned at them, shaking his head.

" You might give out some slips of paper, Mr. Blaney," said Webb : " and we'll see how the tables are getting on. What are they doing now ? "

" They know up to nine times, and the pence table to one hundred," replied Richard,—"at least, I hope so," he added.

" Well, I hope so, too," observed Webb drily ; " they must know their tables or they'll get nowhere." He began to jot down figures on the back of an envelope.

Presently when all the boys had their slips, Webb took up one, and held it in front of him. " Now then," he said, " name on top—no ! no ! not yet ; wait. Name on top, and then : one, two, three, four, five, six, on this side. Turn over. Seven, eight, nine, ten, eleven, twelve on the other. All understand ? Very good. Do it."

Within ten minutes the table-test was over, the slips collected, and Webb sat at the table marking them while Richard continued the lesson.

In a while Webb shuffled the slips together, stood up, and walked over to where Richard was standing by his desk. " Just set them to some silent reading, Mr. Blaney," he said, " I want to talk about these."

Soon the class was bent over its books, eyes glued to the page, but ears alert to catch the low conversation that was beginning at Richard's desk.

" This won't do at all, you know," began Webb, tapping the sheaf of slips with his finger. " One boy with twelve right, two with eleven, none with ten, none with nine, six with eight, six with seven, five with six, eight with five, none with four, none with three, one with two, six with one

CP

and thirteen with none. Average just over four—about 35 per cent. What do you think of it ? "

"Not much," replied Richard, "but it's what I expected."

Webb frowned. "You said they knew them," he remarked.

"I said I hoped so," rejoined Richard.

"Hope is no weapon for a teacher's armoury," observed Webb sententiously.

"It's about all that's left to him," said Richard warmly.

"I'm afraid I don't follow," said Webb.

Richard shrugged his shoulders. "Oh, well ! " he said. And then he smiled. "Hope, why of course : Land of Hope and Glory."

Webb flushed. "I'm afraid," he was saying, when Richard interrupted, "Did you notice the hall floor this morning ? "

"I can't say I did, Mr. Blaney," snapped Webb, his temper fraying ; "what was the matter with it ? "

"It was soaked," said Richard loudly.

"Doubtless," replied Webb, "it usually is on wet mornings. I thought we were discussing this rather deplorable result," and he flapped the sheaf of slips on the desk. "Let us keep to the point."

"That *is* the point," said Richard. A flush began to mount in Webb's wrinkled face, but Richard went on rapidly. "The kids don't know their work. I agree, they don't. To expect them to do so is to expect the impossible. They're underfed, ill-fed, badly clothed and deplorably shod. Their physical condition renders them unfit to profit by instruction. You're asking the impossible."

"Indeed," replied Webb ; "well, Mr. Blaney, the impossible is being performed in all the other classrooms of the school. How do you account for that ? "

Richard looked at him narrowly. "Do you want me to account for it ? " he asked savagely.

" Of course," replied Webb.

Richard flushed. " By God, then," he began and stopped. " I'd rather not," he said lamely.

" That's wise of you," commented Webb. He tore up the slips of paper and dropped them into the waste-paper basket. " Well, Mr. Blaney," he said, " the impossible must be done in this room as elsewhere. And, while we're on the subject, there are a few other matters. It's not merely tables that are unsatisfactory. The arithmetic is bad, the geography is bad, and the drawing, well," he spread his hands, " frankly, I don't understand what you're driving at with the boys. I grant you are a clever draughtsman yourself, but," he shrugged his shoulders. " Finally, the discipline in this classroom is *bad* ; there's no other word for it. There's always a noise in the room. It can be heard in the corridor. Has it not occurred to you that this one factor is the cause of the others ? "

" You think the discipline's bad because the boys are noisy ? " asked Richard calmly.

" Obviously," replied Webb ; " what other explanation can you offer ? "

" This," said Richard ; " they're quiet and attentive when I want them to be. In odd moments I see no reason why they shouldn't talk."

" There shouldn't be odd moments," replied Webb.

" Hell," said Richard softly.

Webb reddened angrily. " I beg your pardon ? "

" Oh, nothing," said Richard.

Webb fingered his drooped tie. Richard's fingers itched to take the creased piece of silk and tie it decently. " Well, Mr. Blaney," Webb said, turning to move away, " if the boys are quiet and attentive when you want them to be it is, I think, a pity you don't want it more often."

He moved with short tripping steps toward the door. To

Richard's eyes his back view seemed pompously triumphant, smug, hypocritical. Webb opened the door, passed
through, and was closing it behind him, when Richard
strode after him, and putting his head out, said furiously,
" Mr. Webb, this is my room, and while I'm in it I shall
teach as I think fit. If you object you know what to do."

Webb looked over his shoulder. " Thank you, Mr.
Blaney, I can assure you I need no reminder on *that*
point."

As Richard closed the door and walked back to his desk
a buzz of subdued conversation broke out. He made no attempt to suppress it, but stood staring out over the
chimney-pots of the surrounding tenements.

As Webb went down the corridor with his little strutting
bird-like steps a faint smile hid itself behind his bushy
moustache.

2

The Blaneys usually reached home in the evening round
about six o'clock, and had their meal at seven. It had in the
beginning been a sort of high-tea, was referred to as tea,
and was eaten as soon after six as they were ready. In the
course of time, however, the hour had gradually become
seven, the tea side of the meal vanished, it was called, and
was, in fact, dinner. Since the war Richard had developed
the annoying habit of a warm bath before this meal, an
affectation which the builder's peculiar economy of combining bathroom and lavatory rendered exasperating to his
brother and sisters. But indeed the whole family life was a
series of petty annoyances and exasperations, and it was
only the accumulated inertia of years of living together
which prevented at least the two men from breaking away.
That George, who was quite comfortably off, and could
easily have afforded a flat of his own, should put up with a

poky little bedroom, and share a sitting-room with an uncongenial brother, was a source of constant amazement to his friends. That Richard, whose untidy habits, downright opinionativeness, preoccupied egotism, and occasional brutal franknesses of speech, should not have been turned out long since was equally amazing to the somewhat prim, precise and virtuous respectability of his sisters' friends.

Nevertheless this seven o'clock meal was usually a sociable and pleasant enough affair. It began quietly, and with a certain slight tension, for all were tired and hungry. But, provided the first ten minutes were achieved without disaster, it generally progressed into an enjoyable half-hour. George drank whisky with his meal, and under its influence developed an affable if rather trying facetiousness. Richard drank hock or sauterne, when he was flush, and at other times a small Guinness. The two sisters drank milk, and all four ended the meal with coffee. While her children ate, Mrs. Blaney sat by the fire sipping weak China tea, listening to the talk and adding to the general conversation her contribution of household news, tradesmen's chat, the doings of Peter the cat, and the misdoings of Jerry the Irish terrier. When these were exhausted she would, if the opening occurred, tell her dreams of the previous night. Her dreams were particularly noteworthy for their extreme vividness, their inordinate length, and their utter incomprehensibility.

But this cold October evening things went wrong all the way. George, who was going to the theatre, wanted to shave in the bathroom at the very moment when Richard was stretched out comfortably boiling. They were both late down for dinner, and were both annoyed to find their soup had been served and was half-cold.

" We thought we heard you coming down ten minutes ago," said Jane, as Richard pushed his soup aside and began crumbling his bread on to the cloth. " But mother will heat it for you. Is yours cold, George ? "

" Iced bouillon ; I like it ! " grinned George, who had poured himself out a generous three fingers of whisky, and was prepared to overlook all minor troubles.

" Don't bother," said Richard. " Any fish ? Hake, my God, I *loathe* hake, it's like eating flannel. Can't you get sole in this benighted place, mother ? Or even plaice wouldn't be so bad."

Mrs. Blaney shook her head. " No," she said. " I don't know what tradespeople are coming to ; it's take it or leave it these days. They don't care whether you have it or not. He had some dabs, but they were such wretched little things I wouldn't have them. He wanted four shillings for eight, and I remember the time in Blymouth when we could go on the beach as the boats came in and get a bucketful for a few coppers. That reminds me ; I was dreaming last night ; a very extraordinary dream it was, I can't explain it at all, for I don't, I'm sure, know anyone, and I never have, with the queer name——"

" All right, mother," laughed George, " tell us later ; the hake's not too bad. Is the joint in the oven ? Now don't move ; I'll see to things. Dick'll carve. Why don't you let Annie stay and look after things. It's a daft idea to let her go at five. You've done quite enough work in your time——"

" I like doing it myself," interrupted Mrs. Blaney ; "and when I'm no longer able to I hope I'll die. Annie ! I'm glad to see the back of her. But they're all alike. You can't trust them to do anything unless you're watching them. I remember your poor Uncle Robert—why, how queer now, Robert was in my dream ; it's only just come back to me. He was saying——"

" In the dream, mother, or at the time you're remembering ? " asked Jane patiently.

"Who? my dear," replied Mrs. Blaney, who having once begun a narration was quite unable to think of anything else but the way the tale was to go.

"Poor Uncle Robert," snapped Richard, who had finished carving, "never mind him, mother, he's dead and done for. This meat's not too bad. It's vile looking stuff though, meat. I loathe butchers and their wares. The amount of sheer ugliness——"

"Did the inspectors come in after all, my dear?" said Mrs. Blaney to Jane. "You look as if you'd had a worrying day."

Jane shrugged her shoulders and nodded. "Yes, and if Jackson, the head-inspector, hadn't been jolly decent about everything I don't know what would have happened. I'd two of my staff away sick, and one turned up an hour late this morning owing to the fog. However, it was all right, and the children really excelled themselves. Mr. Jackson was very pleased."

"The pleasant little fellow!" commented Richard; "you must be singularly fortunate with inspectors in your quarter, for all I've known have been ferreting swine, especially the subs."

"Inspectors are like other people," commented Jane; "they're what you make them."

"Thanks," mocked Richard; "if it's a joke I'll take it, but if you mean that as a serious proposition, why, it's all footle. People aren't what you make 'em, they're what they make of themselves. Do talk sense, Jane."

"There's such a thing as looking for the best in people and getting it out of them," interrupted Agnes, pouring herself out a second glass of milk.

"You'd have a hell of a job finding goodness in a bad egg, however long you looked," derisively. "But it's nice to see the milk of human kindness flowing so readily. I hope you treat those poor devils of girls under you accordingly."

" It's a pity a poet with your wonderful vocabulary," observed Jane coldly, " is forced to use so many oaths."

" Quite wrong, Jane ; I'd swear better if I were a better poet. Do you remember the tale of Swinburne and the cabman ? The cabby said——"

" We don't want to hear it, thank you," interrupted Agnes. " We've heard it before. What point there is in a string of dirty words I never can——"

" Poets ! " roared George boisterously, " they're damn fools, all of them. We're doing Bronson's new book of poems, and we got Bulake to do a dozen decorations and a dust cover. Bronson saw all the drawings and approved. We next sent him pulls of the drawings, and this morning he wrote to us and said he's decided the drawings were all out of tune, and that he'd prefer the poems to appear in all their naked beauty. I'm quoting his mush. With anyone else we'd make him foot Bulake's account, or take his stuff elsewhere, but Bronson is Bronson, curse the little boomster ! and so——"

" And so," broke in Richard, " because he's a versifier whose stuff sells by the ten thousand you'll swallow his nonsense, lick his boots, and——"

" Publishing is business," interrupted George ; " there's no room in it for sentiment or high falutin rot. A writer, poet, novelist or whatnot is a mine. If the mine's likely to yield a good percentage of ore, why then, we'll lay down the plant and work it. If it's been salted we drop it and cut our losses as soon as we can. Why, I'd recommend old Fawcett to publish *your* tripe if I thought it would sell."

" I've no doubt Fawcett takes recommendations for books from his workmen," said Richard unpleasantly.

" There's some difference between a workman and the head of a department," observed Agnes tartly.

" Don't take any notice of him ! " snapped Jane ; " We don't want a repetition of last Sunday ; we've heard enough socialism or bolshevism or whatever it is to last us a life-time. Is the coffee ready, mother ? "

" But there's a tart," cried Mrs. Blaney anxiously.

" Good for you, mother," cried George. " Forward tart."

" Pah ! " scoffed Richard, " what, after all, *is* George but a workman ; and you, too, both of you. We're all mem-bers of the working-class (God, what a name !) I suppose because you're the boss of a slum school you think you're a cut above it. Well, I'm in a slum school too, for that's what it is, to be honest about it——"

" I don't follow you," Jane was beginning, when Richard laughed harshly : " Precisely what Webb said to me this morning. ' Mr. Blaney,' he said, ' I'm afraid I don't—— ' "

" Anyway, what was it he didn't follow ? " said George indifferently, going over to the hob for the coffee-pot.

" I've half-forgotten now," went on Richard ; " but the gist of the business was a row we'd had over my kids. He said they didn't know their work——"

" And did they ? " interrupted Jane coldly.

" They didn't," continued Richard ; " that was the point, or rather the point was (and I not only showed him the point but I shoved it into him) the point was——"

" Let's hope you were quicker coming to it than you are now," said Agnes.

" The point, apparently," commented Jane, rising and taking her coffee with her, " was, according to your own showing, that Mr. Webb was right and you were wrong."

" Wait till I've finished," replied Richard flushing. " You know what a rotten morning——"

" Sorry," said George, standing up and pulling a pipe from his pocket, " no time now, I must be off." He grinned. " Write a poem about it and read it to us as a soporific."

Jane had left the room, and her feet could be heard mounting the stairs. Agnes sat sipping her coffee. George was lighting his pipe and looking at the clock. Mrs. Blaney poured herself out another cup of tea.

Richard got up and turned his back to stare out of the window. He felt, as he often did with his brother and sisters, like a small boy suddenly snubbed. He turned toward Agnes and George. He smiled faintly. A sudden boisterous cheerfulness invaded him. " Well, damn your eyes," he said with a grin. He walked to the door and opened it. Then he turned to his brother. " A pleasant evening, George, and a soldier's farewell to you." He slammed the door behind him, and was turning in to his sitting-room when the postman knocked, and he heard a letter fall into the box. It was for him, from Rachel. He smiled happily, lit a cigarette, and entering the sitting-room pulled a big arm-chair up to the fire, put his feet on the mantelpiece, and opening the letter began to read.

DARLING,—Mr. Sayers is back in town and so I am now at Adelphi Court and have closed the flat for the time being. I don't think he's back for long, as at breakfast this morning he and Mrs. Sayers were talking of a most princely offer from Hollywood. Offstein, the film-millionaire, is prepared to pay the great John Henry twenty-five thousand pounds if he'll go to Hollywood for a month and write a play for him. J. H. pretends to sniff at it but I think he'll go. There's a terrible lot of correspondence to get through just now—the accumulation of six weeks. There's all the business with Stonehurst over John Henry's collected edition, and there are about a gross of rude postcards to be written to autograph hunters, importunate poets, would-be playwrights, sharks and begging-letter writers. Most of all this falls on me, and therefore I simply can't come to *The Royalty* with you on Friday. It's a pity about the tickets. You could take Jane, couldn't you ? She'd appreciate the attention —you're not *very* brotherly are you ? Or if you won't I expect the box-office could get rid of them. The public have taken to Maddison's play and every seat's been occupied for the last six weeks. He was here to lunch yesterday, and was terribly pleased with himself.

He made one remark to J. H. which would have annoyed you. "There's no need, that *I* can see," he said, chumming asparagus with his great horse-teeth, "no need at all to *offend* people. Truth by all means, my dear Sayers, but not all of it, hey ? The truth about the other fellow, but no home-truths ! "

That's not *your* way at all, Dick, is it ! Truth at *any* price is your motto. The only thing is, Dick, what *is* truth, as P.P. and a thousand others have said. Is any man's truth absolute truth ? I often think people confuse truth with mere brutal, hurting frankness. After all these downright blurtings are a bit smug, aren't they ? Now, don't be silly, Dick, I don't mean that you're smug, but my pen was running away into generalities.

By the bye, I read your poem *The Schoolmaster* in *The New Era*. It's a bit obscure and there's just the faintest soupçon of omniscience about it. Well, hardly that ; I don't know exactly what I *do* mean—I'm dullish at the moment. But there were some fine lines in it, and plenty of meat. Real sincere good stuff—but of course it was, if you wrote it, darling. Come along on Sunday afternoon. I'm writing this tucked up in bed. I'm indelicate enough to wish you were here. My feet are cold. I'd let you kiss them. Well, good-night darling. Do come along early.

Ever,

RACHEL.

Richard folded the letter and put it in his pocket. He lit another cigarette, and sat watching the smoke. He felt vaguely unhappy. He turned over in his mind some of the phrases in Rachel's letter. Was he like that ? Was that how he appeared, even to Rachel ? Was he wrong then, and everyone else right ? He thought of his snubbing at dinner. Had he provoked it ? And Webb. Was he wrong about that business too ? What was it Dale had said ? He couldn't remember. What an irritating, intolerable smug he must appear to people. No wonder he was always in trouble. He ceased to think at all and closed his eyes. The cigarette burned slowly away. He sat up suddenly as it stung his lip, and removing it gingerly, flung it on the fire.

" I'm damned if I'm not about fed up with all this," he said sourly. " Why the devil don't I clear out ? I would for two pins—or three." He grimaced, and going over to a bookshelf took down Canton's *Invisible Playmate* and was presently absorbed in its pages.

3

At a quarter to nine the next morning a group of men stood round the fire in the staff-room of Banton Lane school. Dale was one of them, and he held open in his hands the current issue of *The New Era*. The other men were Manning, a tall, dark, stooping dyspeptic in the early forties ; Foster, a red-headed, burly youngster who had just arrived on a motor-cycle ; Clarke, a short, stout, grey man nearing his retirement ; and Lester, a gloomy, saturnine-looking fellow in the fifties, unshaven and generally dishevelled. Opposite the group, in a chair in a far corner of the room, sat Richard.

Dale was grinning mockingly. He flicked the pages of the review with his finger. " Here, just listen to this," he said. He began to declaim in a ludicrously pompous voice :

" *The Schoolmaster,*
by
Richard Blaney."

He paused for a moment, and his glance strayed over toward Richard. Richard smiled non-committally. " Go on, Dale," he said, " don't mind me."

The rest of the group showed but a languid interest. Young Foster, who was looking out of the window into the playground, cried angrily, " Damn those kids, they're at my bike again." He grabbed his cap from the table and hurried out.

Dale turned to the review and continued :

> " *Now, with averted face*
> *In this young-teeming place,*
> *Far from my vanished ways*
> *Of Truth's long sensuous days,*
> *I watch, aloof, a crowded solitary,*
> *This little world of uncontrolled desire.*
> *I am the sentinel upon a tower*
> *Wherein myself lies captive and alone ;*
> *The ruler of an unremembered hour ;*
> *The hidden priest before an altar fire.*
> *I know not these who know not me ;*
> *I am a voice that whispers down the wind ;*
> *A water-drop upon unquarried stone ;*
> *A hand that seeks in darkness ; a mad mute*
> *With voluble fingers talking to the blind.*"

Dale broke off with a chuckle and looked at the three men who were listening perfunctorily.

" Marvellous, isn't it ? " said Dale. " What metre's this masterpiece in, Blaney ? " he asked.

Richard smiled again, but made no reply.

" One of his own, eh ! " ventured Manning.

" Arithmetical Progression *I* should call it," said Clarke ; " each line a bit longer than the previous one. Did you notice that ? "

" In that case," said Manning facetiously, " thank God it ended where it did."

" What do you mean, *ended* ! that's only the first fit. Here we go now ; but I'll miss a page or we'll have the bell go before I've finished. Now then :

> *Authority whose sword is Punishment,*
> *And Dignity the buckler at its breast ;*
> *Vulnerable to the weanling and the fool,*
> *Yet proofed and panoplied against the world ;*
> *Under whose banner I usurp the place*
> *Of pure Omniscience. I review*
> *A thousand generations at a glance ;*
> *Judge and condemn ; and with my little rule*
> *Measure the secrets of unnumbered wombs.*

"The indelicate little feller ! " sniggered Dale, his glance once again straying over to Richard, who picked a newspaper off the table and began looking at the pictures.

" Well," went on Dale, " I'll bet you didn't comprey that little lot, Lester. Why not send it up to the Browning Society."

Lester made no reply. He withdrew his pipe from his mouth, spat in the fire, and wiped his lips on the back of his hand.

" I wish you wouldn't smoke oakum under my nose, Lester," said Clarke querulously, " it turns the stomach so early in the day and I'm feeling not too jolly ; we'd a wet night at the club last night."

" Shut up," cried Dale ; " here's the best bit and it's the last verse. I've left out whole chunks. I didn't want to spoil your own reading. Lend me your ears :

> " *We are the keepers of posterity ;*
> *Our land a realm of make-belief beyond*
> *To-morrow's dawning. Distant Yesterday*
> *Forgets us, and To-day remembers not.*
> *We are but shadows in a shadow-play*
> *More unsubstantial than the frailest dream.*
> *Whether the years shall ravel-out the plot,*
> *And mock, with things that are, the things that seem*
> *We shall not know ; but they who know shall reap*
> *Us in a thousand harvests while we sleep.*

"Amen, videlicet, id est, ad lib.," mocked Dale ; " Now then, young Blaney, wotchermean by it ? "

" Webb's in the playground," replied Richard ; " you'd better get out, Dale ; you're on this week."

Dale hurried out with the review under his arm. A bell jangled harshly. Clarke and Manning followed Dale. Lester walked to the door and, as he reached it, he half turned and said morosely, " That last bit was dam' good, Blaney. Dale's only sick because *he* can't do it."

Richard smiled. " Thanks," he said, " I say," he added hurriedly, as Lester was closing the door, " see my kids up, will you ? My hands are filthy, simply must wash."

Lester nodded and closed the door.

A hour later Richard sat in his classroom marking books. The class was busy with six arithmetical problems that were written up on the blackboard. A subdued buzzing marked the progress of calculation and low conversation. Here and there a few boys who had finished were sitting on the hot water pipes. One of these sybarites was eating his lunch. Several boys were playing noughts and crosses, half-a-dozen were " copying " with engaging frankness, and one very small urchin was fast asleep.

There was a knock at the door and a big boy entered and approached Richard with a folded slip of paper. Richard opened the paper and read in Webb's sprawling fist. *H.M.I. on the building.* Richard nodded, returned the paper to the boy, and went on with his marking.

In the early days of elementary education inspectors appointed by the Board of Education visited each school in the country on an appointed date to examine the children. The salary of the headmaster depended upon the result.

The evils of such a system were so obvious that by the time Richard began schoolmastering there had been a complete and fundamental change in the method of testing the work of the schools. Two inspectors were given charge of a district (a head-inspector and a sub-inspector), and they carried out surprise visits to all schools in their area. They could come a dozen times in a year or not at all. The essence of the method was surprise.

In Richard's article in *Progress* he had dealt with the inspectorate in violently partisan terms. " It was inevitable," he had written, " that the inspectorate came to look upon itself as a body part inquisitorial, part magisterial, and part punitory. It was equally inevitable that teachers came to regard them as spies, fault-finders, enemies. This unhappy result was due mainly to the fact that the head-inspectors were usually affable incompetents. They were drawn from Oxford or Cambridge men, penurious, of no family, and with no social pretensions. They were rarely of high academic attainments and they were entirely ignorant of the working of an elementary school. It was to counterbalance the futilities of these amiable nincompoops that the sub-inspectors were appointed. These were men of a very different calibre. They were drawn from the same class as the elementary scholar and teacher, and were, indeed, more often than not ex-teachers. Their boast was that they knew the ropes and couldn't be bamboozled. They were, in fact, a very efficient and hard-working body of policemen. This unfortunate alliance of smiling incompetence with frowning espionage largely nullified the serious efforts of the few real educationists in Whitehall. The attitude to-day of the inspector to the teacher is suspicious, that of the teacher to the inspector secretly hostile, but on the surface either abject, flattering, or recklessly truculent. The inspector is a person to placate. In the last resort he holds one's bread-and-butter in his hand, as an adverse report from him often leads to the teacher's dismissal."

Ten minutes after Richard had read Webb's warning note his door opened, and Hanley, the sub-inspector for the district, walked in. Richard stood up, smiled, held out his hand, and said " Good morning, Mr. Hanley."

Hanley took Richard's hand gingerly and released it. He nodded but did not speak. He sat down at the table and regarded the class. A dozen or so of the boys put down their pens and stared at him. " Don't stop your work, boys," he said. " What are *you* doing ? " pointing to a small boy still on the hot water pipes.

" Sums, sir."

" Do you do your sums sitting on the hot-water pipes ? "

" I've finished, sir."

" Been finished a long while ? "

" Yes, sir."

" You've been reading a book since ? "

Dp

" Yes, sir."

An indignant voice cried out, " Please, sir, he's been eating his lunch, sir." Another more indignant voice added smugly, " He's been playing noughts and crosses, sir."

" Oh, indeed," said Hanley ; " and what have *you* been doing ? "

" Nothing, sir."

" Nothing ? Have you done your sums ? "

" No, sir."

" Why not ? "

" I can't do them, sir."

At this point three helpful voices very self-righteously proffered the information, " He always copies, sir."

" Why can't you do them ? " asked Hanley.

No answer.

" Do you know your tables ? "

" Yes, sir."

" Well, what are four sevens ? "

No reply.

" Come, that's easy. How old are you ? "

" Nine, sir."

" Nine, well you know what four sevens are surely, eh ? "

" Yes, sir."

" Well, what ? "

" Twen'y," hesitatingly.

" Yes, twenty what ? "

" Free, sir."

" Sit down. No, *not* on the pipes. Go to your desk. Get on with your work, boys. If you've finished take out a reading book."

Hanley turned to Richard, who was lolling against the cupboard, his hands in his pockets and a nervous smile on his lips. Hanley frowned. " Er—Mister—er——"

"Blaney," said Richard, not changing his attitude, and smiling broadly.

"Mr. Blaney," went on Hanley; "what class is this?"

"Lower two," replied Richard.

"Poor material?" said Hanley.

"The average of the district," replied Richard. "What can you expect?"

Hanley without replying looked at the books on the table which Richard had been marking when he entered.

"Do you usually mark English exercises during Arithmetic?"

"Very rarely," replied Richard. "I'm rather behind with the marking this week."

Hanley turned the pages of some of the books.

"How many times a week do your boys do English composition?"

"Twice, Tuesday and Thursday."

Hanley sat looking at the books for some few minutes. "You omitted the composition last Tuesday, I see," he said presently.

"There was a medical inspection that morning," replied Richard smiling.

"You couldn't fit it in somewhere else? It's an important lesson."

"I follow the time-table," said Richard abruptly. He was watching Hanley's long red hands with their dirty finger-nails. He felt a sudden rush of anger at this inquisition. Yet Hanley was perfectly justified. It was his job, but somehow he seemed to make it a nastier business than it need be. Further, Richard was conscious that both he and the boys had come badly out of the inquisition. And it was entirely his own fault. Why the devil hadn't he pulled the kids together before Hanley entered. He'd plenty of time.

He shrugged his shoulders, and stared down at the top of Hanley's bald head.

" I find your boys ill-disciplined," said Hanley suddenly and sharply.

" You don't know them as well as I do," replied Richard calmly ; " they are, in fact, very well behaved."

" I fear that our standards differ," said Hanley unpleasantly.

" Obviously," replied Richard, nettled.

Hanley stood up. " I'll have your arithmetic books and drawing books down in Mr. Webb's room, if you please. Immediately." He walked to the door and was gone.

At a quarter to twelve Webb came into Richard's room. He began without any preliminaries. " Mr. Hanley is distinctly dissatisfied with your boys, Mr. Blaney."

Richard nodded but said nothing.

" He said, too," went on Webb, " that your attitude was discourteous, truculent and offensive."

" That's not true," replied Richard warmly.

" He mentioned," continued Webb, " that you stood lounging against the cupboard with your hands in your pockets while talking to him."

Richard laughed. " It's probably true ; but I really was not aware of it. I'm doing it now as a matter of fact. I should be sorry if I thought you believed that I meant it offensively. It means nothing whatever. Sheer forgetfulness. Anything you like but nothing discourteous, I assure you."

" It's not a proper attitude to assume before an inspector," persisted Webb.

"Good Lord, why not ! " cried Richard. "Are we in the Army ! " Again a sudden rush of unreasoning anger swept over him. He flushed. " Hanley's not my boss. Nor are you, for that matter, Mr. Webb."

"A masterless man, eh?" smiled Webb, not ungenially; "well, Mr. Blaney, men without masters are often men without jobs."

And suddenly, swiftly, as if a light had flashed, Richard saw his way clear before him. It came to him that the past five years since his demobilisation had been leading up to this point.

"I agree, Mr. Webb," he said, "I'm going to the office at lunch time to resign. My month's notice will terminate on the last day of November."

Webb stared. "That's rather rash, Mr. Blaney," he said slowly. "May I ask what you're thinking of doing, if it's not a rude question?"

"I'm getting a school in the country," replied Richard, who, one minute before, had not the remotest notion of doing anything of the kind.

Webb drew down his lips. "Teaching in the country is not all jam. I've had some. Too much, in fact. Take my advice and don't be in a hurry. Think it over for a day or so." He nodded and walked out.

That evening Richard replied to an advertisement in *The Schoolmaster* for a post as senior assistant master at Portway Street School, Welling, Meadshire.

The following morning he handed in his resignation, giving the usual month's notice. He knew it was risky, as it was very doubtful if he would get the vacancy at Welling. But his luck held. A fortnight later he received a letter notifying him of his appointment to Portway Street, his duties to commence on Monday, December 1st.

On Friday, November 28th, he said good-bye to Banton Lane, and the next day he caught the noon express from Paddington and reached Welling at half-past four.

CHAPTER III

OF WELLING, THE PINES, AND SUNDRY PERSONS

I

The cathedral city of Welling, in Meadshire, lies along the left bank of the Teal at the point where that slow and muddy river begins to widen out into the estuary.

Welling is one of the oldest and certainly the smallest of the cathedral cities of England, its population at the last census being only 8,568.

Built in the form of a semicircle whose diameter is the Teal, its arc is Market Street, with the High Street describing a chord mid-way between. The High Street runs directly north and south.

The High Street leads at its north end into Bridge Street, which bifurcates into an east road over Belton Bridge, thence by a quiet highway to Queenstown; and a west road to Melcombe, the well-known summer resort. The south end of the High Street narrows into Tilly's Lane, widening a few hundred yards farther on into the old Roman road to Darum, the county town, twelve miles away.

The Market, which is situated to the west of the High Street, is bisected by Gay Street; and the section of the city between the river and the High Street is split into three more or less equal parts by Portway Street and The Arcade. Portway Street emerges from the Cathedral precincts, the north and south close both entering the High Street.

A policeman is always on point duty by the bandstand

near Belton Bridge, and another at the beginning of Tilly's Lane.

The plan of the city on page 2 will assist the visualisation of the strange happenings that began at the end of 1924, ended so calamitously in January 1926, and in that brief period gave to this sleepy yet prosperous little city a world-wide fame—to avoid the invidious word.

For a decade before Richard came to Welling its name had become a news item—not for itself, however, but because the Dean of Welling was the celebrated Henry Perseval. Dean Perseval was not merely the despotic master of St. Matthew's cathedral but the dictator of Welling. Dr. Strang, the Bishop, held a very secondary position, and during the whole of Richard's time there he was abroad seeking health. Dr. Hellewell, bishop of the neighbouring diocese of Selbury, who acted as suffragan during Dr. Strang's absence, was a nonentity.

The one opponent worthy of the Dean's steel in Welling, and indeed one of the few men who stood up to him, was Owen Jones, the proprietor-editor of *The Welling Sentinel*. Jones, a fiery Welsh methodist, lived in an old tumbledown house abutting on the south close, and but a stone's toss from the Deanery.

It would be difficult to find two men more sharply contrasted than this fiery little editor and the Dean. The Very Reverend Henry Perseval was over six feet, while Jones barely touched five feet two inches. Perseval was a fine burly figure, with sparse lank black hair, and a bald patch like a tonsure. His cheeks were raddled, his nose large and fleshy, his eyes almost black and very brilliant, his mouth small and slightly pursed. His chin jutted out like the ram of a battleship. He had a rich, sonorous, " fruity " voice, an impressive presence, and long, beautifully shaped white hands. Jones (he was familiarly O. J. to everyone in Welling) was thin and frail, his pale face, with its sharp blue eyes, pointed nose and small cleft chin, was dwarfed by the immense mop of bright red hair that crowned him. He limped badly from a congenital short leg, his voice was a fluting sing-song, he was a vegetarian, a water-drinker, a non-smoker, a rigid radical and perhaps the hottest gospeller of methodism that ever came out of Wales.

Andrew Banks, the Mayor, was a stout, dark, middle-aged, good-tempered ex-tradesman. He had made a fair fortune from Banks's Non-Slip Suspenders, had been mayor for three successive years, and lived in the Manor House opposite the bandstand. He was a slow-witted, open-pursed dullard, with a leaven of shrewdness in money-matters. He feared Owen Jones, yet admired him, despite official mayoral denunciations of *The Sentinel's* notorious editorials. Perseval he courted, flattered, supported and loathed.

Colonel Bowers and Captain ffoliot who sat on the bench with the Mayor were both retired soldiers of the regular army. Bowers was a tall, white, baldish man of sixty-five, with florid cheeks, a veined and slightly vinous nose and a drooping moustache. A simple, amiable, half-smiling expression was habitual with him. He usually wore tweeds of a very wide check, and was master of the North Meadshire Staghunt.

Captain ffoliot had been invalided from the army in 1922 after serving in Russia. He had a small pension, some snug investments, and cultivated flowers and vegetables in a four-acre garden, worked, in theory, by himself, but in practice by his old batman and an ex-corporal of sappers. He was a tall, scrawny, pallid man of forty. He stooped, always wore cord breeches, leggings, and a shooting jacket, and walked with his hands clasped behind his back. He stammered when excited or moved.

Colonel Bowers' neighbour in the north close was Clarence George, the well-known nature writer. George was a tall, thin, pink-faced, peering albino, whose short-sighted eyes stared through immense horn-rimmed spectacles. He wore tweed jackets, flannel trousers, and sandals, winter and summer alike, lived chiefly upon garden produce, but had not infrequent drinking bouts at *The Crown*. He spoke with a hoarse, gasping articulation, in an affected accent, and cleared his throat after every sentence. He had been a best-seller for years, and his somewhat sentimentalised stories of wild life were admired and devoured both in England and the United States. He was married, with seven children. He denounced fox-hunting, but occasionally accepted a mount with the North Meadshire Staghunt. An illicit relationship with a touring company actress playing at the Theatre Royal some three years previously was a prideful memory and was the burden of his conversation with his few male intimates. He took it as a proof of the sensible frankness and simplicity of his character that he was not averse from discussing this solitary amative aberration before his wife.

2

The Pines, situated opposite the Mayor's house, facing the Square and bandstand, was an old seventeenth century mansion, with later additions and annexes as haphazardly placed as the parasitic excrescences upon a barnacle.

It was run as a boarding-house, or superior lodging-house, by the two Miss Oveys, Miss Lettice and Miss Alison.

The Miss Oveys were in the early fifties, Lettice being two years the elder. They were the only children of one of the residentiary canons of the cathedral, who, at his death, had bequeathed them eighteen hundred pounds and his invalid wife. The Ecclesiastical Commissioners sold them The Pines for fifteen hundred pounds as a special act of grace, and their mother shortly afterward following the canon, they were able to devote their energies to the one undertaking in the world that may be pursued without knowledge, experience, vocation or ability. They trusted to counter-balance this lack by gentility, prayer, and the intervention of Providence.

After eighteen months muddling they were saved from bankruptcy, and put upon the road to wealth and prosperity, by the advent of a gross, common and low-born person masquerading under the protective title of Mrs. Robbins. Mrs. Robbins had never known the amenities of matrimony, and by that lacked experience some man had been denied a rich possession. She was a short, plump, greasy-faced, black-haired woman with little merry eyes, a button-nose, a wide-lipped mouth, a clutch of chins, and a vast bosom. She was an omnivorous gossip, slatternly, loud-voiced ; she laughed continuously and raucously at anything, at everything, at nothing. She was an ardent chapel-goer, a royalist with a wide knowledge of the world's monarchies ; she loved porter and gin to excess, and in excited moments used language of a rich and all-embracing foulness. She was, in short, a troublesome person and most uncongenial to the two Miss Oveys. But she was a cook of unbounded and prodigal genius, and within a year of her arrival The Pines was earning a profit of 20 per cent. on the purchase price. When Richard became a boarder the annual turnover was larger than the whole of their original outlay.

The two sisters were both little women, but while Lettice was plump and grey, Alison retained her chestnut hair and the slim straight figure of her girlhood. They quite honestly considered their prosperity due entirely to their own exertions, plus a certain assistance from God that was owing to the daughters of a residentiary canon.

The staff of The Pines at this time consisted of Mrs.

Robbins ; Polly, a scullery-maid ; Ethel, a kitchen-maid ; two parlour-maids, Mary Bassett and Kate Churchill ; two chamber-maids, May Whitley and Doris Stocks ; John Hicks, the gardener, groom and driver of the old brougham that still took guests to and from the station ; and Alfred, the odd-job boy.

There were generally about ten permanent boarders at The Pines ; and there were usually three or four birds of passage, commercial travellers, summer visitors, Americans, or, very occasionally, a touring actor or actress from the Theatre Royal.

The scale of charges varied from thirty shillings to five guineas a week. For thirty shillings one had simply a small bedroom, took meals in the common refectory, and was tolerated but not welcomed in the drawing-room, billiard-room and lounge. This last was a large, untidy room, given up to dilapidated arm-chairs, a sofa, and a piano. Here smoking, not permitted in the refectory or drawing-room, was allowed.

For two guineas a boarder had a small bedroom, and a half-share in a tiny sitting-room. Three guineas acquired a sitting-room to oneself, and further rooms were a guinea a week each. In all, including the parasitic excrescences, there were thirty-nine rooms at The Pines.

It was rare for a room to be vacant at The Pines, even in the depth of winter. The Miss Oveys were become ladies of substance. The bow of the bank-manager avoided obsequi-ousness by the narrowest possible margin. Colonel Bowers was a frequent caller. The Mayoress often dropped in to tea. Clarence George never failed to present them with an autographed copy of each new book from his pen.

All these material splendours they owed to the genius of Mrs. Robbins.

They paid her £48 per annum.

3

Richard began work at his new school on Monday, December the first. On the following Sunday he wrote a long letter to Rachel who was now back again in her small flat in Maida Vale, Sayers and his wife having decided upon the Hollywood adventure.

I have now (ran the letter) been in Welling just a week ; I've seen—I suppose—most of the inhabitants, and I've done five days work in my new job. Let me clear that away first.

I'm enclosing a picture-postcard giving a panoramic view of the place. Most of the buildings you'll be able to pick out yourself but I've marked The Pines and my school with crosses.

It's a small school, only about two hundred boys, is called Portway Street Council School, and is on the right side of Portway Street as one comes from the Cathedral. From my classroom window I can see out over the estuary, and away to the north-east the smoke of a remote passing ship occasionally smears a line above the horizon. You will notice that the railway runs between the school and the quayside. The distance is barely fifty yards, and I find the noise of the trains very trying. I imagined country life would at least be quiet !

The headmaster is an oldish man of about fifty. He's very ordinary in size, manners, colouring and so on. The staff consists of two men, not counting me, and a woman. Bailey and Roding are the men, and a Mrs. King the woman. There's nothing about them worth describing. As for the kids, well, they're the same as all the others I've ever had anything to do with, and for that matter so is the school and everything in it, about it, and around it. In fact, I'm fed up with schools and everything connected with them. It's a school and I'm in it—let's leave it at that and get on to something more interesting.

Welling itself? Well, it's a bit early to give any impressions. I doubt if I have any. It's not an impressive sort of place. It's small and dirtyish and provincial (whatever that may mean exactly—do you remember how we laughed over Belloc accusing H. G. Wells of being provincial, H. G. having been born in one small provincial town, and Wells's retort that Belloc of course had been born all over Europe. I mean we laughed over the retort). Where was I ? Oh, provincial, well, perhaps that's not the word, but for one of the oldest cathedral cities it seems strangely lacking in dignity, somehow cheap and sort of childish. I'm afraid this isn't a bit clear but I'm not clear about it myself. I can't think of the one illuminating word that *would* paint it for you. Oafish ? No. Amateurish ? Nearly. It *is* a sort of amateurish looking place. Planned by amateurs, built by them, inhabited by them—a sort of second-rate amateur theatrical show. Even that doesn't describe it. Well, it can't be helped ; perhaps when I've been here longer I'll make a better fist of it.

I thought the Cathedral a pinchbeck thing when I first saw it, but I'm not so sure now—it grows on you.

You'll be wanting to know about the great Perseval. Of course I've seen him. It's impossible not to. He's all over the place. I've not spoken to him, but I've been at his elbow when he was speaking to someone else. A perfectly poisonous type, hefty, over-fat, mauve cheeks, a " rich " voice (over-rich, like German cooking), the proud prelate to the life, in fact, just a trifle *more* than the life—more a caricature of himself than himself. But you know my sudden hates at first sight. I probably malign the man.

There's a queer little red-polled character you'd love. He's the editor of the local sheet, is Welsh, radical, methodist, is named Owen Jones, never misses a chance of swiping Perseval (whom he calls the Pope of Welling—you know what a red rag papistry is to Perseval !) and is apparently going to be a bright spot in the humdrum life which is likely to be my portion here.

There is a Theatre Royal but I've not yet been. There's been a revue on during the week . . . ! Nearly opposite, however, is a very jolly little pub called *The Crown*. I've spent most of my evenings so far in its bar-parlour. Although it is a smallish and rather disreputable-looking pub it is *the* pub—the house of call of the panjandrums of the city. You'll always find one pub like that in every place in England. What rules this choice I've no notion, but there it is, and *The Crown* is *the* pub in Welling. In the five evenings I've spent there I suppose all the leading lights of Welling have called in. It is run by a plump, small, short-sighed ex-soldier named Daniels. It is a free house (you know what that means ?) and sells the best draught Bass I've drunk since before the War. By the bye, I've noticed that *the* pub in any town is usually a free house. Is that the explanation ! Daniels is mild, affable, witty and hen-pecked. He's about my age I should say. His wife looks much older. She is a tall, thin, pale, mousey, flat-chested creature, bad-tempered, shrewish, and frightfully virtuous and respectable (a way these women often have). She won't allow cussing of any sort and as for a bawdy tale—well, I can't imagine anyone even thinking of one while she's in the offing.

The Mayor (one Banks a suspender magnate) is a bit of a character by all accounts—he's in every evening. There's the military in the persons of a Colonel (or General—I forget for the moment) Bowers, and a Captain Folliot (I hope the spelling's correct) ; the local police superintendent, a colossus named Haynes, has been in twice,—I don't know whether on or off duty, but he'd a couple of pints each time.

He's an immense creature, well over six and a half feet and burly with it. I gather he's not liked, but I've heard no spicy details yet.

Then there's the new tenant at Denacre Hall, the largish Tudor-cum-Jerry mansion about a furlong from my digs. He only arrived on Thursday. I've not seen him and have heard nothing about him except one amazing rumour which is probably a lie : that he is *the* great David Hartley ! ! However, I've no grouch against rumours—they lend a touch of salt to life, and we'd have died without them during the War—or cut our throats.

You'll want to know about my digs. Well—oh, but just a moment. I'd forgotten our celebrity—no, *not* Perseval, but guess ? You can't. Why, *Clarence George.* Never heard of him ? But darling ! Never read *The Toad's Odyssey ? The Questing Mole ?* The—the—but I forget the rest. Well, anyway, he's a writer of nature books. He's the queerest looking fish, an albino. Wears sandals and horn-rims. Eats lettuce and dates and so forth. However, Clarence apparently drinks like a sponge, for he's in *The Crown* every night for hours and guzzles all the time. Perhaps he's merely resting after a masterpiece and needs a diversion. I've not spoken to him yet. But my digs ! They're worth a new paragraph !

The Pines (opposite the bandstand ; I've marked it with an X) I won't describe as far as its architecture goes, I hope you'll come down one of these days and see it for yourself. It's a big lodging-house and caters for all purses, provided they are respectable. It's kept by two unbelievably *nace*, genteel (*that's* the word) spinsters named Ovey—Miss Lettice and Miss Alison. Lettice is the elder. She's grey and plump as to person, but for mind, morals and manners—God ! darling, she's incredible. She's smug caste incarnate, the perfection of gentility, a crème-de-la-crèmer. Alison, the other, is not so bad, She's younger looking and much more human. Their late da was a local parson, a residentiary canon I think they call it. If Lettice takes after the canon his reverence must have caused a flutter in Heaven on his arrival. Do you remember that yarn about Shaw going to Heaven and coming to God seated in majesty upon the celestial throne. And Shaw having introduced himself, God stood up, saying, " I beg your pardon, I'm afraid I have your seat." God will abdicate when Lettice arrives.

There are about a dozen people in The Pines just now. I've only spoken to one or two, as I share a sitting-room with a man named Mason, and we have our meals served there. I've not a bad bed-room, and for that and the half-share of the sitting-room, I pay two guineas a week. I'm afraid I'll have to spring another guinea if I can manage, and get a sitting-room to myself—Mason's an infernal gasbag, and you know how keen I am on privacy.

Mason is quite ten years older than I am, and looks more. He's an old Winchester boy, but you'd never think it. He's a looseish sort of bird, and as far as I can gather is neither quite in nor quite out of the social swim here. He runs a small book-shop in The Arcade, and contributes a weekly local-gossip column to *The Sentinel*. He uses the pseudonym *The Gargoyle*. He's not like one but is, I should say, a handsome bloke. But I never know when a man's handsome and when he's not. He's a frightful gossip and has already told me more scandal than I've heard for years. He's the sort that simply must have someone to gossip with, and that, I'm sure, is the only reason he shares a sitting-room, for he seems to have plenty of money. He told me he prefers congenial company to his own. *Any* company is, I expect, nearer the truth. He gives the impression of being well-read, knows all about the latest books, and yet there's not a volume of any sort among his chattels (it's mostly his furniture in the sitting-room), and I've not seen him reading anything but his own article in *The Sentinel*. This sheet comes out every Saturday. It's rather a scream. O. J., as everyone calls him, seems to have his knife into half the inhabitants of Welling and apparently doesn't care a damn for Perseval or anyone else. I'll send you next Saturday's.

It's time I stopped. It's after midnight, and Welling's been asleep for hours. Some of the boarders here I think you'd like. There's one Irish youngster named Kevin Pearce, for example, a bank clerk ; there's Captain Lacy (ex-merchant skipper) who's a pleasant old cock, and Miss Thatcher a schoolmarm very keen on him ; there's Mrs. D'Arcy L'Estrange a " vidder " of the most mysterious ! Mason says—but if I begin to tell you Mason's libellous scurrilities I'll not get to bed to-night.

Good-night darling. I kiss your feet. I'm returning Walpole's *Jeremy*. Not so bad. Perilously near slop once or twice. Bye.

EP

CHAPTER IV

UNPRECEDENTED CAREER OF DAVID HARTLEY AND OTHER MATTERS

I

When Jamie Hartley, minister of the Wee Free Church at Buckie, Banffshire, listened in relief to the first bellow of his only son David on a chilly December dawn in the year 1866, the famous Hartley second-sight was in abeyance. Had not agitation for the time being swamped the family gift Jamie might well have hesitated before mounting the winding stair-way to greet so extraordinary a prodigy, for this son of the manse was talking at ten months, reading before he was two, and at six was correcting his father's Latin and the local dominie's mathematics.

The ancient and beloved Dunedin Academy took young David to its arms when he was thirteen, and set itself to shape him. And, as once before in history, David faced, fought with, and overcame Goliath. What shaping there was, young Hartley did, and it is said that the celebrated Academy still bears the marks of that struggle.

David Hartley possessed every characteristic that goes to the making of a genius, except that swift, reckless impetuousness that so often leads to disaster. Therein, perhaps, he fell short of genius, and remained only a man of stupendous and unparalleled talent.

The coruscating splendour of his scholastic career must be read elsewhere. It is enough to direct attention to the list of books, mathematical and medical, that follows his name in the British Museum catalogue under the dates 1886-1890.

At the age of twenty-nine he was a consulting surgeon in Wimpole Street, with an income of five figures. A year later the reigning monarch of a central European State collapsed from a duodenal ulcer at a banquet in London. The sufferer was a gross, overfed, chronically costive man of sixty. Hartley found the duodenum ulcerated for a length of eight inches. It was not an uncommon practice for a surgeon to remove short pieces of the duodenum in severe cases, and to trust Nature to pull the patient through. Nature responded to the appeal about thrice in a dozen cases. Hartley removed the whole of the duodenum, joined up the pylorus and the jejunum, and had his royal patient out and about in seven weeks, a slimmer, more active, and vastly healthier man.

The following year William Olwen the American multi-millionaire brought his fourteen-year-old imbecile son to Hartley's surgery. Young Olwen's disability resulted from a fall as a child of two. There was some cerebral lesion, and the father had discovered during twelve heart-breaking years that even his vast wealth could not buy a surgeon to perform the impossible.

Seventeen weeks after landing at Southampton, Olwen sailed for home in the *Balgania*, taking with him a cheery bright boy, who, it was true, knew little more than a baby of two, but who was striding through the ordinary schooling of young children at the rate of a year a week.

The curious may read the case in Hartley's *Surgery of the Brain*.

Hartley refused a royal appointment and a baronetcy, and the following year left England for a voyage of several months, from which he returned in the early days of 1898 to be called to the Bar.

Two years later The Belton Oil-Shale Corporation briefed

him as leading counsel in the international dispute over oil-concessions that came to be known years later as the Belton Bubble. The fee marked on his brief was £30,000 and Hartley earned it. The Belton Corporation won their case and with it concessions worth hundreds of millions sterling.

At forty Hartley entered Parliament as Conservative Member for Caston, and at forty-four he had refused the Lord Chancellorship in Banningtree's Government, had resigned his seat and had been appointed a Judge in the Court of Chancery.

A year later he abandoned law, was ordained a curate in the Church of England, and for a few months worked in the east end of London. Shortly afterwards he was inducted into the living of St. Joseph's Church, Mayfair, and was appointed Chaplain to the Bishop of London the following spring. He was suffragan bishop to Dr. Harple, Bishop of Belcaster, from 1918 to 1921, and a year later returned to the metropolis as Bishop of Farling, the newly formed diocese cut out of the ancient St. John's.

Hartley had frequently crossed polemical swords with the notorious Bishops Bowes and Mottram, and with Deans Sayl and Perseval, from the pulpit, in Press articles and in books, and the country was not unfamiliar with the unorthodox views of these clerics. The average man, in relation to these frank discourses and arguments, was in turn annoyed, bewildered and disgusted. A third-leader in *The Daily Echo* probably voiced the national sentiment when it asked pointedly : *Why don't they get out ?* That was the caption of the leading article, which went on to ask very plainly why, for example, Dean Sayl, who denied the divinity of Christ, found himself able to remain in a Church whose first dogma was the assurance of that divinity, and further to take £2,000 a year from that Church for work he was obviously not doing.

It was true that *The Daily Echo* was a scurrilous sheet owned by the Jew Jabez Schaffer, that it owed its circulation to its habit of rummaging in dirty linen cupboards, and that it was utterly venal, corrupting and open to corruption. Yet once in a way it seemed to be saying the frank thing simply if bluntly.

Hartley alone had in his polemics used so discreet a tongue and pen that it is doubtful if a dozen people had really grasped what was implied in his guarded utterances. Certainly *The Daily Echo* and its readers, who howled " atheist," " Judas " and more obscene epithets at Sayl, Perseval and Bowes, together with the more restrained controversialists in the respectable columns of the *Church Times* and other Anglican organs, would all have been readier to grant Hartley the old title Defender of the Faith than even to question his staunch orthodoxy.

It was then with a sense of stupefied bewilderment, of anger, of disgust, of something indeed approaching outrage, that the congregation in Cheyne Street Church heard the Bishop of Farling's sermon on Christmas morning in the year 1923.

It was perhaps fortunate that no papers were published the following day, and that the writers of leaders, editorials, captions, and cross-heads, had time to see things in their right perspective. That Press-indignation which boils so easily doubtless owes much of its heat to the friction of speed. Twelve hours is usually ample for that indignation to go off the boil and to become a mere gentle simmer. In twenty-four hours indeed the hell-broth may be cold. Even with this cooling period, however, the newspapers on the morning following Boxing Day were definitely warm.

But the fashionable congregation, who caught Hartley's words fresh from the mint, had no such period to collect themselves. The words, as they fell from Hartley's lips, might have been pellets of sodium dropping on to water, so hissing and stormy an agitation followed their descent. The fashionable, unemotional and restrained congregation of Cheyne Street in all but utterance swooped suddenly to the level of the debased yahooings of *The Daily Echo*. If only Hartley had played decently, it was thought, it would not have been so bad. If he had mounted the pulpit and made his frank disavowal straight away, much might have been forgiven him. As it was, however, the outraged listeners were as ready to shout " Master Executioner, light your fire " as any of their forbears had been in those less complex ages of simple faith, unsullied by doubt honest or otherwise.

For Hartley had for ten minutes preached a plain, unpretentious, orthodox Christmas Day sermon. So simple indeed as to be without savour, so plain as to be unappetising, so unpretentious as to reflect upon the culture of the congregation, and finally orthodox to boredom.

And then in the same tone, with no alteration in inflection or pitch, Hartley said, " That is, of course, a tale for children."

A stirred bee-hive, an upset anthill, a tumbled hornets' nest, are similes deserving a decent and grateful interment. Unluckily there is nothing else so vividly descriptive to replace them. The interior of Cheyne Street Church after the fall of that quietly spoken sentence can be described no more aptly than by the assistance of those old and tried familiars.

Hartley's voice went on smoothly. " Children, it must be added, either in mentality or in physique. The physical child, the true child, the being of a few brief years, may be allowed to continue for a while to believe in his tale. But it is time that the mental child be shaken out of childishness. It is high time that the adult world, or that part of it which calls itself Christian, should wake to the fact, or if already it has woken, should acknowledge the fact that the resurrection of Christ did not take place. It did not because it could not. Life once destroyed cannot renew its existence. The dead flower will not bloom again. Christ died, and the vital part of him ended for ever, as the vital part of you will end when you die. There is nothing in you that will exist, or can exist, once the body has seen corruption.

" Christ was human and mortal. He was a man conceived, fathered and mothered, as we all are ; and because of his common mortality his life was that of all mortals : it passes and is gone.

" It is because I believe that the Church which I serve must shortly take its stand upon the *mortality* of Christ that I still call myself a Christian. It is because I believe that the implications of such a truth demand statement, that in the name of the Church I would ask you to face the truth and reality of your own mortality. Christ was mortal ; he did not rise from the dead. You are mortal ; you also shall not know resurrection. You will not have any other life beyond this. Are you honest enough, are you brave enough, to accept that ?

" This is not the time to discuss the existence of God. I had hoped that it would be possible for a Bishop of the English Church to ask that question in this pulpit, and to voice it as an hypothesis to be probed. Finally, I dreamed to have the Church with me, beside me, supporting me, in an honest denial of the existence of God, if that denial were serving the aims and purposes of absolute truth.

" I have said that I still call myself a Christian. I leave my justification to your judgment—your calm and leisured judgment. I have said that I believe the Christian Church will soon take its stand upon the *mortality* of Christ. Up to this point I am still a son of the Church, and in that Church's communion. I have further told you what I have dreamed. It is because I realise that it is only a dream that I now declare myself no longer a son of the Church and without her communion."

Hartley raised one hand, paused a moment, as if collecting his thoughts before proceeding, and then turning suddenly he descended the pulpit steps.

Decidedly David Hartley, ex-surgeon, ex-judge in Chancery, and now ex-bishop of Farling, had a good Press the day after Boxing Day.

The Daily Echo headed its editorial *The Wolf Leaves The Fold.* The last paragraph of a vituperative commentary on the already famous sermon ran : " Within the sheep-fold there are still many wolves. It is true they wear over their mangy pelts the sheepskin of orthodoxy, but to the discerning eye the fur shows under the wool, the sheepskins are slipping off. Where is the shepherd who will strip these dissimulating raveners and drive them from the flock ? "

The Times in a very temperate leader under the title *The Bishop of Farling and Orthodoxy*, remarked : " . . . it is a long way from the affirmation of Jesus' mortality to the negation of atheism, and we think his lordship is likely to find himself a solitary wayfarer."

The Morning News had an exclamatory article by Dean Perseval, and a symposium giving the views of a banker, a neuropathic specialist, a Jesuit father and the Chief Rabbi. In all these conviction seemed to be waiting upon discretion.

The Evening Portent printed a page article by Pastor Jones, the Welsh revivalist, and had collected the deliciously outspoken if irrelevant views of a jockey, a prize-fighter, the Attorney-General, George Bone, the famous cricketer, Alfred Robinson, the captain of the Association Football cupholders, and Miss Claire Lotte, the comedienne.

Before the New Year dawned the country learned that Hartley had left the Church, had resumed his private life, and had left the country under an assumed name for a voyage of indefinite duration.

Three days after Richard Blaney arrived at Welling a three-line item of news in the Press announced that Hartley had returned to England, and had gone to live at Denacre Hall, a small estate he had recently purchased at Welling.

2

Upon the Monday evening following David Hartley's arrival at Welling Richard sat in the bar-parlour of *The Crown*. A picture-paper was in front of him as a protection against gossiping intruders. The bar was not uncomfortably full and there was a pleasant buzz of conversation, which, with the regular grinding jar of the cork-extractor, the smooth swishing of beer-engine handles, and the intermittent jets of laughter, made up that attractively familiar atmosphere common to all the bars of the world.

Clarence George leaned against the bar counter, a tankard of ale at his elbow, and a short briar-pipe between his teeth. He was talking ostensibly to a local tradesman beside him, but his hoarse, gasping voice rose loudly above the common chatter, and his glance wandered from face to face, watching anxiously the effect of his carefully chosen words.

Captain ffoliot drooped over the cheese-basket on the counter, discussing winter-greens with Daniels the proprietor.

Mrs. Daniels wiped glasses with slow mechanical regularity, and replied to the remarks of customers concerning the weather in the impersonal and monotonous tones of an automaton. She rang the changes upon three phrases, " Very unseasonable," " too muggy altogether," and " most unhealthy."

Richard was busy with his own thoughts, and only occasionally a word or phrase separated itself from the general noise and drew from him a momentary attention.

Kevin Pearce, the young bank-clerk from The Pines came in, and seeing Richard, looked over to him with a shy nod of greeting. Richard hooked a chair round with his foot. Pearce came over and said, " Terrible froust in here after the street. It's rottenly cold to-night."

" Cold," said Richard, smiling, " I gathered from the landlady that it was muggy, unseasonable and unhealthy."

" That was the last time she was out," laughed Pearce ; " it's the only tune she plays ; will you have something ? "

" Thanks, a draught Bass," replied Richard ; " I've not got acclimatised to your bitter yet ; there's a vinegary smack about it I don't fancy."

" You should try the cider," rejoined Pearce, " and *then* go back to our bitter. You'd probably like it. But then you'd like anything after draught cider." He moved away to the bar, and returning presently with the drinks, sat down and raised his glass.

" Know any of this crowd ? " asked Pearce when they had drunk.

Richard shook his head. " I know one or two by sight, and I know the names of a few, but I've done no more than give them a good-evening. I know Flemming from the newspaper shop, and the man who's talking to him, Brown, the tobacconist, isn't it ? "

Pearce nodded.

" And I've seen Clarence George about a good deal," went on Richard ; " and the military chap, Folyot isn't it ? And that big fellow by the door is Haynes, the police boss, isn't he ? "

" Yes, that's Haynes, the superintendent. You've surely heard the yarn about him ? "

Richard shook his head.

" He came here," resumed Pearce, " about four years

ago, with a big reputation for efficiency and all the more notorious police virtues. Welling very soon didn't like him at all. One of his reforms was to sweep away the street traders, toy-vendors, and stall-holders. His next was to round-up the gipsies from the moors and get them moved. Both these stunts were from his point of view successful. Many of the gipsies cleared right away, but a few of them came into Welling and rented houses or got lodgings.

" Two of the gipsies, brothers, Bob and Henry Surrell, got fourteen days each for resisting the police. The resistance had been no more than a bit of cheek, but cheek from gipsies was too much for Haynes, and he trumped up the whole business, supported, naturally enough, by a sergeant and constable, who were with him at the time.

" A week after the brothers came out of clink the constable was set upon in the dark and severely handled, not injured, but well thrashed. The following night the sergeant was belted into a daze, and his helmet smashed down over his face.

" Haynes had no doubt at all about the matter. He didn't wait for his turn, or for warrants or anything of that sort—perhaps he didn't need them, I don't know anything about police regulations—but took a sergeant and a constable with him the next morning and called round at the Surrells' house. They couldn't get a reply to their knocking, but after a time Bob Surrell put his head out of a top window, and told Haynes to get to hell along out of it.

" Haynes's goat rose at this, and he told Bob that he and his brother were under arrest, and would have to come along to the station. ' Open this door,' he ended sharply and very nastily.

" ' You go and —— ! ' jeered Bob Surrell, and slammed down the window.

" Haynes sent the sergeant round to the other side of the

house to mark time on the back door, dispatched the constable to the station for two more peelers, and took up his position on the pavement under the Surrells' bedroom window.

" I don't know if Haynes dozed, or what, but the Surrells, a few minutes later, slipped the window up softly and tumbled a large marble clock on to Haynes's head. He dropped like a pole-axed bullock, and when the constable returned with the reinforcements Haynes lay knocked silly on the pavement—it was a back-street—and the birds had flown. They got them some weeks later, just about in time for Haynes to be fit to give evidence. The bench assumed that the Surrells had been responsible for all these bashings —as they probably had—and gave them six months apiece on each count.

" Haynes looked down his nose at these sentences, as he'd boasted he'd get them five years. But he looked further down when old Colonel Bowers said to the two other magistrates, ' Concurrently, I think.' Banks the Mayor, and ffoliot (over there talking to Daniels), agreed, and the Surrells grinned themselves out of the dock.

" Clarence George who was in here a night or so after the case was tried, (he's a neighbour of Bowers) said that the old boy had laughed so much over the clock business he'd have let them off altogether if he'd had his way. I don't think it very dam' funny myself do you ? "

" Well, I don't know," replied Richard, " I've seen less funny things roared at on the stage."

Before Pearce could make any further comment the hoarse, gasping, affected voice of Clarence George rose above the general level of sound in the bar. " Yes, there's not the slightest doubt it's the great Hartley himself."

" Who's this Mr. 'Artley, Mr. George, sir ? " asked one of the men standing by the bar.

" Who's Mr. Hartley, Tom," beamed George amiably, " ever heard of the king ? "

Tom grinned. " I believe I have, Mr. George, sir, now I come to think of it."

" And the late Napoleon," continued George, " and Shakespeare and er—and—er—shall we say our good superintendent. Now roll all these eminent gentlemen into one and *then* you'd be somewhere near Mr. David Hartley. Tom, I'm amazed at you. You must cut out the drink. You're getting addled, Tom."

" Rich, eh, Mr. George, sir, is he ? " asked a short, dapper little man in leggings and brown velvet breeches.

" Beyond riches, beyond riches, Fred," replied George with jocosity, " he's——"

" He don't spend much, then," interrupted a heavily built man with a rough red complexion that merged into purple over the cheekbones. He was drinking hot rum and spitting continuously into a spittoon between his feet. " I hear he's only got a chauffeur and one manservant who's his vally, cook, dishwasher and whatnot. He came to my shop this morning for some cutlets. The vally-chap I mean. The chauffeur drove him down in his boss's car. The car cost a bit but this Mr. Hartley's not throwing money about. What do you think he bought, eh ? Two lamb cutlets, total one-and-a-kick. For three men, eh ! P'raps 'twas only two for the chauffeur don't live in. He's staying at The Pines, so *his* job's not too dusty for a working-man. I'd not much care for the vally's job, shut up in that great dam' barn of a place all alone, as you might say. Not even a maid for a bit of fun ; although he didn't look the fun sort now I come to think of it. A washed-out scowling sort of fellow. But you can't tell. The gloomy ones are often nuts for the women when they get half a chance, eh, Mr. George ? Now the chauffeur looks a different sort of chap altogether. Big straight youngster. Been a soldier I should say. R.A.F. lad in the War I'd not be surprised. Pint of mild missis."

Both Pearce and Richard had been listening in a desultory way to the butcher's rumbling voice. At the mention of the chauffeur staying at The Pines Richard recollected on the previous Friday seeing a stranger standing in the door of the billiard-room. The man was wearing a dark green livery and appeared to be waiting for someone.

Pearce had evidently been following a similar train of thought. He caught Richard's eye. " Did you hear that about the chauffeur ? " he asked.

" I was about to ask you the same thing," laughed Richard ; " it's queer how minds run along parallel paths when they receive the same impulse. Yes, I heard it, and I was thinking that I had a faint recollection of seeing a well-set-up, biggish sort of chap in the billiard-room a few evenings back."

" He's a bedroom (a large one) and a fine sitting-room," continued Pearce; "I didn't know chauffeuring was such a paying game. If there are many jobs like that going I shall chuck banking and take up driving. I'm sick of the bank anyway. There are too many girls in it now. It's a girl's job, I suppose."

" I should say that jobs like Hartley's chauffeur's are rare," replied Richard ; " but then Hartley, if it *is* Hartley, is a rare specimen."

" I'm afraid I don't know anything at all about him," went on Pearce diffidently : " he was before my time, I expect; I'm only two and twenty. Do you know anything about him ? Clarence George's rot was of course all bunkum."

" Our eminent fellow-citizen *under*-stated things, believe me," smiled Richard ; " a year ago Hartley's name was everywhere. You *must* have seen it."

Pearce shook his head. " I never read the papers," he

confessed, " except for football and cricket results, just the sports page, you know. Who was or is Hartley ? "

" Hartley was," replied Richard, " Dr. Hartley of Wimpole Street ; he was also one of His Majesty's judges in Chancery ; and he was the Bishop of Farling."

Pearce looked bewildered. " You're pulling my leg ? "

Richard shook his head. " It's only a minute or so to time. Let's be off and I'll tell you about Hartley as we go along."

3

It was a little after eight o'clock the next evening. Richard and Mason had just finished their dinner, and the maid, Mary Basset, had brought their coffee, asked if they wanted anything more, and smiled over her shoulder at them as she closed the door.

" She's an attractive chit, in a homely sort of way, isn't she," said Mason, warming the brandy in his glass between his large hands ; " when she's busy in here in the firelight and lamplight I get an infernal hankering after domesticity with wife and kids and all the rest of it—all things I'd hate to be cumbered up with in the clear unromantic hours of daylight."

Richard filled his pipe, making no reply.

" Sometimes," continued Mason, " when I've been alone here, and she's been tripping round setting the table, I've sat watching her trim little figure, the assured poise of her body, her slim ankles, and the rounded curve of her breast under her tight frock, and I've been afraid, ashamed I suppose, to say a word to her because I knew my voice was not under control. You know that hunger of desire that gets hold of you at times for anything that's feminine—sheer animalism, I suppose, just lust. Or is it something a little better. Where does lust end and love begin, or are they inextricably mingled ? It seems to me that so many people dodge the issue by calling lust passion. Is there any difference ? Probably, but perhaps not, human beings are such humbugs."

"There's supposed to be, obviously," said Richard; "people talk of passionate love, but never of lustful love. I often think it's a deliberate avoidance of facts, we're ashamed of the beast in us. Our physical functions embarrass us, to put it mildly. And I don't think it's an acquired, a civilised embarrassment. It seems to be a human instinct. Humanity will always seek privacy both for the final intimacy of love and for the excretory processes."

"Always is a long while," commented Mason, "and as a matter of fact it's partly a question of geography. If you're at all high-stomached it's very easy to be disgusted in continental villages, to go no farther from home. But I agree about the privacy that love demands. Doesn't it even go further than privacy, and seek darkness ? When I was a youngster the most vivid picture ever conjured up in my mind by poetry or prose was Tarquin putting his foot on the candle before he seized Lucrece."

Richard nodded. "It's queer how words make pictures and get you when you're young. I was made a captive before I was twelve by a feebler thing altogether : *And her bosom white as the hawthorn buds.* That commonplace lit me and fired me to a real sexual hunger. That's another thing we ignore, or pretend to, the sex-life of children. I was at nine madly, passionately, frenziedly in love, more deeply than I've ever been since ; and when the girl turned me down, I lay on my bed and screamed, biting at the sheets and the pillow. This fury of despair was followed by weeks of an empty misery of desolation that I'm sure I'm incapable of feeling now."

" Of course," agreed Mason, " I'd a dozen love-affairs before I was twelve ; and at thirteen I was crazily in love with one of the maids at home, a girl of twenty. It was the Christmas holidays before I went to Winchester. It was no mere calf-love business so often grinned at by adults. I loved her joyously, frantically, miserably. Perhaps that's why I've now a partiality for maids—or anyhow for Mary. What do you think of her ? "

" I've not noticed her much," replied Richard ; " she's not my type ; I like fair-haired, slim, white-skinned girls—everything she's *not*, in fact."

" You'd like Mrs. Clarence George, then," said Mason ; " or you would have done when she was younger ; she's slim, with corn-coloured hair, and a skin so smooth and white that dazzling's the only word for it."

" I was listening to George holding forth in *The Crown* last night," replied Richard. " What sort of a fellow is he ? "

" What do *you* think ? " asked Mason.

Richard shrugged his shoulders. " A bit crude. The loud-voiced type. Everything about him a semitone too high. I prefer his tales to himself."

" He's not too bad, really," smiled Mason, " he's shy and nervous, as a matter of fact, and frightfully conscious of his albinism ; he thinks it sets him apart as something unnatural. He's fond of talking though. He'd do a far better gossip-column in the old *Sentinel* than I do. What was he on ? Foxhunting or flyfishing ? "

"The new tenant at Denacre Hall, mainly ; I suppose it is *the* David Hartley."

" Yes, it's the great man himself," nodded Mason. " I'd a list of over a dozen books from him this morning ; they were all biology and psychology. He wants them by the end of the week. He'll be lucky if he gets them, as I've to send to London for them. A couple of them are

Fp

two-guinea volumes, and the rest vary from fifteen to twenty-five shillings. I've found a good customer at last. I've not seen him yet, have you ? "

Richard shook his head. " I'd certainly like to meet him. He'd be worth meeting. Since he's been supreme in three rascalities he must be the world's finest rascal."

" Rascalities ! " commented Mason laughing, " why, what's the matter with them. We must have medicine, we must have religion, and we must, I suppose, have law. You may think them all humbug, but they're easier to do with than without. Religion especially. If you're going to have a God, he's omniscient and omnipotent, and therefore to be worshipped. I won't say placated. If worshipped, it's more convenient to have a set form of worship, hence——"

" Why have a God ? " asked Richard.

Mason laughed. " We're in for it now. I warn you I'm a Catholic. A bad one, but," he raised his hands with a whimsical gesture. "Why have a God, eh? Well, here's the world ; who made it ? "

" Here's a watch, *a posteriori* there must be a watch-maker ! That old mumbo-jumbo ! " grinned Richard. " It's not even an analogy."

" Well," went on Mason, " I'm afraid I don't see how you're going to avoid the necessity for the existence of *something* to make the universe. There's surely an architect, a designer. It doesn't affect *me*, you know ; I *believe* there is. I'm trying to see what you're driving at."

" The power to design is immanent in every cell, in every protoplasm," rejoined Richard, " which means that a single cell is capable of producing a whole universe in course of time without any external assistance from a God."

" Marvellous ! " chuckled Mason. " And where, by the bye, did the cell come from then ? "

" Why from anywhere ? " asked Richard. " Why not that

it always existed. If matter is indestructible—a thing I don't believe, by the way ; it's one of the many laws of the scientists that are always faked for demonstration purposes —but never mind, we'll say it's true. If matter then is indestructible, it will last for ever, and a logical corollary of *that* seems to be that it has therefore always been in existence. Assuming that this is true, and also that the power to design is immanent, inherent, in all matter, why then, exit God."

" Exit your grandmother ! " scoffed Mason. " Here, try mine," proffering his pouch, as Richard was about to fill his pipe, " if you can stand pure latakia."

" I can stand anything but liquor," replied Richard, taking Mason's pouch. " I've a theory about boozing. I believe that if three or four generations are hard drinkers, able to carry a barrel without spilling any, about the fifth generation or so the children are unable to stand more than a hen's beakful ; the line has reached saturation point, and so is bludgeoned back into temperance. My father, my grandfather, and my great-grandfather were all boozers, my grandfather especially soaked and pickled himself for years. Well, my brother can't touch beer at all, and a double Scotch will do him proud for hours. Spirits lift my roof right off, and a pint of beer is enough to put me at least on the road to tightness."

" I'm sorry to wreck a good theory," laughed Mason ; " but my people have been a hard-drinking crowd since God-knows when, and here am I, the last of my line, and I can't get even moderately elevated. A bottle of whisky in an evening would do no more than spoil my appetite the next day. Brandy's the only stuff that really moves me. I've never been drunk in my life, and I've seen lusty drinkers under the oak. But we've got away from God. Do you want to return to him ? I don't mind, you know, but I'm not a bit interested. My standpoint is outside argument, outside reason, if you like. I believe in God. Just instinctive, perhaps. Or a sort of protective covering to keep away the horror of annihilation. Or just mental inertia. Or my Catholicism, which I don't practise. What's your grouch against medicine ? We'll agree, shall we, that all lawyers are rascals, and that a law that needs a specially trained and congenitally cunning mind to interpret it is a bad law. Hence all laws are bad laws, all lawyers specious and artful dodgers, and Justice all flim-flam. But doctors, you know ! Haven't you ever been to one as a last hope. They've their limitations but——"

" When I run for a doctor," interrupted Richard, " I hope he takes my case, diagnoses my complaint, (wrongly, of course), treats me and kills me as a punishment for my utterly childish credulity."

" Wait till you're married, and the kid's dying," said Mason, stooping to put coal on the fire.

" I'm not so sure there'll be any kids," replied Richard. " I can't afford any ; I can't afford marriage at all, for that matter."

" Don't worry," chuckled Mason, " no one can until they want to. You'll marry, if the right moment gets you."

" It never got you," said Richard.

" It did," answered Mason, soberly ; " it got me, and I took what I wanted without benefit of clergy. And then I was mad to marry the girl, hungry's not the word. Devouring madness. It's true. Not the accepted belief, is it ? Well I can't help that. I wanted her a dam' sight more then than I did before. But she wouldn't marry me. Said she did love me but she wouldn't marry me now as she'd always have the deadly thought gnawing at her that I'd married her from some mistaken feeling of doing the right thing. That's no like the old romances, eh ? Don Juan generally bolts for it with the seduced maiden trailing after him and dying by the road. But my case is not uncommon, I'm convinced of that. But it was birth-control we were discussing. Or at least not having kids was your point, wasn't it ? Or one of them. It amounts to the same thing. Well, here my unfortunate catholicism comes in again. It's not permitted, although, if I married, I'm pretty certain I should practise it ; thousands of catholics do. Of course, one can split hairs, and say of certain practices that they are not birth-control but self-control. All my eye. They are, in fact, self-abuse, and I'm not using the term in the particular sense which has now become so narrowed as to refer simply and solely to an unnatural practice. I mean that many marital practices that are lauded as the control of self, are so harmful as to be abuse of self."

" Unnatural is a dangerous word to use," ventured Richard ; "we might sit here all night before we came to a common agreement as to what we mean by nature. And when we reached that common agreement we'd have to admit that all birth-control was unnatural."

" Well it *is* isn't it ? " asked Mason.

" I suppose so ; but it doesn't follow that it is harmful, at least physically. But really I don't know, and I'm afraid I'm not particularly interested just now. I'll not worry about it till it's a matter of urgency."

" When it's usually too late ! " laughed Mason. " Good lord ! it's past nine, and O. J. wants my column by breakfast time in the morning. I've not half done it and I've about as many ideas as a snake has legs."

" There's Hartley," said Richard ; " Isn't he good for a few paragraphs ? "

Mason wrinkled up his nose and pursed his lips. " I'm a bit nervous of Hartley as a topic," he confessed. " I'd rather see which way the cat jumps before I get my sling ready. We've always been cautious with Perseval (at least *I* have, O. J., as boss, pleases himself) but the Dean's very small potatoes compared with Hartley. Throughout his career queer rumours have gathered about him like a flock of carrion crows."

" That's certainly news to *me* ; I'd an idea it was a halo, rather than carrion crows, that was about his head."

" A bit of both," suggested Mason ; " why not ? But what are you referring to ? "

" Well, it's most of it hearsay, certainly, but yours is only rumour. One fact I'm sure about : he treated dozens of poor folk for nothing, and ran a clinic for crippled children out of his own pocket."

" A well-stocked experimental station, uh ? " said Mason. " Like hospitals. But that's stealing your thunder. What else ? "

" Nothing very definite, nothing definite at all ; but somehow or other Hartley's name has always been connected in my mind with extraordinary acts of generosity, with real decency. There's been an associated sense of things that are fine and gracious and—er—noble," he ended on a faint note of embarrassment.

Mason got up. " That's the other face of Rumour, isn't that all it is ? She's a two-faced lady. And Hartley's therefore very much like the rest of us, except for his brains. Well, I want to get to the library before it closes. I must grub up something or other for O. J. You're not coming along ? "

Richard shook his head, and as Mason went out, he poked the fire into a cheerful blaze, re-filled and re-lit his pipe, picked up Butler's *Way of all Flesh*, and after a glance at the clock settled himself for a comfortable hour.

CHAPTER V

UNSEASONABLE CONDUCT OF A WORSHIPPER

I

Henry Perseval, Dean of St. Matthew's, Doctor of Divinity, Doctor of Laws, former fellow and tutor of Christ Church, Oxford, was a disappointed man. He had never been accorded his deserts. That was his considered opinion and many thousands of his fellow-countrymen agreed with him, although the constructions put upon the phrase were many, varied, and widely (even wildly) contrasted.

For ten years domestic chaplain to the Archbishop of York he had achieved in his ample leisure a reputation as a ripe scholar, a distinguished littérateur, and a religious controversialist of extreme modernity.

Toward the end of his chaplaincy his particularly provocative book *Some Aspects of The Councils of Nicea and Constantinople—A Modern Commentary* informed that section of the public deeply interested in such matters that a new light, if not a new force, had arisen in the world of militant ecclesiasticism. In this frank little book Perseval, who had doubtless subscribed to the thirty-nine articles before his ordination, lopped and clipped and pruned these dogmatisms to a mere two dozen. In passing he rejected the Trinity, and cast dubious glances at the divinity of Christ.

That portion of the lay Press which noticed the book were divided into three camps : the vituperative, who knew nothing of Nicea and cared less, but who welcomed any opportunity to shout " Judas " simply because it liked shouting scurrilities ; the judicially hostile, who opposed the agnostic

tendencies of churchmen because they considered such
tendencies subversive of the safety of the state ; and the
judicially friendly, who thought that a modern reformation
in the Church was long overdue. There was indeed a fourth
party who could not follow the learned Dean's verbal antics,
and querulously demanded to be told in plain English :
Did he or did he not believe such and such.

Dr. Perseval's next book *The Humanity of Jesus* should
have left, in the least suspicious mind, no doubts as to his
beliefs and opinions.

The Deanery of St. Edmund's, London, fell vacant just
then, and not only Dr. Perseval himself, but a strong body
of opinion in the country, considered his claims to the prize
could not be ignored. Had he not every qualification ?
However, Perseval's claims were overlooked in favour of the
more decorative ones of Dr. Alfred Sayl, and Perseval had to
content himself with the Deanery of St. Matthew's, Welling,
which he accepted the year before the war.

Dr. Strang, the Bishop of Welling, was already at that
time a notorious free-thinker, and Perseval undoubtedly
set himself to become, not the power behind the episcopal
throne, but the throne itself. He determined, moreover,
that the tide of freedom of thought which he believed would
shortly sweep the country should carry him upon its crest
to the height of his ambitions. His third book *The Empty
Sepulchre* was planned and written solely to that end. It
came from the Press at the end of July 1914 and, as many
another and better book, fell still-born in that period of
excited and loquacious pugnacity which marked the early
months of the war.

Nevertheless the Dean, balked of his larger ambitions,
set himself to rule his minor kingdom. He was a man of fine
presence, handsome and distinguished, and the rich sonority
of his voice, his undoubted oratorical gifts, and his daring

tilts at orthodoxy, packed St. Matthew's on the occasions when he preached.

He had, indeed, by the end of the war completely over-shadowed Strang, and the Dean of Welling was as familiar a name to the lay public as that of the Dean of St. Edmund's.

A year or so before Richard Blaney came to Welling the Dean had begun his world-famous weekly articles *A Modern Churchman's Causerie* in *The Saturday Universe*, that red-covered purveyor of literary fireworks, owned, controlled and edited by Abraham Rosenberg, the Hebrew banker.

It was said by the malicious that this last straw was too much for Strang, and his subsequent breakdown was ascribed to jealousy. Certainly about this time began the Bishop's frequent long voyages in search of health. The Suffragan Bishop, Dr. Hellewell, was no match for the redoubtable Dean, and indeed a local wit remarked that Hellewell in the Dean's presence was a modern elucidation of a hitherto obscure verse in the Bible referring to the Almighty and the Mouse.

Dr. Perseval married in 1903 Grace, the only daughter of Sir George Dew, head of the distillery firm of that name ; and by her he had three children, Gillian born in 1905, Freda born in 1915, and Maximilian born in 1917.

2

On Christmas morning 1924, St. Matthew's Cathedral might well have roused envy in the heart of at least one of the worshippers assembled to hear the Dean's Christmas sermon, and to pray. It is conceivable that this solitary worshipper, Mr. Lou Bellairs, lessee and manager of the Theatre Royal, might well have surveyed the fashionable crowd enviously, and have remarked with the gloomy scorn of the unsuccessful professional for the gifted and popular amateur : " Capacity—and for a one-man show ! "

By such a remark Mr. Lou Bellairs would have been guilty of no irreverent forgetfulness of his Maker, for decidedly Dean Perseval, and neither God the Father nor Christ the Son, had been the magnet to attract so large, so patient, so well-dressed, and so excited a multitude.

Welling was now very much alive to the exhilarating fact that for a month there had been dwelling on its borders, occasionally walking its streets, eating its produce, breathing its refined air, the notorious, the unparalleled, the world-shaking David Hartley.

On that Christmas Day Welling, or that portion of Welling which could crowd into the Cathedral, was deliciously and thrillingly aware that it was during his Christmas Day sermon twelve months ago that Hartley had made his devastating avowal. Two questions agitated them. Would their Dean loosen the sword of scepticism from its scabbard of traditional decorum and, drawing it, emulate, nay outdo, Hartley by such cutting and slashing at the body of Mother Church as would leave that ancient lady *in extremis*. That was the major question. Would Hartley be there to listen was the minor one.

Hartley's pew was empty when the service began, and it was empty when at five minutes before noon Dean Perseval mounted the steps of the pulpit.

As the Dean bent his head in prayer nine hundred of Welling's adult citizens, and almost as many of its children, settled themselves in all the stages of comfort that lie between the perfect and the uneasy—this last indeed, in the persons of the wriggling young, had jumped the border-line, and was definitely with the discomforts.

The Dean raised his head and faced the congregation. He looked indubitably great. He stood silently while twenty might have been slowly counted. The hushed expectancy was an intoxicating wine which he drained eagerly, yet with sufficient slowness to savour its bouquet. There were not a few in that multitude, and these not children, who at that moment became unconscious atheists, inasmuch as it seemed preposterous that a being could exist so glorious as to command and receive the worship of Dean Perseval.

The Dean gave out the text, and that richly sonorous voice seemed to leap out of the sounding board behind and above him as singing birds released into the sunshine, as a handful of jewels scattered in largesse by a conqueror. " The twenty-third verse of the first chapter of the Gospel according to St. Matthew. *Behold the Virgin shall be with child, and shall bring forth a son.* And St. Luke the twelfth verse of the second chapter. *Ye shall find the babe wrapped in swaddling clothes and lying in a manger.*"

The Dean repeated the texts, and then resting his hands upon the pulpit rail and bending a little forward he said, " The prophecy and the fulfilment. A fulfilment which gave to the world a prophet, a gospel, a God, faith, hope and——"

There was a stir in a pew not thirty yards from the pulpit and directly facing it. A youthful, frail-looking man was seen to be standing with outstretched arms.

A rustle of mild excitement ran over the congregation, quickly followed by a murmuring of indignation. Interruptions were no new thing in the experience of the congregation of St. Matthew's, although lately they had become very infrequent. The Dean's sermons provoked them, deliberately fished for them, it was said. They occasioned the merest half-glance of amused tolerance, a patient waiting until the wardens removed the offender. But here was a matter for indignation. The Dean interrupted in the first sentence of the long waited sermon. It was intolerable. Where *were* the wardens !

The Dean looked away over the head of the young man whose hands were stretched up to him. Was it a gesture of appeal ? There was nothing menacing in that motionless figure.

And then a voice of amazing volume shook the congregation into bewildered and outraged attention. " Come down, plump prelate ! " roared that mighty voice.

The Dean looked over the heads of the assembly ; five wardens converged upon the brawler ; the congregation craned necks.

But the decorous and dignified pace of the wardens gave that obstreperous voice exactly fifteen seconds' grace. " Come down ! " it boomed and bellowed and re-echoed, " prince of the Church of Christ who was born in a manger, who gathered corn by the wayside for his food—when have you eaten so frugally ? Who succoured the poor—what poverty have you relieved ? Who healed the sick and comforted the desolate—to whom have you brought healing and consolation ? Who was betrayed then as you betray——" Two muscular hands took the interrupter by the shoulders, two by the legs, two gripped his waist, one smothered his mouth, and a rough arm encircled his neck. A dignified, if flushed and panting procession moved slowly down the aisle, the noise of an opening door was heard remotely; the spirit of silence, who had fled abashed, returned, and with her came reverence and awe, her other selves.

The Dean, unmoved, calm, unflurried, his hands still resting upon the pulpit rail, his head a little up-thrust, continued as if there had been no interruption, no hiatus, not even a brief pause—" and charity."

There followed a sermon of such suave and bland orthodoxy that, before its close, the expectancy of clerical indiscretions had given place to the not less exciting expectancy of appetite.

The congregation devoured its traditionally mighty repast that day without dreaming that the Dean had substituted the word " charity " for " illusion " when he resumed his interrupted sentence. That the whole tenor and argument of his sermon had to be recast, remoulded, changed utterly and completely at a second's notice, was equally unguessed by them. To the Dean, a master of extempore oratory, such a task had presented no difficulty that he did not surmount with supreme and admirable facility.

3

It was perhaps rather unfortunate that Christmas Day fell on Friday, for the local magistrates did not meet until the Monday, and the brawler in the Cathedral, who gave his name as Alfred Smith, was kept in custody over the week-end.

At ten o'clock on the Monday morning the Mayor, Colonel Bowers, and Captain ffoliot sat at the magistrates' table in the little courtroom awaiting the arrival of Mr. Isaac Downer, the clerk.

" Small sheet this morning, eh, Banks ? " smiled Colonel Bowers, looking up from *The Times*.

" A few drunks, an assault, and the Cathedral fellow."

" Ah, yes, Smith, isn't he ? Does anyone know anything about him ? Any visible means of support, or just a tramp ? He looked a ragged-backside sort of wastrel to me ; but I wasn't very close."

" I've had a few words with Superintendent Haynes," put in Captain ffoliot, " and he says the fellow's a stranger. He had nothing to identify him on him, and not a cent in his pockets. He refused to answer any questions, except to give his name as Alfred Smith, an alias of course. Haynes puts his age at anything between thirty and forty-five, says he speaks like a gentleman, and to judge by his hands has never done any rough work."

" Gentleman ! " snorted Bowers, " his voice had a canting

whine to my ear; he's probably a discharged clerk, one of these socialist or communist rascals. What's the charge, Banks?"

" Brawling and creating a disturbance in a place of public worship, resisting arrest, and wandering without visible means of support," read out the Mayor, who was running his fingers down the charge-sheet. " Downer's very late this morning. But he's always late. It's very annoying. He does it purposely, I'm convinced of that. He's nasty, too, if one mentions it."

" He's insolent," grumbled Bowers, " and too damned cock-sure by half. But I don't see that we can do anything about it. He knows all the tricks of the trade and we don't. He's here to instruct and advise us, and he's no intention of letting us forget it. I hate dealing with these upstarts. He'd no school you know ; went to a Board School, and then as office-boy into a solicitor's, and just *grubbed* his way up. But it's the same everywhere now. Once, if a man were a solicitor, a medical man, a padre, or in the services, you could be certain he'd a school and came from decent people, had some breeding about him, but nowadays—my God ! "

" It's worse than that, Bowers," said Captain ffoliot, " when you get down to the workers these days what do you find but shiftlessness, scowls, insolence, and a lot of canting rot about e-q-q-quality. This Smith blackguard had the nerve to ask Haynes what he was doing for the sick and the d-d-d-destitute. Told him too in the same breath that no man was good enough to be another man's master ; and added that Jesus C-C-C-Christ said so."

" You say Haynes knows nothing at all about him? " asked Bowers.

" Nothing. The only man who'd seen him before the Cathedral incident was Thatcher Burnett, he's a hedger and ditcher too, who said that he'd noticed him on Christmas Eve prowling about near Denacre Hall."

" Has Haynes seen Mr. Hartley ? " asked the Mayor.

Captain ffoliot grinned faintly. " No ; Hartley's not an easy man to approach. Haynes thought it unnecessary. Hello, that's Downer's car, I think. Shall we open now ? Are we taking the cases alphabetically ? "

" I propose," interrupted Bowers, " that we have this blasphemous rascal in first. We can dispose of the drunks afterward ; they won't take long ; can't blame a man for an extra glass or so at this time of the year. What's the assault, by the way, not a criminal one ? "

" No, common," replied the Mayor ; " just a neighbourly squabble, the Mahons and the Fergusons in Gay Street ; bad language, words, and a black eye or so. Ah, good morning, Mr. Downer ; good morning, Superintendent. Constable, open the door of the public entrance, and bring in Alfred Smith in two minutes."

Some dozen or so citizens of Welling filed in, shuffled along the narrow gangway, and settled themselves with much scraping of chairs and clearing of throats. A cold, damp wind blew in through the open door. " That'll do, Constable ! " snapped the Mayor irritably ; " close the door. Alfred Smith."

There was no dock in the small court-room. The prisoner entered and stood by the reporters' table, facing the magistrates in their chairs on the platform. A constable stood immediately behind him. Seated close to Superintendent Haynes were the four witnesses, two wardens from the Cathedral, Thatcher Burnett, and Butcher Wainwright who had been sitting next to Smith in the Cathedral.

The proceedings were farcically irregular. The four witnesses remained in court throughout the proceedings, the prisoner was badgered to reply to questions that were not allowable, while the magistrates, and even Haynes, prompted witnesses, argued loudly, and at length, or appealed to Downer sotto voce. That gentleman sat with a grin on his face, watching the burlesque of justice through half-closed eyes.

Haynes read the charge and described the arrest.

" Lies from beginning to end," observed the prisoner calmly.

There was a humorously appreciative murmur from the public gallery.

The Mayor looked at the figure standing in an attitude of careless disregard before him. Smith's glance caught and held the Mayor's, stared insolently, unblushingly. The Mayor felt himself becoming embarrassed, reddened, and lowered his eyes to the charge-sheet. But in that long glance he had taken in the man's ragged clothes, his thin straight figure, pale clear face, bright brown eyes, and tousled hair. There seemed nothing minatory about that almost frail, and certainly wholly destitute and powerless figure ; nevertheless, as the Mayor's eyes fell, an extraordinary sense of fear swept over him. He was not quite sure that it was fear. He could not indeed find a word to express it. Anger was it ? No, not that. Awe ? Well, what exactly *was* awe ? Reverence ? Nonsense ! What the devil was he thinking about. Disgust ? No, it was not that. It *was* fear, or something so like it that the effect was the same. The gobbling voice of Colonel Bowers broke into his thoughts.

" That will do, Smith. What do you plead ? "

The prisoner merely shook his head.

Bowers stared at him angrily, and then turned and whispered to Downer, who nodded indolently.

" We'll have the first witness, Superintendent," said the Mayor.

Thatcher Burnett was sworn, and in reply to Colonel Bowers, said that just before five o'clock in the afternoon of December 24th he had seen the prisoner near Denacre Hall.

" You're sure of the time ? " asked Captain ffoliot.

" Yes, sir," replied the witness, his s's blurred to z's and his vowels open and drawn-out. " I know it were near five because I knock off at five. I get the time from the Cathedral clock, sir."

" It was nearly dark, then, Burnett," said Colonel Bowers, " you couldn't see the Cathedral clock from that distance."

" It'd struck the three quarters some time since, sir," replied Thatcher Burnett.

Bowers nodded. " Go on."

" I was doing the ditch for Mr. Hartley, sir, the ditch behind the hedge, Melcombe side of the big gates ; I'd just put my hook down and was fastening my dinner things to the bike, when that young fellow came through the hedge, looked at me a while, and then made off toward Melcombe."

" Do you mean he came from the grounds of the Hall ? " asked the Mayor.

" Yes, sir, pushed his way out through the hedge."

" How was he dressed ? "

" About same as now, sir, on'y not so mucked."

" All right, Burnett, that's all, thank you."

The two wardens gave identical evidence of the brawling in the Cathedral, and Wainwright the butcher, who had been Smith's neighbour in the pew, corroborated the statements of the wardens. Asked if he could remember what Smith had shouted Wainwright shook his head. "I only remember the beginning, and I'm not quite certain of that. I think it was, ' Come down, plump pirate.' "

Downer smiled broadly. " Prelate, I think—er—er—Wainwright, prelate."

The Mayor and his two colleagues conferred together for a few minutes. Several times they looked toward Downer, who was leaning back in his chair and staring at the ceiling.

GP

Presently the three nodded their heads almost simultaneously, and the Mayor rapped on the table with his finger, and said, " Alfred Smith, the magistrates find the charge——"

The prisoner took one step forward before the restraining hand of the constable fell on his shoulder. He smiled faintly, shrugged his shoulders, and with his two hands thrust out level with his waist he began to speak rapidly. That vast deep voice that had seemed to fill the Cathedral crashed and boomed and re-echoed in the tiny court-room.

" I found in the temple of God lies, treachery, sophistry, worldliness and betrayal ; a worship of mammon, a denial of Christ ; all that I found where there should have been truth, loving-kindness, faith, charity, gentleness and meekness.

" I find in the temple of Justice——"

The Mayor's hand descended heavily upon the table. " Silence ! " he said loudly, staring over toward the prisoner, but avoiding his glance. " The magistrates find the charges proved. If you have anything to say concerning those actions which we have found you guilty, er—guilty of —we are prepared to listen. But we cannot listen to a rigmarole——" At this point the Mayor looked up, caught Smith's glance, was held by it until he shivered and dropped his eyes. " . . . to a er—rigmarole about er—we don't want any socialism here," he ended lamely.

The prisoner turned his back upon the magistrates, and surveyed the court. He then faced round and stood quite still.

Bowers and ffoliot were whispering together. Bowers spoke softly to the Mayor, who nodded.

" Six months' hard labour," said Banks gruffly, and looked down at the charge-sheet.

Downer, with an expressionless face, leaned from his seat, and whispered across Bowers.

Bowers stirred uneasily, and fidgeted with a pen-and-ink stand. The Mayor slightly raised his eyebrows. " Twenty-eight days," he amended.

Again Downer whispered.

The Mayor flushed. Captain ffoliot said a few quick words to Bowers, who smiled, and repeated them to Banks. The Mayor smiled also and said huskily, " Er—that—is : Fifty-shillings or twenty-eight days."

" I have no money," said Smith simply ; " you will pay for me."

There was a burst of sniggering laughter from the public gallery.

" Don't be insolent ! " snapped Bowers, " or you'll get more. If you've no money you must go to jail. Have you any ? "

" I have no money," repeated Smith, " but you have plenty. What have you——"

Bowers waved an impatient hand.

" Constable," he said, " remove——"

A chair scraped in the gallery. A man stood up. It was Daniels, the owner of *The Crown*. " I'll pay the fine, Mr. Mayor," he said. And fishing out a wad he marched down the steps and put three notes on the table in front of Haynes who glared at them angrily.

It was not yet noon when the last case had been dealt with and the court cleared. The Mayor stood chatting with Downer. Bowers and ffoliot, who were going to Sapton links for a round before luncheon, came over to them.

" Well, Banks, we're going over to Sapton ; can we drop you anywhere, or you Downer ? But I forgot, your car's here, hey ? What about you then, Banks ? "

The Mayor shook his head. " Thanks all the same but I'm walking ; I want to make a few calls too."

" All serene, then," replied Bowers ; " damned queer of Daniels, wasn't it ? "

" Queer," said ffoliot, " it was damned insolence ; did you see his g-g-g-grin? When's he up for his licence again?"

" Heh ! I'd forgotten that," commented Bowers ; " April I think, eh, Banks ? I think we'd better have a word with Haynes."

Downer smiled sardonically. " It didn't strike me as an insolent grin, ffoliot. Ever seen the drawn gape of a rabbit fascinated by a stoat ? And the licence business wouldn't do, Bowers ; too—er—personal, shall we say, or not suffi- ciently disinterested."

" I don't quite follow you, Mr. Downer." He hated Downer calling him Bowers, and emphasised the Mr.

" No ? " said Downer. " Bates & Bates, the Darum brewers, have been trying to buy out Daniels since 1916. He's too cute and won't budge. Doesn't want to. *The Crown* was his father's, and a free house, and it's going to be while he's alive, he boasts. Well, you are a director of Bates & Bates, ffoliot has shares, a fair holding, eh ? That's all right, I've some too. The Dean has quite a lot. But, well——" he spread his hands. He turned away ; the door closed behind him, and a minute later they heard him cranking up his car in the street below.

Bowers drew down his mouth so that his teeth showed under his drooping moustache. It was as much a grimace of annoyance as a half-sheepish grin. " Blast that fellow ! " he growled. " Come along, ffoliot. Well, good-day, Banks."

4

On Tuesday evening the customers of *The Crown*, at least those frequenting the bar-parlour, had the good fortune to be present at the first night of a spectacle that was to be an ever fresh topic of conversation for many months, and was ultimately to take its sequential place, small yet important, in the strange happenings at Welling that are now as important a landmark in human history as the birth of human speech. Had it been realised that the performance was for one night only, and a curtailed performance at that, doubtless *The Crown* itself would have fallen under the invading feet of the curious.

The affair began quietly. The early customers soon after six found to their amazement that the bar-parlour staff was increased by one. Mrs. Daniels always served behind the bar, while Daniels both served there and strolled around to the tables to chat with and to take orders from customers who were seated in small groups about the room. But on this evening a thin, frail, brown-eyed man, with a shaggy head of hair over a face of remarkable pallor, paraded among the tables, wearing a white apron and carrying a tray. The first two customers stared for a moment, but obviously did not know the new waiter. Presently three others entered, eyed the waiter, walked to the counter, and stood drinking. One of them, however, followed the waiter with curious eyes, and at last said something to one of his companions. All three now stared at the frail stranger walking slowly in and out among the tables entirely unconscious of the interest he was arousing. Several fresh customers arrived, and presently the astounding truth was out and about. The new waiter was Alfred Smith.

Colonel Bowers entered for a gin and vermouth at twenty-five minutes past seven. He strode to the counter, and being served, raised his glass and half turned to look about him. The edge of the glass was at his lips when he started abruptly, shaking some of the liquid over his hand and up his arm. For a dozen seconds he glared angrily, the half-empty glass poised six inches below his quivering moustache. Then he drained the glass, placed it on the counter, wiped his mouth, his hand, and his arm, with a large blue silk handkerchief, and with an amazed and angry snort strode to the door.

By eight o'clock the bar was full and Smith was carrying out his duties under the battery of a hundred absorbed, surprised eyes. Clarence George was gasping hoarse nonsense to Captain ffoliot, who was not listening. Richard and Mason were there; Haynes was in his favourite corner; Crowson, the chauffeur from Denacre Hall, was talking busily with Joe Barentz, the proprietor of the new garage on Broad Walk at the quay end of The Arcade. "Major" Browning and Fletcher, the retired builder, had tired of the quietness of The Pines billiards room and had dropped into *The Crown* for more varied fare. There were also a sprinkling of the tradesmen in the city, the cashier from Barlow's, and one or two mechanics, shop-assistants and clerks.

By nine o'clock the interest had become milder, and by nine-thirty the crowd had thinned considerably, and those who remained were discussing with exaggeratedly friendly gestures the topics that on such occasions formed the mainstay of their intercourse—cattle, football, crops, business and divers complaints. Alfred Smith remained upon the stage as unregarded as a familiar drop-scene.

At exactly a quarter to ten Kitty Baxter, one of the youngest and prettiest of the half-dozen or so professional prostitutes of Welling, entered the bar-parlour and took a seat at an empty table. This was sheer bravado on the part of Miss Baxter, and she had obviously primed her courage with drinks at other houses. No prostitute was ever permitted in *The Crown*, alone or accompanied. It was not the sort of happening that seemed within the bounds of possibility. As well might *The Crown* habitués expect the ascetic O. J. to enter and call for a pint.

Miss Baxter's effrontery won for her a *succès de scandale*. It was a furore, a triumph brief but glorious. She sat unnoticed for the space of five seconds. And then Alfred Smith approached her, bowed, smiled, and asked for her order. " A Guinness, darling, and be quick, there's a good boy," said Kitty. It was not until Smith was returning with the drink to Kitty's table that Mrs. Daniels noticed her leprous presence. The landlady dropped the glass she was polishing. " Smith," she called, " what are you doing ? Bring that glass back."

Smith stared from Kitty to Mrs. Daniels with a puzzled frown. Kitty smiled at him softly, and then directed an impudent grimace at Mrs. Daniels.

" I'm serving this lady, madam," said Smith haltingly.

" Bring that glass here, you fool ! " snapped Mrs. Daniels. " Get out, you slut ; how dare you ! "

Smith put down the glass in front of Kitty, and turned once more toward Mrs. Daniels, who had lifted the counter-flap and was coming toward them.

" Cheerio, darling," smiled Kitty, raising her glass.

Mrs. Daniels towered over the table. " Get out, you ! " she said icily, and raised her hand.

Smith put out one arm, as if to ward off a blow from the girl. " What are you doing ? " he asked in a distraught voice. " She is a good woman ; it is easy to see that. I have seen few better in——"

A resounding slap was heard all over the bar. In the silence, fallen so suddenly that the small clock on the shelf above the bar was heard ticking clearly, the shrill angry voice of Mrs. Daniels rasped and fretted the nerves like a saw upon a hidden nail. " Get out, both of you, *now* ! "

Kitty rose slowly. She was still smiling. Smith stood with one hand up to his smarting, flushed face. He stared stupidly from one woman to the other.

" Out ! " said Mrs. Daniels, beside herself, and jerking a thumb towards the door. Smith looked over to the landlord, who, with one arm resting on the handle of a beer-engine, was apparently looking into the ullage trough. " Out with you ! " shouted the landlord, without looking up. Kitty put a hand upon Smith's arm. She staggered a little. She looked at him with a foolish drunken smile. " Come on, darling," she said ; " see me home, there's a sport." She moved unsteadily toward the door, constraining him to follow. As she passed the landlady she spat in the saw-dust at her feet and flung at her so vile a phrase that Mrs. Daniels went white, stepped back a pace, and put up a hand to her mouth.

The next moment the door had slammed behind the couple, and the bar-parlour became loud with excited voices.

Daniels, who was serving Captain ffoliot with a final drink, noted with relief that it wanted but three minutes to time. ffoliot, whose potations had mellowed him, said amiably, if somewhat reprovingly, " Well, Mr. Daniels, you'd a bad b-b-bargain there, eh ? Can't understand why you did it."

" You can understand just about as much as I can, Captain ffoliot," replied Daniels in a puzzled voice. " Why I paid his fine is a mystery to me, except that I caught his eye when he turned round in court, and after that I didn't seem able to help myself. It was the same afterward. Don't ask me to explain ; I can't. Well, thank God he's gone ; no one's more pleased than I am to see his back. I hope we've seen the last of him."

Mr. Daniels's hope was realised ; but, strangely enough, that realisation brought the keenest disappointment to a number of citizens of Welling, not the least important among them being Superintendent Haynes.

CHAPTER VI

IMPERTURBABILITY OF THE DEAN

I

Welling awoke on the morning of New Year's Day to the excitement of a mystery. For the more important citizens of Welling it was an uneasy waking, a stirring of drowsy limbs, a turning of aching heads and a licking of parched lips : such was the price they paid for social eminence, the price of being numbered among the two hundred chosen adults who graced the Mayor's New Year Eve Fancy Dress Dance at the Town Hall. This annual merrymaking was originally a children's party, to which a few important adults were invited to keep the fun going. As many as a thousand child dancers had been known to pack the floor of the Town Hall. In the course of time the affair lost its purely juvenile character, more and more adults came in, the masks and noses donned by the pioneers to amuse the children grew into costumes more and more grotesque, lovely, or resplendent, and at the time of the Mayoralty of the patentee and sole manufacturer of Banks's Non-Slip Suspenders the festivities were frankly in the nature of a Fancy Dress Ball for adults, in which, by special grace, one hundred youngsters were allowed to participate.

The awakening then of these revellers upon New Year's Day was uneasy and late. The " lesser breeds without the law," up, out, about, and at work some hours earlier, had been recompensed for their loss and rewarded for their virtue by having to themselves the first draught of the heady and foaming cup of mystery. It was theirs to take the top off.

The Cathedral had been broken into and desecrated.

The famous twelfth century tapestries in the apse had been torn down, shredded and scattered. The altar rail was bent and twisted, the altar steps fouled, and the rich altar-cloth rent to rags.

In the lesser transept Justus van Helsing's Stations of the Cross had been ripped and " worried "—no other word so aptly describes their condition. Three of the John panels in the western transept were splintered, pews were upset, hassocks scattered, books torn, with their frail leaves lying over the floor as if there had taken place the deciduous mating of a host of gigantic ants.

Nothing had been stolen, nothing utterly destroyed ; it seemed to be a mere wanton act of imbecility, stupid, haphazard, apelike.

2

Venning, one of the minor canons (he was precentor), arrived at The Deanery while the Dean was still in his bath, and was restrained with difficulty from shouting his news through the keyhole.

Having learned that Venning had not yet breakfasted, the Dean suggested he should stay for breakfast, and tell his news then.

Twenty minutes later, interminable ones to the precentor, the Dean, Mrs. Perseval, Gillian and Venning were seated in the pleasant room looking out over the Teal.

It was after nine, and a pallid sun had just clambered over the mists beyond the estuary, and was competing in a half-hearted fashion with the blazing fire on the hearth. Long before the meal was over it had given up the unequal contest and retired for the day.

" Well, fire away, Venning," said the Dean, stirring his coffee composedly. " An outrage in the Cathedral, I gather ; I've heard something about it. Tell us the details. Presently,

presently, feed first, there's no hurry. Who's there now?"

"Canon Hoyle was there with Superintendent Haynes when I came away," replied Venning.

Dr. Perseval frowned and made a slight sound of annoyance. "Hoyle, tut! tut! h'm, well, of course. H'm. And Haynes was sent for? Of course, yes. Some more coffee. Well, well, Venning," jovially, "tell us now if you really can't wait."

"Yes, that's pretty bad," commented the Dean, when the recital was over. "You don't know what Haynes says? No, of course not. I suppose it's pretty clear."

"You mean that dreadful brawling fellow, dear?" asked Mrs. Perseval.

The Dean nodded. "It seems pretty obvious, eh, Venning."

"I don't believe it, father," said Gillian. "Canon Venning has just said it looks like the work of a maniac or a monkey. Whatever that poor creature Smith was I'm sure he was quite incapable of such wicked and stupid vandalism."

"I probably know more about the fellow than you do, darling," replied the Dean gently, sure that the ugly affair at *The Crown* could not have reached Gillian's ears, and would indeed have been incomprehensible if it had.

"Perhaps you do, father," smiled Gillian, equally sure that such matters were not the sort of things the Dean was likely to know. "But, really, was there any sign of violence or madness about Alfred Smith? It wasn't true, of course, but I'm sure it seemed true to him. He appeared sincere enough. After all, to a tramp, and he was that, wasn't he, we must seem to live a very luxurious and scarcely Christ-like life. I mean that he's probably a Bolshevik or Communist or whatever it is, believes all men are equal and so on. Or that's a Socialist, isn't it. Well, it doesn't matter; I can't see much difference. Anyhow, when people believe *that* sort of thing, why then it seems to me bang goes the church, at least as regards popes, cardinals, bishops, deans, and all the splendour, wealth and ceremonial that attaches to them. It must be jolly hard on——"

The Dean rose. " Yes, darling, of course. Things *do* seem like that at nineteen. I didn't mean to interrupt you, but it's over the half hour, and we really must be off."

" *That*," said Miss Lettice Ovey, at luncheon in the refectory, "is what comes of treating these people leniently. One disgusting outrage follows another, of course ; and will continue to do so until the rascal's laid by the heels. I've no patience at all with such softness. That's what's the matter with everyone these days—the country is emotionally bankrupt and is living upon sentimental overdrafts."

" You'd have a job, Miss Ovey, to get an overdraft if you were bankrupt," grinned James Fletcher. " We've had some, eh, dear," turning to his wife. " But," he went on, nodding toward Miss Ovey, " you're quite right. That brawling tramp should have been put away for a couple of years. A fine state of affairs now, isn't it. There's more discipline wanted, more firmness, we want more cat used. A touch of the cat and these fine fellows would mend their ways, eh, Major ? "

Ex-Sergeant-Major Browning nodded gloomily. " Same everywhere nowadays, Fletcher," he said. " Army too, glad I'm out of it. The only way to get the best out of men is to put the fear of God into 'em, and it's the only way too to keep down the worst. Relax discipline, and what happens ? Thanks ? Not likely. Gratitude ? No fear ; oh, no. I'll tell you —Bolshevism, murder, any beastliness. This fellow who's done all this is tarred with *that* brush. It was plain enough, I should have thought, and then he goes scot-free. I wonder they didn't give him something out of the poor-box."

" It's not proved, you know, that he'd anything to do

with this Cathedral job," said Captain Lacy mildly. " For my part I don't believe he did. He seemed a decentish sort. After all, what did he say that hundreds of people haven't thought. I can't see it's much of a crime to say what you think—even in church and out loud. It's time someone answered the parsons. But that young man hadn't the physical strength to do the damage that was done in the Cathedral. I thought he looked about all-in in court the other day."

" Oh, I *quite* agree with you, Captain Lacy," smiled Miss Alice Thatcher ; " perhaps not *altogether* about shouting in church what one thinks. If folk did that, why, the children would soon be copying the example of their elders, and shouting loudly what they thought in schools, and that would be *too* dreadful. They're naughty enough now, in all conscience. No, I mean that the poor young fellow looked ill. I had the good-fortune to be sitting quite near him in the Cathedral, and only a few minutes before the disturbance I was watching his face, and thinking what an interesting, poetic-looking face it was. A distinguished face, even. It reminded me of dear Haydn Coffin singing *Motherland*. There was a sad sort of look in his eyes, a sort of——"

" Well, Miss Thatcher," interposed Miss Ovey tartly, " you may be right, but *I've* no patience with all this softness, and I hope nothing happens to any of the children under your care from this wretch. None of us can feel safe with a wild beast at large. I doubt if Captain Lacy was so soft when he'd a crew to govern at sea."

" I left that to the mate," Lacy smiled amiably ; " but he was pretty easy. I never saw him do more than smack the boy's head. But the work got done without much cursing. All yarns of brutality at sea are mostly faked. Brutality doesn't pay nowadays, that's the long and short of it. Perhaps it never did. No one's been arrested yet, have they, Browning, Fletcher ? "

The two addressed shook their heads. " Arrested any-one ! " scoffed Fletcher. " Haynes ? I'll gamble you, Lacy, he'll never find that brawling scoundrel."

" Do you mean Smith ? " asked Lacy.

" Who else ? He's the man they're looking for, isn't he. If *he* didn't do it, who did ? "

Captain Lacy moved back his chair and stood up. " No," he said, " I give betting a miss nowadays, otherwise I'd be glad to gamble you that Smith had nothing to do with last night's business."

Richard and Mason sat at tea in their sitting-room.

Mason had been writing his *Sentinel* column during the afternoon, and half-a-dozen loose sheets lay on the sofa.

" No lack of meat for your column these days, eh ? " said Richard.

Mason poured himself out a second cup of tea. " You mean the sacrilege affair ? I've hardly touched it. O. J.'s doing a leader. I've contented myself with merely mention-ing it, and have spread myself over Banks's Circus."

" Has O. J. a clue then ? " scoffed Richard.

" Clue ! O. J. doesn't worry about technical matters, concrete things, reality. No ! he's up against the conscience, the soul, the trend of spiritual things, and guff of that sort."

" Guff ! " cried Richard, " that's a bit thick for a Catho-lic, isn't it ? "

" I meant that it's guff in O. J.'s hands, but for the love of Mike don't start on theology again. The question is : Who killed Cock Robin ? "

" Well, who do *you* think ? "

" Everything points to Smith," replied Mason, " but I'm sufficiently a gormandiser of detective tales to know that everything *never* points to the guilty person."

" Not in tales, no," said Richard, " but this isn't a tale. But aren't there any other suspicious characters ? "

Mason shrugged his shoulders. " Search me. Who else *could* it be ? What object——"

" *You're* not altogether free from suspicion, you know," grinned Richard ; " and there are some twelve hundred folk in Welling that fall equally under the same cloud."

"Beyond me," said Mason. " How do you make that out ? "

" Welling Cathedral was stolen from the Catholics, eh ? Isn't that what you say ? Well, what could be——"

" We're not likely to injure any of our possessions," mocked Mason, " which are merely being looked after temporarily by our estimable if extremely dull lost brethren. I'm afraid your theory, like most of your theories, won't wash. You're a far more suspicious character—a confessed atheist. Who more likely to commit sacrilege, and to enjoy an orgy of destruction of holy things. There's Hartley, too ; he's another, isn't he ? "

" Pah ! bunkum ; the convinced atheist wouldn't pay churches such a compliment. The man who commits sacrilege is always intensely religious, intensively religious I might call it. I reckon he's permanently pathological but only transiently sacrilegious, as the lover who strangles his mistress is permanently pathological but only transiently murderous."

" I'm too tired to follow you," yawned Mason, " but I'd not be surprised if you're right. Well, I must hop down to the office with my stuff before dinner. Cheerio."

Shortly after nine o'clock that evening Clarence George leaned a negligent elbow on the bar at *The Crown* and wagged a derisive finger at Captain ffoliot. George's chocolate and white spaniel Larry lay flattened at his feet. It was mangy and bore obvious signs of neglect. George worshipped it in print and thrashed it in the seclusion of his garden. Larry was a good gun-dog, and George, despite his white-lashed peering eyes, was a first-rate shot.

Standing between the two men, but behind the bar, stood Daniels, polishing glasses.

George's throaty gasping tones were loud above the low massed growling of voices. " All my eye, ffoliot ; I don't believe for a moment that poor little rat had anything to do with it."

" I'd answer that if you were to be taken seriously," rejoined ffoliot, carrying off his annoyance with an air of faint amusement, " but you can't expect me to t-t-treat your cursed flippances with any respect."

" I'm as serious as an owl," went on George ; " you fellows have no knowledge of character, no insight, no essential understanding of the subtleties of impulse. You need an artist on the bench to advise you. That misguided Smith fellow was an artist in his way ; that's why you didn't understand him, and treated him in the traditional way the English treat their artists."

" They don't seem to have treated you too badly," said ffoliot ; " I wish I'd your leisure. But as for your artists, I know a little about this artistic t-t-temperament. Do you know what I call it ? Humbug. Half the shiftless rascals, the work-shys, the tricksters, the sharks, the seducers, rapers and p-p-p-perverts mouth a lot of damned rot about the artistic t-t-t-temperament and plead it as an excuse for any of their blackguardisms. As for Smith, in the first place he was a damned little, work-shy, spouting Bolshevik, and in the second place he's the obvious p-p-p-perpetrator of the outrage at the Cathedral. And if Haynes doesn't shortly lay him by the heels you can look out for some worse things than sacrilege. What do you think, Daniels ? Have another drink, George. Bass ? "

The landlord reached down for the bottles. When he

stood upright again his face was flushed. " I think you're quite right, sir."

George, who either had not heard of the end of the Tuesday evening affair or was purposely ignoring it, stared at Daniels. " Why, dammit," he croaked, " I thought you were about the one bright spot in the whole nasty muddy business. Who's been getting at you ? On Monday you pay his fine and cherish him like a brother. On Friday rub his nose in the dirt. What d'you mean by it, Tom Daniels ? Middle name Peter, eh ? I'll never pray for a publican again. Ever heard of the Vicar of Bray. Dammit you ought to be in the Church."

" There are some things, Mr. George," said Daniels, gravely, " that are not so easy as they look. What I did for the man I did, and that's that. Why I did it is another thing. What I thought about him, and still think about him, you've just heard. And if the two don't seem to fit, I can't help it. But if Smith didn't do it, who did, sir ? "

" Who ? There're dozens of people in Welling who might have done it. I'd have done it myself if I'd thought of it, and had the pluck, but I've got to keep respectable or my publishers would get annoyed. Alienate my readers. But what about ffoliot ? He's no need to run straight. And why not the great Hartley ? Or the Dean. If you think about it you'll see that suspicion should certainly point to the Dean. Always look for motive. Well, here you have it. First the reverend one's love of the limelight ; second, the restoration-fund badly needs a fillip ; third, more love of limelight, and so the fourth, fifth and sixth. If Haynes were a man he'd arrest the Dean. What a panache, eh ? for the Superintendent. And, by the bye, no one has suspected it may be the work of a woman. There are quite five hundred women in Welling capable of it. If you look at the thing closely you'll see it's obviously the work of a

Hp

woman—a virgin spinster. All that ripping and tearing and scattering. What's that ? Why, repressed sex ; the chained and thwarted libido ; the frustrated creative-urge. *Too* obvious, isn't it. What does Freud say ? You don't know, ffoliot. You ought, you have all the marks of a Freudian subject. I'll tell you. Frustrate the creative-urge and it becomes the destroying, the annihilating urge. See Freud's *Sex-Repression in Infants*, Chapter nine-hundred-and-six. I'd lend you my copy only it's a signed first edition, countersigned by Jung. Well, I can't stay. What about some shooting on Saturday, ffoliot ? Larry's getting lazy, aren't you lad ? " He stooped to pat the spaniel, who cowered down and backed away. " My God ! misunderstood as usual. It's a curse to be sensitive. Damn you, Larry, take that, you ungrateful, slinking, lecherous bastard. No shooting, eh ? Well, 'night ffoliot, 'night Daniels. And, mark you, the Dean's the man."

The Welling Weekly Sentinel, which was on sale by 10.30 on Saturday morning, contained a leading article by the editor headed *Seedtime and Harvest*.

The deplorable and regrettable outrage (it ran) at the Cathedral need occasion no surprise to the thinking reader. Who sows tares will not reap wheat. Rather, who soweth the wind reapeth the whirlwind. Surprise and indignation is being expressed that the criminal has not yet been brought to book. To these natural expressions of emotion the kindred one of fear is fast being added. We consider, however, that any such feelings are unnecessary, further, they are invidious. Superintendent Haynes has the matter in hand, and we do not speak without the book when we say that developments may shortly be expected and an arrest made. *The Sentinel* is not the bar of justice, and we do not presume to prejudge any issue, but we may be allowed to summarise the events of the last week. What were they ? The brawling in the Cathedral (curiously enough we had almost written " the lashing of the money-changers in the Temple ") the trial and sentence ; the affair at *The Crown* ; the sacrilege.

We put these events in sequence, not to point to any person as the perpetrator, but because we would put our readers in logical mood.

For those of our readers who have been happy enough to sit at the feet of Dr. Perseval during the last ten years (for ourselves we have not experienced that happiness) the sacrilegious act which has shocked not Welling alone but all England must appear as an inevitable result.

We submit that sooner or later the passionate, if misguided, anger of some unhappy worshipper in that wonderful house of God was bound to display itself in violence.

We say without any fear of contradiction that there is a logical sequence in these events but that *the brawling was the end and not the beginning of a chain of events*. Further, and with equal conviction, we will add that the sacrilege that followed so closely upon the heels of the brawl *was merely coincidental* and in no way connected with it.

We trust we have made ourselves perfectly clear.

Do we then exculpate Smith ? Not necessarily. Smith may be the guilty party. Time and Superintendent Haynes will doubtless show. We reserve our opinion. Frankly the matter is much bigger than it appears. The waif Smith is no protagonist in a sordid drama but a simple passer-by sucked by chance into a whirlpool of tremendous events— a speck of dust in the eye of Hercules.

Who then, it may be asked, is the protagonist in this vast drama to which we allude. With full consciousness of our words and of all their implications we reply : *The Church of England*.

The police-court proceedings will be found on page 6, and an interview with Canon Venning is on page 4.

We would call our readers' attention to the charming nature story on page 8. This is reprinted from *By Hedge and Ditch*, the recently published book of our distinguished citizen Clarence George.

3

At half-past nine on Saturday evening Superintendent Haynes rang up the Deanery, apologised for the lateness of the hour, and asked Dr. Perseval if he could spare him five minutes.

Shortly afterwards the Superintendent sat in a comfortable chair before a blazing fire in the Dean's study.

" Well, Superintendent," enquired the Dean genially, " any news ? "

Haynes shook his head. " Nothing to go on, sir. What is puzzling us is not so much where Smith is *now*, but what he did with himself between Wednesday morning at nine o'clock, and the early hours of Friday morning, when he broke into the Cathedral—if he *did* break in."

" Is there anyone else you suspect ? "

" Well, sir," smiling, " it's a policeman's duty to suspect all sorts of people provided they fulfil two necessary qualifications : have they a motive ? Have they an opportunity ? In these cases, and in many others, of course, we have to take into consideration the maniac and the drunk. In such cases there is no necessity to look for a motive, and opportunity is the only qualification. Well, sir, it's pretty plain that the opportunity to break into the Cathedral is a qualification, if I may call it that, possessed by most of our citizens, yourself, and myself included. There is then only motive to consider, and in religious matters it is a difficult job to tackle. I therefore ruled out religion for the time being and considered the whole affair as one of personal spite. It is here that you can help us. Is there anyone——"

"A moment, Superintendent ; you don't think then that Smith is the man you want ?"

"I can't go as far as that, sir ; he may be ; quite probably is. He's being well attended to, but while we're searching for him it's possible that the real culprit may get away. Now, of course in confidence, sir, do you know of anyone locally who might be harbouring feelings of revenge toward you. A dismissed servant, say ?"

The Dean shook his head slowly. "I have many enemies, or so I am credibly informed, but they are rather in the church at large than in Welling. Perhaps I might say in the world at large."

"You know nothing about a Richard Blaney, for example ?"

"Never heard the name. Who is he ? Why do you mention him ?"

"He's a young schoolmaster who's only been in Welling a few weeks. We know nothing against him, and I merely mention him because a newcomer is at least always worth enquiring about."

"Then Mr. Hartley's is the next name on the questionnaire, eh ?" smiled the Dean.

"It *was*, sir," laughed Haynes, "but I see I needn't bother. There's his chauffeur and manservant. I suppose . . . ?"

Dr. Perseval shook his head. "I don't think we need consider them. I don't think the line of personal spite will lead us anywhere. It seems to me the work of a maniac, or perhaps a religious fanatic. That seems to point to the man Smith. You were saying . . . ?"

"About Smith being in hiding from Wednesday morning

until Friday ? Yes sir. If we could unravel *that* we'd know something. I questioned the woman Baxter. She admitted—you'll excuse a few er—sordid details, sir—she admitted that Smith went home with her on Tuesday night, but says she was too drunk to remember very much. She does remember him putting her to bed, and then turning in on the floor with all his clothes on. ' He never touched me,' were her words, which perhaps you'll not understand——"

" You can take it, Superintendent, that I'm not unfamiliar with life in most of its aspects. Go on."

" ' He never touched me,' she said, ' and he woke me up just about eight to drink a cup of tea. And when I'd drunk it he took the cup, leaned over me, and gave me a kiss like a kid would, and hopped it. And when I got up after a fag I found he'd left me a quid note.' That was all she'd to say, sir. She did not see him again, and no one that we've questioned has seen him since. The pound note was queer. I thought it must be a lie, for he'd not a cent on him when he was in court. I sent Constable Baxter along to *The Crown*, but it was all right. Daniels had given him the note as an advance to buy a few things."

" Which means he left the woman's house penniless ? "

Haynes nodded. " Unless he'd been helping himself at *The Crown*, which is no easy job with a cash register."

" And Mrs. Daniels ! " laughed the Dean. " Well, Superintendent, I'm afraid I can give you no assistance. I confess I'd have fewer misgivings if it had been a question of personal spite. A maniac is another matter. We don't want some terrible sexual outrage. There is always that horrible possibility with a maniac at large ; and I'm afraid the fact that, for the moment, religion seems to be the impulse is no safeguard. Good night, Superintendent ; *do* please keep me informed from day to day. *Good* night."

CHAPTER VII

THREE NIGHTS

You say (began one of Richard's letters to Rachel, dated January 9th) that there's never any news in my letters. I like that! Don't I tell you about myself, what I've been writing and thinking, how I'm feeling, and why. What more can any girl want!

You don't want me to talk about school, do you? I've enough of that from 9.0 till 4.30, and after that I do my best to forget it. For sixteen years I've laboured with child (as someone put it); I began keen, energetic and quite fond of kids. I've nothing to show for sixteen years' work (except the sack, for that is just about what my hegira from town amounted to); I'm no longer keen or energetic, although I still like youngsters; and I feel ten years older than my age. If I'd just one more ounce of pluck than I possess I'd chuck the job and chance my arm. That's the curse of a safe job—after a dozen years or so of a regular screw—however miserable—one hasn't the guts to clear out and make a fresh start. It would be a livelier world if everyone were sacked automatically after five years in a job.

No, *fiche-moi l'école!* which is, if I've spelt it right, a very low oath, but no lower than the subject deserves.

Scholastic news barred then, and my personal news exhausted, what else is there to write about in a small-sized somnolent city like Welling. Nothing at all, darling. NOTHING did I say? Gawd! haven't you read the papers? Or perhaps it's not in them. We've had about eight days of such excitements that I hardly know where to begin.

I told you in my last letter all about the Smith affair—

you remember, the brawl during Pious Persy's Christmas Day oration ? Well, that, apparently, was the beginning. You remember the fellow disappeared after a dust-up in *The Crown*. Good ! Well, now we come to New Year's Day, and I'll need a new paragraph in which to spread myself.

About eight o'clock on New Year's Morning Venning (he's a minor canon in charge of the music, precentor, isn't it ?) found that the Cathedral had been broken into and left in a pretty condition. John panels, mediæval tapestries, screens, paintings, altar-cloths, stained-glass windows, books, pens, hassocks and much of the other organised paraphernalia of mechanical worship had been smashed, torn, ripped, ruined, scattered and upset. (The only thing *not* upset, by the bye, was Holy Henry.) As you may guess, seethings of excitement in Welling all day and for days.

Obviously, said Welling, it was that bloody little brawling Bolshie, Smith. Hue and cry for Smith, the chase led by the unwieldy Haynes—luckily for H. not literally led. The perfect bureaucrat (literally !) he sat in his bureau and hounded on his myrmidons (don't you love that word—it has thrilled me ever since I first came across it as a small kid in Cockton's *Valentine Vox The Ventriloquist*—' sinister ' is another thriller from those romantic days) his myrmidons (I must write it again) to trail, take and hold in duress the unfortunate Smith. The bloodhounds however failed. Friday passed and Saturday dawned but still there was nothing to report. On Saturday morning *The Sentinel* appeared with a leader by Owen Jones (O. J.) in which that rufous little hot-gospeller, in what he doubtless conceived to be a well-disguised, tactful and lucid (in reality the wildest of confused and bigoted dithyrambs) homily, admonished the Dean as the cause of the outrage. However, I sent you the copy yesterday—I meant to days ago but forgot—and you can read him yourself. To-day's issue I've not yet read, but

will post it on Monday, and you can use it to check the
following world-shaking events. But before going any
further I must mention that to date (Saturday evening)
Smith is still at large, although he was seen by—but I'm
coming to that.

Welling's palate for sensation, tickled so pleasantly on
Christmas Day and New Year's Day, received another and
keener titillation last Sunday morning. Soon after dawn,
and just about the time the early-servicers were trotting on
their empty stomachs to kirk, P.C. Gale found the Welling
War Memorial not only upset but broken. It was a poor
imitation of the Whitehall Cenotaph, a weak copy in which
austerity had become insipidity, and grandeur a mean
pretentiousness—like a cretin wearing the dress of a
gladiator. Welling should have welcomed the fact that
dwelling secretly among them was an artist of spiritual
conviction and physical strength (the thing must weigh
fifteen hundredweight). But no ! Welling became hysterical.
Insult to England's dead. And so on and so forth. Smith
again of course ! Tremendous howls of indignation levelled
at the puerility of the local police (Welling hates Haynes
who is, in truth, a pompous and tyrannical windbag). But
that was merely a beginning. Some time during Sunday
night all the windows of the Baptist chapel were smashed
(Mason said it was a divine intervention to let in the light !
these Catholics ! !). But worse, the statue of Eleazer Atkins,
the founder of Welling Grammar School, had been hurled
from its pedestal, and lay in ten or a dozen jig-saw pieces
across the roadway. The statue (a damned nuisance to
traffic it always was—surely Jehu rejoiced that day !)
stood in the middle of the small circus formed by Market
Street, the south end of the High Street and the beginning
of Tilly's Lane. And only thirty yards away from the Police
Station ! !

We now come to Monday night. Hold your breath! we're only just getting warmed up. You'll see how appropriate the verb is in a moment. Well, on this never-to-be-forgotten Monday night there was a disgraceful and outrageous attempt to burn down my school ! ! All those who have the best interests of the nation at heart will be glad to know this despicable act of incendiarism was unsuccessful. But the clod, the lout, the clown with a phial of phosphor in his fob (as Lamb said in one of his not-too-understanding moments) proceeded thence to the Natural History Museum (the pride, the nestling, the darling, the apple's-eye of Welling, with its statues of Jefferies, White, Audubon, Thoreau, Walton, Darwin, Laplace, Newton and Lamarck, its stuffed dead birds (including a chough !), otters and badgers, its butterflies, dragonflies, and blown birds'-eggs, *and* its presentation copies of the works of Clarence George—dear God, dear God, all these !). Where was I darling? I've just turned over the page and am too lazy to go back. Well, anyhow, the Natural History Museum opposite the bandstand, and quite near dear old Banks's mansion, was burnt out, gutted, utterly destroyed. How Rima must have sung !

It was an exciting night for the Bankses, and for us at The Pines for that matter. My joint-sitting-room looks out over the Square, and from three a.m. till dawn (whose coming the flames mocked) Mason and I sat supping bottled Bass and watching the conflagration (that's the correct word—see *The Sentinel*).

By now, sated of these second-hand excitements and alarums, you will be yawning and hoping it's the end. Madam, the end is not yet.

On Tuesday, about dawn, or just before, the aforesaid clown (or another, or even one not in the clown category) delivered a promethean assault (O. J. again !) upon

Denacre Hall—*you* know, the great Hartley's residence. It was only in the jerry built portion, and unoccupied at that. Not much damage was done, except to dignity, and in fact tempers produced more heat than the flames.

The local brigade turned up accompanied by most of the early birds of Welling. They found the fire out and well under ; but the Captain (a fire-eater rather than an extinguisher), a pig-headed sidesman in one of the bethels, insisted upon making assurance doubly sure (his phrase) and despite the protests of the valet, he (grimy but exalted from his victory over the flames) got the hose ready, and was on the point of forcing an entry (once more I quote O. J.). There was some excuse for Captain Herbert, as there was still a lot of smoke, and all sorts of cracklings and creakings and groanings from wood and iron-work. The arrival of Hartley himself (or rather of his head, shoulders and voice from an upper window) began the fun. Hartley told Herbert in the nastiest of voices (I know this completely contradicts everything that one hears about Hartley, but I was there—yes, at eight, on the foulest of January mornings !—and it was undoubtedly a nasty, provoking, insolently imperious voice) told him to clear out and to take his rascals with him.

Herbert, like a fool, attempted to argue, and then actually asked to be allowed to enter and look round. You've heard the phrase " convulsed with rage " ? I used to think it journalese. Well, at Herbert's suggestion Hartley's face at the window fitted that phrase as the eye fits the socket. He looked demoniac. He used a foully offensive epithet. " —— off ! " he shouted ; " my God, Bates," to the valet, " where are the dogs ? Go and loose them. Dammit ! get out while you're safe."

Hartley's Alsatians had earned an unsavoury reputation in and around Welling, and long before their joyous morning baying was heard Denacre Hall grounds were as deserted as the site of ancient Babylon.

Well, darling, that's all to date. Since that Tuesday morning nothing else has happened, and Welling is just beginning to calm down.

There are two small items of interest—or they may prove to be later on. The attendant on duty at the bandstand reported to Haynes a day or so ago that on Wednesday, just before midnight, he was leaving the bandstand (that's last Wednesday week, of course—the day before New Year's Eve) and he overtook a man just beyond the Mayor's house. A light burns outside there all night and the attendant swears the man was Smith. He watched him cross Market Street, when he disappeared. I've forgotten what the attendant was doing at the bandstand at that hour—it was something about a lost handbag. Rather dull, eh?

The next item is even less interesting. The valet at Denacre Hall is convinced that just after three o'clock on Tuesday morning, the 5th, he saw a misshapen, stooping, heavily-built man clamber over the railings of the drive, and come toward the main-entrance. Bates's room (that's the valet) commands only a partial view of the approach, and the figure was hidden when still about thirty yards from the door. It was quite moonlight on Tuesday—at least it was here. Bates was awake and up with neuralgia. How I came to know anything of it was from Crowson the chauffeur. He digs here, I think I've told you. Bates, of course, told Hartley in the morning, suggesting that the figure he'd seen was that of the incendiary. Hartley merely smiled, but pooh-poohed the notion.

So there you are, darling, and all the records broken (a) My own—for longest letter, (b) Welling's—for the most exciting week and (c) Yours—for patience in reaching the end.

It is well after midnight. There is a confused medley of snores haunting what would otherwise be a romantic silence. Thank God to-morrow's Sunday. I shall not get up before mid-day.

A fine love-letter this ! But when I gave you love you demanded news. Having now had a surfeit of news you may have regained a healthy appetite for love. But it's too late now. Next time.

Mais, je t'aime quand même !

PS. I'd nearly forgotten ! There have been *no* arrests of any sort. Haynes is terribly peeved. Welling, despite its fears, chuckles—at least by daylight.

CHAPTER VIII

AN APHRODISIAC INVASION

I

Punctually at nine on the following Tuesday morning Miss Lettice Ovey entered her small bureau. She changed the date on the new almanac from 11 to 12, noted with pursed lips that the daily motto was : *She that is loved is safe—Jeremy Taylor*, lifted oddments and ornaments from desk and mantelpiece to check the thoroughness of the dusting, sat down, opened her account book, and rang for her morning cup of tea and dry toast.

Five minutes later she paused in the middle of a column as Mary Bassett knocked, entered, put the tray by her side and said, " Is that all, ma'am ? "

Receiving an impatient nod by way of reply Mary withdrew, closing the door softly behind her.

Miss Ovey dipped a finger of dry toast in her tea, transferred the dripping morsel dexterously to her prim mouth, and was about to pick up her pen when a guffaw of laughter, followed by a softer peal, brought a frown to her brow.

She began to drink her tea with little rapid sips. The apple slid up and down in her corded throat like a marble on a child's abacus. Presently she put down her cup, and removing the receiver from her desk telephone, asked for a number, and presently was through to her correspondent. At the end of a brief conversation she replaced the receiver, and leaning back in her chair rang for the maid.

Mary Bassett re-entered, and picking up the tray, was eaving the room, when Miss Ovey said, " When you've taken the tray to the kitchen, Mary, I want to speak to you. Please be quick, as I am very busy."

Mary returned presently, a little breathless and flushed. She stood beside Miss Ovey, waiting.

"Sit over there, Mary," said Miss Ovey, moving her chair, so that she could watch the girl's face. "I have an unpleasant task before me."

"I am sorry to hear that, ma'am," replied Mary demurely, but with a touch of anxiety.

"I will be as brief as possible," went on Miss Ovey. "It is this, Mary; I do not find your attitude toward the boarders all it should be, especially to the gentlemen. No, please don't say anything until I have finished. As far as the ladies are concerned there is no very grave fault, just a slight lack of respect, a mere *gaucherie* perhaps; but as regards the gentlemen the matter is very different. In short, Mary, you are much too familiar with them."

Mary flushed. "I don't understand, ma'am; I'm sure I've done——"

"I'm quite sure you've done nothing wrong, Mary," interrupted Miss Ovey; "it is simply an undue and unfitting familiarity on your part that I complain of."

"I've done nothing, ma'am, I'm——"

"Undue familiarity," interrupted Miss Ovey, "joking and laughing."

"But, ma'am, I only laugh when they make jokes. That's no harm. It would seem so—so—unfriendly if I didn't."

"Friendly or unfriendly are not terms that are fitting to your position as a maid. Only a moment ago I heard you laughing on the stairs with one of the boarders. Who was it? Mr. Mason?"

"Yes, ma'am."

"You are often laughing and talking and joking with Mr.

Mason, and with Mr. Blaney, and Mr. Pearce, to name no others. It must stop."

"But what can I do, ma'am? It is the gentlemen who ought to stop. It's not fair to put it on me, ma'am."

"I beg your pardon, Mary, what do you mean by that?"

"I only mean," doggedly, "that I can't help it, ma'am, or stop it; it's not my fault."

"Indeed, then how do you explain the fact that the gentlemen seem to reserve their jesting for you. I have no fault to find with Kate."

"I don't know, ma'am."

"You must know; it's perfectly plain. The least you can do is to be honest——"

"I am honest, ma'am, I——"

"I've not finished. The least you can do, I repeat, is to be——"

"I *do* know then." Mary rose hurriedly from her chair, her cheeks red and her eyes wet. "I *do* know, Miss Ovey. The men like me and I like them. Is that any harm? Is that my fault? And they don't like Kate. I like talking to them and joking. Who else is there to joke with here? I don't work the worse for it. They're just like schoolboys, and I've three brothers at home. There's no——"

Miss Ovey opened a drawer at her elbow and took out some notes. "I did not expect insolence from you, Mary. After this, of course, you cannot stay after to-day. You will be paid in lieu of notice. I have nothing more to say. Send Alfred to me. Oh, and your reference will be ready before you go. I trust——"

"Keep your reference, Miss Ovey," said Mary quietly. "You'll pay me the money because you've got to. I've nothing to thank you for in that. I sha'n't need a reference. No references are wanted in the job I'm going to. And——"

"I hope you've not been foolish——"

" Hold your tongue. It's my turn to speak now. Who are you to tell me not to be foolish ? And if I *was*, what's it got to do with you. Well, I *am* going to a better job : I'm going to be married. And *that's* a job you'll never get. You're a dirty-minded old woman."

" Thank you," said Miss Ovey, calmly. " Please close the door softly when you go out, and send Alfred to me."

By ten-thirty Mary Bassett had departed, flushed, bright-eyed, and defiant ; and as the door closed behind her Miss Ovey in her bureau rang up the servants' Registry Office for the second time that morning. She spoke for a moment, then listened for a considerable time, nodding her head and occasionally interjecting abrupt staccato affirmatives. At last she said, " Very well then, as soon as you can send her along. Yes, oh, certainly, before noon. Thank you. Good-bye."

Just before twelve o'clock Miss Ovey and Miss Alison sat side by side in the bureau. Two half-empty glasses of a highly intoxicating cowslip wine and a plate of biscuits, were on a small table near them. Sitting opposite the two sisters was a strikingly lovely girl of about twenty-two. The absurd, helmet-like hat could no more disguise the pale beauty of her face than could the cheap fur coat hide the alluring grace of her body.

" Take off your hat, child," said Miss Alison.

Released from the hideous constraining shape of straw a mass of black curly hair sprang into a sudden and silky loveliness about the bewitching face.

Miss Alison caught her breath. She looked for a moment at the girl's vivid scarlet mouth and black flashing eyes and

I P

looked away. Her sister tapped upon the desk-top with a pencil.

" How old are you ? " asked Miss Ovey.

" Twenty-four, ma'am."

" And you have no references ? "

" I have never been out before, ma'am."

" What have you been doing ? Not in a factory, I hope."

" I've been at home, ma'am."

" You don't live in Welling ? "

" No, ma'am. I came here for a holiday. I live in Silchester. And I liked Welling and thought I'd like to stay for a while. And so I went and put my name down at the Registry. Only this morning, just after breakfast."

Miss Ovey looked enquiringly over to her sister, but Miss Alison remained silent.

" Were you—are you staying with relatives, relations ? " resumed Miss Ovey.

" No, ma'am, I'm staying over Clarke's the confectioners, in the High Street."

" H'm, yes. Have you been to Welling before ? Do you know Welling ? What made you choose it for a holiday ? "

" My mother used to come here when she was a girl, ma'am."

" Indeed. What's your mother's name. No—not Mrs. Brown. I mean before she was married."

" I know, ma'am ; Ann Nankarrow, ma'am."

" Oh, yes ; and you're Ann too. Is there anyone in Silchester would give you a reference ? You go to church, of course. Who is your vicar there ? "

" We don't know anyone," shaking her head, " at all, ma'am ; we've only been in Silchester a few weeks. You see we used to travel about a lot. We don't live in a house. It's a caravan. Or it was. Dad was a——"

" A gipsy ? "

" Well, no, ma'am, not exactly a gipsy ; he called himself a travelling salesman. We sold everything for the house, pots and pans and carpets and brushes and all that. But Dad died when we were nearing Silchester and so we stayed there. Mother has sold up and is in lodgings. If I don't stay here I'll go into service when I get back. Perhaps we both will. Mother doesn't look old."

" Is she like you ? " asked Miss Alison.

" Yes, ma'am."

" Well, Ann, my sister and I would like to talk it over. You had better have your luncheon in the kitchen, and by then, doubtless, we shall have made up our minds. Alfred will take you down. Ring for Alfred, please, Alison."

The door had scarcely shut behind Ann and Alfred when Miss Alison turned hastily to her sister with outspread protesting hands. " My *dear* Letty, we really can't. You're not thinking, surely, are you ? "

" I don't see why not, Alison."

" You're going to introduce that—that—that simply incredibly lovely and provocative creature into this house with half-a-dozen men in it, about whom we really know nothing. My *dear* Letty——"

" She's a pretty girl, but that's neither here nor there. I'm convinced she went to that Registry Office by the direct intervention of Providence. You noticed her tale seemed a little lame. Of course."

" I don't understand you, Letty."

" Why, the poor child hadn't the slightest notion of remaining in Welling. But, our need arising, Providence, I am perfectly sure, inspired her for our benefit. She is pretty and—er—I suppose provocative to men. Well, we must see that nothing is provoked. As for refusing the assistance of Providence, when it is proffered so graciously and so abundantly, it's out of the question."

Miss Alison shrugged her shoulders. " I can't, I fear, Letty, hope to understand such things, but it seems to me that if Providence wished to assist it might have chosen a more suitable instrument than a gipsy."

" Nonsense, Alison, the girl's no gipsy ; she's quite respectable. Trade is respectable enough these days. Her father was, after all, a merchant. A little mediæval perhaps, but we should not object to *that* in a Cathedral city of the age of Welling."

" You dismissed Mary because she was too attractive to the——"

" I dismissed Mary for insolence. And in any case Mary came to us in the ordinary way. All this is quite different. You know, my dear, where it is a question of Providence I am never at fault. Providence inspired me to take The Pines, and has inspired my conduct of affairs ever since. We owe our present position entirely to that, you must admit. Mary Bassett was an insolent little flirtatious baggage, coming from nowhere and returning thither. Ann Brown is a different person altogether. I look upon her as especially chosen by Providence, by God, to be a help and a comfort to us. I am sure, when you have given it longer consideration, you will agree with me."

" In that case I will agree with you now, my dear Letty," replied Alison drily. " I must see cook about the savouries. Shall I tell Ann ? "

" Do dear."

2

" Boy, a peacherino ! *Gott in Himmel !* have you seen her ? "

Mason, who in moments of excitement spoke the language of O. Henry, grinned amiably as Richard entered their sitting-room about half-past four the same afternoon.

" Who ? What ? No, I've seen no peaches. I'm dirty and I've a throat like a red hot saw. Ay, ring for tea, I'll be down in ten minutes."

" If you'll take my advice you'll make it five," chuckled Mason.

It was more than ten minutes later when Richard returned to find tea waiting, and Mason eating bread-and-butter, which he was spreading thickly with Gentleman's Relish. " You've missed it, my boy," he said indistinctly.

" My God ! I don't know how you can stomach that stuff as you wolf it," said Richard. " A little of it goes a long way with me."

" I eat it for its beneficial effects ; by nine o'clock I shall have acquired a princely thirst which——"

" What's the ' it ' I've not seen ? "

" The new maid."

" Good Lord ! is that all ? What a randy old devil you are. You've too much leisure. If you worked harder you'd have less hankering after wenches. Well-fed, idle folk are always lustful. And given the opportunity they are not only uxorious husbands or adulterous bachelors, but promiscuous. Obviously so. It's an engaging occupation, given average luck, and provided one hasn't to work for a living. The finest of all the parlour games we used to call it in the army."

" What the devil are you blethering about, Blaney ? Have an egg. No. Bread-and-butter. Well, try the cake—a new one, God bless us."

" It's you that's blethering, isn't it ? New maid. Curse new maids and old maids, tall and short, fat and thin, the whole boiling . . . "

" Have you finished ? Give me a cigarette. I'll ring. Now shut up, sit still and watch."

Ann Brown entered with a tray. She placed the tray down

and leaned over the table to gather up the cups and plates. She did not look at the two men by the fire. Presently the tray was full and she turned toward the door. Richard sprang up and held it wide. He kept his eyes averted until she had almost passed him, and then he looked at her half-shyly. She looked into his eyes for the briefest moment and was gone.

Richard sat down again by the fire. Mason looked at him with a faintly derisive smile. " Eh, my boy ? What——"

" Shut up ! " irritably ; " do shut up. Christ ! what a lovely thing." He sat very still staring into the fire. Presently without raising his eyes, and mumbling a little over the stem of his pipe, he began to quote :

> " Come with bows bent and with emptying of quivers,
>   Maiden most perfect, lady of light.
>   With a noise of wind and many rivers,
>   With a clamour of waters and with might ;
>   Bind on thy sandals, O thou most fleet,
>   Over the splendour and speed of thy feet ;
>   For the faint east quickens, the wan west shivers,
>   Round the feet of the day and the feet of the night."

" Precisely ! " commented Mason. " Swinburne, isn't it ? Lovely, lurid stuff he wrote, and they say he never had a woman in his life. And now apologise for your abuse. Isn't she a peacherino ? "

" She's—she's—hell ! what isn't she. Sorry I droned out that mush. Pah ! a wax doll beside a child. Ay, I'll apologise for anything. I'll believe in God next ; nothing else could have planned her. The new maid. A maid. Think how we've corrupted that lovely word."

" M'm ! m'm ! m'm ! " grunted Mason, filling his pipe.

Having cleared away in Richard's and Mason's sitting-room Ann had to serve a rather late tea in the refectory for three of the women boarders. They were Mrs. James Fletcher, Miss Alice Thatcher and Mrs. D'Arcy L'Estrange.

As Ann went out Mrs. L'Estrange began to pour out. "No milk, I believe, Miss Thatcher? Isn't she a bonny lass. Mary Bassett was pretty, but this new girl is positively lovely. I hope the men will leave her alone. But who could blame them, especially the younger ones."

"Young or old, they're much the same," commented Mrs. Fletcher, out of the experience of sixty years of a quiet life. "There's not one of them to be trusted. Nature never intended them to stick to one woman, and they certainly have every sympathy with Nature's view. Not that I doubt Fletcher's fidelity : I don't."

"But surely, Mrs. Fletcher, you don't mean to say that conjugal fidelity is merely lip-service on the part of men. It sounds too disgusting."

"You're not married, my dear, and I'm not saying it unkindly ; your turn will come, and then you'll perhaps think differently. You can't know men until you've lived with them. I'm sure Mrs. L'Estrange will tell you the same. Brothers are not much help. I was brought up with a family of brothers and found I knew nothing of men till I was married. You've got to live with a man in all the intimacy of married life before you know much about them. Don't misunderstand me : I've no patience with folk who pretend that men and women are entirely different creatures. That's bosh ; they're far more alike than unlike. But you'll find that men are more childish, more sentimental, more sensual, more imaginative, more cautious, and more emotional than we are."

"In other words," smiled Mrs. L'Estrange, " that they are, when all is said and done, a slightly superior piece of workmanship on the part of the Creator, more delicately balanced, their nervous system more sensitive, their steel of a finer temper. The notion that women bear pain better than men is true in fact, but the reasoning is fallacious, the blunt truth being that women don't feel pain so keenly as men ; they simply are unable to, their nervous system, coarser, duller than men's, will not let them."

" Isn't all that old-fashioned ? " said Alice Thatcher. " Surely women have proved to-day that they are men's equal in everything."

" Don't you believe any such nonsense, my dear," smiled Mrs. Fletcher, " men are annoying, shiftless, lazy, dirty, untidy, anything you like that's distasteful to a diligent, conscientious and fastidious woman ; but, taking it all round, men can do most things better than women, and without half the expense of energy and nervous force."

" I can't agree," shrugging her shoulders, " but, curiously enough, when you use the word fastidious I'm bound to go further than you. I've taught boys and girls, separately and mixed, from all ages between five and twelve for many years, and I must confess that in grain boys are more fastidious than girls. I know small boys have the reputation for being dirty, and in fact they can be filthy little beasts, but I have found them far more fastidious with themselves over small personal intimacies than girls, they seem to have a keener sense of the privacy of their own minds and bodies than do girls. It may——"

" We're all saying the same thing," interrupted Mrs. L'Estrange. " I heard a woman, a very well-known composer, say that humanity is an instrument, the creator is the master-player, and that all the loveliest, deepest and truest effects are obtained from the male strings. That's not precisely how she put it, but it's the gist of it."

" Do you think women are the more beautiful ? " asked

Alice Thatcher. "Even that seems to be pooh-poohed nowadays."

"Yes, I've read about it scores of times," said Mrs. Fletcher, "and I've never been able to make head or tail of it. I don't know what it means. What do you think about it, Mrs. L'Estrange?"

"I think there's a terrible lot of humbug talked about beauty, and I agree with you that I don't quite understand what is meant by women being more or less beautiful than men. To artists? To one another? To some non-human observer outside the world? If much of beauty is sexual, and I don't see how you can escape that, why then men find the supreme beauty in women and women in men. We'll leave out all the other beauties, which are, after all, only poor or rich relations, whichever you prefer. There may be things of loveliness which would appeal equally to men and women, as far as we can judge, but even then who's to know whether they are re-acting similarly. I think it's one of those insoluble questions, insoluble because there can't be an answer. But I'm getting out of my depths. I'm not sure I follow my own reasoning. Even the new maid is not absolutely lovely, and I'm using absolutely in what Mr. Mason calls the highbrow sense. Neither absolutely nor universally."

"I doubt if Mr. Mason would agree," observed Mrs. Fletcher drily. "It was he who led to Mary's——"

"We're coming round in a circle, aren't we?" commented Mrs. L'Estrange. "I was about to defend Mr. Mason by saying that they were all doubtless equally attentive, and then I remembered we began like that."

"All talk about really deep things does that," gushed Alice Thatcher, "don't you think? I think it proves that there are some things we can never know, either we're not meant to, or our minds are not big enough. Well, I've a lot of exercises to mark before dinner. This little chat *has* been delightful. And now I'll make a confession. I don't think Ann beautiful. There's a word which describes her better if only I could think of it. Not alluring, not enticing. No, it's, dear ! dear ! ah, *luscious, that's* the word. Like a gorgeous cherry bursting with juice. That sounds horrid, but it's the way she impresses me."

" Play you a hundred up, Lacy," said "Major" Browning in the lounge that evening after dinner. " What a night. I thought it was *February* fill-dyke."

" Make it a foursome," suggested Fletcher ; " here's Mr. Pearce with nothing to do for an hour. Come along."

They filed into the billiards room, and while Browning practised shots, the others hung up jackets, re-filled and lit pipes, chose cues from the dozen in the rack with the care of professionals, chalked them and presently tossed for partners.

It was noticeable that the three older men called one another by their surnames, but all mistered Pearce, who was secretly hurt at this, but was himself scrupulous to use the title in replying to them.

" H'm, Browning and I, Lacy and Mr. Pearce. Come along, then. You break, Browning."

" What do you think of the new girl, eh ? " asked Browning, as the two balls followed one another aimlessly from cushion to cushion. Browning always broke as if driving off a tee. " What we used to call *tray bon for the troops.* I can't understand Lady Letty. She sacks a pretty piece for flightiness and then takes on this real peach. You'll have to watch your step, Mr. Pearce. Your shot."

Kevin Pearce smiled self-consciously, but making no reply, he played his ball, and scored a difficult cannon. He followed this by potting the red twice, and finished with a pretty five by a cannon and going in off the red.

" Well done, Mr. Pearce," said Lacy. " As your partner I'm glad to see your skill, but," jocosely, " as an old man I can only look askance at such evidence of misspent hours."

Fletcher followed, but failed to score, and then Lacy made seven. " Ample for a man who's had to work for his living," he commented. " Yes, she's a very pretty girl, Browning. I've never seen a prettier. So *that* was why Mary went. What nonsense. But I don't think you're right. If *that* was the reason, why engage some one much more dangerous—I'm referring to you young fellows. I'm immune."

" There's no doubt that is why Mary went," said Fletcher ; " the wife had it from Kate. And from all accounts Miss Ovey heard a few home truths before Mary left."

" Of course ! " grunted Browning, " as we were saying the other day, all that sort of insolence is on the increase. I didn't know you'd any time for that sort of thing, Fletcher."

" Well, I haven't, as a matter of fact ; I'm all for discipline and the more rigid the better, but I always make an exception in the case of anyone getting the sack. I saw Arthur Roberts getting the sack in a sketch over fifty years ago, and after ten minutes listening in meek silence, he made for the door, and then turning round, delivered himself of things he'd apparently stored up for years. I've forgotten every word of them, but if you've seen Roberts you'll guess. Well, ever since then, sacking has been a comic business to me. Whenever I've had to do it I've always had a sneaking hope the poor devil would turn on me, but I've never had any luck. Dammit ! I'd have taken him back if he had. But I thought you were sweet on the schoolmarm, Lacy ? " he ended irrelevantly.

" Eh, what ! " exclaimed the startled old sailor ; " don't spring those shocks on me, Fletcher ; I'm too old, and my heart won't stand it. Do you mean Miss Thatcher ? "

" Ay," grinned Fletcher.

" The boot's on the other leg," put in Browning ; " it's the lady who's sweet—unrequited, though, eh, Lacy ? What's the score. Seventy-eight, fifty. Good Lord ! and I won the handicap four times in succession at Aldershot— mess handicap, you know. I'd run up a hundred in seventeen minutes in those days. Best break one-o-eight. *Now* look at me. Your shot, Mr. Pearce. Well, pints round we beat you yet. We'll run along to *The Crown* when we've finished and toast the bright eyes of the new wench. Good shot, seven ; splendid, ten ; oh dam' good ! dam' good ! twelve, fifteen, ah, *that's* a difficult one ; I'd play it off the cush. Let's see, only seven wanted, oh, dam' good ! eh, Lacy ? Youth will be served, what ? Game ! Well, pints it is. Dam' the rain ; hark at it ! Come along, lef' right, lef' right."

CHAPTER IX

A WEEK'S HAVOC

I

It was about ten o'clock on the following Saturday evening. A moon near the first quarter shone palely through the bare branches of the trees that surrounded the garden of The Pines. The rains of the past fortnight had ceased and all day long a pale wintry sun, as new and frail it seemed as the year itself, had endeavoured to warm the sodden earth. The day had been windless, the temperature high, and toward night-fall a faint mist rolled in from the estuary, drifting like a thin, gradual smoke about the streets, over the buildings and among the naked trees.

The Pines was in darkness, except for a low light in the hall and in the lounge. The Miss Oveys, Mrs. Fletcher, Mrs. L'Estrange and Miss Thatcher had accepted an invitation from the Mayoress to share a stage-box for the last performance of *A School for Scandal* at the *Theatre Royal*. The men boarders were about their several occasions, and the staff were at the pictures.

As Kevin Pearce crossed over Bridge Street, the unlit façade of The Pines, gloomy and shadowy in the mist, seemed strangely uninviting. He felt homesick, very young and isolated and alone ; Dublin seemed far away. Despite the bull-dog pipe jutting so jauntily from the corner of his mouth he felt himself no more than a little boy ; he thought of the pleasant Saturday evening fireside of the small house in Dublin, of his mother listening to his exploits, his father smoking and nodding an emphatic agreement, tiny

Cathleen sitting silent upon his knee in an ecstasy of worship. He hated Welling ; he hated The Pines. An utter misery pervaded him. A hungry emptiness crawled in his belly. He wondered if he were going to be ill. Something was the matter with him. A sudden rush of self-pity moved him to a checked sob.

" God damn," he said huskily, " what's wrong with me ! "

He put his latchkey back in his pocket, and leaving the short drive, walked along the path that circled the house, and came into the garden. The small, squat summerhouse loomed out of the mist vague and unreal. He came to it, and stood for a moment leaning against one trellised side, to which brown writhed ropings of creeper still clung. A faint stir within startled him. He came round to the entrance and peered inside. In the dim light that seeped through the lattices he could at first see nothing. And, then, near the corner, standing looking at him, was Ann.

She still wore her maid's black, demure dress, but her head was bare.

He did not know what to say. He stood at the entrance staring. Soon he could see her face. She was smiling and looking him in the eyes. His heart began to thump against his chest. His mouth was dry. He moved a step inside and waited. She came toward him, put her hands upon his coat, and looked up into his face.

Her loveliness overwhelmed him. " Aren't you—you'll catch—aren't you cold ? " he managed to say thickly. He watched her slow smile, felt her hands moving over his coat, and then she put her fingers to his mouth. They were smooth and cold.

" You're frozen," he said. She bent back her head, and her hands caressed his cheeks. His arms went about her, pressing her body to him. She drew his head down, and slowly, softly, caressingly, she put her mouth to his, drew herself closer into his embrace, and then was still.

Presently she stirred a little and shivered slightly.

" You are cold," he said. " Wait." He took off his coat. He pulled open a cupboard door at the back of the summer-house, and taking out a pile of cushions, made a rough couch upon the floor. He knelt down and held out his arms. She knelt beside him and put her face to his. Presently they lay down and he drew his coat over them. He felt her hands about his neck, the slow even coming and going of her breath upon his face. He shook with the thumping of his heart. " Ann," he whispered, " Ann, Ann." He shut his eyes. His self drifted away from him on a tide of dark confusion, sank, was gone. His self stirred, awoke, came back to him. He was drowsily aware of Ann. He lay still in a delicious langour.

When the Miss Oveys installed a bathroom in The Pines after purchasing the property from The Ecclesiastical Commissioners, they considered (and Tyler, the builder, who did the work for them, was of the same opinion) that they had added the last touch of luxurious modernity.

At the end of two years their verbal instruction to Tyler for the installation of a second bathroom was a masterpiece of restrained and genteel *savoir faire*. Tyler received it with a perfection of mingled surprise, admiration and humility.

The commission for a third bathroom a year later came to Tyler through the post. It was as well. The perfect expression of emotion meet for both parties had already been achieved. To risk a repetition would have been to court an anticlimax.

Nevertheless the three bathrooms were inadequate. Richard and Mason both wanted cold baths in the morning and hot ones before dinner. Young Pearce also seemed to be after one at the most inopportune times, while the hopeful comings and annoyed departures to and from the bathroom of the other boarders was a source of constant and increasing friction and bickering.

And so there appeared one day neatly printed Bathroom Regulations hung up in each bedroom. They dealt in the main with hot baths. Each bedroom was allotted two weekly half-hours, and at the bottom of the card there was a note to the effect that all other times could be considered as vacant. These spare times were mostly between seven and eight in the morning, and during mealtimes.

These ablutionary details explain the slippered, pyjamaed and dressing-gowned progress of "Major" Browning toward the bathroom at exactly a quarter past ten on the evening of Monday, January the eighteenth.

The ex-sergeant major entered slowly, turned on the hot water, lit a cigarette, and was about to lock the door when he noticed that the two clean bath-towels, which should have been on the rail for him, were missing. He was already flushed from the bottled stout he had been drinking and from the warmth of the room. As he glared at the omission the flush spread from cheeks to throat and round to the back of his neck in a wave of indignation. " Why dammit-all ! " he growled, gherked frothily, and rang the bell.

He sat down in a white cane-bottomed easy chair, and throwing back his head, stared at the whorls of cigarette smoke drifting up through the steam. There was a knock at the door. "Who's there?" mumbled the "Major." "'Sat you, Ann?"

" Yes, sir."

" Well, dammit, where are my towels. Good Lord, come inside ! d'you think I'm in the bath. Now, look, not a stitch. Where are they ? "

Ann smiled at him provocatively. " It's Mr. Pearce, sir. He's been boxing at the Institute, and came rushing in half an hour ago for a cold sponge down. He must have used your towels. Look." She opened a cupboard beside him, and there, in a tall basket, were two wet, bedraggled towels.

She had to bend partly over him to reach the cupboard. The curve of her breast was within six inches of his hand. He stared at her, moved his hand toward her, and then plunged it into his pocket.

As she stood upright she remained near him, just touching him. She smiled down at him. " I'll bring you two, sir."

" That's a good girl, Ann." He put his hand on her wrist, and began to rub his finger along the soft white underside of her arm that showed through the opening in the sleeve. "You're a pretty lass, Ann," he said. "And don't you know it."

" Now, then, sir, please. You'll run the water over." She moved over to the bath and turned off the hot water. " You're a bad man."

" I'd be good to you, Ann ; give me a kiss."

" You rang for towels," laughing. " In two minutes." The door closed softly behind her. Browning drew a deep breath, and began to fidget with the neck of his pyjamas.

He heard her quick step on the carpeted corridor. He rose quickly and hid behind the door, a half-sheepish, half-wolfish grin on his broad heavy face.

There was a knock and Ann entered with the towels. She stared at the empty chair, and then turning suddenly faced Browning with wide provoking eyes and lips a little breathlessly apart.

" Thank you, my dear," he said hoarsely, and moved against the door. " Put them on the rail and give me a kiss before you go."

She dropped the towels on to the chair, and coming over to him said, " You must let me go. I've an awful lot to do. You're a bad, wicked man." She struck him lightly upon the

KP

mouth, laughed, and brought her fingers stingingly across his cheek.

He let out a low, grunting laugh. He put his arms about her, crushing her against him, so that her feet lifted from the floor. She raised her face to him, laughing, and freeing one hand from between her breast and his, she struck him again and again.

He bent his head swiftly downward, with a twisting thrust as a hawk striking. He fastened his mouth upon hers greedily.

With his eyes shut he raised one hand and groped blindly for the switch.

In the darkness his fingers fumbled with the rope of his dressing-gown.

About half past nine on Wednesday evening Captain Lacy stumped irritably up the flight of stairs to his sitting-room. He was sure the fire would be out. His evening was wrecked. It was too late for *The Crown* now, and he didn't fancy the Club on Wednesdays—it was market day, and a very mixed bag usually occupied the favourite chairs and corners, laughed noisily, and drank itself into maudlin affability before the bar closed.

Captain Lacy sighed as he opened the door of his sitting-room. Confound Miss Thatcher, did she think he'd nothing better to do than to stand at her elbow and turn over music for over an hour. He'd feed up here in future. Fire out, of course, and room like a refrigerator. He switched on the light. " I wonder if the maid left any kindling about. No, of course not ; never when you want it. Well I'm not sitting here for a couple of hours in this cold. I'm sorry, but there we are." He rang the bell, and going over to the sideboard, mixed himself a stiff whisky and soda.

There was a knock at the door, and at his call, Ann entered.

" Hello ! I thought Kate was on, Wednesday evenings."

" Kate particularly wanted this evening, sir, and so I'm taking duty for her. You're awfully cold here, sir. Why, your fire's out. I'll get some kindling ; the scuttle's full. Was that what you wanted ? "

" That's nice of you, Ann ; yes, it was why I rang. I'm really very sorry, but I was kept downstairs much later than I expected. If you just bring the kindling I'll attend to it."

" And a nice mess you'd make. It's all right, sir ; it'll not take me five minutes. Of course you can't sit here like this. You'd catch your death."

She returned in a few minutes with kindling wood wrapped in newspaper.

" Let me help," said Lacy, putting out his hands for the bundle.

" Please sit down, sir," pushing away his hands, " and smoke your pipe. I'll do it much quicker without help."

He sat and watched the graceful, girlish figure crouched at the hearth. Presently the ashes were swept under the grate, the new fire laid and lit, and with a pleasant crackling of wood the flames sprang up the chimney.

She rose and turned half toward him, so that in the leaping firelight her face was a play of light and shadow. She looked down at him and smiled. " There, sir, the room'll warm up fine soon. Is there anything else, sir ? "

Lacy stood up. " Nothing, thank you, Ann." He fumbled in his pocket and held out half-a-crown. " And thank you very much."

Ann drew back flushing. " Oh, no, sir, please, no. It's quite all right about the fire."

" Nonsense ! " laughing lightly, but with an unaccountable shakiness in his voice. " Pooh ! pooh ! you mustn't mind taking a little gift from me. I'm only an old seaman. You don't lack any gifts from the young fellows, I know. Come."

He took her hand, and placing the coin in her palm, closed her fingers upon it and held them close with his own. " There, for chocolates." The shakiness of his voice took him by surprise. What was the matter with him.

Ann stood still, looking up at him. " Thank you, sir," smiling shyly. " Is there anything else ? " She moved as if unconsciously nearer to him. " Please, sir—sir—you're—hurting—my—hand."

He took her hand and held it in front of him. He unclasped her fingers one by one. Upon the coal-grimed palm and across the fingers the edges of the coin had made red indentations. He stared at them. The coin fell to the floor and rolled away under a chair. He raised her hand to his lips, and began kissing the reddened palm and fingers slowly and then more quickly, more roughly. The grime marked his lips and chin.

" Ann, will you marry me ? "

She did not reply.

" Ann, could you love an old fool ? Ann, will you marry me ? "

She bent her head, sighed, and then looking up at him laughingly, she drew down his head, and kissed his lips.

He held her close, kissing her eyes, her hair, and presently her lips. She drew herself more closely into his arms. He stooped and, lifting her, carried her over to the sofa at the other side of the fireplace. He sat down holding her in his arms. " Ann, Ann, will you marry me ? "

She half opened her eyes. " Perhaps ; kiss me, old silly. Hush, keep still."

He rose with her in his arms, blundered toward the door of his bedroom, pushed it open with his foot, entered, and closed the broken-latched door with his back. A moment later the key turned in the lock.

The Fletchers, a decent couple, and rigidly Church of England with high leanings, observed every Friday as a fast-day, during which they substituted fish for meat at luncheon and dinner. But, as Mr. Fletcher pointed out, it is a well known fact that weight-for-weight fish contains far less nourishment than meat, and one must keep one's strength up. Hence, in place of the steak or two cutlets or a chop of his ordinary luncheon, he consumed three or four plaice, or a large chunk of that scavenging fish courteously and humorously named rock-salmon by the fish-monger. As wine, said Fletcher, goes better than ale with fish, he drank with it a half bottle of a sour and flatulent Graves. It followed invariably that Mr. Fletcher grew somnolent after his Friday luncheon, and as sleep is as good as food, the lacked nutriment was replaced by a nap from two-thirty until such time as the body had renewed its vigour and was able to cope with the labour of living. Mrs. Fletcher, who always ate sparingly, and on Fridays merely pecked at a tiny sole, found that what new vigour she needed was best obtained by an afternoon visit to the Mayoress or some other gossiping crony.

The Fletchers had been married forty years, and not one night during that happy period had they slept apart. For well-nigh fifteen thousand times had the Fletchers kissed, murmured sleepy good-nights, snuggled up together, and drowsed into oblivion. Not once had James gone astray in those forty years ; and never had the cuckoo justification for flying above their roof-tree uttering his derisive cry. Jimmy and Jenny were a faithful couple.

But upon this fateful Friday all things conspired against the continence of James. The half-bottles of Graves were finished and he had foolishly drunk a full bottle of a cheap and sickly Sauterne. The fish was smoked haddock, of

which he was inordinately fond, and of which he had
devoured with gusto and growing hilarity some two pounds.
He had accepted from Captain Lacy a long, evil-looking
black cigar, which he smoked to the bitter end by stuffing
the last inch into his pipe. After two-thirty The Pines was
deserted except for the staff—even the Miss Oveys were out
upon domestic business. Finally, it was Ann's afternoon
in.

James Fletcher woke from an uneasy and nightmare-
haunted slumber as the Town Hall clock boomed four
o'clock. He gherked noisily and made a wry face. " Damn
that wine." His mouth was sour, his throat hot and dry.
His head seemed stuffed with cotton-wool.

" Phew ! " he said, drawing his hand across his face,
" a spot might pull me together. Better not, perhaps. I'll
try a pot of tea and a bit of cake." He rang the bell, and
three minutes later Ann tapped at the door and entered.

She was radiant, her face flushed as if from sleep, her
eyes bright, her lips red, soft, and inviting. The plain black
frock was a foil to the startling loveliness of her body.

She smiled down at Fletcher, who sat in an arm-chair by
the dwindling fire. He was picking his teeth with a pipe-
cleaner, and for a moment or so, engrossed in the effort to
dislodge a particularly baffling piece of haddock-gristle, he
did not look up. And then, suddenly, he grunted with
satisfaction, and raised his eyes to Ann's. He stared at her
stupidly, as if she were a stranger. His glance ran over
her from head to foot. Of a sudden, and for the first time in
his life, he was vividly aware of the beauty of a human
body. There crept disloyally into his consciousness the
vision of Jenny's meagre shapelessness. A gnawing sense of
having been cheated by life invaded him. Against the double
invasion of beauty and self-pity loyalty fled the field. He
grinned ingratiatingly. " Tea, my dear, tea, *that's* what I

want. I'd like a large pot, a jug of hot water, and some cake. Do you like it here ? "

" Yes, sir, thank you. I'm very happy."

" You'll make someone happy one day, I'll be bound. Perhaps you have already, hey ? "

Ann smiled provocatively. " Perhaps, sir."

" He's a lucky dog, then. Don't you ever wear pretty frocks ? "

" Don't you think this pretty, sir ? " turning half away from him, and raising her arms so that the short skirt lifted.

" It's pretty when you're in it," hoarsely, " would you like some frocks, eh ? Something flimsy. You're a pretty young woman. Never worn low-necks for dinner, I s'pose. It's a shame to hide those pretty arms." He took her hands. " Aren't in any hurry, are you ? "

" Your tea, sir," said Ann softly, leaning against his knees.

" Pooh ! hang the tea. Give me a kiss, and we'll see about those frocks." He suddenly shifted his hands from hers, slipped his arms around her, and dragged her on to his lap, so that she sat facing him *à cheval*, her laughing face very close to his, and her hair brushing his forehead.

He began to tremble violently. He forced her roughly against him, and put his mouth to her neck. There was a vast rushing in his ears. He fell headlong into unsounded depths. His body thrilled to an unimagined rhythm that seemed to beat from the incalculable remoteness of outer space.

He rose up slowly from great depths. He emerged. He stared at Ann savagely, bitterly, disgustfully. He thrust her from him. " Tea," he said brutally, " tea, get my tea."

She went out slowly. He leaned forward in his chair and put his hands over his face. " God forgive me, God forgive me," he mumbled miserably. " Jenny, Jenny, I didn't mean it."

2

Richard lay in bed. He could not sleep. A reading lamp was upon a small table beside him, and face downward on the bed was a volume of Lamb's letters. He moved restlessly, and flung the eiderdown to the foot of the bed. With an impatient exclamation he switched off the lamp, and lay staring at the moon-bright ceiling, as the room gradually lightened to his eyes.

A distant clock struck one.

A chill gust blew in from the window. " Blast it ! " he cried fretfully, and sitting up, dragged the eiderdown over him and lay back again. He gave up trying to sleep, and lay with closed eyes and hands clenched by his sides.

He was tied fast to the wheel of passion, and as it turned and turned endlessly he was slowly broken.

Behind his lids a vision of Ann was painted in a thousand maddening and alluring images.

He groaned, switched on the lamp, and lay with open eyes fixed upon the opposite wall. But the images stayed ; they passed before him an endless procession of loveliness.

For a while he found peace and a spiritual release. The wheel ceased to turn. He lay inert. The images left him. He poised drowsily, delicately, upon the brink of sleep.

And then, flooding back, the visions overwhelmed him. The wheel turned once more. He reached the limit of endurance. He cried out distressfully and surrendered.

He got out of bed slowly, put his feet into slippers, wrapped his dressing-gown about him, opened the door, and on cautious feet tip-toed along the corridor, down a short flight of stairs, turned to the right, and stood outside Ann's bedroom door, breathless from the ungovernable thumping of his heart.

He turned the handle of the door softly, pushed the door

open, entered noiselessly, and closed the door as quietly.

After the darkness of the corridor the moonlit room hid nothing from him. He turned his glance to the bed. Ann lay with open eyes watching him.

He moved swiftly toward her, unable to speak. But she sat up suddenly, and throwing back the clothes, put her fingers to her lips. He saw that she was naked ; and stopping abruptly he remained motionless, one knee bent, his body drooped forward, his arms hanging.

She laughed very softly, and slipping from bed, came over to him and put her arms about his neck.

His arms went round her. Under his hot hands her body seemed cold and smooth as marble. She stroked his face with little tender gestures, whispering so low that he understood nothing.

He lowered his head and began to kiss her breasts very gently. She was so small and frail, so incredibly lovely. Lust drew off from him. A surge of emotion went over him, part compassion, part love, part something he could not understand. " Ann," he said softly, his lips against her breast, " Ann, Ann."

She shivered and drew herself closer. " I'm cold," she said. " I'm cold. I love you, I love you." She clung about him weeping. A tear ran down her breast, touching his lips.

Stooping, he gathered her body into his arms, and holding her tightly, walked unsteadily towards the bed.

Two hours later he left her. He loved her. A tenderness toward her, warm, fragile and delicate, flowered in his heart. He could not bear to think of losing her. Every thought of her was lovely and precious. She was so sweet, so gentle and loving. He thrilled again at the memory of her caressing, of her soft lips, her breath upon his face, of the little foolish things she had whispered to him. He must marry her. The thought of losing her was an unbearable torment.

Christ, how fragrant she was. Round and round in a circle of enchanted blisses his thoughts revolved. No God ? There must be God. God was very good to him.

He reached his own room and flung himself upon the bed, the dressing-gown wrapped round him. He did not want to sleep, although an intoxicating languor was creeping over him. He lit a cigarette, and lay a long while in thought, living over again the ecstasy of the past hour.

A woman's voice raised stridently, furiously, shook him from his spell. He rose from the bed and stumbled to the door. He ran along the corridor. Heads were poking out of doors, and sleep-hazed eyes stared after him. He came to the little landing, and looked into the angry face of Miss Ovey. She stood some distance from the open doorway of Ann's bedroom. Ann, wrapped about with a gay-coloured garment, outfaced her from the threshold with a defiant smile. Mason, a step behind Ann, stared at the floor, a grin of sheepish rage twisting his mouth.

Richard turned away and walked back to his bedroom. He removed his dressing gown, kicked off his slippers, and stepping into bed dragged the clothes over his head.

3

The small bureau of Miss Ovey had witnessed strange happenings during its existence, had watched the play of human emotion throughout most of its gamut, had seen laughter and tears, had listened to impassioned appeals and irrevocable sentences ; minor comedies, petty tragedies, yet differing only in degree, in scale, from a cosmic catastrophe.

But that Sunday morning, when most of the occupants of The Pines were at Church or out walking, the tiny bureau saw staged a swiftly moving and swiftly ending play-let that its previous experience could not parallel. But which of the Muses, Thalia or Melpomene, presided is too difficult a question to decide.

Miss Ovey sat on her swivel-chair, with Miss Alison beside her on a cane-bottomed arm-chair brought in from the lounge for the occasion.

Ann Brown, who had refused a seat, stood facing them. She had discarded her maid's frock, and wore a dark blue dress with a bunch of artificial red poppies at the waist. She had threaded one of the poppies in her hair, an oriflamme of defiance. Her hands were clasped loosely behind her back, her chin was tilted slightly upward, and she was smiling. She looked little more than a child, but a child of such insurgent beauty that Miss Alison sat throughout the interview watching her in dumb wonder.

" Have you anything to say beyond what you said last night ? " asked Miss Ovey, speaking with the icy detachment of painfully bridled anger.

" What do you want me to say ? "

" *Want* you to say ! *want* you ! Is there anything you *can* say to us. It is to God you need——"

" God, yes. To God who gave me my beauty. What would——"

" Don't add blasphemy to harlotry. If——"

A low laugh interrupted Miss Ovey. Ann stretched up her arms. " God made me beautiful. I am glad of my loveliness, glad of my lips and eyes, glad of my white body, glad, glad, do you hear. Glad because all men love me——"

" Love ! be quiet ; how dare you talk of love. Is that——"

" All men love me. Shall I tell you how they love ? Your fat Major, your greedy Mr. Fletcher, Captain Lacy, young Pearce——"

" That boy, you shameless wanton ! Have you——"

" Boy ! he was as good a man as any of them. Love ! What do you know of it ? *You* my mistress ? I have no

mistress, no master. I am love and beauty, desire and lust ;
all things to all men. Ask them how I loved them. I am
alive and you are dead. Dead like a stone, earth, mud. You
have never been alive, but when I die I shall die as flowers
die, as fire dies. Do you think I care for you, for what you
think. Wanton, am I ? So is the wind, the sea, the rain and
all the flowers. *You* turn me out ? When I go there is not a
man here that would not follow, run to me, crawl to me, if
I lifted a finger, because I am all things to all men, to each
the dream of his heart. I am love, I am lust, I am the
world's desire, I am life." She stood for a moment trans-
figured, with flushed face and pouted laughing lips. She
looked from one to the other, her fingers playing with the
red poppies at her waist. Her breath came quickly. She
seemed about to break out again into vehement speech ;
and then, turning away abruptly, she was gone.

Miss Alison put out her hands towards her sister in a
gesture of infinite bewilderment. " My dear," she gasped,
" my dear."

Miss Ovey swept one arm outwards as if thrusting away
some obscene and horrifying vision. " It was indeed a gift
from God," she said, " but it was a cross and not a crown."
She straightened herself suddenly, and sat very upright.
" Well, that is over."

" What—what—are we going to do ? " asked Miss Alison
timidly.

" Do ! do ! why nothing ; she's gone. What do you
mean ? "

" The gentlemen, dear, what——"

" Just nothing, Alison ; ignore it. What else *can* we do ?
It will be simple enough. Who will want to remember it ? "

" Perhaps," sighed Miss Alison ; " it may be. *I* can never
forget. My dear, where did she learn to talk like that ? Who
could blame the men. Almost, as she spoke, I could have

loved her, I could have cried. Even now I am dreadfully shaken. I have never heard such words. Pour me out a glass of wine, dear, please."

" Words ! " snapped Miss Ovey, unlocking the little cupboard, where the cowslip, dandelion and elderberry wines were kept, " words ! she's no doubt been talking to wild young men all her life, poets and artists and such like. Don't upset yourself and be stupid. Drink this. I think a small glass will do me good, too."

4

Mason looked over to Richard after Kate had cleared away their evening meal. It had been a strained and silent half hour. " It's all serene, I gather," said Mason, " by-gones are to be by-gones. The dead past is to bury its dead. Very wise of Letty and Ally, I must say."

Richard slowly filled his pipe but did not reply.

" It's about the rummest business I've ever——"

" Shut up ! " said Richard softly.

" Eh ? What ? "

" I said shut up."

" Why, damn it all, Blaney, we're all in the swim. I don't want to talk——"

Richard sprang up, white and trembling, and stood over Mason. " Shut up, Mason ! " he said in a thick harsh voice. " Do you understand ? " He stood there for a moment, menacing, malignant, murderous. And then he turned his face aside quickly, pushed his way in a groping fashion past the chairs, and snatching swiftly at the door was gone.

Mason picked up the pipe that Richard had let fall, turned it round and round in his fingers, put it carefully on the table, whistled softly, and then shrugging his shoulders stooped for the poker and stirred the fire into a blaze.

CHAPTER X

A LUNCHEON AND A TEA

I

A day or so later David Hartley sat in his small study before a log-fire, with a large red cloth-bound manuscript book upon his knees. He was writing up his journal, and the occupation appeared to afford him some amusement, to judge by his smile; and some difficulty, if the accentuation of the Michaelangelo crease between the eyes had any significance.

Occasionally he read back, turning over pages as if for verification. He frequently consulted small red note-books beside him, and added pencilled marginalia to the manuscript.

A low-pitched buzzer sounded from the large office-desk behind him. He removed the receiver from the telephone, listened a moment, and then said, " Very well, show him up here, Bates."

It was a fad of Hartley's to have all the rooms in Denacre Hall connected by telephone, with a switchboard in the valet's apartments.

Hartley pushed his journal and note-books into a drawer, drew another chair over to the fire, and as the door opened, and the Dean entered, he went over to him with an outstretched hand. " This is an unexpected pleasure, Perseval ; a unique one almost, I believe. Come over to the fire ; the cold is abominable."

The Dean sat down and held his large fine hands to the blaze. " I wonder why *my* logs never burn," he said, with a smile.

"You probably don't store them; a year's dry storage is the very minimum. I found some three or four tons in the cellar which have been seasoning for five or six years I should think. Notice the mauve flame and the absence of smoke. Hotter than coal, too, isn't it? My predecessor here was a wise fellow."

"He was a very annoying old man," commented the Dean, "an epileptic. He shot himself in the end, and the Hall stood empty for three years before you came."

Hartley nodded. "I heard the story from the bailiff. A trifle macabre, wasn't it; shot himself with a butcher's humane killer. How did he come to have such a weapon?"

"It was left with him by Clarence George, the nature-writer. You knew he lived here? Well, George is very much anti-slaughter in all things, and he was trying to interest old Betherton over a parliamentary bill to insist upon the use of humane killers in the French and Belgian abbattoirs to which our worn-out horses are sent. Betherton, by the bye, was an uncle of Lessing, then Home Secretary.

"George had borrowed the weapon with a couple of cartridges from Wainwright, the butcher, and after explaining its mechanism to Betherton, had left it with him at the old man's request. His man found him in the morning shot. He had been dead about eight hours, so he had turned the thing on himself within twenty minutes of George's departure."

"Suicide? It seems more in the nature of an accident," said Hartley. "What was the verdict at the inquest?"

"Accidentally shot. George was in a blue funk about it all, but Betherton's fingers were rigidly glued to the butt. I don't mean that George was ever suspected. It was just awkward, an unfortunate mess. I said suicide, just between ourselves. Betherton was a most unhappy old man, and he'd only made a will the previous week——"

"Not very evidential," smiled Hartley; "unhappy senility is not uncommon, especially if sickness is added to age. The will was probably coincidence. The facts seem rather to square with the coroner's opinion. However," slightly shrugging his shoulders, "I am the gainer." He picked up a *Times Literary Supplement*. "I see your new book is expected from Fawcett & Green's in the Spring: *The Way of Rome*. Rather near Belloc's title, isn't it?"

"Designedly," said the Dean; "and it was about my book that I called. I hope I'm not keeping you from more important matters——"

"I've no important matters. I'm a pensioner," smiling. "Look here, I'm having an early lunch, almost at once, why not join me and talk then. I like talking when I'm feeding; I think it aids mastication, and slow mastication inspires both thought and caution. Do you mind cold stuff? I believe there's a tart. Bates is a clever fellow, an extraordinarily gifted person. I pay him five hundred a year, and thereby cheat him abominably. That belauded Neapolitan Benito at the Alcadi hasn't half his skill. Bates could command ten times the salary I pay him if he weren't so ferociously English. And he's quite agreeable to valet me into the bargain. I don't know if that's the innate simplicity and modesty of the true artist, or the result of early environment. Well, come along, we'll go down.

"Speaking of Benito," said Hartley, a few minutes later, "these tomatoes and the cucumber came from Naples by air only yesterday. There's something to be said for progress. I wonder, by the bye, how far back in history dates the knowledge of the esculent qualities peculiar to various popular foods, especially on the vegetable and mollusc side; it would make a pleasant little book. But your book, Perseval. I don't like your title. I prefer 'path' to 'way.'"

Perseval nodded. "But, I'm employing it figuratively,

you know. I've allowed myself, by the bye, to be persuaded by Fawcett & Green to let it go into their *Modern Thought Series*. I dislike the notion of a series intensely : the square peg has to be rounded to fit the hole and loses a lot in the process. But it's a fine series——"

" And you're in good company."

" Yes. You know the series ? Of course you would. Well, each volume has a foreword ; this is a prominent feature. I wondered——"

" If I'd do it," laughed Hartley. " Aren't you taking a Jonah on board ? What do Fawcett & Green say about it ? "

" They're more than agreeable, delighted. I'm asking, I know——"

" Nothing at all, my dear Perseval ; you're very welcome. How long ? When do you require it ? You must let me see your MS. or proofs."

" I've proofs with me," said Perseval. " The foreword is to be quite short, about fifteen hundred words. By the middle of March, if that's not pressing you too much. I've not been through the proofs myself yet, but Gillian's corrected the more obvious errors. She's rather a dangerous proof-corrector—corrects *me* at times, by George ! "

" Your daughter ? I've not I think had the pleasure——"

" Yes, my elder girl. She's been acting as governess to my two other children—a most unsatisfactory arrangement, but professional governesses are too terrible. I've decided now to get a tutor for these two youngsters. Freda is nine and Max seven. They both need a firm hand, but it must be a cultured one. It's an insoluble problem, for the type of man I want wouldn't dream of taking the post. That's not my only worry just now. Venning, the precentor is leaving us. He's been the making of the music at St. Matthew's for the last ten years, and there's no one to replace him, simply no one. It means getting a new man. I hoped to get the

LP

vicar-choral from St. Bedes, but," smiling wryly, " there was a difficulty at the last moment."

Hartley had been tapping his glass very softly with his nails, listening apparently to the faint musical percussion rather than the Dean's words. A shadow of annoyance was beginning to cloud Dr. Perseval's florid face, when Hartley said very abruptly, " I may be able to help you on both counts."

" I should be extraordinarily grateful. You know some-one then——"

" My nephew, Roy. He's eight and twenty, and, I understand, an exceptionally brilliant young man. He's been holiday-making in the south of France but is expected home at any time. He is coming along here, and, I think, could be persuaded to visit the Deanery for a few hours a day. He will be here, if I read his letter aright, to-morrow. If this seems helpful I'll send him——"

" My dear Hartley, it's too good of you ; it's more than helpful, it's Providential. I'm most grateful."

" He's a fine musician," went on Hartley ; " his setting of Olaf's eighth mass is reckoned first rate. Why not let him take on his shoulders the burden of the Cathedral music. He'd jump at the chance."

" It's extraordinarily kind, Hartley, but the irregularity —I'm afraid——"

" Pooh, man ! he's ordained. A temporary measure. In any case——"

" Yes." interrupted the Dean, " why not. I really am grateful, Hartley. If he'd only bridge a month's gap it would be an inestimable boon."

" Don't thank me before you've tried the pudding, however," smiled Hartley ; " the boy's three parts a catholic."

" Roman Catholic ? "

" Are there any others ? "

" *We* are the catholic church, my dear Hartley."

" Are we ? I thought we were the Anglican heresy," smiling. " But—well—I'm afraid you'll find him with a distinct bias Romeward, shall we say. You'll also find he's read all you've written. That may prove annoying, eh ? I really believe he's read more widely than I have. Are these insuperable obstacles ? He's not in the least a difficult person for his years. There is, in fact, a bland mellowness about him at times, that is positively patriarchal. He'll be here to-morrow, I hope to luncheon, but in any case not later than dinner. Shall I send him along to see you on Monday. Just a friendly visit. I'll say nothing of your difficulties."

" Send him along to tea on Sunday. He can then make the acquaintance of Mrs. Perseval and the children. I really am grateful, Hartley. No, no, thanks, no coffee. It makes me sleepy—extraordinary that, isn't it. Would you care to dine with us to-morrow. There'll be just ourselves, Bowers, and Hailsham the Canon in residence."

" I'd be glad if you'd not press me. Just now I'm——"

" Not at all. Well, some day a little later on. Perhaps with your nephew—er—he's a Hartley ? Er—Guy, was it ? "

" Roy. Roy Hartley. Yes, we shall be delighted. Thank God the weather shows signs of being warmer. I'll come to the lodge gates with you."

2

At a quarter to five on Sunday afternoon Roy Hartley entered the pleasant fire-lit drawing-room of The Deanery. When he left at half-past five he had made captive the hearts of three ladies, one of tender years, and had antagonised two gentlemen, one also of tender years.

Roy Hartley was one of those cosmopolitan, ageless, and

de-nationalised men, who at twenty are completely mature, assured and unselfconscious, and at fifty differ little in appearance and manner. He was of average height and build, with crisp, dark curly hair, heavily marked eyebrows, bright sparkling eyes, fine features, inbred to a suspicion of delicacy, a naturally pale complexion now deeply bronzed, and a wide full-lipped mouth whose crimson was accentuated by a slight black moustache.

He walked, stood and sat gracefully, his gestures were easy, his voice low and deep, his intonation cultured, and his language simple, direct, and vivid in a slightly mocking way. His voice when addressing women had a caressing quality that annoyed other men. He was a professional in that art in which most men are stumbling and gauche amateurs : he was a master lover.

The Dean sat facing Mrs. Perseval at the head of the table. Gillian was on her father's right. Freda next to her ; Roy Hartley sat opposite Gillian, with little Max on his left. Max, as he gobbled through his bread and butter, with his mind on the cake and biscuits, watched the visitor out of the corner of his eye.

" You think you could manage that young man, Mr. Hartley ? " smiled the Dean nodding towards Max, whose face was hidden in his cup, his eyes staring unblinkingly over the rim. " And the young woman opposite ? "

" I expect so, eh, old man ? " said Roy genially, tweaking Max's ear, to his annoyance. " And as for the young woman, no doubt she'll manage me." Max, swallowing clumsily, choked into his cup and flushed with embarrassment. Freda blushed prettily, hung her head, and looked up through her lashes at Roy. It was going to be lovely to be taught by Mr. Hartley ; he looked like a prince. " Have you been to Africa ? " she asked shyly.

Roy's hand went up to his face. " It *is* rather a deep

shade," laughing, " but it was not the African sun. Nothing so romantic ; just the south of France, which I found uncomfortably hot."

" How did you go, Mr. Hartley ? " asked Mrs. Perseval, whose slender figure and artistically and skilfully treated complexion, aided by the friendly lamplight, subtracted at least twelve years from her five and forty.

" We motored (I had a friend with me, a man who was at Winchester with me, Robson—son of Robson, the cancer-man) from Boulogne to Bordeaux, and from Bordeaux we used Shanks's mare. We were walking, I should say, about five or six weeks."

" You're fond of walking ? " asked Gillian.

" Well, I'm not," laughing, " not the actual walking ; what I do like about it is the sheer sensuous joy of tired muscles relaxing at the end of a day's tramp. I can imagine few things more intoxicating than the reward of a twenty-five mile tramp with fifty pounds of kit. I mean the stretch-ing out in a hot bath, the languorous thrills that run over one's body from crown to toes, the cold shower to follow, clean clothes, a pleasant little meal with a bottle of decent wine, coffee, kummel and a green cigar : the seventh—the seventy-seventh heaven."

" An enervating one, isn't it ? " asked the Dean, who thought these bodily ecstasies a little out of place.

" I hate cold showers," said Max, wrinkling up his nose.

" What ! not like a cold tub ? " cried Roy, in mock horror. " I can't have you cutting that now I'm in charge."

" You're not," said Max, flushing, " and I shan't."

Mrs. Perseval interposed to bridge an awkward pause. " Where did you go to first after leaving Bordeaux ? "

" We'd intended to average about twenty miles or so a day," resumed Roy, " and decided not to stay anywhere

longer than a night. We were on the way to Lourdes.
Robson, who's a Catholic, had a rendezvous there with his
brother, a priest from Kerry. However, on the second day,
blazing days they were too, we reached a little coast water-
ing-place to the S.W. of Bordeaux called Arcachon. It was
the middle of last August, and you remember what the
weather was like all over Europe. I've never experienced
anything more tropical ; we were simply baked, blistered,
burnt brown. We sat down outside a small café-restaurant,
and just sagged. The patron brought us Pernod and soda,
with ice bobbing up and down on it. We drank greedily,
and he replenished our glasses. We drank again and a third
time. Do you know Pernod ? It's a yellow, harmless enough
looking stuff, but it rapt us away into Paradise. Or maybe
it was the ice. I really don't know. But we sat there for over
an hour, lolled rather, smoking acrid Maryland cigarettes,
which seemed to fume with an intoxicating aroma we'd
never before experienced, and about seven Robson observed luxuriously, ' We might stay here a day or so ; this
seems a comfortable sort of place, and the patron doesn't
want to talk. Let's have dinner, and if the grub's equal to
the silences of monsieur le patron, why, then, I think,
eh——? "

" We stayed in Arcachon ten days. I confess after three I
was bored and wanted to push on. Robson, however, who
was heavyweight champion at Winchester, and again at
Oriel, found a crony in the town he'd met in London the
previous year. This was a French professional heavyweight
named Paul Journée, a big fair rather loutish looking chap
with a broken nose and badly mauled ears. He had been in
London for a bout with the Englishman, Wells, and Robson
had had three rounds with him in the gymnasium of the
International Club. Journée had a physical culture academy
in Arcachon where he promised clients *beauté, santé, force,*

if his notice-board were to be believed. He was an amiable giant of a fellow and hugged Robson ecstatically."

" Did he win ? " interrupted Max, who was now showing some interest in the proceedings.

" Did *who* win, old chap ? "

" Porjornay."

" Do you mean against Wells ? " patiently. " No, Wells beat him, in the fourth round I think it was."

" No, not Wells, but the——"

" Don't interrupt, darling," said Mrs. Perseval, who found herself listening eagerly to Roy's chatter about a pastime she had hitherto classed very near the unmentionable things of life.

" It's all right, Mrs. Perseval. You mean Robson, eh ? Well, they didn't fight, you know. They had a bout or two of friendly sparring each morning, just to keep the muscles limber."

" While you drank Pernod, Mr. Hartley ! " smiled Gillian.

" Not as bad as that. I certainly left Robson to his fellow pug, but I had a find myself. Down by the Cinema near the Punch and Judy stand——"

" Oh, is the French Punch and Judy," Max was beginning excitedly, when his father caught his eye and frowned him to silence.

" I found a small café whose patron had been a waiter in Paris half-a-century before. He was at the Coq d'Or, three doors beyond L'Opéra, for twenty-five years, and he told me that two or three evenings each week for about a year there came in for dinner—whom do you think ? "

" Napoleon," ventured Freda.

" Bigger than that," laughed Roy.

" Hugo," suggested the Dean.

" Zola, Dumas fils, Baudelaire—oh *do* tell us, Mr. Hartley," said Gillian.

" No, you're getting quite warm."

" Guy de Maupassant," said Mrs. Perseval, surprisingly.

" Yes, and my ex-garçon never tired of talking of him. He'd a queer theory (M'sieu le patron, I mean) that people only wrote about the things they'd a passion for doing themselves."

" Which would make de Maupassant a horrid person," observed Mrs. Perseval.

" Oh, I don't know, mother, many of his stories are lovely things, fine things, soaked with pity. Do you think *Boule de Suif* his best tale, Mr. Hartley ; I don't, in the least."

" No, I prefer *Mouche*. *Boule de Suif*, in my opinion, is extraordinarily trite and obvious."

" I think the loveliest of all his tales is, well—I've forgotten the title, *Chouette* I believe. About a poor mite of an Indian girl child who is tied in a sack and flung into the moat because——"

" That will do, Gillian, please," grunted her father, " pitchers have ears even in these enlightened Freudian days." The Dean disapproved of the trend of the conversation. He was amazed that Gillian showed such knowledge of de Maupassant, whom he considered a mere lewd pander without any genius at all. " I rather think, Mr. Hartley, that there was a spark of reason in your patron's theory. De Maupassant died young as a result of evil living, and his tales decidedly portray such living. We have a writer living in Welling, Clarence George, the writer of nature-tales, who also lends a touch of truth to the hypothesis, shall we call it. George is a terrible fellow for fighting all the cruelties of the world in his books, but it has always seemed to me that he describes the sufferings of trapped rabbits and badgers, wounded birds, and the other maimed and hunted things of the wild, with an amazingly lickerish gusto. He refuses to spare us one heartrending cry of agony.

He lays bare each quivering nerve, displays each drop of tormented sweat. The great friend of the dumb and the friendless, eh ? Well, he thrashes his dogs and his children, and simply flays his wife with a searing tongue. You'll meet him, I expect—a queer fellow, an albino."

Roy nodded. " Most people suffering from physical disabilities are sadistic, actually, or in dreams. As for——"

" Tell us about the French Punch and Judy," blurted out Max, who was weary of the unintelligible jargon of the adults.

" Well, old fellow, it's not much different from the English, and the children who gather round are about the same as the English children, perhaps a little noisier. By the bye, sir, there *is* a difference between the English and French versions. The French retains much more obviously the original plot, which, of course, centred round Punch as a cuckold."

" Did he have a cuckoo ? " asked Max.

The Dean frowned. " You may leave the table now, Max ; Please don't make too much noise overhead. Freda, cut along to the nursery as well."

The two children left reluctantly, Roy's nod and smile being received shyly and coyly by Freda, and with a certain hostile dubiety by Max.

" It's extraordinary," pursued Roy, deliberately or unconsciously avoiding the Dean's stare of disapproval, " how cuckoldry as a theme persists. Originally almost the sole theme of tale, conte, mystery-interlude, and ballad, it still holds pride of place in the Latin countries, if not here and in the States—and I shouldn't care to wager very much upon their immunity."

" So much the worse for the world," commented the Dean, to whom the meal had been an increasingly annoying ordeal. He found himself disliking Hartley intensely ;

and he decidedly disapproved of cuckoldry as a tea-time topic, especially with Gillian and his wife there.

"Oh, but, father, it really *is* funny, and after all it has biblical authority. Why should——"

"Where did you go to after Arcachon, Mr. Hartley?" put in Mrs. Perseval tactfully. She knew more about Gillian than her father did, and also was not averse from enjoying a discussion of the married woman's one great traditional joke, but she observed that the Dean was flying danger signals, and thought it better to climb on to safer ground, if young Hartley were not to lose his opportunities as tutor at The Deanery and temporary precentor at the Cathedral. She did not want him to lose that opportunity.

"After Arcachon? Oh, Lourdes, on foot. It took us just ten days, which was of course slower going than we'd intended, but the weather was, as I've said, unprecedented. I was utterly fagged and done up when we reached Lourdes. Robson was quite fresh. He's one of those iron indefatigable sort of persons. You've been to Lourdes, sir?"

"Yes, several times. Did you find it repaid you for the labour of getting there?"

"Well, yes. I'm glad I went. It is true I was a bit disgusted at the huckstering there, but the catholics don't bother about that side of it. Robson, when I put it to him, just grinned and said, 'Well, why not; a man's none the worse a catholic for being a good business man. You want to divorce religion from life, pack it away in cotton wool, and only take it out for a reverent squint on Sundays. We don't. Religion is life and life is religion; and there's nothing in life that can hurt religion and vice versa.'"

"The usual sophistry," smiled Dr. Perseval. "He convinced you, eh?"

"Well, he didn't, as a matter of fact; I found Lourdes

depressing, sordid, and horribly pinchbeck by day. But at night, and viewed from the heights, with a torchlight processional snake four miles long winding through the streets, and the rest of the town darkling, the hucksters shops closed, the raucous voices stilled, the predatory hands no longer clutching, the cozenage, the shouting, the dust and clamour forgotten, why, then Lourdes seemed a place somehow set apart from earthly things, and I could almost believe in the miracles."

" And do you still ? "

" Well, yes and no. I believe, in fact, there's no doubt about it, that wonderful cures are effected, but I do not believe in the miraculous element, in the intervention of God. But that's really neither here nor there. I had a wonderful emotional experience when I left Lourdes alone by train, about ten one evening. Impossible to explain it to myself afterward. The whole thing, looking back, seems cheap, tawdry, theatrical, a child's device to trap a child's fancy ; but there it is. As the train cleared the town and steamed slowly westward, I put my head out of the carriage window, and looked back at Lourdes. The night was dark, and the town was no more than a black, faintly-starred huddle in the valley. And then I looked up, and caught sight of the lighted crucifix on the mountain-top above the town. I had a queer moment of emotional exaltation as I watched that remote bright symbol. Even at the time my feelings were indescribable, and now they seem far less real than a dream, I have indeed forgotten entirely *how* I felt. But it was an unforgettable moment. My dear Mrs. Perseval, do you know I've been chattering here for nearly three-quarters of an hour. I don't know how to apologise. This is not my usual habit, I assure you. I fear I open too readily to warm sunshine. You must all forgive me." He rose, and taking his leave with an easy charm of manner that the Dean found somehow irritating, he was soon striding quickly along the South Close toward the High Street.

The Dean, who had accompanied him to the gate, did not return to the drawing-room, but made for the haven of his study. He avoided for the rest of the evening any opportunity for a discussion. Nevertheless, by breakfast the next morning Mrs. Perseval told Gillian that Mr. Hartley was coming for two hours every morning as tutor to the children. The matter of the Cathedral appointment, however, hung fire. "Your father thinks Dr. Strang's absence makes things difficult," she said non-comittally.

Gillian smiled. "It won't last, mother. The Dean of St. Matthew's not master of his own Cathedral ! My *dear* Uriah."

CHAPTER XI

CUCKOO

I

Roy, who commenced his tutorship on the following Tuesday, was by the end of the week lord and master of Freda's heart. She loved him to the point of embarrassment, and asked nothing better than to sit at his feet, a diligent and adulatory bondsmaid. He came each morning at ten, and left at noon, and those two hours were the whole of the day for Freda, and the inspiration of her dreams at night. In her anxiety to win his approbation she became a pathetically assiduous little blue-stocking, haunting her father's library, where she knew knowledge lay entombed in a thousand volumes, badgering him with questions, committing to memory poems, dates in history, mathematical tables, and an indigestible hotch-potch gleaned from the encyclopædia. And suddenly romance budded in her heart, and presently blossoming, led her to a delectable country whose inhabitants she recognised as her true kin. It was the country of romantic literature, and here, in the persons of Jane Eyre, Maggie Tulliver, Lorna Doone, the Lady of Shalott, Christabel, Amy Robsart, Hereward's Elfreda, Gerard's Margaret, Helen of Kirkconnel, and a host of others she found kindred spirits with whom she was at once on terms of delightful intimacy, an intimacy which sprang from a close mutual understanding, and a sharing of the same spiritual adventure.

To these friends, soon becoming more real and alive than the people around her, she could repeat without shame the treasured sayings of her hero, whisper her dearest desires, bring her tears and heartache, her joys and hopes.

To Max there came no such budding and blossoming. He remained aloof and hostile, a hostility which, as the days passed, surrendered grudgingly to a reluctant admiration for Roy's prowess at games and his willingness to draw freely upon a store of enchanting stories, which were none the worse for having at times a historical or even a mathematical setting.

It often happened that a story was unfinished by noon, and Roy, agreeably continuing until virtue was rewarded and wickedness punished, was invited to stay to luncheon.

The Dean not infrequently lunched away from home, and the delayed climaxes to Roy's exciting narratives chanced many times to coincide with the Dean's absences. To Mrs. Perseval and to Gillian these meals soon became as exciting and as romantic as any of the tales to whose accommodating duration they owed their inception.

Dr. Perseval had forgotten, or designedly pushed aside, his first misliking for young Hartley, and had come to enjoy the few periods he was able to spend in his company. He found him an amusing and stimulating companion, combining a wide and penetrating knowledge of men and books, with a taking modesty in his own attainments, and a deferentially admiring attitude towards the Dean's achievements.

It was on the morning of St. Valentine's Day that the Dean had to leave home for the Church Congress at Exeter, and it was by the last post the previous evening that the final proofs of his new book arrived for revision. The Congress was to last for ten days, and the proofs were urgent. If he took the proofs with him and sent them off from Exeter, he would have to take with him some half-dozen or so works of reference, for many items needed final verification.

There was one way out of the difficulty, and the Dean took it. Roy had helped him with the previous revision, had indeed suggested various emendations ; he knew the book thoroughly, and was as competent as the author to see the book through the Press.

Unluckily it was a Sunday, and Roy was not expected. A hurried note invited him to lunch, and before the Dean left at two o'clock, it was arranged that Roy should do the final revision of the proofs at the Deanery, where he could consult the necessary authorities.

" It will have to be in the evening," said Roy. " I'll come along about nine and put in say a couple of hours. If I begin to-morrow it should not take me longer than till Thursday. That will leave ample time for the return of the proofs, sir ? "

" Splendid," said the Dean. " Why not come to dinner for this week and combine business with pleasure. And eleven is rather late to go stumbling along that unpleasant footpath of your uncle's. Stay over the night until you've finished the wretched things. Better still, come for the week, eh ? "

Roy shook his head. " It's awfully hospitable of you, sir, but I can't be away from the Hall just now. Uncle David is not at all well. As you know he's not been out except for a short walk or so since I came, and our evening meal together is one of the small diversions to which he looks forward as eagerly as I do. No, I'll come along after dinner, as soon as I can, and put in a couple of hours. As for the wretched footpath, I've a torch, you know, and a good pair of boots, and I'm a tried and seasoned wayfarer."

" Who only walks for the good things at the end," said Gillian, mockingly.

" Exactly, both ends," smiling. " You and Mrs. Perseval at this end, and my bed at the other. If there are——"

" As you like, my boy, as you like," interrupted the Dean's rich voice. " Don't overdo it, you know. Last post on Friday will be time enough to send them off. What's wrong with Hartley ? He was fit enough a month ago. I hope our mists aren't getting into his bones. There's only one thing for that : rum, the real Jamaica stuff."

" No, he's as indifferent to climate and as unaffected by it as I am," replied Roy ; " his heart is not too strong, and it's bothered him just lately ; nothing more than that, but it's left him with a disinclination for physical exertion of any sort."

The Dean nodded. " Well," glancing at the clock, " Congresses, like time, tide and eternity, wait for no man, and I confess that to eternity they bear more than a fleeting resemblance. You've never had the inestimable pleasure of attending one ? No ; you've missed much, then. Well missed. No more interminable spate of chatter ever afflicted man since Babel."

.   .   .   .

Roy, yawned, put down the proof he was revising, looked at the clock, and lit a cigarette. He'd do another half-hour before he went. He glanced appreciatively round the cosy study. The Dean certainly forgot nothing in the way of comfort. He took the coffee-pot from the electric heater, poured himself out a cup, added three lumps of sugar and sat stirring slowly.

A gentle knock at the door was followed by the entrance of Mrs. Perseval. She apologised for disturbing him. " I'm sure I shan't sleep, so I've come down for my bed-book. It's the most amazingly ambulatory volume in the world. Unless I hide it, it walks down here a dozen times a week, and has the exasperating habit of occupying a different place on a different shelf every time I come here for it."

Roy followed her glance over the two thousand odd

volumes. " And the name of this annoying bedfellow ? " he smiled.

" The delicious Pepys. It's volume two I'm looking for. No, Mr. Hartley, you're not to bother. Please *do* sit down." She put a hand upon his arm and led him back to his chair. " It's too bad of me. Here's Evelyn, who'll do almost as well, although he's not the sleep-giver dear Pepys is." She busied herself at the shelves for some moments and then softly moved towards the door. " Good-night, Mr. Hartley."

" I'll look Pepys out for you before I go, Mrs. Perseval. Volume two, you said ? Shall I leave it on the little table outside ? Are you likely to be asleep ? Shall I bring it up to you ? Perhaps one of the maids . . ."

" I'm afraid I shan't sleep with old Evelyn. You'd be an angel if you just dropped it outside my room. I'm afraid the maids are abed and asleep this hour past, and Gillian and the children. This is a house of the seven sleepers. I hope you won't feel too much like the Prince in the fairy-tale."

" I might if you were sleeping, you know," laughed Roy. " You shall have Master Pepys by eleven." He paused and looked at her with eyes that made no attempt to hide an admiration of her physical charms, or a frank avowal that it was only those charms that drew him. She returned his look, and for a long moment they watched one another.

Roy picked up the proof. " I'll bring the book in to you," he said. " I'll tread like Agag lest you are asleep."

He opened Mrs. Perseval's bedroom door. Under his arm was the Pepys. He had found it easily. It was quite near the gap in the row of the Evelyns—a presentation set printed on parchment in an almost fulsome binding.

The room was in darkness save for a small circle of light over the back of the bed. Mrs. Perseval reclined against a

MP

pile of pillows. A filmy silken dressing-jacket clung precariously about her shoulders. Her hands, lightly clasped, rested on the quilt, and her book lay face downward beside her.

Roy walked quietly over to the bed, proffering the Pepys without speaking. She stretched out a hand and the dressing-jacket slipped from her shoulders on to the pillows behind her. Her bare arms, neck, throat and breast were shadowed by her movement.

Roy placed the book on the bed, sat beside her, took her hands in his, and said with a low laugh, " I have not kept you a hundred years."

She held his hands tightly. Her heart began to beat and struggle against her breast. She breathed rapidly and with an increasing sense of suffocation.

He bent over her. She closed her eyes, waiting, her heart thunderous, her blood surging tumultuously in her ears. She felt his breathing near, put up half-reluctant arms and drew him down to her. His hair brushed her forehead. She felt the strain and stress of his body, and with sudden abandonment she gave him her mouth.

2

The Dean's new book was published on March the thirtieth, and at noon on that day, when the van of the station carrier failed to stop at the Deanery, the author's fretting impatience exploded into mild profanity. Besides his six free copies the Dean invariably purchased from his publishers three dozen copies at the usual discount. A few of these he dispatched to friends and the remainder to the Press, accompanied by a letter addressed to the reviewers, drawing attention to important passages. This quaint procedure had been Dr. Perseval's custom since the publication

of his first book. This book, as its successors, had received
a good Press, but the Dean, hungry for praise and in-
tolerant of any criticism, considered it had been scamped.
He had therefore written some score or so letters of complaint to various periodicals. The few replies he received
did nothing to appease his wrath. Thereafter he character-
ised all reviewers as a set of venal hirelings, or alternatively,
a pack of indolent and ignorant rascals. Employing a
modern version of Morton's fork he therefore sent all
important publications a signed copy of each new book,
addressing it, with a covering explanatory letter, to the
reviewer. It says much for the good humour of the reviewers
that they ignored the implications of the Dean's invidious
methods, and dealt with the books upon their merits,
which, indeed, were not few.

The Dean's parcel of books, which usually arrived upon
the day of publication, was so bulky that it came by train
and was delivered by the station carrier. When, therefore,
upon that bright March morning the Ford railway van
failed to stop outside the Deanery, where the Dean, hidden
by the drawing-room curtains, stood impatiently awaiting
its arrival, a feverish activity displaced the usual mid-day
calm of the Persevals' dwelling.

Harper, the chauffeur, was dispatched hurriedly to the
station with an abusive letter to the stationmaster, and
instructions to bring the parcel back with him.

Harper returned without the precious books, and with
a verbal message from the stationmaster, a truculent rascal
much liked in Welling, and with a standing in his free-
mason's lodge that rendered him indifferent to the Dean's
tempers. This message, diplomatically watered down by
Harper, denied any knowledge of a parcel and hinted at
previous packages wrongfully addressed. Harper on his
return journey, while turning into Portway Street, collided

with a dustcart, smashed his windscreen, and cut his face and hand.

As Harper backed into the garage the Dean hurried down to receive his volumes, with Roy, who was just leaving, a pace behind him. Harper, mopping his cuts with an oily and greasy handkerchief, delivered the ill tidings in a morose monotone.

The Dean pshawed and tutted pettishly, and at the end of the short recital, packed off the wounded chauffeur to be patched up by Dr. Forde.

At that moment Gillian came out with a handful of letters that had just arrived by the noon post. Among them was a notification from Darum Station Goods office that a parcel addressed to Dr. Henry Perseval awaited immediate removal. A curt printed footnote to the effect that " After two days the merchandise will be subject to warehouse, wharfage, demurrage or siding charges in addition to the charges shown hereon," seemed to the infuriated Dean a personal and malignant affront.

Gillian's attempt to save the situation, by offering to run the car over after lunch and pick up the parcel, merely caused the fire to flame more furiously.

" Nonsense ! You know I won't have you drive by yourself. And if you *could* be trusted the car's smashed, ruined probably. I shall sack Harper. It's sheer da—da— deplorable carelessness."

" Let me run the car over to the new garage in Broad Walk," said Roy. " Barentz is a smart fellow and he'll vet it for you and put it right in a couple of hours. I'll call for it this afternoon, and as Harper's not fit to drive to-day, I'll run over to Darum station, collect the parcel, and you shall have it by tea-time : it's only twenty-five miles there and back."

" Well, that's good of you, Hartley," mollifying slightly,

" but I don't want to monopolise your day in this fashion. I'm very grateful, none the less."

" That's all right, sir ; we'll consider it settled."

" And I'll come as your guide," said Gillian, with a trace of diffidence.

" I was about to beg that favour. I'm rather a duffer at direction, and once off the high road it's a maze of a route."

" Look here, my boy," went on the now soothed Dean, " you look in for tea, bringing the car with you, if it's ready, and then the pair of you can go off about five. You should be back by—— ? "

" Six, sir, to leave a wide margin for accidents," smiling.

Dr. Perseval frowned. " Better leave a wider margin still, and avoid them altogether. Well, six-thirty, h'm ? We'll then run over the book, sure to be errata, I've never seen anything like the carelessness of printers these days, and you must join us at dinner, and perhaps a rubber afterward, eh ? " The Dean was now once more disposed to admit the existence of a pleasant side to life.

" Thank you, sir. Is that agreeable to you, Gillian ? Good. Then I'll come along soon after four with the car."

When Roy called at Barentz's garage at four o'clock the car was ready, with the exception of the wind-screen wiper. " Leave that till to-morrow, Barentz, we'll get no rain to-day," Roy said impatiently.

Barentz cocked his eye at the wrack packing low down over the estuary. " I'm not so sure, sir ; it's April weather though it's still March. It'll not take more than twenty minutes. I've had to send over to Queenstown as I'm out of stock. Brooker is due back now. I'll send him along with the car when it's ready."

" No, can't be bothered. I'll look in with it to-morrow. It'll not rain."

Doubtless the missing wiper may be absolved from responsibility for the whole of the disastrous journey, but it was without question the cause of the first mishap, one indeed that by fraying the driver's nerve may have set the whole stage for troublous times.

It was raining heavily when they started, and at the beginning of the narrow neck of Tilly's Lane, they bumped into and upset a small boy who darted off the kerb at a moment when the blurring of the screen was at its densest.

The child's protesting howl reassured everyone but his mother that he was unhurt. That lady demanded compensation with threats of violence, accompanied by innuendoes directed at the Church of England and young women gadding about with curates. Finally the policeman on point duty at the end of the High Street had to bring his notebook into action before honour and cupidity were satisfied.

Four miles from Darum, in the centre of an intricate maze of narrow winding lanes, the off back tyre collapsed with a particularly malevolent report. Roy removed the muddied traitor and fitted the Stepney. He had no overalls and the rain still fell steadily.

A furlong further on began the notorious Darum hairpin, a winding hill with a gradient of one in six for the last hundred yards. Roy drove up carelessly on top gear. The last dozen yards were enlivened by a violent knocking of the engine, and at the top the car stopped dead with a smoking radiator.

Roy grinned ruefully. " Big end gone, probably." Fortunately it was less serious, but the trouble, a badly choked jet, took Roy nearly an hour to locate, and twenty minutes to repair. The one bright spot in the gloom was the cessation of the rain.

They reached Darum station at three minutes past seven to find the goods office closed and the man in charge departed. A shilling tip to a youthful porter going off duty however brought the departed back, and a half-crown persuaded him, contrary, as he pointed out, to the regulations, to deliver up the merchandise.

While these illegal actions were afoot Gillian rang up the Deanery, gave a short account of their tribulations, begged them not to wait dinner, as she and Roy would get something light at Darum and have a supper as soon as they got back ; about nine o'clock, she ended hopefully.

Bribery is a diplomatic amenity and may not be hurried. It was therefore eight-thirty when the car left the lights of Darum behind and plunged into the labyrinthine lanes beyond. Darkness, intensified by a mist, had fallen, and the rain again fell torrentially.

Three miles from Darum, uncharted in that black misty sea, Roy drew in to the grassy side of a lane and confessed himself lost.

He got out, and looking in through the window at Gillian snuggling sleepily into her furs, suggested that he should walk along the lane in quest of a cottage, an inn, a wayfarer, or a signpost. Gillian agreed, and a moment afterward put out her head to watch him disappear into the darkness. The small hand of the clock beside the speedometer had just slipped over the Roman nine in hopeless pursuit of its taller brother.

The long hand was within half-an-inch of lapping its slow competitor when Roy returned.

Gillian jumped from the car to meet him. " Oh, where have you been ? I've been so frightened. I wondered if—I thought."

Roy took her outstretched hands and rubbed them briskly between his own.

" You're frozen," he said ; " where are your gloves ? "

" I don't know. In the car. Where have you been ? "

" Half over Meadshire in a blind circle, I should think. I've seen neither cottage, inn, light, signpost, chick, duck, hen, nor child. Get in. We'll push on slowly, and perhaps you'll get your bearings presently. I must depend on you now."

" I knew that last turning was wrong," said Gillian dully. " I tapped on the window, you know, but you took no notice."

" I'm sorry. I ought to have stopped. But I don't think it would have made any difference. It was before then we made the mistake. But all these lanes look alike in this gloom. Do get in d—er—get in, Gillian. You're shivering."

" I'll sit in front with you."

" No, it's much too cold. I'll listen for your taps this time—and obey them. Please get in, Gillian."

He held the door open and peered inside. " My aunt ! it's ten o'clock. We're benighted." He laughed and bowed mockingly, motioning with his hand toward the step.

" Oh, don't laugh. Can't we go back to Darum and go round the longer way ? "

" Well, there's no room to turn, and three miles reversing in this inkiness is no joke. But we'll try. Do get in. I'm awfully sorry, Gillian. Are you angry with me?" He had put out one hand to assist her. His fingers rested lightly upon her arm. She turned and looked up at him. " No," she said, " no." Her lips quivered. " No," she said again tremulously, haltingly, as if it were the only word she knew.

He saw that she was near to tears. He withdrew his hand from her arm. She turned toward him with a low cry. He put his arms about her and she drew herself into his embrace, weeping softly for gladness, for forgiveness, for love, for she knew not what.

Two hours later a motor cycle popped its way along the muddy lane. Roy hailed its rider, an engaging youth dressed as if for a prolonged aerial sojourn over arctic wastes, and was offered a pilotage to Cressart, a small market town about seven miles from Welling.

The reached the Deanery just after one, and found various search-parties about to set out.

Roy accepted a bed and a night-cap. As he raised his glass he said to his host, " I won't apologise, sir, for opening the parcel ; the book was such a Godsend during those two hours we were hung up that an apology would somehow seem ungrateful, ungracious."

" Welcome, quite welcome, my boy," smiling with great affability. " And did you find any errata, h'm ? Or were you too lazy ? "

" Peccavi ! but it was not laziness, sir ; we were much too interested to remember to watch for them."

3

The first and second Tuesdays in June each year were set aside for the children's picnic given by the Mayor. The picnic took place at Barton Sands, the children of seven and under going the first Tuesday, and the over sevens the following Tuesday.

Barton Sands was a wide, flat, shining stretch, running in a five mile arc from Cairn Head to Formby Point. Midway of the arc, and about half-a-mile back from the sea-mark lay the village of Barton Olney, and behind the village Barton Olney Woods spread patchily over the moors up to the ruins of Welling's ancient city wall. A six-inch naval gun could very comfortably have shelled Welling from Barton Sands, yet the distance by road round the wood was over twelve miles.

The younger party usually numbered about seven hundred children and the other something under a thousand. With each party went a small army of helpful adults, and to recruit these amiable volunteers the Mayor and Mayoress spent many busy weeks of cajolery beforehand.

Each of the two days were whole holidays for the schools, and the teachers transferred their activities from the classrooms to the sands. The army of helpers bore many resemblances to an army in war time. It had its G.O.C. in the person of Andrew Banks ; its officers, represented by Bowers, ffoliot, Clarence George, Dr. Forde, two or three residentiary Canons, and the Canon in residence for June ; its N.C.O.s, the teachers ; and its rank and file consisting of able-bodied spinsters, small shopkeepers, nonconformist parsons and a host of well-meaning mothers. The analogy may be strained a little further, for it was the N.C.O.s who bore the literal heat and burden of the day, and ensured its success.

Aloof yet affable, as Jehovah with the smoke of the burnt-offerings in his nostrils, loomed the Dean. He was, as it were, above the battle, yet his presence lent to it a cere-monial dignity that inspired the staff, overawed the children, and flattered the rank-and-file.

In all the eight years since the inception of these gala days Alice Thatcher had not once been absent from her place with the under sevens. This spare, flat-chested, sucked-dry, little woman of forty, for all her twenty years of teaching, had lost none of her ardent enthusiasm in the care of other people's children. She liked children, she found them interesting, fascinating, inspiring even, and despite her apparent severity and quite blunt refusal to stand any nonsense, the children responded to her eagerly. They knew where they stood with her. She had complete control over her temper, her affections and her tongue. She liked her job and she overworked herself.

At forty her hair was beginning to grey, her complexion was muddy, her eyes dingy and wan, her lips faded. She suffered from sickness and headaches due to chronic constipation, and toward the end of a day she was often miserably in pain.

She had always wanted a child of her own ; she had wanted a lover, a husband, a home, and all the little tender commonplaces, humdrum and warm and strangely moving, that are a part of this everyday human relationship. Lacking these intimacies she would have made do with affection.

In all her life no one had loved her. She had been brought up in an institution ; from there she had gone to a training college, and thence to an appointment at the age of twenty-one to the post she still held in Welling. The fickle, fleeting cupboard-love of children she might have had, had she relaxed her severity, loosened the rein she kept upon herself, been responsive to warm if ulterior overtures. In her early days of teaching a fear of favouritism and a fear of encouraging familiarity had kept her aloof, correct, and unsmiling, and now habit had moulded her beyond change. The children liked her, responded to her, worked for her and did not play her up ; but what little affection they had to give to adults they lavished upon more showy and ingratiating mistresses.

It was a day such as only June can bring to a festivity. At nine o'clock, when the children clambered into the twelve gaily decorated charabancs lined up outside the Mayor's house, the sun blazed down from a cloudless sky, the faintest of warm breezes lifted the leaves of the trees around the bandstand, and under Belton Bridge the gulls drifted lazily seaward, white speckles that vanished and re-appeared as the water-glitter winked and blinked dazzlingly.

Alice settled herself comfortably in the back seat, quelled the most boisterous among the shouting enthusiasts wriggling, twisting and jumping around her, and, as a bugle blew called warningly to the children to be seated.

There was a sudden uproar of machinery springing into life ; the charabancs began to tremble ; young voices swelled uncontrollably into screams of excitement, and old ones reiterated messages of good advice, good cheer, and good wishes.

The three charabancs ahead jolted suddenly into motion. Alice saw the chauffeur stoop, heard the crescendo of the engine, and as the great coach broke its inertia with a jerk and began to gather speed, the door beside her was flung open and Roy Hartley sprang in.

He smiled at her confusion.

" Wrong coach. I know. Forgive me if I startled you. Thought I'd lost it altogether. Which *is* my coach ? Must wait now till we get to Barton, unless you have me flung off." He spoke breathlessly, and dropped into the vacant seat beside Alice with a sigh of contentment.

The children turned round in their seats, craning their necks, smiling at Roy, watching Alice curiously, glancing from one to another, with an interest that faded rapidly, passed, and was replaced by the excitements of the open country now spread so enticingly ahead of them.

" My first trip," said Roy, " but not yours, Miss Thatcher."

" My eighth, and this is the finest day of them all. A wonderful day, even for June."

> " *A noise like of a hidden brook*
> *In the leafy month of June*
> *That to the sleeping woods all night*
> *Singeth a quiet tune*,"

quoted Roy.

" That is very lovely," said Alice softly. " I daren't think of lovely things on a beautiful day like this, lest too much beauty make me mad."

" And would you mind ? "

" Mind ? Being mad ? "

" Yes, mad for beauty's sake."

Alice laughed. " I don't think I should like it very much. Perhaps it depends upon the sort of madness. Although all madness, it seems to me, must be dreadful ; there is an unnatural, an unhuman, horror about it, akin to the horror we should feel if a dog suddenly burst into blasphemous ribaldry, or made love to one with human speech and half human gestures."

" Beastly, yes. What is the programme when we arrive ? This is all new to me, you know."

" Well," laughing, " there is a programme of organised events, but it rarely takes place as planned. Usually there's bathing and paddling and so on for an hour or so after we arrive. Then the children eat their lunch—those, that is, who have not eaten it en route. Some, by the way, look, are already eating it, and it's not yet half-past nine."

" Too excited to eat their breakfast. Please go on, Miss Thatcher."

" In the afternoon there are sports and games, enlivened by the band. Tea follows at half-past four. Then more games, distribution of prizes, and finally, although it won't be dark, fireworks. The start for home is generally begun about half-past eight to nine—a little later sometimes, a little earlier at others, depending upon the weather."

" I don't feel myself likely to be at all useful. I shall appoint myself your subaltern. May I ? "

"You'll feel happier as a free-lance." Smiling, " you needn't worry about being useful ; you'll *have* to be—the children will see to that."

The last few of the children, replete and distended with cake, buns and unnumbered cups of tea, had rushed shrieking off to the sands, where the after-tea amusements were beginning.

" What duties now ? " asked Roy. " Do we, as the apostles, gather up the fragments into twelve baskets. And who washes up ? And who——"

" No," laughing happily, " we're off duty now until the bugle goes for the general assembly and lining up for the charabancs."

Roy looked at his watch. " Three hours, then, perhaps four. That's fine. Are you tired ? "

Alice had never been less tired in all her life. Her eyes were radiant, her sallow face flushed ; there was a joyous urgency stirring in her blood that drove back the years and retrieved from those ravishers some shreds and tatters of her stolen youth. She smiled into his eyes. " I'm not in the least tired. Are you ? "

" A fountain of energy. Let's go exploring in Barton Woods."

" Tea first."

" Tea ? "

" Of course. In the big marquee over there. Aren't you hungry ? I am and I'm simply dying for a cup of tea, *boiling* hot."

Roy jumped to his feet. " Stay here, and I'll bring tea and cakes and things."

She shook her head, laughing. " And nice and hot the tea would be by the time you got here. We'll sit outside the marquee at one of the tables, and then afterward, if you're still a fountain of energy, we'll explore Barton Woods."

As they approached the first belt of scattered trees Alice said lightly, " Have you a nose for direction ? The wood's terribly dense as you get into it. There are all sorts of harrowing tales of lost and strayed wayfarers, beginning in

the days of King John and ending only last year, when two
boy scouts spent some sixty-odd hours finding their way
out."

" That's all right. I'm perfectly wonderful upon uncharted seas and so forth."

" A newly acquired sense, isn't it ? "

Roy raised his brows inquiringly.

" The little bird of Welling tells a tale of a knight and
lady benighted in a car some months ago. The little bird
further says——"

" Oh, *that* ! " laughing, " that was Gillian's fault. I shan't
lose *you*."

" No ? Poor Gillian, this is the first Barton picnic she's
missed. She'll hate being ill. What's the matter with her ?
No one seems to know anything about it."

" It's not very much, just sickness, biliousness probably,
or indigestion. She looks queer, though, run-down, blood-
less, in need of a change probably. I'll ask Uncle David to
prescribe for her. He practised once, you know."

" Practised once ! Is that all you can say about the great
David Hartley ! But I suppose uncles have no honour
among their own nephews. We're getting into the thick of
the wood now. Don't let your sense of direction slumber and
don't let's turn too often. Keep straight on as well as we
can judge."

" There's a better way than that," smiling.

" Yes ? "

" We can sit down in that bracken ; it looks a desirable
couch." He knelt in the bracken and swept a space with his
hands. " Delicious. Feel." He put his hand in hers and drew
her down beside him. She began to tremble. He lay at full
length and she sat very still looking away through the
trees.

Presently she lowered her eyes and looked shyly at him,

avoiding his glance, but watching the youthful beauty of his face.

She tried to look away but constraint or desire prevented her. She met his glance ; his eyes smiled into hers.

She returned that gay glance gravely, steadily, humbly.

He put out a hand and drew her toward him. For a moment she struggled against the compulsion of his strength and of her desire. And then she bowed herself over him, laid her face beside his upon the arm that pillowed his head, drew him close and kissed him.

He began to play with her hair, and to stroke her face with caressing fingers. Presently his fingers sought her breasts, and his free arm went round her roughly.

Time stood still. When again it moved she heard faintly, as if it fell from immense heights, a thin calling note. It was a wisp of sound so frail, so tenuous, so incredibly remote, that it did not touch to understanding her drugged and drowsy consciousness. Again and again it called, incredibly remote, incredibly frail.

Roy stirred, loosed her arms, withdrew himself from her embrace. He sat up, pushed the fingers of both hands through his hair and smiled down at her negligently through the frame of his arms. " Isn't that the bugle ? Come along."

She knelt up and drew his hands down and held them against her lips.

He put her away from him, not ungently. " Hark at that racket ! We shall be late." He stood up and helped her to her feet. He stooped and kissed her carelessly upon the ear. " There ! Come along."

She walked beside him with but half of her consciousness awake to reality. Her body drooped slightly ; her feet dragged. She was aware of nothing but a warm and all pervading joyousness.

CHAPTER XII

COMMENTATIVE

I

July had been a wet dull cold month. It was followed by an August so dry and hot and windless that by the middle of the month the small green apples were become red and plump and full, and before its close the apple-harvest was over, while in all the fields the corn was stooked by the second Saturday. For this alone that August might well have remained a vivid memory among people to whom the seasons are the chief givers or withholders of all good things. Strange happenings indeed must befall to relegate the topic of nature's vagaries to a position of secondary importance. That the heat, the rainless thunderstorms, and the unprecedented harvests of that August received but scant attention from the gossips is the measure of the strangeness of the contemporary events.

As great men, despite apocryphal tales to the contrary, invariably show indubitable signs of greatness from their earliest years, so the first day of August was, relatively to the normal quietude of Welling, a prodigious birth.

It was a Saturday. The Theatre Royal had been closed for a month for renovating, and Mr. Lou Bellairs, the lessee and manager, had as a re-opening novelty arranged a grand boxing display for the afternoon. There were to be one 15-rounds heavy-weight and one 15-rounds light-weight contest, five ten-rounds contests at various weights, and a 3-rounds exhibition bout between Fly Platner, the English bantam-weight champion, and Bossy Jordan, the coloured

Np

American ex-world's bantam-weight champion. Further, Tom Mavis, the English welter-weight champion, was to be the referee in all the contests.

Boxing at the Theatre Royal was an innovation and, as it proved, a financially successful one. The pugilists boxed to capacity. Welling found it all a pleasantly exciting experience, but one which, in the normal course of everyday events, would soon have slept in its pigeon-hole of memory along with ten thousand others.

At six o'clock however, Tom Mavis entered the bar-parlour of *The Crown*, and allowed himself to be so hospitably entertained by numerous admirers, that on leaving at seven, his car, which he drove himself, avoided P.C. Baxter on point duty near the bandstand, by so narrow a margin of safety that the constable's outraged if accelerated dignity demanded satisfaction to the point of requiring the English champion's name.

" You know my name all right, all right," said Tom Mavis, with difficulty repressing a hiccough. " Mind I don't help you not to forget it in a hurry."

" Name, please, *and* address," repeated Constable Baxter.

"*I'll* write it," exclaimed the flushed pugilist, snatching the book from the policeman's hand, and skying the official pencil.

There followed in disorderly sequence the attempted arrest of Tom Mavis, the K.O. of P.C. Baxter, the hurried departure of the victor, the belated arrival of reinforcements, and the detention of the pugilist half-an-hour later by the Queenstown police.

From nine o'clock the same evening the bar-parlour of *The Crown* discussed the matter dispassionately, settled it satisfactorily, and passed on to more intimate topics.

" A miss is as good as a mile," observed Captain Lacy, " Baxter shouldn't have taken any notice ; the car didn't hit him."

" That's all right," commented Mason, " but our noble pug was obviously tight, and it was Baxter's job to run him in. A tight man in a powerful car like Mavis's is too dangerous to be at large. What do you think, Blaney ? "

" If murderers must be hanged I think a drunken driver who kills anyone should certainly swing. In fact, seeing what a lethal weapon a car is, I'd charge any man who attempts to drive when tight with attempted murder."

" You *would*, of course," chuckled Mason, " and the passengers with being accessory, I suppose. You'd have arrested Mavis on sight, if you'd have been Baxter."

" God forbid I should have been Baxter—a deplorable sample of crude bumbledom. Most provincial peelers are tarred with that brush. In some parts they add a sort of naïf insolence to their officiousness. East Anglian cops are the finest examples. I once asked a Norwich peeler why the city was decorated so gaily one morning, and he replied, in the maddening Norfolk sing-song drawl, rising to a high falsetto on the final word, ' What ! are you so ignorant you don't know *that* ! ' "

" He deserved a medal. Thank God someone takes you down a peg or two at times. But about drunk and driving ? What do you say in the matter, Crowson ? We've heard enough amateurs on the subject ; let's have the professional point of view."

Hartley's chauffeur emptied his glass and smiled. " This is beer," he said, " and it's my fourth. You'll reckon I see no harm in a glass or two for a driver. Well, you're wrong. I've finished work till Monday or I'd not be drinking. I reckon a single drink takes the edge off a man's driving and makes all the difference between safety and riskiness. I don't touch liquor unless I've got twenty-four hours between me and my next turn at the wheel. Ordinary times I only drink Saturday nights, but since I've been to Welling

I *have* had a few glasses during the week, but only because I knew I'd not be wanted next day. I've more time on my hands at this job than I know what to do with."

" There aren't many men would grumble at *that*," laughed Mason ; " been with Mr. Hartley long ? "

" Only since the first day of last December. He engaged me just before he came down here. It's a queer job."

" Queer ! " Clarence George's gasping voice broke in from the bar, where he was lounging with Larry at his feet, " queer ! all jobs are queer in Welling, old chap, for Welling's the queerest place in England. Isn't that so, Mr. Daniels ? "

" You ought to know, Mr. George," smiled the publican. " Queer enough tales you write about the things hereabouts."

" Oh, come now, good boniface, come now," gasped George, " you're not going to tell us you've forgotten all the queer business of the last few months."

" That's just it, Mr. George, it's only the last few months that queer things *have* happened. In all my twenty years here beforehand I remember nothing out of the ordinary. It's all just lately."

" Since December, eh, Mr. Daniels," said Mason.

" That's right, sir, December began it, as you might say."

" That was when *you* came to Welling, wasn't it, Blaney ? " laughed Mason. " Has Haynes interrogated you yet ? "

" I don't want to monopolise *all* the credit. Mr. Crowson here came about the same time, and Hartley of course."

" He *is* a queer one, Mr. Hartley," said the chauffeur, for whom the beer was beginning to speak. " He shuts himself up in his rooms for days on end, and only Bates sees him. Some days even Bates doesn't get a glimpse, for he gets instructions over the house-'phone to lay a meal in one of the rooms, and to call the boss when it's ready. Bates doesn't like the job at all, and if he weren't paid like a bally prince he'd not stay. Ten quid a week he gets. Three more than me. But he's worth it. I'll say that for him ; he's got a way with grub that I've never met before. It's A.1 at The Pines but it don't touch Bates's."

" D'you hear that, Blaney ? " interrupted Mason. " Now here's a chance to prove one of your pet theories. What is it you say? If genius marries genius the offspring is a dud, but if talent marries talent the offspring is a genius. How's that ? "

" As inaccurate as your renderings usually are. But what do you propose ? "

" Why, we'll marry our amazingly talented Mrs. Robbins to the amazingly talented Mr. Bates, adopt the offspring, who will be a culinary genius, exploit him or her, and live on the proceeds."

" They might be barren. Talented people often are, like mules. Mules are wonderfully talented ; remember the army ones ? You'll have another drink, Mr. Crowson. Pint ? Pint of your best ullage, Mr. Daniels."

" Well, good health, sir," said Crowson, taking a long pull and putting down his tankard. " Bates has no time for women ; he's not much time for *anything*."

" Yes, I should say he'd got plenty to do with Mr. Hartley and his nephew to look after."

" I didn't mean it exactly that way, sir." Crowson always grew deferential in his cups. " I mean he doesn't show any interest in things. I wanted him to come to the scrapping at the theatre this afternoon, but he said he wouldn't waste his time ; they were all fakes."

" Not Baxter's K.O., anyhow," laughed Mason.

" Not that he *has* much spare time believe me, sir," continued Crowson, with the slow careful speech of the man who is aware he's had too much. " Not that Mr. Hartley's nephew makes much difference. No, sir. But the boss is not too well these days and keeps his bed a lot, and that makes work, and he's bad-tempered with it. No, gentlemen, don't think I'm saying that young Mr. Hartley makes work. We hardly ever see him. Come to think of it, I've only seen him twice up at the Hall, and then he was alone and in a damned hurry. No, he's mostly out, what with his job at the Dean's and the choir. Half *lived* there when he first came."

" So I gather, so we *all* gather, eh ? " coughed Clarence George, who was rolling Larry over on his back and rubbing his belly with his foot. " *Persona grata* to the last degree. Especially with Mrs. Perseval and the pretty Gillian." George when drunk was not above the petty scurrilities of local scandal. " The Reverend Roy Hartley is, in my opinion, which has not been asked for, God be praised, is— er—what our rustic friends call a lad. Eh, Daniels."

" Maybe, sir."

" Not maybe at all, good boniface, not maybe, but *is*. Eh, Mason, you journalists know everything. What do you think of the right reverend temporary precentor ? " The beer and spirits he had been drinking had now sloughed from George most of his acquired decencies of social conduct. He was at the moment as vulgarly and maliciously defamatory as any of the gossiping rustics of his books, rustics indeed who had no existence outside George's myopic pages.

" Discretion is the better part of journalism," replied Mason.

" Discretion my backside," gasped George ; " you're a downy fellow, Mason. You'll be discreet next over Queen Anne's death. My good man, it's the talk of Welling. The boy bishop, the Primate in embryo has, I'm prepared to wager you, seduced——"

" Time, gentleman, please ! " cried Daniels loudly, switching off the corner lights. He raised the flap and began to make his round of the tables, collecting glasses with noisy haste. " Time, gentlemen, *please* ! "

2

" I always think," said Miss Lettice Ovey, as she poured out the tea on Sunday afternoon, " that five is the perfect number for a friendly tea-time."

" Just right," agreed Mrs. Fletcher, whilst Alison nodded, Miss Thatcher smiled approval, and Mrs. D'Arcy L'Estrange said, " I once heard a wise old body say of afternoon tea-ers that two was for lovers, three made a gooseberry, four took sides, five was canny but six a crowd."

" One over the right number is always as bad as a crowd," replied Miss Ovey. " I've not sugared ; I always forget who does and who doesn't take it. These are cucumber sandwiches, those tomato, and here are our famous Robbins flead-cakes."

" When I die," smiled Mrs. L'Estrange, helping herself, " flead-cake will be found written on my heart. Mrs. Robbins keeps the recipe a dark secret ? "

" On the contrary she showed Alison how to make them the first month she was here. Alison weighed everything to a scruple, followed the directions implicitly, and certainly turned out flead-cakes, but—well—eh, Alison ? "

" They were dreadful, and yet, as far as I could judge, the ingredients were the same, and I followed Mrs. Robbins's instructions to the letter. It's knack, I suppose ; but it's queer how no two women cook alike."

" Is it any queerer than other things we do differently ? " asked Miss Thatcher. " No two pianists play the same composition exactly alike, no two people write exactly alike— it's all like our fingerprints—the slight difference that makes *all* the difference."

" I'm afraid I'm a dreadful sceptic over fingerprints and such scientific marvels," laughed Mrs. L'Estrange. " I've a notion our men of science play a game of make-believe half their time. They make up a nice theory as a carpenter makes a box, and then they plane and cut and trim the facts to fit it. It's really asking too much to believe that no one else in all the world has thumb-markings the same as mine."

" It's not quite as sweeping as that, is it ? " rejoined Miss Thatcher. " There's about one chance in seven millions of finding a duplicate, I believe."

" One in seven *I* should say."

" I don't think the police would use the method if it weren't sound," objected Miss Alison.

" The police ! " laughing. " Are they infallible ? Are they even very particular ? Are they capable of deciding ? When a body is chosen chiefly on physique other things are bound to suffer. Can you imagine a more stupid man than Superintendent Haynes ? "

" I think all very big men seem stupid," ventured Mrs. Fletcher, " but it's only seeming. Perhaps it's the contrast with the agility of little men that——"

" Pugnacity, isn't it ? " smiled Mrs. L'Estrange, " rather than agility ; but really, our police do seem well—er—ponderous in mind and body, don't you think so ? "

" Well, they're efficient, anyhow," said Miss Ovey, cutting the rice-cake ; " there's nothing but court-cases in the papers these days—even *The Times* gives pages to them."

" It's only the police successes that are chronicled in the Press. I expect their failures would occupy double the space. It's rather queer, but if a crime is committed where one happens to be living, the criminal is simply *never* captured. When I was living in Kilkee there were seven or eight burglaries in ten days, all within a stone's throw of my villa ; not one of the rascals was caught. And all the disturbance we've had in Welling the last ten months—what have the police done ? "

" They've doubtless done all that anyone could do," said

Mrs. Fletcher. " I don't think it can be an easy task to find a man who's disappeared."

" It's hardly *a* man," rejoined Mrs. L'Estrange, " it's several."

" Then you don't think the outrages are the work of a single criminal ? " asked Miss Alison.

" Decidedly not. I should say there are at least three or four in it. In the first place I don't think the man Smith had any hand in the Cathedral outrage. As for the smashings and burnings they were probably by others. Haven't you noticed how these things spread. One criminal is followed by a dozen weak-minded imitations, especially in the imbecile sort of crime like cattle-maiming, window and dress-slashing, hay-rick burning and so on. If the police ever *do* get on the right track they'll probably find they've to do with a dozen or so mental defectives."

" Well, I don't agree, but it *is* a strange business," commented Miss Ovey, shaking the crumbs from her napkin on to the cloth, " but I'm not surprised. Don't you remember, Alison, I said when that notorious Mr. Hartley came here that I knew unpleasant things would happen. I think he's a nasty man. It's disgusting that the Dean should be on such good terms with him, and the way Mrs. Perseval fusses over young Mr. Hartley is even worse. She might be his mother and an over-indulgent mother at that."

" Only a mother ? " smiled Mrs. L'Estrange. " Mr. Roy Hartley seems a very affectionate son."

" And a most loving brother to Gillian," said Mrs. Fletcher. " I don't dislike Mr. Roy Hartley, but I think the Dean's a great ninny to allow the intimacy that obviously exists between them. Gillian's a lovely child, and very young, and well, you know what I think about male scruples."

" I'm sure you're wrong," said Alice Thatcher quietly. " Mr. Hartley's position at the Deanery and in the Cathedral makes it inevitable that he should be on intimate terms with the family. You don't, I hope, mean intimate," flushing, " in any—er—a—in *the* sense."

" I trust not," remarked Mrs. Fletcher drily. " But, well, things have been seen."

Alice reddened. " Gossip," she said angrily, " street-corner gossip. Tea-table tattle. How I hate it. It's all beastly, degrading, humiliating. If we must gossip, can't it be of good and not evil things. I hate gossiping women. I hate myself for being a woman."

" The good things are so *very* dull," said Mrs. L'Estrange.

Mrs. Fletcher smiled indulgently. " Do you think, my dear," she said, " that it is only women who gossip. There's no more slanderous set of gossips than men in their clubs. I know because James comes home and repeats it to me. My dear, after a lodge dinner the house simply reeks with stale, mouldy, rank tittle-tattle. You like Mr. Roy Hartley. Well, as I've said, I don't dislike him myself. On the contrary, in fact. But if I'd a girl of twenty I'd not introduce him into my house, and from what James has said to me there aren't many men in Welling who would be so complacent as the Dean."

" The Dean's quite absurd about that young man," snapped Miss Ovey ; " I heard on the very best authority that he was actually going to allow him to preach this evening. Luckily dear old Canon Manning put his foot down. He's in residence this month you know. He's defied the Dean's authority on more than one occasion and won. People say—but there, it's doubtless only gossip."

3

At three o'clock the following Wednesday afternoon there was a meeting at the Chapter House. It was presided over by the Dean, and there were also present the Canon in residence and seven of the residentiary canons—Halsham, Clarke, Stacey, Devine, Shepperson, Moffatt and Curwen.

It was one of the regular gatherings for the discussion of Cathedral and diocesan affairs, and would probably have runs its normal two hours of tedious discussion, if the Dean had not arrived late and excused himself by the one statement that was evidently a spark to tinder.

" Awfully sorry, Manning, I've been waiting for Hartley. I wanted him to talk to you all about the mass for next Sunday. However, something must have delayed him. He'll come along. We'd better begin. What have we first ? "

Canon Manning folded up the paper that lay on the table in front of him. " I think," he said slowly, " that before Mr. Hartley arrives we had better have a little frank discussion."

" Frankness, by all means, my dear Manning ; but what about ? About Hartley ? "

Canon Manning nodded. " I speak with the fullest sense of responsibility, and the knowledge of the seriousness of my words." He paused.

" Yes, go on."

" In the best interests of the Cathedral and of the diocese I think, we all think, that our precentor should be asked to resign. It——"

" Resign ! " snapped the Dean, " he has no appointment to resign from. His work at the Cathedral is purely a voluntary and temporary affair and we are under the greatest obligation to him. There is surely no question of his ability. What exactly is the trouble ? " angrily.

Canon Manning flushed. " The trouble is, sir, that Mr. Roy Hartley's actions are becoming, have, I fear, become, an open scandal in Welling."

" Nonsense ! " snapped the Dean ; " my dear Manning, this is preposterous. What *are* you referring to ? "

" To put it bluntly, Perseval, the common talk in Welling is that Hartley is living a notoriously lascivious life."

The Dean sat back in his chair, his arms stretched out before him on the table ; the fingers of one hand were clenched, and the fingers of the other tapped the polished surface. He looked round the circle of faces, and saw nothing there to lighten the dark oppression he felt stealing over him. " I really—I'm not—be more explicit, Manning ; what exactly are the facts ? "

" Few, if any, obviously, or you would have been acquainted with them as soon as we knew them. In these matters there can unfortunately only be conjecture and suspicion until it is too late. Briefly, Mr. Hartley is a frequent visitor at the cottage of Thatcher Burnett. Mrs. Burnett is a very pretty and flighty young woman, and the visits are always made when the husband is at work."

" Go on."

" At the Barton Sands picnic—this is a hateful business, Perseval, and I hate to use such evidence, but Hartley and Miss Thatcher were followed, foxed the fellow called it, into the woods and spied upon. It's all beastly and degrading. Such a witness, you may say, is suspect from his very dirtiness. Well, if that were the only——"

" A moment. What happened in the wood. Do you mean there was intimacy ? "

" So the fellow alleges. But, of course, that is not all. Banks came to me the other day and said that Hartley had been round having tea with the Mayoress, and had made the most outrageous suggestions to her."

" Good—good God, Manning, the thing's absurd. Mrs. Banks is old enough to be his mother and—well—she's——" he shrugged his shoulders. " I confess I was beginning to believe there was some fire for the smoke, but really, this preposterous nonsense makes it impossible to take the matter seriously. It is serious, of course, but from Hartley's point of view—sheer slander and defamation. I think we'd better get on with our other business. I don't want——"

" I regret you are forcing my hand, sir," continued Manning in distress, " but the matter has, I fear, come nearer home to you."

" Thank you ; that will do. If you mean the friendship, the warm friendship between Mr. Hartley and my family, I am aware of it, and it has my very cordial, my warmest approbation. I have not the slightest——"

" I am exceedingly sorry, sir. I apologise, gentlemen, for my discourtesy." Roy Hartley walked rapidly from the door to a vacant chair. He bowed. " My uncle, sir, had a slight seizure after lunch, and this has delayed me unpardonably. No, sir, nothing really serious. I've left him comfortably asleep. No, he wouldn't hear of Forde calling. It's awfully good of you ; I've brought the new setting with me."

4

Since that unforgettable night in January, Richard's letters to Rachel had become more and more infrequent, more and more strained, artificial and forced.

Until that night he had been, in the quaint colloquialism, a buck-virgin. He had flirted with many women, kissing, caressing and fondling them, but less venturesome or more fastidious than many young men he had never proceeded to those lengths of toying and handling which are the hallmark of youths who are, in their own phrase, " lads with the girls." And despite various emotional adventures during the war, even including several half-ashamed, wholly revolted and consequently abortive visits to tolerated houses, he had never experienced the final intimacy to which these toyings and cuddlings are but the traditional preliminaries.

That two hours in Ann's arms had been so overwhelming an emotional experience, an act so intense and thrilling, so joyous a breaking down of barriers, a contentment so completely and perfectly achieved, that it had seared the emotional surface of his consciousness to a tormented ecstasy that the passing months exacerbated rather than healed.

He desired with an urgent hunger a repetition of that supreme giving ; he wanted her mouth upon his, her arms about him, the feel of her body against his own, the gossamer caress of her hair and her breathing. In recollection she seemed the embodiment of all lovely and desirable things ; for that loveliness he wanted her ; but beyond and above that he wanted her from sheer passionate hunger ; he lusted for her as a woman, yet it was not woman he lusted for but for her only. She had touched him to so swift and sudden a realisation of beauty that there was about all his thoughts of her a quality of humble adoration that the bitterness of revelation failed to smirch. Resolutely and fiercely he had shut out from his mind the fact of her promiscuity. Wanton, easy, a light o' love she may have been, but only with him. He forced his mind to accept the sophism, barring the doors against truth, and when truth cried loudly without, he shut his ears.

The first fruit of this strange and worshipping humility had been a sonnet, which he had tortured out with a deeper and finer inspiration than he had previously known. He had sent this to Midgeham Murray, the editor of *The Hellenic Review*, who had offered to print it if he would alter the last two lines, which were, in the editor's opinion, "not true to the writer's emotional experience." Richard had damned Murray's eyes and sent the poem with like unsuccess to Tyrrell, that pompous literary jack-of-all-trades who ran *The London Monitor* with purblind omniscience, seeing no good in anything that did not come out of Balliol. It next went to Wrothley who ran the short-lived *Modern Age*. There it had appeared in the July number. It ran :

> *Mother of Men.*
>
> *Dear Wanton, when the moon made light our bed*
> *Last night, and drenched our passion with its gold,*
> *I asked no dreams to lay beside the dead*
> *Dreams that had crumbled to a little mould.*
> *And then I caught a trembling tenderness*
> *Soften your lips, that was not of desire ;*
> *And my hot blood that sought one more caress*
> *Poured to my brows with a transfigured fire.*
> *So that I hid my face where your heart beat,*
> *Feeling your cool breath through my hair. Confest,*
> *And shameful, like a child, I would not meet*
> *Your eyes, but very quiet on your breast*
> *I lay until I slept ; and when the day*
> *Found us my soul knelt at your feet to pray.*

It was this sonnet which had provoked Rachel into the letter she had for a long while been on the point of writing. She had seen Richard's letters becoming fewer and more constrained as the months passed. They were phrased as love-letters, but there was about them an artificiality that Rachel was quick to recognise. Further, Richard had now been at Welling eight months, and not once during that time had he suggested coming to London to see her. His fortnight's holiday at Christmas, his week at Easter and the few days' break at Whitsun had all been spent away from her. It was true he was hard-up, but he could certainly have managed one visit. He had not even definitely invited her down—there had merely been in one of his letters a casually expressed hope that one day she would see Welling herself. For weeks she hesitated upon the verge of a frank appeal for enlightenment ; the sonnet provided the spur to change hesitation into action.

Her letter had begun with its usual complaint about dearth of news in Richard's letters. It had passed easily from that to dearth of warm feeling, to his lack of desire to see her, and had enquired finally and abruptly if he no longer loved her, and whether the sonnet in the *Modern Age* was the key to the whole business. Am I to understand " *Mother of Men*," she ended, as a description of a physical experience, or is it simply a spiritual adventure inspired by some kindred form of beauty ?

Richard's first impulse had been to write by return, making a clean breast of it, and telling Rachel he no longer loved her. He did, in fact, sit down to reply immediately he read her letter, but as he phrased it in his mind, and came to the blunt statement : " I no longer love you," he put down his pen, and thrusting his hands into his pockets, stared out of the window. It wasn't true. He did still, in a way, love Rachel. It was not that urgent and hungry passion that shook him, drenched him, when he thought of Ann. Perhaps it was only a fondness, an affection. He knew he didn't *want* Rachel now as he wanted Ann. He no longer dared let the thought of Ann in his arms invade his consciousness with its lovely imagery ; it meant too many hours of tormented desolation. But he could think of Rachel naked in his arms as something comforting, pleasurable, soothing, an agreeable and affectionate bed-fellow. He did not believe that his love for Ann was the only possible love. Millions married and lived happily together with no deeper feelings than those he had toward Rachel. Perhaps, after all, that was a better basis for marriage than the torturing hunger he had for Ann. Besides, he did not want to break with Rachel. He did love her in a way, after his

fashion. He thought of Dowson's line, " I have been faithful to thee, Cynara, in my fashion." But it was Rachel who
should have been Cynara, whereas in Rachel's arms it
would be, he knew, Ann whose shadow would fall upon
him, whose breath would be shed between the kisses. He
thought of something Kipling had written : Even in your
wife's arms you shall hold the body of your first love.
Perhaps most men suffer that. And Ann had disappeared
from Welling as completely as if she were dead. Perhaps
she was dead. No, he could not break with Rachel. He
loved Ann ; she meant the dearest things to him that love
may mean ; but she was lost, and to fill that blank, desolate
emptiness which she had left, Rachel was necessary to him.
In some moods of distraught self-pity he wanted to go to
Rachel, put his head in her lap, and cry out a confession
like a little boy. But when that momentary weakness was
past he knew it was impossible to tell Rachel.

He received her letter on the morning of August 7th
and replied the same day.

You must not (the letter ran) take the sonnet as a literal
relation. It was, as are all my poems, inspired by a mood ;
the mood was aphrodisiac, and in this case the resultant
emotional adventure was a spiritual experience. Midgeham
Murray of *The Hellenic Review* turned it down because he
said the last two lines were not true to my emotional
experience. I damned his eyes, of course, but he may be
right. How can I tell if I had not the actual experience ?
One day, soon I hope, we shall have that experience
together. I refuse to take your letter seriously. You must
know I love you. But I begin to loathe the inadequacy of
words. What force, what intensity, can one put into words
to compare with the sheer thrilling power of the contact of
lips and bodies. If you were here in my arms you would not,
you could not, doubt that I loved you, wanted you, needed

Op

you. I want you so urgently at times that I could beat my head against the wall. Do you remember my telling you how I used to bite the sheets and scream over my lost loves as a brat of nine. I am the same brat still in all essentials. You say I do not want to see you. You cannot mean it. Do you seriously believe that, Rachel? Look here—chuck your job and let's get married. I know your screw's bigger than mine, that two people can't live as cheaply as one, especially when both have expensive tastes, but I'd go back to writing drivel for the weeklies and Sundays, and we'd rub along on what I make. Anything would be better than these ever-recurring unsatisfied hungers. At the moment I want you here with me in bed more than I've ever wanted anything else in the world.

Richard put down his pen and stared at the ceiling. Suddenly he saw Ann as she had crept naked into his arms. He felt her cool body under his hot hands. He felt her breathing. And then kiss by kiss, tremor by tremor, the torment of memory began.

He groaned and picked up his pen again.

You still complain of no news. (The abrupt transition startled Rachel as she read the letter, but Richard was unaware of the jolting change; his mind had travelled a long way, his emotions sustained a long ordeal, since he had written the paragraph ending with " world.")

Well (he went on), there is a certain amount of news, but it's in the nature of scandal. It's so easy to fall into the habit of gossiping and swapping scurrilities in the country. I don't know why. Probably because we take much more interest in one another.

I told you about the dismissal of our two parlourmaids, one following the other with only a week's interval. Well, most of the news is on a par with that. It begins, it is true, with an air of importance, but it fizzles out with a very small if spicy hiss before the end. By the bye, this is mere local slander, defamation and what not. I don't vouch for its truth.

Briefly then there descended upon the great Hartley some months ago a nephew from abroad. This was the Reverend (sic) Roy Hartley—the "sic" may well be allowed to represent Welling's opinion ! He's a fine dark handsome person (a real Valentino sheikh sort of chap) a bit younger than I am. He was apparently engaged by the Dean to act as tutor to his two younkers, a boy of seven and a girl of nine. Also being a musical whale the Rev. Roy took charge of the Cathedral music, Canon Venning having departed for a wider sphere. All this, apparently, every irregular, but merely a temporary matter—I really don't know much about these things.

Well, darling, to cut the cackle, our noble Roy Rudolph, the world's darling, is alleged by all the back-biting gossips to have seduced the Dean's wife, his daughter Gillian, and some dozen or so beautiful citizenesses—and not *all* so beautiful, by the bye.

The Crown last Saturday night hummed with it. It was a constant topic at school (thank God we're on holiday now— but I really can't afford to go away ; perhaps I wouldn't if I could ; I'm beginning to loathe shifting about—I think one day I'll take to my bed and stay there for good) and if ever you saw two old women, or old men for that matter, standing upon a street corner, noses almost knocking, you could bet your shirt the subject was the Rev. (sic) Roy.

Mason tells me (he got it, of course, from O. J.) that there was a meeting of the residentiary canons of the Cathedral on Wednesday last and that Canon Manning, a bluff, outspoken old boy, told Pious Persy to his face that he was a cuckold. Doubtless this is journalistic hyperbole, but there's summat in it, lass.

I think things are going to happen hereabouts shortly, and although I can't promise you such an orgy of burnings and smashings as I detailed for your edification some months ago, yet I hope my next letter will, at least, be somewhat more exciting than our Parish Magazine.

And so good night darling and don't write (anyhow don't send) me any more such horrible letters as your last.

You must know I love you. If yet you don't try Couéism —say every day in every way he loves me better and better. Wonderfully efficacious, they say. Bye-bye. I kiss your feet.

This letter brought a very brief reply from Rachel by return of post.

I rather think (it ran) I agree with Midgeham Murray. As for the rest we must meet soon and have a talk. Can't you even afford to run up here for a week? I'd come to Welling, but John Henry is in the throes of a new play and I'm indispensable. For your *chroniques scandaleuses* : don't be daft ! do you think all women are ninnies ?

For the present, then, I'll pretend you love me. In haste for the post. Rachel.

CHAPTER XIII

CUCK-CUCKOO

" And when in due time the shells break and the little monsters appear in their divers nests the cuckoo changeth his note and singeth mockingly Cuck-Cuckoo ! Cuck-Cuckoo ! "

Country Tradition.

I

On a dull, grey, rainy morning in the middle of August the maid entered the breakfast-room at the Deanery with the porridge and the mail. As she moved the cream-jug nearer to Mrs. Perseval she said, " Miss Gillian, ma'am, has a bad headache, and is staying in bed till lunch-time."

" Have you taken her breakfast up ? " asked Mrs. Perseval.

" She doesn't want anything to eat, ma'am, but she's had a cup of tea."

" What is the matter with her, Grace ? " asked the Dean when the maid had gone out. " Nothing serious ? "

" Gilly was awful sick this morning, mummy," said Max tilting his plate and scraping off the last vestige of cream and honey. " I heard her."

" That will do, Max. Will you have an egg this morning ? "

Max shook his head. " A banana and an apple, please. Why was Gilly sick. Did she go to a party ? Freda says——"

" *Peel* your banana properly, Max, and don't eat like a little Yahoo," said his father. " And do chatter less. Do you think I'd better ring up Forde and ask him to look in, my dear ? "

Mrs. Perseval shook her head. " It's just biliousness, I expect. I'll run upstairs and see her after breakfast. Don't hold your cup with both hands, Max. Do drink quietly."

" Freda says Gilly's often sick, mummy, and Freda says——"

" Go into the garden and eat your apple, Max," said the Dean. " Go now. Don't argue."

" May I ride my bicycle on the paths."

" As long as you *keep* to the paths. And don't bother George ; and try——"

" May I——"

" That will do. Cut along at once. Have you finished, Freda ? Don't fiddle with your cup. What are you doing ? "

" It's only my lump of sugar, daddy ; I forgot to stir and it's all at the bottom. May I have an orange instead of an apple ? The apples are all turnippy. They make my teeth crawl. Gilly says——"

" Run along now, darling, and don't chatter so much. I want to talk to daddy."

" What *is* the matter with Gillian ? " asked the Dean as Freda closed the door shatteringly. " You don't think she's sickening for something ? The children seem to know more about what goes on in this house than I do. If the child's ill why haven't you had Forde in. You know how I hate sickness in the house, and I can't be worried with it just now. Why——"

" Very well, darling, I'll go and see Gillian at once. No, I'd rather go alone. There's nothing to worry about ; young girls have these sicknesses. I'm sure——"

" Is *that* all it is ! " snapped the Dean ; " you might have said so from the first. Nonsense ! the children wouldn't understand. Hang it, Grace, do you think children are nothing else but little eavesdroppers, always mute, with ears alert for secrets. It's my opinion they never know nor care about anything going on around them unless it directly concerns themselves."

With commendable restraint Mrs. Perseval forbore to point out her husband's inconsistency, and rising slowly, left the breakfast-room and made her way to Gillian's bedroom.

Gillian lay on her back with her eyes closed. She was awake, and opened her eyes as her mother entered. She was pale and her eyes were dark and heavy.

Mrs. Perseval stooped over her, and then drew a chair up to the bedside and sat down, taking one of Gillian's hands between her own. " What is the matter, darling ? "

" Nothing, mother. I'm just sick."

" That isn't nothing, is it. Have you been eating anything ? "

Gillian shook her head. " I'm all right, mother, really. It's just a bilious attack. I think I'm run down. Perhaps I need a change. Do you think——"

Mrs. Perseval had been watching Gillian closely for some minutes. She interrupted her anxiously, almost harshly. " Gillian, is there anything wrong with you ? Are you keeping something from me ? "

" Anything wrong, mother, why *should* there be ? What is there to keep from you ? I only wanted——"

" Freda says you're often sick now, darling. Why haven't you told me ? Will you see Dr. Forde this morning ? I'll ask your father to ring up at once."

" No, mother, no ; it's too absurd ; there's nothing the matter at all. I have been sick once or twice, but it was nothing. You know what Freda is. I'm feeling quite all right now and hungry. I'll get up and have a grape fruit and an egg. Now, honestly, darling, I'm all right."

" How many times have you been sick, Gillian ? When did it begin ? Do you——"

And suddenly, abruptly, Gillian sat up, took her mother's two hands in her own and said with a desperate calmness, " All right, mummy, I'll tell you. I'm going to have a baby."

Mrs. Perseval withdrew her hand, and putting her arm round Gillian, drew her close. " Gillian," she said distressfully, " Gillian. You poor child. Is it—will you——"

" It's Roy's baby, mother."

Mrs. Perseval did not speak. She held Gillian close in her arms.

" Don't ask me a lot of questions, mummy ; I'll tell you as much—I don't want." She stopped, her voice shaking. " Roy knows, mother. I told him when I was first sure, the day of the Barton Sands picnic ; the juniors. He wouldn't believe it at first, but he had to. He doesn't love me. He never has loved me. He laughed at me then and said I was a gauche child. It happened when we went into Darum to get Daddy's books. What shall I do ? Will you have to tell Father ? Aren't there places where girls go ? Perhaps it will kill me. It does sometimes. Perhaps it will die. I hope it will. I hate it moving in me now. I could never love it. I don't care if it kills me. They won't let it hurt me. What am I saying. How can it be wicked. It's stupid for people to say that. What am I going to do, mother ? "

" You're going to sleep, darling ; at least till luncheon. Now don't worry about it. Leave it to me and stop thinking about it. Would you mind Nannie knowing ? "

" No, mother. Could I go to her ? She lives in quite a tiny place, isn't it ? and Cumberland is a long way from Welling. I'd love to go to her. Shall you have to tell Father?"

" I don't know, darling. But anyhow not until you've

gone. I'll write to Nannie at once. I'm sure that's best. Afterwards we must make other arrangements."

" You mean the baby ? Perhaps Nannie would take it. I'd be glad. I hate it. I thought mothers loved children by instinct. It's not true. You won't say anything to Roy, mother."

Mrs. Perseval kissed her. " Now go to sleep, and don't worry. You're sure you want nothing. *Are* you hungry really ? That's right, sleep will do you more good."

Five days later Gillian left home with her mother for a stay of indefinite length with her old Nannie, who lived in a small village at the foot of Sca Fell.

The same evening Alice Thatcher sat in a low armchair in the library at Denacre Hall. Leaning against the mantelpiece, and looking down at her with a faintly derisive smile, was Roy Hartley.

" What do you want me to do about it ? "

" Nothing Roy. I only came to say good-bye. I wouldn't have intruded but you didn't answer my letters, and I've not seen you at all for weeks."

" You're going away ? That's certainly the sensible thing to do. How are you off for money ? "

" I've plenty. Roy——"

" When do you expect the interesting event ? You're sure about it, I suppose ? "

" Not till February. Yes, I'm sure ; I'm going away before anyone suspects. You'll write to me, Roy."

" Of course. What are you going to do about your school ? Will they pay you while you're away ? Won't you have to tell them ? Medical Certificate or something, eh ? "

" I've resigned, Roy. It's holidays, now, you know, but I wrote to the office yesterday and agreed to forfeit a month's salary instead of notice."

" That was silly. You might have stayed on surely. It wouldn't be noticeable in another month. You're as slim as ever."

" I don't want to stay about here, Roy. I want to get away."

" It's probably best. What are you going to do with the child. Farm it out ? "

" I shall keep it, Roy. I've always wanted a baby. I can work for it. I can go back to teaching later on. No one need know. I shall say it's adopted. Lots of women who don't marry adopt children now. It's something—something——"

" Well, I'm really awfully sorry, Alice, and if there's anything I can do, you know. Still, if you wanted a baby. Where are you thinking of going. Far ? You must let me know."

Alice stood up and came to him. She put her hands to his jacket, and began to fasten and unfasten the top button. She did not raise her eyes to his face. " You'll write to me, Roy. Perhaps you'd come down when it gets near. It will be winter time and you could come in the evening and no one would be the wiser."

" We'll see. Yes, of course, I'll write." He began toying with her ear, looking away over her bent head with a frown. " Well, Alice, I've a most annoying lot of work to do this evening. You won't mind if I don't trot along with you. Take care of yourself. You're not angry with me ? I'm really fond of you, Alice."

At this she held up her face to him. Her lips were trembling. He bent his head to kiss her. " You did love me, Roy," she whispered, her voice shaken out of control for the moment. " I love you, Roy, I love you. I know you couldn't marry me. I don't want you to. I wouldn't ask it. I'm glad you loved me. I'm grateful, Roy. I thank God you loved

me. You love me now a little. Still. Say you love me, Roy."
She was crying now, but so softly that he did not know
until he raised her face between his hands, and kissing her
found her cheeks and lips wet with tears.

" Of course I love you," he said, and raising his head
grimaced at a flamboyant Brangwyn panel on the opposite
wall.

When Mrs. Perseval returned from Cumberland she
found that events had taken the initiative out of her hands.
It was no longer necessary to weigh the pros and cons of
informing the Dean immediately.

She arrived back the last Thursday in August in time for
luncheon. But it was in her boudoir, a full twenty minutes
later, that the Dean put his blunt question.

His wife's startled expression told him the truth. Before
she could speak, he put out a protesting hand. " Not now.
I've a note to write. Wait luncheon for me until half-past.
I must have a reply before I come down."

The note to Roy Hartley that Harper took round to
Denacre Hall asking him to come to luncheon, or immediately afterward, was answered by Bates to the effect that his
master's nephew was out and was not expected back until
the later afternoon. Roy on the plea of a chill had not been
to the Deanery for several days.

The Dean received the not unexpected reply in silence,
and with the slightest tightening of his lips walked slowly
downstairs to the dining-room.

2

But Roy Hartley returned sooner than he had intended.
That return was not without excitement : the children of
Welling will tell of it when they are old and grey.

He left Denacre Hall immediately after lunch. At two o'clock he called in at Mason's book-shop in The Arcade to enquire about some volumes recently ordered by his uncle. At a quarter past two he bought a box of chocolate at the small confectioner's next door to Barentz's garage. Five minutes later the caretaker of Portway Street School saw him strolling along the quayside toward Belton Bridge. Thereafter, until his wild irruption into Welling via Belton Bridge at ten minutes to four, he was seen by one person only.

Thatcher Burnett's small cottage was exactly half a mile from Welling. It lay about fifty yards back from the main road to Queenstown. Between the road and the front door was Thatcher Burnett's garden, where he cultivated vegetables, and where his young and pretty wife Amy grew the flowers that used to deck the small kitchen, but had for some time past added a fragrant and gracious touch to more imposing surroundings.

Behind the cottage fields stretched away to the banks of the Teal. Midway between Belton Bridge and the cottage a footpath led off from the high-road, across the fields in a winding circuit to the river, passing on its way within a stone's throw of Thatcher Burnett's back door.

At a quarter to three Roy Hartley tapped lightly upon this back door with his knuckles. The door opened with a jerk and revealed Thatcher Burnett's stocky figure on the mat.

" Come in, zur, come in ; I've been expecting you," said Burnett quietly.

Roy followed him through the tiny kitchen into the parlour which looked out over the garden. " Sit down, zur, sit down."

As Roy sat himself in an arm-chair, Thatcher Burnett walked back to the door and slowly and methodically locked it and put the key in his pocket.

" What's the idea, Burnett ? "

" I think you know, zur ; I think you know. I want a few words with you."

" Well, that's all right, I shan't run away."

" I'll see you don't, zur."

" What's the trouble ? "

" You know as well I do, zur ; what have you been up to with my wife ? "

" Where *is* Mrs. Burnett ? "

" That don't concern you, zur ; she's out of the way, anyhow. I want to know what you've got to say. I've heard her side of it."

" So you've heard her side. Well, perhaps you'll enlighten me. Do tell me what she says, for I can assure you I don't know what you're driving at."

" Lying won't help, zur, nor trying to put it on to her. I believe her."

" Well, go on, out with it ; what is it ? "

" You've had her, and you know it ; not once, but dozens of times, and you're a dirty thieving swine. An' not man enough to face it. Trying to put it on her. She don't tell lies."

" It's a lie from beginning to end."

" You liar, you know it's true. She's in the family way by you."

" Not by you, her husband, of course."

" You'll grin the other side of your mouth in a minute. No, not by me. I lost my chance of being a father in the war. Ask Dr. Forde."

" All the young men of Welling were doubtless not so unfortunate. A young and pretty——"

" Shut your mouth."

Roy Hartley shrugged his shoulders. " Shut up, eh ? I thought you wanted me to speak. Well, I've heard your story, and I'll trouble you to open that door."

" You don't leave here——"

" Nonsense ! open that door, Burnett ; I've had quite enough of your bluster. If your wife's found a real——"

The back of Burnett's hand took him in the mouth as he rose from his chair. He fell back again into the chair and put up his fingers to his cut lips.

" Get up ! " said Burnett harshly.

" Look here, Burnett, don't be a fool——"

" Get out o' that chair."

" Damn it all, Burnett, listen for——"

" Take it where you are, then ! " snarled Burnett, and leaning over the table drove a vicious blow at Roy's face.

Roy jerked himself quickly to one side. The chair toppled over and sprawled him into the fender. Burnett stood over him. " Get up. If you lay there I'll have the guts out of you."

" Stand away, then, you damned fool. Thanks." Roy jumped to his feet, and as Burnett rushed him, he struck the thatcher on the side of the jaw with a flush hit that slewed his head round with a jerk.

Burnett pitched against the table which went over with a crash. For a second Burnett leaned upon his hands, his head swimming. He dragged himself up, slowly at first, but ending with a crouching spring. He swung a punch at Roy, missed, grunted, hooked up his left fist wildly, and taking a terrific jolt that missed the point of his jaw by a hair, went over backwards into the open fireplace.

The thud of his fall shook soot down from the chimney on to his face and body. He lay still for a moment breathing heavily. He rose slowly, a frightful apparition, his face a grotesque mask of sweat and soot, his eyes glaring, his mouth agape, disclosing the stumps of yellow teeth. A trickle of blood ran out of the corner of his mouth.

He looked about him wildly. " You bastard," he said ;

" you bastard," and reached for the double-barrelled gun over the old wardrobe.

Roy hesitated for a second, moved a half-step towards him, and then turning swiftly, put up his arms and sprang head first through the window.

Cursing inarticulately Burnett rushed to the window firing from his hip. Holding his gun sloped across his body he dived through the smashed window in pursuit.

At ten minutes to four by the Cathedral clock P.C. Hanlon, on point duty opposite the bandstand, had just beckoned on a large touring car when, heralded and pursued by shouts and hoarse cries, a wild dishevelled figure came speeding toward him along Belton Bridge. More remote, a stocky bellowing figure waving a gun hove into view.

Constable Hanlon's brain worked slowly. A fraction of a second too late he put out his foot. Six seconds later he made amends in a bold attempt to trip the pursuer. A heavy blow on the ear jerked his helmet over his eyes, and when next he saw things clearly there was a heap of struggling men lying in the roadway outside the Mayor's house.

Butcher Wainwright's man, Harry, coming out of the Mayor's tradesmen's entrance, had inserted a neat foot before the feet of the first runner. In an instant some eight or nine men dropped on to the prone figure as if sucked in by an irresistible force. Dropping his gun Thatcher Burnett flung himself into the press of legs and arms.

There followed in rapid succession a grunting groan, a shrill scream, gasps and a long-drawn howl. Out from among the legs and arms a torn and bedraggled figure squeezed, ran stooping with finger tips almost to the ground, straightened itself, and shot across Bridge Street toward the footpath to Denacre Hall, with some hundred-odd, shouting, bellowing men and boys in scrambling pursuit. Heading the van, and not fifty feet behind the fugitive, stumbled

Thatcher Burnett, his retrieved gun at the slope. Twice his gun barked before a bend in the footpath round the trees hid the chase from the startled eyes peering from a score of windows.

" Tally-ho ! " yelped a wag, standing outside Baley's fish-shop at the corner of the High Street.

Far spent as he was Roy Hartley increased his lead, and was fifty yards ahead of the foremost of the hunt when he vaulted the wall of Denacre Hall grounds. Well over a hundred eager eyes saw that vault. Ten seconds later, when the first wave of the hue-and-cry clambered up the wall and dropped clumsily down into the currant-bushes, Roy Hartley had disappeared.

The crowd, now reinforced by hundreds of the curious from every street in Welling, scattered about the grounds, poking into bushes with sticks, treading over plots, crushing down flowers and plants.

As they drew near the Hall in an ever widening, loosely strung-out line of advance, a window opened briskly, and the angry eyes of David Hartley surveyed the mob.

" What are you doing ? " shouted Hartley. " How dare you break into my grounds. Leave at once. Get out, all of you. My God, where are the police. What do you want ? "

The mob abashed, embarrassed, not in fact knowing at all what it wanted, drew back muttering. But one unit of that bewildered multitude was vocal. It was Thatcher Burnett. He strode out of the crowd and, his gun under his arm, raised his fist and said dourly, " I want to speak to you, zur."

" Indeed, and why have you brought this riff-raff. Ah, Haynes at last. Superintendent, will you be so good as to read the riot act to this gentleman's friends. And perhaps the sergeant will take his gun away. Thank you. When everyone is *quite* gone, Superintendent, I should be obliged if you would accompany my visitor up. You'd like tea, I expect. Thank you." The window rattled down. The sergeant and the two constables accompanying Haynes rapidly dispersed the mob ; and a few minutes later Bates showed Haynes and Burnett into a bright pleasant little sitting-room that looked out over the neglected profusion of the kitchen-garden.

The Superintendent sat down and accepted a cup of tea, but Thatcher Burnett refused both chair and refreshment, electing to stand over against the mantel-piece, leaning his two great brown hands upon the back of a chair. Hartley noted that his mouth was swollen and his knuckles were badly abraded and had been bleeding considerably.

" Well—er—Mr.—er——," began Hartley.

" Burnett, zur, Thatcher Burnett ; Burnett's good enough, zur."

" Thank you. Well, what is it you want with me, Mr. Burnett ? "

" It's the young parzon, zur, I want."

" Do you usually carry a gun, when you look for people ? You seem to have been in a fight. What do you want with Mr. Hartley ? He's not at home. He's been out all the afternoon."

" He's at 'ome all right, zur, and he's been wi' me the afternoon. That's where I got these," touching his swollen lips and his abraded knuckles. " He's my mark on him too, God damn him, if you'll excuse me, or," truculently, " if you won't, 'tis alla same."

" That's enough of that, Burnett," said Haynes ; " you're under arrest ; you know that."

" Ay."

" Well, keep a civil tongue in your head."

" The young parzun's had my wife, zur, all this summer,

Pp

times and times, and she's now gotten a child by him. That's what we fought about, and arrest or no arrest, I'd a killed him, and I will yet, the dirty slinking bastard. Afternoons an' afternoons, he was around with his sly tongue and his chocolates. Here," he took out a crushed box from his pocket. " Brought that along 's afternoon, but how it got into my pocket, God knows." He brushed the back of his hand across his face and stared into David Hartley's eyes.

" Well, what do you want ? I've told you Mr. Hartley's not in."

" He's in, zur ; he jumped t' wall and he's somewhere abouts, right enough."

David Hartley turned an enquiring eye on Haynes, who nodded, and said, " It's quite right, Mr. Hartley, as far as it goes. He jumped the wall with a crowd after him and disappeared. I'd like to see him. There'll be a charge about this, of course."

Hartley nodded and turned to the telephone. He rang through to Bates. " Is Mr. Roy in ? Have you seen him since he left after luncheon. You're sure he's not in my study. What ? Oh, yes, of course." He replaced the receiver. " My man says my nephew is not in ; he's quite sure." The bell rang again and Hartley took off the receiver. " Yes, yes. All right. Yes. Show him up to my study. Well, Superintendent, you'll have to excuse me. I've another visitor. Really I can do nothing for you. Perhaps you'll call this evening. I'm sorry, Mr. Burnett. If there is anything I can do——" He rose, and moving to the door, held it open, and closing it behind them preceded them down the stairs.

A few minutes later he opened the door of his study and greeted the Mayor, who came over to him as he held out his hand.

He noticed Banks's grave face and worried expression, and

as he motioned him into a seat said, " Not more trouble, I hope, Mr. Banks ; there's enough afoot already I fear."

" I'm sorry, Mr. Hartley," began the Mayor haltingly, " it's no pleasant errand I've come on. Perhaps it's not altogether you I ought to see, but maybe it's best."

" Yes ? "

" It's your nephew."

Hartley made a gesture of irritation. " Well ? "

" I want to put it to you, Mr. Hartley, that it will be best for all concerned if your nephew is not seen again in Welling."

" Go on."

" He's a rascally blackguard, and if you'll forgive me saying so, a dirty one, and a disgrace to his cloth. I'm sorry to upset you."

" Please go on."

" Well, Mr. Hartley, to be blunt, there are probably a dozen young women in Welling your nephew has seduced this summer. I don't know how many others he's attempted to seduce, but I do know that he made beastly proposals to my wife, and she's old enough to be his mother."

Hartley's fingers tapped lightly on the table. His glance remained upon his visitor's face, but he did not speak.

" It's only come out this morning," continued the Mayor, " that the schoolmistress Miss Thatcher is in trouble by him, and has left the town. There's young Mrs. Burnett, there's Butcher Wainwright's niece, and there are others I can't mention."

The telephone bell rang. Hartley picked up the receiver. " Yes. All right. At once." He turned again to the Mayor. " You must give me time to face this, Banks," he said. " I can't say how much I regret it all. My nephew is not here at present, but you may rest assured I will do everything possible to make amends. I've another visitor. Perhaps you will be good enough to excuse me now. This evening after dinner I shall be again at your service, if you care to call."

Hartley mounted the stairs after saying good-bye to the Mayor, and opening the door of the library, walked briskly over to the new visitor with his hands outstretched.

" This is a great pleasure, Mrs. Perseval, and a needed one, I assure you. Let me ring for tea."

Mrs. Perseval turned an agitated face to him. She held out a protesting hand. " No, thank you, Mr. Hartley. I really—I'm afraid I've come on an unhappy errand."

Hartley sat down facing her, and crossing his legs, clasped his hands on his knee. " Yes ? "

" You knew Gillian had gone away ? "

Hartley looked at her intently. " Have you come to me about Roy ? "

She nodded. " Do you know then ? "

" I know nothing. I fear everything now. You mean——"

" I mean that Gillian is going to have a baby and that Roy is the father. That is not all. It is very dreadful. It is not only Gillian. There——"

Hartley put out his hands. " Please," he said. " Yes, I know. I did not know about Gillian. It is——"

The telephone bell rang. " No, I can't see him. I'm not well. Yes. This evening. At ten. Impossible."

He turned to Mrs. Perseval. " The Dean has just called, Mrs. Perseval, but I could not see him. I am too shaken. Please make my apologies. I beg you will excuse me now. I will see Dr. Perseval at ten. Yes. It is extraordinarily kind of you. If you will."

But that evening David Hartley was spared further catechism. Bates's dour adamantine face confronted each visitor at the door and his " Sorry, sir, Mr. Hartley is ill in bed, and can see no one," was proof against every importunity.

An hour after the last caller had been defeated, and but a short while before he went to bed, Bates was busily engaged for twenty minutes rubbing at spots on the carpet in his master's study. " If it's not blood it's damn like it," he muttered ; " come out, blast you ! "

CHAPTER XIV

INTERLUDE: THE GARDEN PARTY

The wonder of Roy Hartley's mysterious disappearance outlasted the traditional nine days. It was, indeed, only the approach of the Mayor's Garden Party to be held the last Saturday in September that displaced that astounding evanescence from its pride of place.

In the absence of Roy Hartley the charge against Thatcher Burnett dwindled to one of mere disorderly conduct. More than half the cartridges found on Burnett were blanks, and it was charitably assumed by the Bench that those fired had also been blank. He was convicted of disorderly conduct and fined a pound, which Colonel Bowers promptly paid. Burnett's ingenuous outburst in Court that the cartridges weren't blank, that he'd intended to kill Hartley, and still would if he ever met him, were drowned by Superintendent Haynes's minatory appeals for silence.

The day following Roy Hartley's disappearance, Haynes had been granted permission by its owner to search Denacre Hall. Nothing had been found to throw any light on the affair, and the questioning of Bates and Crowson proved equally fruitless. Bates was especially difficult.

" You've seen many queer things in your time, Mr. Bates, eh ? " asked Haynes.

" Too many."

" And not all of them before you came to Welling ? "

" You're right."

" For example—eh ? "

" Well, there's the bandstand and the War Memorial business——"

" I should have said at Denacre Hall."

" Oh, here ? "

" Yes."

" Ah."

" For example—eh ? "

" Mostly imagination."

" Imagination ? "

" Ay, what's called hallucinations. You see and hear all sorts of things in a big house that's surrounded a'most by trees."

" Yes, of course. But," impatiently, " you've seen and heard things here that have puzzled you, eh ? "

Bates shook his head. A dour grin writhed his lips. " Not that I remember—no ! "

Crowson, who took his cue from Bates, was equally unsatisfactory. " I don't live in, you know," he explained, " so even if there were anything queer, I'd not be likely to see or hear it."

" And if you *did*," commented Haynes drily, " you'd forget it."

The Mayoral Garden Party, held always upon the last Saturday in September, was perhaps the most popular of the three eleemosynary festivals that Welling owed largely to the generosity of Andrew Banks.

The Barton Sands picnics were, except for helpers, definitely juvenile festals ; the New Year's Eve Ball was annoyingly exclusive ; the Garden Party was, however, so catholic that it welcomed all who could squeeze in. Entrance was, indeed, by ticket, but these were not too difficult to come by, and long before the fireworks began the doorkeepers' visits to the refreshment marquees disposed them to regard tolerantly the brazen importunities of the ticketless.

Provided the day were fine there were rarely fewer than fifteen hundred people enjoying the Mayor's hospitality. If fine, six large marquees sufficed for tea, and one for the bar, the Bench invariably granting the Mayor's application for a time-extension for the great day. If the day were wet the number of marquees was doubled, but the increase did not apply to the bar ; one bar was sufficient. It had indeed been diplomatically suggested to the Mayor that on wet days two marquees might be devoted to the service of Bacchus. Banks, on the plea that it would look bad, had gently but quite definitely declined to authorise the addition. He did, however, agree to double the strength of the staff behind the bar on such unfortunate occasions, and to make tolerably certain that the supply of refreshment did not become exhausted.

On dull days, that threatened but did not actually produce rain by noon, the Mayor compromised with nine marquees all told.

The gates were open at one o'clock and not finally closed until midnight. Clarence George had been heard to asseverate loudly and hoarsely in *The Crown* that he knew for a positive fact dear old Banks rarely wrote a cheque for less than five hundred pounds to foot the Garden Party Bill.

This particular Garden Party was a nine-marquee affair.

Round about the magic hour of five a pleasantly garrulous little party were gathered about a table in the large maroon and gold striped marquee that had somehow or other, in the queerest fashion, got itself reserved for the *haut ton* or the Toneys as Mason had labelled them. He had some years previously expanded this gibe into a faintly satirical article for *The Sentinel*, adumbrating his suggestion that Welling should be divided into four classes : The Toneys or *haut ton*, The Droneys or impecunious leisured, The Poloneys or artisan (living, explained Mason, as they do upon poloneys, fried fish and sardines) and The Stoneys who are self-explanatory.

Mason played with the whimsy for the length of a column, pointing out that while The Toneys and The Poloneys never by any chance mixed or mingled, but were for ever as rigidly apart as milestones, The Droneys and The Stoneys were often interchangeable. Further, while the eye of Hymen might approve with charming impartiality the mating of any members of Toneys, Droneys or Stoneys, the Poloneys in this regard were the only pariahs. Mason was careful to point out that no Poloney could ever become a Stoney—the Stoney state for a Poloney was pauperdom. To become a true Stoney one must have once had some pretensions to Toneydom.

Mason's *jeu d'esprit* had, it is to be feared, been accorded a dubious appreciation by *The Sentinel* readers.

The pleasant little party around the table, consisting of Mrs. Clarence George, the Miss Oveys, Mrs. Fletcher and Mrs. D'Arcy L'Estrange had, in the course of the afternoon, disposed of large quantities of ice cream and Pêche Melba, had drunk no small number of glasses of iced claret cup and iced hock cup, and were now putting the finishing touches, as it were, to several huge plates of pastries, and hoping that the pot would stand another cup apiece. This over-fed and slightly stimulated party represented in its perfection the most deadly and devastating of all lethal weapons: the scandalmonger cleared for action.

" Mrs. Thatcher Burnett is, I hear, home again," began Mrs. Clarence George, a tall, slim, handsome woman with saffron-coloured hair, a white face with a large red mouth, and twinkling violet eyes.

" Complacency is *the* virtue of necessity for middle-aged

husbands with young and pretty wives," smiled Mrs. Fletcher.

" He's making the best of a bad job rather than being complacent," commented Mrs. L'Estrange. " He'll take the child too, I suppose. When is it expected ? "

" In November. It's the first of the cuckoo brood, from all accounts."

" Is it certain there are others ? " asked Miss Alison.

" My dear ! the place is alive with them—teeming." Mrs. Clarence George laughed softly. " It has fallen, it seems, upon just and unjust alike. There's that poor child Gillian and Miss Thatcher and Wainwright's niece——"

" It's a disgusting business altogether," said Miss Ovey primly. " I knew from the first he was a rascal. I'm never at fault in these matters. The uncle is a nasty man, worse probably than the nephew if we knew all."

" It's not only the young people he's demoralised," Mrs. L'Estrange said musingly ; " there is dear Mrs. Banks. That, of course," hastily, " was one of his defeats. It began the whole exposure, I believe. And Mrs. Perseval's disclosures doubtless also hastened matters."

" About Gillian ? "

" Well, yes, but I really meant concerning herself."

" My *dear* ! *Mrs. Perseval !* Surely. No. You can't——"

" It's only too true, Mrs. George. You must have heard. No ? But hasn't your husband——" Mrs. L'Estrange's eyebrows went up quizzically.

" Not a word. Men are mum about their adulteries— at least as far as blabbing on one another to us is concerned. Probably among themselves they gossip enough."

" They do indeed," nodded Mrs. Fletcher ; " men's clubs are just hot-beds of defamation. But really, is this true about the Dean's wife ? I confess I'd not heard a word. But we might have guessed it."

" It seems common property enough now," went on Mrs. L'Estrange, " although, I confess, it's merely servants' tittle-tattle. Our dear Mrs. Robbins, you know, Miss Alison."

" Indeed," primly, " we never encourage her to talk."

" We *certainly* do not," added her sister.

" She needs no encouragement," smiled Mrs. L'Estrange; " discouragement is the word. It's probably only chatter. There's our fiery little editor over there. I do hope he'll come and amuse us."

" Then good-bye to our conversation. He's all ears for scandal. A chiel among us taking notes. I never *can* remember that story and Clarence is always quoting bits of it. But I do think some decency should be observed. The man is for ever peering and prowling and prying. I think it's positively disgusting. Of course he's not a gentleman—and Welsh too. Clarence says he and Downer were both dragged up in the same board-school. It's extraordinary how that tells. Ah, thank goodness he's going. But my *dear* Mrs. L'Estrange I really can't—not of Mrs. Perseval. Just what, I wonder, *did* Mrs. Robbins say."

" I shall decidedly ask her about it on our return," said Miss Ovey.

" I shouldn't. Better hear it from me and forget. It's really nothing—compared with the general outrage."

" Well, perhaps so. But how Mrs. Robbins came to know——"

" Simple enough. One of the scullery maids is walking out with George the gardener at the Deanery. That is more than enough."

" Yes," haltingly, " but——"

" Well," smiling, " George's tale is that for some reason or other he was out by his potting sheds or other messes one night last February, and well," shrugging her shoulders,

" briefly he saw Hartley in Mrs. Perseval's bedroom and apparently their attitudes——"

" Yes, yes ! " interposed Miss Alison hastily, " but, as you say, servants' tittle-tattle. But it's all very distressing. Welling is not the place it was, nor are the people."

" It's all popular education, this iniquitous levelling down," snapped her sister, " instead of levelling up. It permeates and poisons the whole of life to-day. Where are the gentlemen that used to sit in Parliament ? Is that great institution anything more now than a mockery—a shame to England. A gang of paid brawlers. As soon as people expect to be paid the whole standard is lowered, debased. Law-making is a gentleman's occupation and as soon——"

" The same applies to cricket, Clarence says ; it's the professionals who've dragged down our national game into the muck of the mart. The gentleman must come back."

" But he won't, that's just the trouble, isn't it," ventured Miss Alison, whose thoughts had been wandering.

" Who won't, my dear ? " said her sister sharply.

" Mr. Hartley, isn't that——"

" Don't be absurd, Alison. You know you don't listen, and then of course——"

" But it *is* the gist of the matter anyhow," put in Mrs. Fletcher. " And have you considered that he's the fourth person who's completely and utterly disappeared in Welling during the last year—less than a year."

" Four ? Mrs. Fletcher, surely not. There was, of course——" ·

" I thought you'd be surprised. There was, of course, as you were going to say, Mrs. L'Estrange, Alfred Smith ; next there was the man who broke into the Cathedral and also did so much damage in Welling."

" The same man, I *still* think," interposed Miss Ovey determinedly.

" That's two. After that there was Ann Brown our very pretty and mysteriously naughty maid ; and now we have the handsome and very openly naughty Rev. Roy Hartley, nephew of David Hartley Esquire, temporary precentor of St. Matthew's Cathedral. Four. And the police ! " She shrugged her shoulders.

" Oh, my *dear* ! Clarence is *so* funny about Haynes. He made up a simply screaming little poem about that dreadful clock affair. I do wish I could remember it. Now how did it go. Not a bit vulgar. Er—Under the village chestnut—no ; but it was a sort of parody of that. Let me see. Under the city— Why, here *is* dear Mrs. Perseval, now *do* join us. Jane, Jane. Bring a fresh pot, please. No, large. For six."

CHAPTER XV

THREE DAYS

I

Richard's school closed for a mid-term break from the fourteenth to the nineteenth of October. Mason was away holiday-making in the south of France, and Rachel accepted an invitation to stay at The Pines over the week-end.

She arrived on Friday in time for tea, and after Dorothy, the new maid, had cleared away, the two sat over the fire talking.

" I wish you could have met Mason," said Richard, " he's an odd fish and I didn't care much about him at first, but there's a queer, engaging likeableness about him that I should imagine would break down any barriers in time."

" There's a certain likeableness about most people if circumstances allow one to find it. Do you like the Dean any better ? "

" The Dean," shrugging his shoulders, " well, I've never met him socially, but he'd probably improve on acquaintance. By the bye, I had a letter from Mason a few days ago which contained an item of news that might conceivably be important if one knew where to fit it in. He's staying at Lourdes just now with his brother, a Catholic priest, who's there from Liverpool with a pilgrimage. His brother introduced him to Canon O'Brien—*the* O'Brien ; d'you remember ? He went from Anglicanism to atheism and from atheism to Catholicism, and then wrote *The Rood of Sorrows* ; I've got it somewhere ; take it to bed with you to-night—well, Mason mentioned to O'Brien that David Hartley had been living here since last November, and O'Brien said that he'd met Hartley at Lourdes just over a year ago."

"That doesn't seem a particularly important piece of news. They say if you wait long enough at Lourdes sooner or later you'll meet everyone you've known in this world."

"Yes. I don't know why it struck me as a revealing piece of news, but it certainly did. It seemed to me a sort of key-piece to a jig-saw puzzle, but *why* I can't say. It's the Welling atmosphere probably."

"How do you mean?"

"Well," smiling. "Welling lives these days in a state of bewildered expectancy. So many things have happened in the last year that the civic nerve is undoubtedly jumpy. It's an intangible sort of thing as all ' atmospheres ' are, of course, but it's very real and it's more or less always present. You get this sensation of waiting, of expectation, of premonition, wherever you go in Welling now—shops, pubs, social gatherings, street-corner meetings, everywhere in fact. I know it sounds daft, but there it is, something very difficult to define, but, as I've said, real enough. I've tried to worry it out and get it clear in my own mind, but the nearest I can get is a feeling abroad that all of us in this small city have become caught quite fortuitously in the net of some abnormal superhuman drama which is moving inevitably to some foreseen goal. No, that's not at all clear. But then I'm not clear in my own mind. Let me take the jig-saw analogy again. It seems to me that some being, let us say some superman, overman, is moving the pieces of a colossal jig-saw to a foreseen and pre-ordained completed pattern. Welling in some fashion has become inextricably mixed up with the pieces, and is willy-nilly shaken and jolted and upset as the giant fingers move the pieces into position. Is that any clearer ? "

" The jig-saw analogy is clear enough, but I don't quite see what you are driving at. You mean——"

" Wait a minute. Let's get the events of the last ten months or so more or less in sequence. Let me put them to you as a more or less continuous action—I mean the continuous action of my hypothetical overman—and possibly by bringing a fresh mind to bear upon it we may get a revealing flash. You see, these events to us here in Welling, being certainly isolated from one another in time, and apparently in kind, make it difficult, perhaps impossible for us to grasp their implication. Now——"

" Just a minute, Dick," laughing. " I don't follow that last sentence a bit. It's frightfully involved. Don't you mean that you in Welling can't see the wood for the trees ? "

" Well, near enough. The trees being so far apart we only see them one at a time and at such big intervals that we're unaware they make up a wood. We just can't *see* a wood at all. Now all the trees we've passed so far in Welling I'm going to display to you in a clump, shall I say, in the hope that you'll see them as at least a part of the wood."

" A chain and not a scattering of links ? "

" Yes. Now lend me your ears. First, there is the arrival of various newcomers to Welling : David Hartley, his man, his chauffeur and myself. We all arrived about the same time. The events began after our arrival, and it is therefore reasonable to suppose one or more of us is the cause. I propose to rule out Crowson, the chauffeur, Bates, the man, and myself. We now have Hartley as the hypothetical cause of the following events. Let's tabulate and enumerate them. I'll write them down as I say them.

1. Christmas Day last year : Brawling in the Cathedral.

2. Sacrilege in the Cathedral a week later followed by

3. Burnings, smashings and general destruction of buildings. A factor that may be noted is that the buildings
   were a school, a chapel, a museum and Hartley's house.
   Whether this factor is a salient one I don't know.

4. Disappearance of Alfred Smith (the brawler) apparently *before* the orgy of destructiveness.

5. Arrival of a new maid at The Pines, her dismissal, and
   her complete disappearance.

6. Arrival of Roy Hartley (a nephew of the great Hartley)
   at Denacre Hall. Roy Hartley is an ordained priest of
   the English Church and a very accomplished musician.
   He acts as tutor to the Dean's two children and as
   precentor. By the bye, *a* Roy Hartley was ordained in
   May 1923. Mason looked him up.

7. He seduces a number of the young women, married
   and single, of Welling, including the Dean's daughter,
   is chased by an enraged husband with a gun to the very
   walls of Denacre Hall. He vaults the walls and when
   the mob follows he is nowhere to be seen. He has not
   been seen since.

" Now there we are. There's one final point to be noted,
or is it three points. Alfred Smith was apparently last seen
late at night near the footpath leading to Denacre Hall. A
big, stooping, crouching sort of figure Bates claims to have
seen prowling round the Hall just before Denacre Hall was
fired. (Smith by the bye was a littlish slim man.) Roy
Hartley disappeared after reaching at least the grounds of
Denacre Hall. What do you make of it all ? "

" Let me have the paper and read them through. While
I'm reading perhaps you'll look me out that book of
O'Brien's, if you can really recommend it as a bed-book.
Sure. Right."

Q P

Rachel read through Richard's jotted notes, but it was several minutes after he had placed *The Rood of Sorrows* on the table beside her and sat down again that she pushed the paper away from her and smiled over at him.

" Well," asked Richard, " got a cloo ? "

Rachel shook her head slowly. " I'm afraid not. Where's David Hartley now ? "

" He's still at Denacre Hall. He's had pretty rotten health, so it is said, most of the summer, seizures I believe. Heart supposed to be bad. Anyhow he was not seen about much. Lately, however, he's been about in Welling a good deal, and has been away with his car for days on end leaving Bates the valet in charge. A dour grim dog is Bates. Hartley's health seems right enough now, but from all accounts his sickness has affected his temper—he's as surly and touchy and temperamental as a fake-Bohemian from the Café Royal. And now do you smell a rat, darling ? "

" I don't, Dick. By the way, what made you include the affair of the new maid's dismissal from here ? Such a trifling affair hardly seems to fit into your one-man hypothesis, does it ? Or were there important details connected with her departure that seem related to the others ? "

" N-o—er—hardly—it was simply that she disappeared from Welling."

" Not unnatural, if she were summarily dismissed. What was the trouble, pilfering, insolence ? "

" A little of both, in that order. The insolence being her counter-attack. Well, now, darling, doesn't that dark welter clarify into something or other, viewed from your heights ? Anything at *all* stand out ? "

" Only one. That you should have the impudence to begin most of your letters to me with that poor overworked excuse for laziness : There's really no news."

" But, darling, I *have* at various times told you all of it."

" Yes, weeks after the event. And then only when I've badgered you into it. You've talked a lot about this hypothetical enigma of yours, but aren't you a little in that line yourself ? No, don't answer. I'm going to unpack and then I've the firmest determination to lie and soak in a boiling bath for half-an-hour. What time is dinner ? All right then, *à bientôt*."

2

" Are you game for twenty miles ? " Richard asked after breakfast the next morning.

" Shanks's mare ? "

Richard nodded.

" What marvel can you offer me to compensate for certain weariness and possible blisters ? "

" First, Barton Sands, a wonderful five mile stretch of perfect sand running between Cairn Head and Formby Point. Second, a really lovely country-side in all the sad beauty of autumn. Third, the quaint village of Barton Olney, where there is a small pub which will feed us royally. Fourth, Barton Olney Woods, and fifth, sixth, seventh and eighth my unique companionship."

" H'm, your catalogue has a mixed persuasiveness. First, the sky may be dull, a cold wind may blow by the sea, and your perfect sands be a perfect nuisance. Second, it may rain and your autumn loveliness turn into a draggled and depressing hag. Third, it being past the holiday season your little pub may have nothing but arrowroot biscuits and mouse-trap cheese. D'you remember that nightmare meal in Surrey ? However, your fourth, fifth, and so on decide me to agree."

" That's really nice——"

" Because I'll have to put up with you wherever we go,

and I've noticed you're less garrulous when walking than when sitting. Arm-chairs seem to turn on all your conversational taps at once. What time must we start? It's now just after nine."

" Can you be ready by half-past? Right. Bring your mac. I'll carry both of them in my pack. Do you want a stick? There's a weird and wonderful collection in the hall stand. Buck up, then, you've about twenty minutes."

The long hand of the Cathedral clock was about to pass its shorter fellow as Richard and Rachel came out of the bottle neck of Tilly's Lane and struck the open highway to Darum.

" We'll follow the high road for a few miles," said Richard, " as far as Creston, when we'll take to the fields. A footpath winds from there past the golf-course to Sapton Sands, which is about the half-way mark. We'll spell there for a bit and wet our whistles at the Sapton Arms. From there it's only about three miles to Creyde, and from Creyde to Barton Olney not much more than a mile and a half. We'll eat at Barton Olney and then trot along to the sands, or vice versa. Tiring of the sands we next explore the woods and afterwards——"

" Thanks, I *loathe* schedules. Let's just mooch along anyhow. Just drift. Does your pipe always make that noise? "

" When it's happy. I'm glad you're wearing sensible stockings. As a poet I delight in silk, but as a tramp I know there's nowt like wool."

" Have you written much lately? "

" Not a line. Not of verse, anyhow. I've written half-a-dozen short stories. I sent them along to Jackson, my agent —at least I share a small portion of him, some odd hundred other literary blokes have the remainder of him. I like Jackson. He said to me very firmly : ' No poetry. I'd sooner handle Bible commentaries.' He's sold a lot of prose for me and he'll sell the yarns I've no doubt."

" Why don't you write a novel. You're only dissipating your energies writing articles and newspaper stuff. You'll never get out of schoolmastering that way. Now with a novel you might strike oil. Or a play. If they *are* a success you make a mighty pile. Look at John Henry, and he's not half your brains."

" You think that because you live with him—familiarity you know. When you've lived with me for a year you'll wonder—oh, a lot of things, none of them very flattering to me. But you know as well as I do that for every best-selling novel there are a small handful of moderate sellers that just about pay their way, and sacksful of duds that lose money all round. And plays are worse. People think John Henry lucky. They see the finished play and it doesn't seem a very difficult feat. Well, it is. You know that better than I. You help in the workshop. For all his bombast John Henry is a finished master-craftsman. I'm only an apprentice. Of course I could write a novel. Any dam' fool who'll spend the time over it can do so. It's just patience. But why add my stone of futility to the heap. You said just now you loathed schedules, and wanted to drift along. Yet you want me to plan my life according to schedule. I prefer to drift. I do what I want to do. I write what I like. It's one of my few virtues that I don't think about pleasing anybody. That *is* a virtue. Honestly I don't think at all about the selling value. But when it's done, and I set about selling it, I screw out the last farthing from the buyer. I'm the true artist. One of the few wise things Shaw ever said. Hello, there's the peeping ploughboy."

" The what ? Where ? "

" You can't see it plainly enough from here. I *know* it's there and so I can see it. Shall we branch off here ? It's just a bit longer than taking the Creston field-path, but it'll take us past the ploughboy and the milk-maids."

They climbed over a stile and began to follow the almost obliterated traces of the stubble-fields. The ground on each side was uneven and muddy, and the Indian-file method of progression forced upon them stopped Richard's chatter for a while.

The path presently grew plainer and widened, emerging at last into a hedgeless lane scored by wheel-tracks, between which the grass grew rankly. They topped a long rise. "There he is," cried Richard. "Meet Mr. Peeping Ploughboy and learn thereby whatever lesson *is* to be learned." He pointed to a grey stone monolith alone in a field away to their left. It was some six feet in height, as thick as a man's trunk at the base, and tapering away slightly toward the apex.

"It's not Peeping-Tom of Coventry, is it?" laughed Rachel. "His fate was rather——"

"No. But you've got the hang of the story. It's the word ' peeping.' Queer how that word has acquired a sort of sexual significance, and a nasty one at that, as if there were only one sort of peeping."

"Don't get serious so early in the day. What *was* he peeping at?"

"What? At what else does a peeping-tom peep? No, I'm wrong there. He usually wants more than this one spied at. There we are. Now you're coming to them." He pointed away to the next field where, near the centre, a group of similar monoliths stood in a rough circle.

"Well?"

"Those are the nine naughty dairy-maids. The local legend states that they learned the delights of dancing naked in the moonlight, and often stole away to enjoy what the legend calls their orgy. As long as they observed the Sabbath the jealous eye of Jehovah ignored their naughty nakedness, but when finally they outraged *all* the decencies by kneeling to Terpsichore on Yahweh's very own day, why, then Nemesis overtook them. The outraged stare of God became indeed Medusa's glare. And there, as a warning to young maids against nudity on Sundays, they have stood ever since."

" But peeping-tom-ploughboy, what of him ? "

" Oh, yes. Well, he'd got wind of the damsel's bare-skin cavortings, and decided to gloat over their shining bodies from the next field. Unluckily he chose the Sabbath, and the wrath of Yahweh smote him also, but whether designedly, or because his poor oafish body got in the way of the power and the glory, the legend doesn't state."

They were now passing the stone maids. " They're only *seven*, Dick. Where are the other two ? "

" Been reprieved ! " grinning. " But perhaps I got the number wrong. Seven it may have been."

" Your legend's about as correct as your number. That's the worst of writers. You half-listen to a tale and then, to help out your memory, you invent and embroider. I happen to know the legend. It's a Cornish one and it's as much like your version as a dog is like a wolf—a family resemblance, and that's about all. Are those bright spots in the sky the sun trying to get through by any chance, or is it my liver ? "

" Sun," laughed Richard. " Liver spots are never seen by two people simultaneously, and I *can* see yours. I'm nursing the beginnings of a royal thirst. That's the worst of kippers for breakfast. I dote on kippers, bloaters and smoked haddock—my low origin, I expect. We used to cure our own bloaters at Blymouth. I can see and *smell* the curing shed at the bottom of the cliff now. Five-year-seasoned oak we burnt I believe it was. But *that* also may be my inventive faculty again. Perhaps we burnt brown paper. There's the Sapton Arms looming over the horizon. We'll be there shortly. What are you going to drink. Mine's gin and ginger-beer."

" Well, that'll do for me, but the less gin the better."

" Ay," smiling, " it's a foul poison. Would you rather have cider—draught cider from the wood. Scours your throat and sandpapers your vitals. A perfectly loathsome potion. But lots like it. No? Gin and ginger-beer, then. Now if it were the end instead of the beginning of our tramp, do you know what we'd both have? Don't bother to guess. Guinness and port."

" It sounds horrid."

" It's the most amazing pick-me-up, and a harmless one, that the wit of man has yet devised. Like Charles Lamb's pipes : one is wholesome, two toothsome, three fulsome (very !) and four, well, noisome, although I've never tried. Do you see that enormous ruin beetling down over poor little Sapton Arms ? That's Blaker's Folly. Blaker was a mad millionaire—but you know the sort of story. There are scores of ' follies ' scattered over the countryside, all built by crazy millionaires. Ever seen Beckford's Fonthill Abbey. There's another of his towers near Bath, I believe."

" I've read his *Vathek*, but failed to find any genius in it. John Henry dotes on it, and advised me to try it. I told him I thought it punk and he said, ' We're all limited in some direction, my dear Rachel. I find *The Diary of A Nobody*—er—punk.' He's rather a nice old thing."

" Does he always call you Rachel ? "

" Of course. The three of us are quite a happy family. But to return to the ' follies.' What is the strong urge that's behind them all ? It seems queer that crazy millionairedom should express itself in the same way."

" But such an obvious way. It's their counterblast to

their defeat by the world. Despite their millions they know themselves defeated, frustrated. They raise therefore a lasting thing to outlive them, confronting the uncaring mockery of the sky with its challenging and perduring stone. The old coves of the middle ages raised their churches and cathedrals from a very similar urge. And indeed the common (or perhaps *un*common these days) belief in personal immortality is quite a recognisable branch of the same tree. Dost foller lass ? "

" No ; and don't lug in all your what do you call it ? metaphysics ? Well, whatever it is, don't parade it now. It doesn't mix with a tramp nor with gin and ginger-beer. Thank heaven we're here."

It was nearly one o'clock when they reached Barton Sands and much nearer closing time than Richard liked at the little pub. in Barton Olney when they entered the bar parlour and asked for a meal.

" We've not very much, zur," replied the host. " We get no callers this time of the year. We've no meat at all. Just eggs."

Richard looked down his nose. " You haven't any bacon, I suppose ? "

" Well, zur, there's a side of streaky but it's home cured, sweet-cured, and maybe you'd——"

" What ! " roared Richard, " sweet-cured. My first love. My only love. D'you hear that, Rachel. It's perfectly gorgeous. Oh, shades of my aunt Jane in Blymouth ! She sweet-cured her own bacon, and it was the only thing I loved about her. What do you say ? "

" Say ? I could eat wood. Anything. Yes, eggs and bacon's always nice."

" Splendid. Eggs and bacon then. Lots. The eggs fried. Bread and butter. Lots, especially butter. Any cream ? "

" Cream, zur ? Yes."

" God *is* good, Rachel. And jam, or have you honey ? "

" Well, zur, not honey ezactly, but there's marrow jam my missus makes with honey. Maybe——"

" Rachel, I can almost believe in the egregious Browning's ' All's right with the world.' And I think I'll have a bottle of Bass. Two bottles, in fact, poured into one of those big china tankards. What'll you drink, Rachel ? "

" Could I have a pot of tea ? "

" Yez, ma'am, zure. A pot for one."

" Oh, no," laughing, " a pot for *four* at least. I'm as thirsty as four, I'm certain."

It wanted but a few minutes to three when they set off again.

" We'll go through the woods," said Richard ; " it's a little longer but it's easy walking, the bracken's like a thick carpet. You're not tired ? "

" I'm fine. Why can't we always have such appetites. That meal was delicious. And just eggs and bacon. Three mornings out of seven I can't face it at all."

" You could that noble sweet-cured," chuckled Richard. " Wasn't it good. We'll reach Banbridge about five. It's a mite of a place. I've been through it once but I don't know anything about it. I expect we'll be able to get some tea there. Welling's not much more than a couple of miles then, and we'll be in plenty of time for a bath and a change before dinner. I felt as if I were wearing fly-papers next my skin when we reached Barton Sands. The bathe pulled me together and swept me clean. It wasn't a bit cold, was it ? "

" It never is in October. These woods *are* pretty gorgeous. Isn't it still. Woods and cathedrals always move me in the same way. Do you notice how I'm whispering ? I can't help it."

" And blokes like Pious Persy desecrate both. Do you

know, ever since reading a queer book by Algernon Black-wood, I've been half-scared of woods, especially at night-time. It was a rather ghastly sort of yarn in which trees were very much alive and gifted with strange powers over men —or rather over a certain type of man. I've really forgotten most of it, but the effect remains as a sort of uneasy shadowy memory, a nightmarish kind of half-haunting. *You* know the sort of thing."

" Yes. You get it with some of Poe's tales. At least I do. I think the response to the stimulation of the horrific is a very individual personal thing. I respond to Poe, but not to le Fanu nor to Bram Stoker."

" The vampire man ? Terrible tripe. I know it, and yet I can still get a shudder from Dracula, but merely because I read it as a boy of fifteen while convalescent from in-fluenza. It is a sort of secondary horrifying, which my maturity rejects as soon as it gets a chance of having its say."

Rachel nodded, but did not reply. For a while they walked side by side in silence. They had been quite six hours together, and for most of the time they had been alone. Yet Richard had not kissed her once, or made love to her, or treated her in any way other than a friend. They might have been two men.

Presently, as they swung along together, their hands touched. Richard caught and held her fingers, twining his between them. He did not say anything. After a while, feeling his fingers relax, she looked at him, and noticed that his eyes stared blankly ahead. She slipped her fingers from his, and their two arms swung side by side once more. He did not seem to notice the change, but strode on as if alone, staring blankly ahead. Not until they reached Banbridge did he rouse himself and set to finding a cottage where they could get some tea.

The plump little old woman in the tiny thatched cottage opposite the church at Banbridge agreeably demonstrated her conviction that she could find them some tea by ushering them into the cosy kitchen, where a small but bright fire winked hospitably through its black polished bars.

" If you don't *mind* the kitchen," she ventured, " nor my company."

" We were hoping you'd let us sit with you," said Richard. " You've a fine garden."

" Too fine, these days ; my man don't grow younger and he finds it hard now to look after it and his work as well. Although, as I tell him, he might as well give up his work ; there's little for a smith to earn these days. Would you like cake ? "

" You're a thought-reader," laughed Richard ; " you take the words out of my mouth. Cake's the one thing I need to make me perfectly happy. And if it turned out to be home-made cake it would be like Paradise."

" It's home-made," replied the plump little woman, her eyes twinkling. " Maybe you've been in Ireland, sir ? I thought you had. For there's no Blarney Stone hereabouts. There we are, sit you to table while I wet the tea, and then I must go on with my darning. And here's some black-currant jam, and that's home-made too. You'd not think a smith would be hard on socks, now would you. Well, there, look at these. You'll not be doing much darning, ma'am ? "

" Not much—yet," smiled Rachel. " That's a quaint, tumble-down-looking old place at the end of your garden. It looks as old as the hills. Does anyone live there ? Pass the sugar, Dick."

The old woman shook her head. " No one's lived there these four years. It's now all to bits. Sad things happened in that cottage. They do say something walks there at times, but I don't believe in such tales. But she might well walk there, poor soul."

" A story ! " cried Richard, cutting himself a huge wedge of cake. " Do tell us. Ghosts and marvels, eh ? "

" Over fifty years ago it all began. I don't mind it, for I didn't come to Banbridge till I married Tom, nearly forty years now it'll be. There was a little lame cripple of a man, Geordie Denyer, owned the cottage. He was born there. He was a dwarf, a bandy, ugly, little fellow with a great head that rolled on his shoulders as he stumped along with the help of a stick. He kept a little huckster's shop there in those days, and he'd a pony and trap with a stool under the seat to rest his little legs on, and he used to take his goods to sell round the villages. The children were all scared of him.

" How he came to marry Jeanie O'Shea was a puzzler. She was a pretty slip of a maid, dark-haired, slim and tall. He came about up to her elbow. Some say it was religion, and the parson had a hand in it, and if he did God forgive him for what he did.

" Jeanie was as much afraid of Geordie as any of the other children, for she was no more than a child, sixteen maybe, when Geordie married and took her home. She was brought to bed in seven months, and the child was his father all over again—a little monster. Doctor Harper says it's a disease that passes from father to son, but I think it's God's curse. Her mother took her the mite after she'd washed it and wrapped it up, there wasn't no doctors or nurses then, and Jeanie said in a frightened voice, ' What—what is it ? '

" ' A boy, fine boy, for all his seven months. His dad all over.'

" ' Show me,' says Jeanie.

"And when she looked at the little dwarf she cried out and turned away and lay still and wouldn't speak. And when Geordie came up presently she hid her face in the pillow, and then she began to scream out, and say she wanted to die. She was like a mad thing, asking God to kill her and the babe. There's plenty of hot water, ma'am, and lots more milk.

"Well, God took the babe, but Jeanie lived. She never had any more children, and she never put foot outside the door until they carried her out to the churchyard six years ago, with Geordie stumping beside the coffin and crying, with his face all working, and his great head rolling worse than ever. He followed her two years afterward, and since then the cottage has gone to ruin. Maybe she does walk, poor soul."

"Or Geordie," said Richard quietly.

The old woman looked at him. "Maybe you're right, sir, maybe; it's a sad, queer world and 'll take a lot of making up for in Heaven."

"For the Geordies and the Jeanies," said Richard. "May I smoke?"

That night, after dinner, Richard and Rachel stood together at the window of the small sitting-room looking out toward the bandstand.

"I'm so tired," said Rachel, "I could sleep for ever. It's been a great day."

"Sure?" putting his arm round her.

She leaned her face against his shoulder. "Every minute of it." She turned to face him, holding the lapels of his jacket, and looking up at him.

He bent his head and kissed her again and again. He held her away from him, and then placing his arms about her, he put his lips to her hair and closed his eyes.

On the darkness, line upon line, the vision of Ann painted itself in all her loveliness. He felt her body in his arms, her breath on his face. His arms relaxed.

Rachel sighed softly, withdrew herself from his embrace, kissed him, and bidding him a quick good-night, was gone.

He sat down before the fire, his legs outstretched, his hands clenched in his pockets. The firelight died down ; the red coals dulled and became grey ; the cinders fell softly into the ashes of the hearth.

The fire was out and the room cold before he rose, and switching off the light, made his way slowly up to his bedroom.

3

The next morning Richard and Rachel attended matins at the Cathedral. The congregation was a large one and in one of the three Denacre Hall pews sat David Hartley. In the pew behind were Crowson and Bates. During the eleven months that Hartley had been at Welling he had aged as by the passing of as many years. The alert vigour, the hale virility of a year ago had given place to an appearance of senility and decrepitude, that was explicable only upon the assumption of the onset of some malignant disease. As he sat huddled in the corner of his pew, his arms folded and his head bent, he looked an old and a dying man.

The Dean preached, taking for his text that fine passage from Ecclesiastes : " Or ever the silver cord be loosed, or the golden bowl be broken, or the pitcher be broken at the fountain or the wheel broken at the cistern."

His sermon differed only in technique from the hundreds that have been preached from that much-annotated text, but he took the occasion to deliver an attack upon modern superstition, especially in its spiritualistic aspects. One particular outburst made Richard smile. " The medicine-man with his ju-ju is blood-brother to the medium with his hopping tambourine and his disgusting ectoplasm. Mumbo-Jumbo and spiritism are interchangeable terms."

As they walked home Clarence George passed them. In the bright October sunshine his pink peering albinism seemed as revolting as cretinism, female facial hirsuteness, or the artificial horrors of human castration. As he went by he lowered his head with a twisting, snakelike motion of his thin neck, and stared into Rachel's eyes. He nodded at Richard.

" Clarence George," said Richard smiling, as soon as that artist in egoism was out of ear-shot. " What do you think of him ? "

" His work ? "

" No. Clarence the man, in his visible externals."

" It's a horrid thing to say, but he seems loathsome, like a white slug or an etiolated worm. It's a dreadful handi-cap ; a frightful thing for a sensitive person, and he's certainly that, I should judge."

" Yes, his work shows that, at its best. At those rare times when he's on the top of his form he writes lovely and sensi-tive English. Unfortunately, he's rarely on top of his form, or anywhere near it. Being born is a terribly chancy thing, isn't it ? "

" How do you mean ? "

" Well, look at the number of things one might be born —dwarf, imbecile, hare-lipped, cross-eyed, deaf, blind, lame and God knows how many more horrors. It seems a miracle that any babe escapes."

" And yet it's the abnormal that is so uncommon as to be almost a miracle."

" Apparently. By the mercy of Providence, as our Miss Lettice says. But even if a babe manages to be born *compos mentis* and hale and sound in wind and limb, half the world seems to conspire to kill the poor brat. Even the trained nurses that minister to the villagers round here pooh-pooh the child's natural grub, the breast, and advise the mothers to bottle-feed."

Rachel laughed. " You *are* funny, Dick. Since when have you been an apostle of mothercraft ? "

" It's Mason, really," grinning, " or rather O. J. That fiery little Welshman is nuts upon infant-welfare (he owes his lameness and semi-invalidism to ignorant mishandling as a babe) ; he runs a Mothers' Column and pillories all the folk who disagree with him. He headed the column some weeks ago with the one word *Dummies*, and in the course of a biting paragraph mentioned that in half-an-hour's walk he had counted twenty-seven babes sucking those poisonous comforts. More, he rubbed it in by stating that in at least three instances the local district nurse had herself advised them to keep the poor brat quiet. ' The babe,' ended the article ponderously, ' is first inflated and distended by overfeeding and then, when naturally its pain grows vocal, it is outraged by the insertion of this poisonous anachronism.' "

" They suck their thumbs if they don't have dummies," laughed Rachel.

" Not," with mock sententiousness, " if they're properly fed. Again I quote O. J. The dummy, ses 'e, is to the babe what the filthy pipe and the accursed booze is to the man. The healthy man neither smokes nor lushes, according to O. J. The desire for drink is due to indigestion, and the desire for smoke to—er—well, some other complaint which I've forgotten. However, long live drink and in with the dummy, for all I care. If mothers and nurses will murder children (this is another excerpt from O. J., on flies, I think it was) why let 'em. The less cannon-fodder for

RP

the next war. What did you think of Holy Henry's diatribe ? "

" I'm afraid I wasn't listening much. I was watching Mr. Hartley. He looks terribly ill. But I did gather that the Dean dislikes spiritualists."

" Spiritists, darling, that's the word, I believe. It's the only thing about which Persy sees eye to eye with Roman Catholicism. What do *you* think of it ? "

" I just don't. I'm not interested, really. I'm not sure enough in my mind that there is another life at all to bother about folk already enjoying it, or claiming to. Of course, you think it's punk."

" All footle. Existence after death for any creatures seems to me so utterly nonsensical that I can't take it seriously enough to argue about it. But I find the spiritists funny. They're so naif. Their chief battle cry seems to be : Look at the great men, etc., etc., and then they enumerate five, always five, the same five, the Big Five I suppose. Crookes, Lodge, Barrett, and a couple I've forgotten. As if a clever physicist couldn't possibly be childishly credulous when off his subject. But I suppose belief in a future life is necessary for humanity at this period of evolution. Helps it not to kick over the traces and bust things up. Keeps down its childishly exuberant destructiveness, comforts its unhappinesses, gives an air of fair play to the wild and wanton bludgeonings of chance, levels up Tom in the charity school with Thomas at Eton, makes the undertaker a friend, and the hangman no worse than a clumsy surgeon, while even the Reaper himself wears the smile of the pander rather than the grin of the esurient tiger. What shall we do this afternoon ? It's warm—a real Indian summer day. I'll row you up to Bender's lock, we'll get some tea there, and drift back in time for dinner. Or supper as we call it on Sundays—heaven knows why. No, don't tell me ; I'm sure there's a good reason, but I'd hate to know it. Is the pro-gramme agreeable ? Splendid ! "

Richard had drawn up their chairs to the fire after supper, and had arranged them side by side, almost touching. As they sat in the firelight he took her hands in his own, stroked them, and after kissing the fingers, laid them against his cheek. Presently he leaned over and began to kiss her gently at first, and then wildly.

She sat still under his kisses for some time ; and then smiling she kissed his forehead, pushed him with mock roughness back into his chair, and said, " Let's talk."

" Yes," uneasily, " you mean——"

" Nothing, except what I said : let's talk."

" You mean more than that. I know. It's always the same and always has been. When people are going to say or do unpleasant, unkind, hurting things they always begin that way. Let's talk, or I want to talk to you, or menacingly, I want a few words with you. My father used to begin like that before he thrashed me ; my mother, before she delivered me over shrinking, scared and craven to be thrashed ; my sisters before they blabbed on me ; Elman, my teacher, before he tormented me ; and, since I've grown up, my employers, before they told me my work was bad. And now you. What have I done ? " Ruefully, " Am I right, sir ? as Datas used to say."

" Well, you *are* right, Dick. I'm not sure I meant to say what I will say now, when I said ' Let's talk,' but since you expect the worst why, then, we'll out with it."

" Must you ? We've had two such happy days. Haven't you been happy ? I have. I thought you were."

" That's just it, Dick ; you thought I was because you think I'm blind, that I don't notice things, that I don't know."

" Don't know. What don't you know ? Why do——"

" That I don't know you no longer love me ; perhaps you never did. I'm as much——"

" It's not true, Rachel ; it's not true. But what's——"

" Listen, Dick, please. Let me say what I have to say first. May I ? I'm *sure* you don't love me. It's nothing you've done or left undone, but the sense of intimacy, the delicate *something* or other has gone out of our association on your side. The spirit has gone out of you. You play the lover with me. You force yourself. Even when you are kissing me as a lover, passionately, I know it is sham, you seem to be striving to put something away from you by the very intensity of your kissing. I'm not blaming you, Dick, you can't help it. I have been happy these two days, but it was only pretending. A game of make-believe. In a letter I wrote to you some time ago I said : I'll go on pretending you love me. And so I've gone on, and now play-time is over. I've said I don't blame you. How could I ? There's no blame to be allotted in such things. Only you might have told me yourself. Was that too difficult ? I'm not going to ask you if you've a lover. Tell me if you want to." She drew the ring from her finger and put it beside his pipe on the table. " I'm tired, Dick. I think I'll go to bed. I've to be up early in the morning. Kiss me good-night."

Before she could rise Richard had pushed back his chair, and was down on his knees beside her, snatching at her hands, his face in her lap.

" No, Rachel, no ! don't ! it's all wrong."

To her dismayed horror she realised that he was crying. She let her hands remain in his, saying nothing, watching the slow heaving of his shoulders, listening to the sobbing choked breathing that is so pathetic in a child, so piteous in a woman, so shocking in a man.

It was a long while before he spoke. " It's not true,

Rachel. It's not true. I do love you more now than I've ever done. But if you don't believe me what can I say? Except that it's true. If I've seemed different, it's only seeming. I don't know why. Don't spoil everything now. If you'd only marry me you wouldn't doubt me then. Will you marry me, Rachel? Say you will. Don't turn me down. I can't lose you. I can't bear it if you leave me." His voice began to break and she felt his body trembling.

Dreading another outburst of that unbearable sobbing she began to stroke his hair. " Hush. All right, Richard. It's all right. I've been mistaken. Hush please, Dick. We'll get married——"

" When? " raising his head and looking at her half-ashamed, pathetically appealing, childish, with his flushed face and tousled hair.

" Soon. Now, will that do? "

" This year? "

" Heavens, Dick! " laughing, " have mercy on John Henry. As it is he'll be desolated. In the spring."

" Say February."

" February, then. Where's my ring. Put it on for me. I must go to bed. I'm so tired. And we'll spend to-morrow morning in town looking at the furniture shops. Will you like that? And we'll lunch in Soho, for John Henry doesn't expect me back until the evening." She stooped and kissed him. " Now you smoke a pipe and make yourself comfortable for half-an-hour, and don't be daft any more."

For a long while Richard lay sleepless after he had gone to his bedroom. Rachel's room was next to his, and several times he thought he could hear her moving about.

He played with the notion of making a clean breast of it all then and there. He lay seeing himself creeping to her door, knocking, entering, confessing. And then his mind strayed to that other night. The direction of his thoughts changed abruptly, tormentingly. He wondered miserably if in Rachel's arms he would find release. He sat up in bed on a sudden decision to go to her. She would not repulse him. He wanted her, needed her. For the moment he was persuaded that he loved her. And then vividly, warmly, the image of Ann invaded his mind, crept into his arms. And he knew that in Rachel's bed he would find awaiting him not Rachel and love and content, but only Ann's ghost, an unbearable memory, and frustration, and hunger unappeased.

He lay down again, pulling the clothes over him and burying his face in the pillow. His manhood sloughed from him, leaving him a little boy of nine, biting the sheets in childish misery because of some small fickle maid who would no longer go sweethearting with him.

CHAPTER XVI

THE ABHORRED SHEARS

I

For a full week before the New Year's Eve Fancy Dress Ball the Mayor and Mayoress had been busy with the invitations. The hundred children were a simple matter—a mere question of balloting at the schools, with a few odd invitations to the youngsters of personal friends. But the adult guests were a more difficult problem.

Morning after morning toward the end of December Andrew Banks retired after breakfast to his " den," with paper, pens and the local directory, to wrestle with his invidious task. Inventing, manufacturing, and marketing his famous non-slip suspender was, in comparison, mere child's-play, a mere question of supplying a known need. But this allotting of two hundred tickets among at least two thousand citizens needed diplomacy, tact and judgment. There were, fortunately, several thousand citizens who did not need consideration, being below that rigid social line which mayoral dignity is bound to draw.

The harassed Mayor endeavoured to lighten his labours by preparing four preliminary lists marked Certainties, Probables, Possibles and Doubtfuls. The Certainties were simple : these were all the professional men of Welling, the clerical gentlemen of all denominations, the local stockists of the non-slip suspender, the local councillors and city officials, the chief tradesmen, and finally three teachers from each school—these last being necessary evils invited as having expert knowledge in dealing with riotous youth, and chosen by lot. The married certainties brought their wives and the adult portion of their families. The Probables included minor city officials, small tradesmen, the three dentists and two veterinary surgeons of Welling, and the smaller fry of banking and commerce. The Possibles comprised the good Mayor's after-thoughts, and the slippery customers who had dropped through the meshes of the mayoral net at the first haul. The Doubtfuls were, it must be confessed, chiefly those annoying folk whom the Mayor heartily disliked, and were mentally subdivided by his worship into two classes : those he could offend with impunity and those he could not. Few of the first class ever graced the festivity. At the top of the second class stood the names of Owen Jones and Mason. The Mayor had once tried the bold experiment of barring *The Sentinel's* editor and chief contributor, but the facetious article in the next issue headed *Banks's Circus* did not encourage a repetition of the experiment. Nevertheless, although the two journalists' names might well have stood at the head of the Certainties, their relegation to the Doubtful list was a pleasant little piece of make-belief on the Mayor's part, which saved his self-approval from the too sudden buffets of reality.

Among the hundred fortunate children were Donald Petit aged seven, and Amy Robson, aged nine. Donald was the only child of Widow Petit who lived on a small municipal pension in a small municipal cottage, just at the junction of Market Street with the south end of the High Street. The Town Hall, where the Ball was held, was but fifty yards away round the corner. From the front window of Widow Petit's cottage Donald, had he been bold enough, might at any hour between six a.m. and midnight have successfully bombarded with his pea-shooter the policeman on point-duty.

Little Amy Robson lived at the other end of Market

Street, within a few doors of Baley's, the fishmongers. She also was an only child. Her father was a hand in Barentz's new garage in Broad Walk at the end of The Arcade.

The Ball began at eight and, unless New Year's Day fell on a Sunday, continued until an hour after midnight. Parents or friends usually set off to call for the children just before the Cathedral clock roused itself to proclaim the newly arrived year. " Auld Lang Syne " was sung and the children were then expected to leave, the ensuing hour being the *clou* of the evening. The Adult merrymakers, freed from the stare of critical and astonished youth, and invigorated and exhilarated by the profusion of liquors, abandoned themselves to the joy of living and the all-surrendering worship of the jollier gods and goddesses of mythology.

The old year had but ten minutes left of life. In the persons of most of the men lounging in the improvised bar it might well be said to be staggering to its end, a vinous and effusive, if slightly querulous, old reprobate.

Clarence George had reached the stage of staring truculence, a truculence rendered inarticulate, or at least difficult of articulation, by that unruly spasmodic behaviour of the diaphragm which is still a national touchstone of humour.

Near him, sitting upon a high stool, was the redoubtable Owen Jones. George's control over his faculties was by this time insufficient for him to risk a whole sentence, and his hostility toward the little hot-gospeller had to content itself with a stare, which the Welshman's choice of refreshment enabled George to reinforce with a verbal pleasantry combining offensiveness, necessary brevity, and utility. Jones was drinking dry ginger. He was thirsty, and was consuming vast quantities of this unexciting beverage. Each time he drained his glass and said, " Dry Ginger,"

George slapped *his* upon the counter, and solemnly and carefully pronounced " *Wet* whisky." Jones's dress as a Welsh bard and George's as Don Quixote did not somehow seem inappropriate to their solemnly clownish by-play.

So crowded was the bar that these sportive amenities passed unnoticed. Richard as Charles Lamb, Mason as Richelieu, and Captain Lacy as Drake, sat squeezed into the corner on a red-plush lounge. Richard, flushed and excited, was talking rapidly and boisterously. The voice of Captain ffoliot, the M.C., called loudly : " The New Year Waltz." As the orchestra broke into the first bars of Stellini's *Blue Dusk Waltz* Colonel Bowers edged his way through the emerging crush at the door, and said loudly, " Any of you gentlemen seen a little girl dressed as Red Riding Hood ? "

" Three at least, quite three," said Clarence George owlishly.

" That's probably the one," commented Mason drily.

The globular, suffused eyes of Bowers wandered over George and away from him in a questioning stare about the room. Neighbour and friend as he was of George he made no effort to conceal his contempt for that popular favourite's condition, a contempt rooted perhaps in the Colonel's consciousness of his own power to drink his mess under the table on gala occasions in the good old days when he was a power in the regiment.

" No one ? " asked Bowers again, looking round inquiringly. Receiving only friendly but unhelpful noises in response the Colonel turned away, the few remaining occupants of the bar falling in behind him as he moved toward the door.

As Richard and Mason entered the ball-room the waltz ceased abruptly as the great clock at the far end whirred warningly. The dancers linked hands. The chattering and laughter fined away to complete silence as the clock began to chime. With the last stroke the orchestra also linked hands, while the first fiddle mounted a chair, and unsteadily and a little flamboyantly, played "Auld Lang Syne." By the end of that quaint barbarism the tremulous self-conscious pipings of the dancers had given place to an inharmonious babel that was at last no more than an inane corrupted repetition of "Syne m' dear" like the maddening reiteration of a damaged gramophone record.

Long before the last voices were hushed an uneasy sense that something was amiss had begun to invade the revels. Here and there were groupings of nodding, gesticulating, and whispering dancers. Officialdom, discarding hurriedly its fripperies, emerged pale of face from doorways, strode across the floor portentously, flung out hands of anxious yet dignified gesture, shrugged bemused shoulders, and vanished mysteriously into darkling corridors.

And then Captain ffoliot mounted the dais behind the orchestra. " Ladies and gentlemen," he said, " it is my painful duty to inform you that one of the ch-ch-ch-child guests is missing. A search party is about to set out to look for her. In these circumstances you will realise that it would be unseemly to c-c-c-c-continue our festivities. His Worship the Mayor, who is greatly distt-t-tressed, hopes that you will——"

The remainder of ffoliot's speech was drowned in the excited buzz and hum of conversation. Officialdom was sought out and interrogated, and within a few minutes had reluctantly disclosed the facts. The lost child was little Amy Robson. Her father was to have taken her to the Town Hall, but as he was delayed at the garage several hours beyond his ordinary time, the child had persuaded her mother to allow her to run along to Baley's fish-shop for her little friend Doris, and to go on with the Baley party to the dance. Amy left her home at a quarter to eight. It was snowing slightly and she wore over her Red Riding Hood Costume a fawn mackintosh with a roomy hood. She did not call at the Baleys', was not seen at the Town Hall, and when her father arrived at the Town Hall a few minutes before midnight no one had been able to give any information concerning her to the distracted man.

There were still nearly a hundred people in the ballroom when at seventeen minutes past twelve Widow Petit arrived and asked if anyone had seen her little Donald. He was dressed as a Red Indian chief, she explained, her hand fluttering up to her mouth, as she stared at the grave faces around her.

Before the half hour had struck further search-parties had set off to seek the missing boy, and Widow Petit, red-eyed, tear-stained, wringing her hands with pathetic helplessness, was telling her story to Superintendent Haynes. She had been busy after tea, she said, making some shirts for the little lad. She had not noticed the lateness of the hour, and when she discovered it was after half-past seven, and she neither washed nor dressed, her Donald had implored her to let him run along by himself, since if he waited for her to accompany him, it would all be over. As it was but a step round the corner, just past the police-station, she put on his raincoat, gave him her umbrella to protect his feathered head-dress from the snow, kissed him good-bye and let him run along. She'd expected friends would bring him back as they passed on their way home. As no one came, however, and it was well after midnight, she'd popped on a few things and gone round to the Town Hall to find that Donald had not been seen during the evening.

2

Dozens of Welling's citizens spent the hours of darkness scouring the alleys and by-ways and combing the countryside with the help of dogs. They saw the ashen winter dawn creep over the estuary, paling the torches and lanterns to golden yellow blurs, and touching to blank whiteness the snow-covered folds of the stubble fields sloping steeply to the western moorland. Before dawn had finally conquered the street-lamps the number of the searchers had increased tenfold, and Rumour, thousand-tongued, went side by side with the searchers, roused belated sleepers from bed, sat at innumerable breakfast tables, peered into shops and offices, whispered to men on the way to work, to women at their early household duties, to children at play.

Yet it fell to two men about their ordinary tasks to silence Rumour with a Reality that stunned the city to horrified whispering.

At half-past eight Herbert Baines, delivering newspapers on his bicycle to some scattered groups of cottages about half a mile from Welling along the high road to Darum, found the body of Amy Robson huddled under the far side of the hedge. It was the vivid red of her cloak against the white snow that had caught his glance through a gap in the hedge. It took Baines but a trifle over two minutes to reach the police-station, and before nine o'clock it was known that the little girl had been strangled and outraged. Rushton (the police surgeon) and Dr. Forde were agreed that she had been dead at least ten hours.

The city was not unprepared for the worse news which followed. John Maxton, a farm labourer, just before nine o'clock found the body of little Donald Petit in a bed of nettles by the river side, about half-a-mile beyond the point where the other body had lain. The little boy had been strangled and mangled so brutally that his appearance at first glance suggested savaging by a horse or pig. It required, however, but the briefest examination to show that this also was murder. Doctors Rushton and Forde again agreed that the child must have been killed well before midnight, Forde even putting it as early as nine o'clock, the probable hour of the other murder.

Welling, after the first shock of horror, did not fail to remember that it was a year ago to the day that the Cathedral had been desecrated, the first of a series of violent acts culminating in the firing of Denacre Hall.

By ten the hue and cry, official and unofficial, was out for the murderer, or murderers, over twenty square miles of countryside ; and by noon the whole of Meadshire, and presently the counties about its borders, swarmed with a host of avenging searchers.

Welling closed its shops and business houses before the morning was over, and while the great bell in the Cathedral tolled dismally hour after hour, little groups of men at street-corners, in clubs and public-houses, discussed and argued and gesticulated omnisciently ; and little knots of women by doorsteps, outside shop-windows, or by twos over garden walls, shook heads sadly and wiped streaming eyes of sympathy.

Long before the early dusk gathered the city had drawn in its treasures of women and children to the security of comfortable firesides, while reluctant boys in early adolescence protested volubly against such an enforced haven.

At three o'clock *The Sentinel* published a special edition, rushed through the streets by vociferous and brawny young men.

Dark-fall found Welling streets deserted, and its citizens once more at the mercy of Rumour. Rumour, having no arrest to report, was soon reinforced by her ugly sister Fear.

CHAPTER XVII

POINTS OF VIEW

I

The special late edition of *The Welling Sentinel* contained the following leading article.

Murder Most Foul

" The appalling outrage which has destroyed two young lives, and made of Welling a city of mourning, is but the culmination of a series of violent deeds unparalleled within living memory in these parts.

" Never before in the long history of our city has the dawn of a New Year broken upon so distressing, so awful, so harrowing a scene of tragedy.

" In all death there must always be a touch of pathos, but in the untimely cutting off of young lives that emotion is intensified a thousand-fold. We may well weep at the fall of the oak, but the destruction of the sapling is a tragedy too deep for tears. We know all too well that the Reaper reaps blindly, but when that random stroke hews down our little ones we pass beyond the ministrations of human comfort, and must seek our consolation from the Divine Compassion.

" As if to add one last touch of awfulness, of pathos, the Reaper struck at these little ones clad in their gay festal robes. At these thoughts the stricken heart cannot but wonder why the majesty of death could not spare these babes their playtime. It is at these sad moments that we discover how inadequate are words to console the afflicted ;

they seem but an intrusion upon hopeless grief, adding to, rather than taking away from, the burden of sorrow.

" Yet, while not presuming to offer consolation, we must extend to the grief-stricken parents our deepest and most heart-felt sympathy.

" But while the blood of these outraged babes cries from the ground unavenged, there can be no rest by day or by night for the men and women of Welling. A ravening beast in human guise is abroad in the land, and until that beast is destroyed we shall know neither peace nor security nor a surcease from dread.

" No one need question the fact that our local police are efficient, painstaking, and untiring, or that in Super-intendent Haynes we have an official second to none in the country in determination, zeal and energy. Are these sufficient ? We will not at the present juncture labour this query. It is but fair to remember that the dastardly crime is not yet twenty-four hours old, and we may well hope that before another day dawns the wretch will be laid by the heels.

" This is neither the time nor the place to refer to past events, but it may not be irrelevant to remind our readers that the mystery of the desecration of our Cathedral is still unsolved, and the perpetrator still uncaught.

" In all sympathy we would ask our readers, and especially the sorrow-stricken parents, to ponder that wonderful poem of Robert Louis Stevenson beginning *Yet, O stricken heart, remember O remember* which will be found printed in full on page 4.

" The inquest we understand will be held on Monday and the funeral will take place the following day."

2

Miss Ovey, Mr. and Mrs. Fletcher, Sergeant-Major Browning, and Mrs. L'Estrange sat in a corner of the lounge after dinner. Their conversation was carried on in whispers, as if death were in the room. The two men and Mrs. L'Estrange were smoking, Miss Ovey was giving only the most perfunctory attention to a game of patience, while Mrs. Fletcher was busily knitting a sock.

" I don't like Mr. Jones, and I don't like his paper," said Miss Ovey, " but for once he's saying what all decent people are thinking."

" About the police ? " asked Mrs. Fletcher.

" Yes," nodding. " I'm not one to be always running down our local men, who, I think, in fact, are as clever as any, but I certainly think in such a case as this assistance should be called in. Don't you think so, Major ? "

" Absolutely. I'm afraid I've not the faith in Haynes you have, Miss Ovey ; but even if he were the best man in England this is too big a job for him to tackle ; it's not a one-man job at all, eh, Fletcher ? "

" You're right. It's a job for the whole of England, and the sooner it's put on the right footing the better."

" It ought to have been a year ago," said Miss Ovey, sharply.

" You think," began Mrs. L'Estrange.

" I'm sure. If that evil little rascal Smith had been laid by the heels we should not have had this horror in Welling, nor any of the other happenings of the last year."

" Well," gravely, " you know we differ about that ; and, indeed, many of the—er—well—unfortunate things that have occurred in Welling recently cannot possibly be laid at the door of Alfred Smith. You might as well blame Mr. David Hartley."

SP

" I *do* blame Mr. Hartley. I think it was an unlucky, an evil, day for Welling when he came to live among us, and I'm convinced that we shall never return to our former tranquil times while he is with us."

" He's much too sick a man to be responsible for anything these days, isn't he ? " ventured Fletcher, putting the end of his cigar into his pipe. " He's bedridden half his time, and certainly has not been out since October."

" You're not suggesting Mr. Hartley is the murderer, surely, Miss Ovey ? " said Mrs. L'Estrange.

" No, certainly not ; I'm merely saying that his coming to Welling coincided with the beginning of the trouble, and if it were not such a wicked wish I could hope that his sickness might be a fatal one."

" I'm inclined to think," continued Mrs. L'Estrange, " and the Dean thinks the same (for I met the Mayoress this morning and His Worship had already had two interviews with Dr. Perseval), that it is more than possible the desecrator of the Cathedral and the murderer are one and the same person ; but certainly, as far as I'm concerned, not that poor little Smith, although I believe the Dean suspects him. He says that the two very distinct acts bear so close a resemblance to each other as to make it possible to think they are the acts of one man."

" A bit far-fetched, isn't it ? " said Browning. " I'm afraid, as a plain man, I don't see much resemblance myself."

" The Dean is convinced they are the work of a maniac, and he says that it is a well-known fact that what I believe he called a religious maniac is liable at any moment to become a sexual maniac. It——"

" It is all disgusting," interposed Miss Ovey hastily, " and however correct Dr. Perseval may be, and you too, Mrs. L'Estrange, I confess I should sleep more comfortably if Smith were in jail. Unless that comes about it will be only by the mercy of Providence that we shall not all be murdered. Although, indeed, Providence so far has never failed me. I suppose Scotland Yard will be called in. I'm sure we should all feel safer."

" I'm afraid not," said Mr. Fletcher, sucking noisily at his pipe, " Haynes is the sort of chap who thinks it a confession of failure to consult anyone else. Unless worse things happen Haynes will carry on himself. Don't you think so, Browning ? "

" Absolutely. Mind you, in one way, I don't know that I blame him, although I've no opinion of his brains. I can't see what Scotland Yard can do that *he* can't. When Scotland Yard comes into a case it always reminds me of the regiment—the Colonel got all the praise but it was the Sergeant-major who *made* the regiment. Well, Scotland Yard comes in, and if the man's nobbled, gets all the credit, while it's the local man who's done all the ground-work."

" Personally, Major, I really think it is iniquitous," remarked Mrs. L'Estrange, " that Scotland Yard, who are, or are supposed to be, experts, must wait to be called in by the local self-important nincompoop before they get to work. It's one of the queer things no woman can understand. In a reasonable world the expert body would automatically take control on the discovery of any really serious crime. Doesn't it often work out in practice that four or five days, valuable days for the criminal, elapse before Scotland Yard gets to work ? What in the name of common-sense is gained by that ? "

" It's a mistake to look for reason or common-sense in the conduct of public affairs," smiled Mrs. Fletcher. " Take divorce, for example. Can you——"

" Well," interrupted Miss Ovey, rising abruptly, " this really won't do ; I'm becoming really too fond of gossiping after dinner. All those things are best left in the hands of Providence, and when Providence considers that Scotland Yard should be called in, doubtless Scotland Yard *will* be called. But I trust it will be soon."

3

Never before on a Saturday evening had the bar-parlour of *The Crown* been so deserted. Most of the habitués had remained at home at the request of their families, and the few men clustered about the bar spoke in low voices, and wore an air of gloom that had about it nevertheless some elements of funereal enjoyment.

Clarence George, with Larry and Nell at his feet among the spittoons, alone lifted his voice above the level of the reigning decorum. He was nearing the end of one of his periodic drinking bouts, and was drinking " dog's-nose " from a tankard with the intense determination of one who races against time.

Daniels leaned against the back of the bar polishing glasses. His wife sat in a small bureau, between the bar-parlour and the private bar, checking the week's accounts.

Captain ffoliot, with one elbow on the bar counter, and his face half turned toward Daniels, carried on a desultory conversation with him, to which George occasionally added a comment.

Richard and Mason sat in the near window-settle, with Captain Lacy on the other side of their table.

" I'm more than ever convinced, Daniels," said ffolio " that if Haynes had managed to arrest that little cathedral rascal, Smith, we'd have been saved this shocking b-b-b-business."

" I'm afraid you're right, sir."

" Haynes's initial mistake was not to take the matter

seriously enough. He lacked foresight, or he'd have foreseen this, or something very like it."

" That's a fact, sir."

" It's well known that religious mania and sex-mania often go together. You remember the Ripper murders ? Well, Bowers was a subaltern at the time and he tells me that their M.O. was convinced the Ripper crimes were the work of a religious maniac. He was so keen on his theory that he wrote to the police to know if there were any secret records of sacrilege, or even simple church-breaking, in London. The police p-p-p-probably thought *he* was mad, and anyway Bowers's regiment left for India shortly afterward. But I'm pretty well convinced there's a good d-d-d-deal in it."

" Seems likely, sir. The only doubt I've really got about Smith is that he was a littlish frail sort of chap, perhaps not really little, but somehow he looked it, a waxy sort of face, if you remember ; well, he didn't seem the sort of chap to be strong enough to do all that smashing business of last year. And then these poor children. Haynes says they must have been carried all the way, although how he gets that, seeing that snow fell most of the night, is beyond me. But if it's true, well, Robson's little girl was nine and big for her age, and from her house to where she was found was nearly a mile ; no light job for a weakish chap like Smith. Then, you know, poor little Petit's arm had been torn off—it's true, sir, wrenched right out of its socket. I can't see Smith doing that."

" First sensible remarks I've heard all day, boniface," gasped Clarence George ; " fill up the sparkling bowl. ffoliot, I hate a consistent man. Because you said a year ago that Smith was the man, it's still Smith. Smith yesterday, to-day, and for ever. Rot. All dam' rot. Sh'll I tell you what I think ? It was an elemental."

" A *what* ? "

" Elemental. Spook. Don' cher know ? An earth-bound spirit of evil. I've a theory that all the more horrible crimes are done by elementals ? Ever read Montague Winters on 'em ? Wonderful fellow, a bit prosy in his style, *you* know, no fire, no artistic guts, but for *facts*, horrible and loathsome facts, real bloodcurdlers, why, give me Montague for a bedmate. *Elemental*, that's the solution."

" Have you told Haynes ? "

" Well, not yet ; as a matter of fact, I only arrived at that solution a couple of minutes ago. In sooth our fair boniface put me on the track. No footprints, eh ? All covered up with snow ? All my eye. The elemental, being a spirit, made none. I should say——"

" But seriously, sir, you don't think it was Smith either ? "

" Don't you keep a diary, my poor friend ? You don't. It's a pity, but it's not too late to begin. You might still be my Boswell. Well if you *had* kept one you'd find in it, under a date of about a year ago, that I visited this over-rated hostelry, drank its dubious liquors, and told our dear ffoliot to his face that he was barking up the wrong tree, and that Smith was a misunderstood and sensitive artist, as I am, also, quite incapable of such disgusting crimes as he imputed to him then and imputes to him now——"

" If I remember rightly," interrupted ffoliot, " you very helpfully suggested that the Dean was the guilty p-p-p-party, or failing him, Hartley, or some hundred-odd women."

" You misunderstood me. Not odd women. Normal ones. It's the normal women who do the odd deeds. And I still stand by what I said."

" That's going rather far, sir. Mr. Hartley, sir, perhaps, but the Dean——"

" And Mr. Hartley, sir," mimicking, " was once a bishop,

good vintner, and if, as *you* say, perhaps a bishop, why not a Dean. I'm convinced. Hartley's the man."

" Since when ? "

" Weeks, ffoliot, weeks ; I saw this coming off. Hartley's the fellow, mark my words."

" Hartley's not been out of Denacre Hall for over a month. He's practically bedridden, a d-d-dying man. Don't be dam' silly, George."

" Roy Hartley. Hey ! *That* startles you. So obvious, isn't it, now it's mentioned. Obvious libertine, religiously and musically minded, disappears after a perfect orgy of rape——"

" Rape, be—— "

" Seduction, then, seduction, don't interrupt, ffoliot ; where was I. Oh, yes. Disappears absolutely. Pah ! He was in hiding. The libido needed recuperating. He hibernated, as it were. And then the libido being refreshed and renewed, the urge recharged, why, then, he emerges a ravening wolf. But as I've told you before, the libido may become aberrant, turn aside into—— "

" God ! how that fellow drivels on," said Richard softly. " We've time for another. Same again ? And you, Captain Lacy ? " He beckoned to Daniels, who, at his nod, brought three Guinnesses to the table, collected the used glasses, and returned to his shoulder-rest.

" It's not quite the drivel it sounds, is it ? " said Mason. " There aren't many flies on Master George. The difficulty is to separate the grain of real hard sense from all his chaff of intentionally flippant nonsense."

" And the grain here ? You don't surely think Roy Hartley—— "

" Good Lord, no ! " laughing. " I was merely thinking of his generalisations about potential murderers. There was more than a grain of truth in *that*. But the real fertile grain was his defence of Smith. He should be ruled out by any sane person. Don't you think so, Lacy ? "

" I'm afraid it's beyond me, Mr. Mason, but I agree about Smith. But, as far as that goes, it seems to me that it's all so queer a business that you'd have to rule out everyone, if you're simply going to be reasonable and—er—logical."

Richard nodded. " A case for intuition, eh ? inspiration ? There are worse things to work by. Yes."

" You see," continued Lacy, " there's nothing reasonable, hardly even human, at all, about not only these last horrors but the events of a year ago——"

" But we're agreed upon a maniacal perpetrator, aren't we ? " asked Mason.

" Yes. And that seems to me to offer the least hope of nailing the fellow by ordinary logical means."

" Set a maniac to catch a maniac," laughed Richard. " Isn't that what you boil down to ? Sounds, if I may say so, a bit fantastic. I'm inclined to think myself that the more mentally abnormal the criminal is, the simpler it is to spot him by sheer deduction."

" And your deduction is ? " laughed Mason.

Richard shook his head. " Logic's not my strong point ; inspiration and intuition *are*. So if the criminal were assumed to be a master of logic, then by my own argument, I *should* be the man to lay him by the heels. As it is," shrugging his shoulders, " you may search me. What about you, Mason ? "

" I'll leave it at that. Hello ! Daniels is getting ready for his famous impersonation of a London potman. And there's the Cathedral striking. Can you manage another before we go. No ? You Lacy ? Well, come along then. We'll go home like the ivy, lest worse befall."

As they buttoned up their coats Richard said, " Well, now, look here, we're three men of, I suppose at the least, average intelligence. We confess this business flabbergasts us. Ergo : What chance has Haynes who is—well, isn't he now ? "

Mason nodded. " Leave it to our Miss Letty's Providence, eh ? Who fights on the side of the big battalions."

" *And* the big numskulls. Should we otherwise ever have won the war. I suppose we did win it ! Numskullism is the G.C.M. of soldiering."

" Which means ? "

" We hadn't a monopoly."

" How did we win, then ? You're right, Blaney, logic is *not* your strong point."

CHAPTER XVIII

THE OFFICIAL STANDPOINT AND THE EMOTIONAL

I

And now Welling and its citizens, as a news item, began to creep into the national newspapers. The sedater Sunday papers gave the double murder three lines in their news items column, while *The News of the Globe* gave it a column headed *The Welling Horror*. The London morning papers on Monday were about equally generous with their space *The Morning Clarion* allotting six lines, *The Wire* nine, and *The Daily Leader* eight. *The Wire* used the tragedy as a text for a short leader upon the folly of abolishing capital punishment. All these journals suggested that the local police had the matter well in hand, and an arrest might be expected at any moment. No journal spelt the name of Superintendent Haynes correctly, and *The Wire* seemed hazy over the city's geographical position, the sub-editor apparently confusing it with Welwyn.

Satisfied and convinced as the country at large (as represented by its newspapers) might be that the local constabulary were dealing competently with the affair, the citizens of Welling by no means shared this conviction or satisfaction.

Albert Robson, the father of the dead girl, attended the inquest on the Monday, and at the end of his brief evidence of identification drew upon the store of a limited but vivid vocabulary to denounce the inefficiency of the police.

The funeral of the two children took place on Tuesday, and the next morning Robson was at work as usual in

Barentz's garage. With two mates, Alfred Bennett and John Riley, he began dismantling a car, and during the morning shift the three men worked in silence. It was toward the end of the afternoon, when the job neared completion, that Robson said suddenly, " I'd sooner go on working all night than go home and face my missis. It's about half-killed her."

" It's always worse for the women," commented Riley ; " housework don't stop you thinking about other things, like a tricky job with an engine does."

" And it's being *in* the house where the kid was makes it worse still," said Bennett, scratching the contact breaker with a horny thumbnail.

" Ay," dully, " she says she'll not sleep till that devil's been caught. Christ ! " savagely, " if I on'y had him here. Ay, *if*. Just about as likely to have him here as Haynes is to get him."

" You give him the straight griffin at the inquest, Bert. It's what everyone's thinking, isn't it, Jack ? "

" You're right. Haynes ain't fly enough to catch a kid scrumping apples. This is a job for Scotland Yard."

" 'Course it is. That's what I was going to tell the coroner if I hadn't been shut up. For I *was* shut up, for all his soft speeches. There's no square deal in this country or any other for a working man. They shut your mouth up. And if you won't shut it, why, out you go, out of your job and in clink 'fore you know where you are."

" Why don't you go round and see 'Aynes ? " asked Bennett. " See him to-night, and say, polite and all that, that you think the Yard ought to give a hand."

" 'Twouldn't be any good," doubtfully. " B'sides, he wouldn't see me."

" He would, Bert. They *got* to, you know. Can't refuse. It's like the army and refusing to take the C.O.'s punishment and asking for a D.C.M. The C.O.'s got to give way;

it's Army regulations, and it's the same with the police. He'll see you all right. That's right, isn't it, Jack ? "

" That's it. They're our servants after all, although you wouldn't think it to see their swank and the handy way they've got with their bleedin' truncheons. You take Alf's tip, and go and see him. If he 'on't do anything, there's no harm done, and he might. Stands to reason he ain't feeling none too cushy about it ; 'd like to call in the Yard, p'raps, and 'd be only too dam' glad to be shoved into it. You hop along after a bit of tea and a wash."

" Have a couple at *The Crown* as you go along, if you're frightened of him."

" Frightened be ——. I don't want any dope to face 'Aynes. I've right on my side, 'aven't I. I've a dam' good mind to. I'll talk it over with the missis, and see what she says. Maybe I'll sleep on it to-night."

" Well, *I* wouldn't, Bert. I wouldn't waste another bleedin' minute ; 'd you Jack ? Have a talk with the missis is all right, but you see Haynes 'fore you go to bed. An' have a couple with us after. We'll be in *The King's Head* at 'r past nine. I can't stick *The Crown*—too much swank and collars and cuffs there, to say nothing of old mother Daniels. Now what do you say ? See Haynes say about eight or so, and meet us in *The King's Head* at 'r past nine, or nine if you like. Now what do you say ? "

" I'll do it. Nine sharp. That's the buzzer. But I'll have a word with the missis first."

2

" I've been talking things over with Alf Bennett and Jack Riley, said Robson to his wife, as she poured him out a cup of tea and took the kippers from the oven.

" Have you, Bert ? " listlessly.

" Yes, mate. They thinks the same as I do."

Mrs. Robson said nothing, but sat looking out through the rain-smeared panes at the bare trees around the bandstand.

" Think I ought to go and see Haynes, and straight away. What do you think ? "

" *Will* he see you, dear ? "

" Oh, he's got to. That's the law. I know that all right. Like the army. Some things they *got* to do, like 'em or not. I'm going to see him and put it to him straight. The straight griffin. What about Scotland Yard ? I'm going to say to him, see ? What about calling in the Yard ? "

" You'll have to be careful, Bert. Mr. Haynes is a hard man. And it don't pay to offend the police. Dad used to say they always got you if you did, and did it on you something cruel when they got you in the cells."

" Don't you worry about *that*, old girl. He'll not get me on the hop. I know as far as I can go. I can do the polite all right. I'm going to say, ' Don't you think the Yard ought to know about it, Mr. Haynes ? ' See ? Friendly advice, like. There's nothing wrong with that, is there."

" Seems all right, Bert." Anxiously, " you won't go drinking before you go ? You know how it goes to your head. And he may be nasty, you know, and then——"

" Not a drop, mate, not a smell. I'm not such a fool. I'm going to meet Alf and Bert afterward just for one at *The King's Head* and a bit of a chin-wag about it, but no a drop before, Old China, don't you worry."

" Let me come with you, Bert."

" What ! to the pub ? Hey, chuck——"

" To the station. I'd rather, Bert. I'd feel easier. Besides it might help to persuade him. And he won't be so nasty, and then you'll not lose your temper and get swearing. Do, Bert. I'd like to get a bit of fresh air, too. I been feeling so bad all day," biting her lip. " All the time I keep on thinking," breaking down suddenly, and giving way to unrestrained sobbing, " keep on——"

" Christ ! don't take it so hard, old girl, don't take it so hard. Here." He went over to her, putting his arms round her shoulders, and laying his face against her hair. His mouth was twisted grotesquely. " Cheer up ! " shakily, " ay, we'll go along together. Aren't you going to eat nothing. Let me boil you an egg ? You got to eat, old mate. You'll on'y get ill. Now come on now. Let me pour you out a nice hot cup ; this is all cold. That's the ticket."

" Sit down, Mr. Robson, sit down, Mrs. Robson. Quite all right. Quite. Yes, yes. I'm only too sorry I can't give you more than five minutes," looking at the clock, " hardly more, I'm afraid, I've a hundred things to do before nine o'clock. Now what can I do for you ? I'm sorry to say I've no news, no real news that is, although I think we're within reach, yes, I think I may say we're——"

" That's just it, sir," interrupting with obviously abrupt decision, " that's just what we've come about."

" News ? Well, you know, as I've said, there is no definite information, nothing very tangible yet to go upon. But I've every hope——"

" No, sir," interrupting desperately, " it's not news we've come after. I know you couldn't give us that just yet, if you had it. I know the law, sir. No, sir ; we thought, the wife and I, that maybe a bit of help wouldn't come amiss. Sort of lion and the mouse, sir, you know."

" Oh, yes ; quite. All help is help. Now what is it you think—— ? "

" Well, sir, we thought perhaps it wouldn't be amiss if the Yard knew about it."

" The *Yard* ? Oh, yes. Of course. You think Scotland Yard ought to know."

" That's right, sir."

" Well, Mr. Robson," with grave good temper, " I can assure you that Scotland Yard *does* know."

" That's fine, sir. Thank you. I might have guessed. And perhaps the Yard's already on his track, sir."

" Well, not yet, you know, Mr. Robson. Not just yet. Scotland Yard is of course aware of the terrible tragedy——"

" Then isn't it time, sir," interrupted Mrs. Robson, with agitation, " that they done something. It'll be a week Saturday, and that wretch——"

" *We* are doing everything that is humanly possible, Mrs. Robson, you may depend upon that. At any moment——"

"But," put in Robson doggedly, " you said Scotland——"

" I said," suavely, " that Scotland Yard knew of the tragedy, but you did not give me time to explain that the Yard is satisfied with our competence to deal with the matter, and will not therefore interfere unless requested."

" Two heads are better than one, sir."

" Not always, Mr. Robson. Please don't think me unsympathetic. I feel very deeply for you, but you must realise that in these matters it is the head and not the heart which will bring the criminal to account."

" But Scotland Yard," more doggedly, " *is* the head of the whole country, sir ; I don't want to interfere in what's your business, and as you say it's heads and not hearts. But Scotland Yard's got the best heads——"

"Well, Mr. Robson," drily, " I'm really afraid I've given you all the time, more, much more, in fact, than I can spare. I must really ask you both to excuse me now. You may rest assured——"

" It's our child that's dead, Mr. Haynes," angrily, " if it were yours you'd not——"

" Sh ! Bert, it's no——"

"All right, Min, all right, but I'll have my say. Now look here, Mr. Haynes, I'm the father of the child and I've got a say in it. I'm not saying you're not doing everything, but I *do* say, and I'm not the only one in Welling by long chalks, I say it's a job for Scotland——"

"I'm sorry, Mr. Robson," rising and turning to the door. "Perhaps another——"

"Sorry hell!" furiously, "if you won't do nothing then we'll find someone who will. No, and *that* won't wash. I'm not going to be shut up by anybody. I know my rights. If you won't call in Scotland Yard I will. And there's hundreds in Welling 'll back me up. All right, *all* right, we're going. Come on, Min. It's time *we* did something 't any rate."

"Ah, here you are, Bert, we'd given you up. Thought 'Aynesey 'd clinked you. What 'you having? Right. Get that down you. Here we are, let's have a sit down."

"A-h-h! that was a bit of all right. My throat was like a file. Yes," nodding, "I've had some backchat with Haynes. Proper up-and-a-downer. I'll tell you in a minute. What are you going to have?"

"'S all right, Bert, they're on us to-night. Same again, Mr. Peters. Well, did you give him it straight?"

"I did that. The straight griffin."

"What did he say? Lost his wool?"

"Not half. Tore his shirt off. But all very 'aughty; you know."

"Yes. How did you start?"

"Did the polite. I took the missis along. Very polite and quiet. So was 'Aynes. Toffs both of us."

"Go on."

"It was the wife stuck him the first one, a real gutser. Ay, she did that. The first real one. 'Isn't it time,' she said,

' if the Yard knows all about it ' (he'd told us the Yard knew ; one up to him *that* was) ' if the Yard knows all about it that they *done* something. *Done* something,' she says. Real nasty.

" He didn't like that, and he began to get nasty. ' We,' he says, ' *we*,' very important, 'are doing everything human beings *can* do, Mrs. Robson.'

" But I lugged him back. ' But what are Scotland *Yard* doing ? ' I asked him. ' Two heads are better than one.'

" And then he give the whole show away. Took the wind out of our sails, and no error. What d'you think ? "

" Gawd knows."

" Says the Yard won't interfere until he *asks* them."

" 'Struth. What did you say ? I know what I'd a' said. What about you, Jack ? Ay, that's it ; *and* me."

" And that's just about what I *did* tell him. I said, ' Look here, I'm her father, and I'm not satisfied. It's too big a job for you, and I'm not the only one 'at thinks it, not by a long chalk.' "

" That was a nasty one."

" Ay, and he bit it. Got up and showed us the door. Polite still but nasty. But I give him another one, one for his knob, as we went out. Told him I was going to write to the Yard myself, and that there were hundreds in Welling who'd back me up."

" That's the stuff. What did he say to that ? "

" Dumb as a fish. All doggo. Well, that's that. I won't stop too long. It's lonely for the missis."

" Are you writing to-night, straight away ? "

" Well, not straight away. Wants a bit of thinking over."

" You're right. *An'* thinking out. You won't have another ? Sure ? Well, cheerio Bert."

" Ser long, Alf ; ser long, Jack."

TP

CHAPTER XIX

PELION UPON OSSA

I

" It is high time we took the gloves off over this business,"
Owen Jones remarked to Mason on Friday morning.

Mason nodded. " Yes, and put on knuckle-dusters. Shall
I do the slugging ? "

" Leave it to me."

The editor of *The Welling Sentinel* usually gave two hours
each Friday afternoon to the building (his own word) of
his weekly leader. At least upon this occasion the two hours
were well-spent.

" Seven days have passed (began the editorial, headed
Plain English, in the next day's issue) since foul murder
struck down two innocent young children in the very heart
of our city. Seven days. And the blood of these two babes
still cries to Heaven for vengeance.

" What are our local police doing ?

" What has Superintendent Haynes done ?

" The mills of God grind slowly. Is our Superintendent
waiting for God's mills to grind ? Let us give him another
text : God helps those who help themselves.

" We have peculiar opportunities of knowing the feelings
of our citizens in most matters that concern their welfare,
or the welfare of their city. An editor is, by virtue of his
office, the recipient of many confidences ; he has his finger
upon the pulse of the city's heart ; and of that heart he
often knows the deepest, the sincerest, the dearest thoughts.

" We say without fear, without hesitation, without favour,

that the people of Welling are not satisfied that everything which could be done to bring the murderer to justice
has been done.

" We say quite frankly that the citizens of Welling demand that the experts from Scotland Yard shall be asked to
take the case, and asked *without any further delay*.

" We say that Welling will not hold our own police guilt-
less if the dastard be allowed to escape. Already the sands
are running out ; already it may be too late ; already fresh
deeds of horror may be planning ; *already one or more of our
little ones may have seen its last dawn*.

" In the words of *Ecclesiastes* : To everything there is a
season, and a time to every purpose under the heaven ;
a time to be born and a time to die ; a time to plant and a
time to pluck up that which is planted ; a time to kill and a
time to heal . . . a time to keep silence and a time to speak.

" Those words, and we refer our readers to the full passage, are as true to-day as when they were written.

" In speaking as frankly as we have done we have followed
their teaching. We commend that teaching to Superintendent Haynes.

" We need the assistance of Scotland Yard.

" That assistance we must have.

" *At once*."

2

It was the Dean's invariable custom to rise at seven on
Sunday mornings. The maid took early tea for two to Mrs.
Perseval's room a minute or so before seven and knocked at
Dr. Perseval's door. The Dean then joined his wife for tea
and a chat before going for his bath.

Mrs. Perseval had, however, spent the Christmas in
Cumberland with Gillian, who had some weeks previously

given birth to a baby boy. Mrs. Perseval had prolonged her stay into the New Year, and was not expected back before the end of January.

The Dean had therefore, during his wife's absence, had his early tea brought in to him at seven on Sundays, and at eight on the other days of the week.

A light and uneasy sleeper, his somewhat irritable "Come in" always followed close upon the sound of the maid's tap, so close indeed, and so unvarying, that the girl's hand slipped to the door handle without a pause.

Upon this Sunday morning, however, she had turned the handle automatically before realising that the habitual "Come in" had not been spoken. She allowed the handle to revolve back and knocked again. After waiting a moment she put her ear to the door. Then she knocked sharply.

She stood uncertain what to do. It was a new experience, a new problem. Ought she to enter, or would it not be best to take back the tea to the kitchen, and explain things to the housekeeper when she took up her tea? She was young and new to service, and the question of making decisions had not often troubled her.

She knocked again very loudly.

And then, with sudden determination, she turned the handle and entered.

The tray fell with a crash. She screamed twice on a high-pitched hysterical note, and emerging panic-stricken, with a hand to her mouth, she ran blindly downstairs into the arms of George, who was making for the kitchen for his own tea.

George, an ex-soldier, morose, silent, and completely disillusioned over the wiles and charms of women (he'd more paying hobbies, as he expressed it) took the frightened girl by the arm and held her roughly. " What the devil——" And then he saw her white, scared face.

" Here, what's bit you ? " he asked, releasing her.

At the end of her first stammered sentence he again took her arm, and pushing her with a sort of rough kindness into the kitchen, said, " You make yourself a cup of tea. Now stop crying. Not a word to anyone. Leave it to me."

He went up to Dr. Perseval's room, pushed the door wide and entered. He stared at the tumbled bed and whistled between his teeth. He had seen many trench shambles in France, but somehow this mess in a pleasantly furnished room of a familiar house turned his stomach over.

He came out on tip-toe, removing the key from the door. Then, locking it from the outside, he pocketed the key, and hurrying downstairs, set off for the police-station.

The sergeant on duty listened to him in silence. " You locked the door ? " he said at the end of the recital. " Sure ? Good. Have you the key ? Thanks. Well, wait, will you, a few minutes." He turned to the desk telephone and in a few seconds was speaking with Superintendent Haynes.

Nineteen minutes later Haynes, Dr. Rushton, the police-surgeon, and Constable Baxter entered the Dean's bedroom.

The dead man lay sprawled across the tumbled bed. His pyjamas had been stripped from his body and lay a small bloody bundle of rags upon the carpet. Sheets, blankets and eiderdown were torn and drenched with blood. The pillows lay in a corner.

The dead man's skull was smashed in ; his face beaten and pulped out of all resemblance to humanity ; his throat and chest were torn and savaged as if by the attack of a beast. His left arm, twisted and broken and partly wrenched from its socket, was doubled under him.

After the briefest examination the three men left the room, locking the door behind them.

Before the Cathedral clock struck nine the news had leapt in hushed scared whispers from house to house, from lip to ear, in every street, road, and by-way of the city. Haynes had had a long telephone conversation with London, and while he had sat waiting for his trunk call to go through, the Dean's car with Max and Freda inside, bewildered, a little scared, but very excited, was bowling along the Darum road *en route* for Salisbury where their grandmother lived. They knew something had happened, but then so many things had happened lately ; first Gillian went away, and then mother, and it really did not seem to make much difference ; if anything it was nicer, for they'd far more freedom without Gillian's and mother's watching eyes. And now here was an unexpected holiday with Gran at Salisbury. Gran, whose house was ever so much bigger than the Deanery ; Gran, who allowed them lots of pocket money, and who didn't mind how many sweets they ate. And there were ponies there, too, and bicycles. And Gran had three cars and hundreds of servants. What tremendous luck ! when they hadn't dared to hope they'd see Salisbury and Gran for quite a year.

3

At five minutes past three that afternoon a special train from Paddington pulled into Welling Station. The special had done the two hundred and fifty miles in something under four hours. Out of the single Pullman coach stepped Superintendent Allen and Detective Sergeant Greer from Scotland Yard.

Haynes was there to meet them, and after a brief visit to the Deanery, the three men repaired to Haynes's office at the police-station.

Before the three officers had left the Deanery the news of the Scotland Yard men's arrival was common knowledge. Welling, dangerously near the border-line dividing sanity from that queer incalculable state of wild and terror-fraught hysteria known as panic, breathed a vast sigh of relief, the comforted relief of the frightened child who, huddled alone and terrified in bed, hears his father's footstep without, and whispers to himself that now all is well.

" We'll see first if I've got the hang of things, Haynes," said Superintendent Allen, as they sat down and Haynes rang for a constable to bring them tea. " I may say we expected your call a little sooner, eh, Greer ? Well, now, roughly, things are something like this : you've been at Welling five years. Apart from trifles, Welling, up to about a year ago, was a well-behaved peaceable place—no crime at all in fact. And then, a year last Christmas I think ? Yes. A year last Christmas begins a series of criminal acts—a connected series probably, anyhow possibly. These were : brawling in the Cathedral ; followed by sacrilege ; next some dozen or so acts of destruction and incendiarism during a single week. There is then a pause of how many months ? Nearly twelve. That's so. And then, in the space of a week, we have two children murdered and Dr. Perseval. That embraces all the violent acts, I believe ? "

" There was the pursuit of Roy Hartley by a local workman. It was certainly violent and in intent murderous ; the fellow had a gun."

" Yes. But a separate business. Not in the sequence. Or do you think . . . ? "

" I'm uncertain. This Roy Hartley business was queer. I think I've told you all of it."

" Yes. Queer, certainly, but—well, we'll not rule it out altogether, but for the moment we may omit it, I fancy. You've never managed to get on his track since he left Welling ? Nor Smith ? No. There was a maid who disappeared. Did you get anything there ? "

Haynes shook his head. " She'd only been here a week.

Her story was a lie. She was supposed to have a mother at Silchester and to have been leading a sort of gipsy life for years selling goods with a caravan. There were her mother and father and herself. Her father was supposed to have died at Silchester."

" Yes ? "

" Tissue of lies. No one answering in any way to their description known at Silchester."

" H'm. Y-e-e-s. But wasn't she a prostitute—or at least of that class ? You said——"

" Well, yes. A little trollop, anyhow."

" Yes. Well, they're birds of passage. Of course they lie. She may be connected with the affair, as may Roy Hartley, but just now we'll leave her out. Roy Hartley was a young clergyman ? "

Haynes nodded. " Yes. I've two items of information regarding him ; perhaps three. He was ordained in 1923 ; he has not been seen in England since, according to his bankers, in fact, since 1923 he is said to have been with a big American party excavating on the site of Babylon ; he was supposed to have spent several months in the South of France during the summer of 1924."

" Supposed ? "

" Well, if he's been with this excavating expedition——"

" Yes, I see. But of course he might—— However, we'll leave him for the time being. These violent acts by a coincidence seemed to synchronise with the arrival of newcomers at Welling. David Hartley, his two men, and a young fellow named Blaney, a schoolmaster. Anything about him ? "

Haynes shook his head. " Nor Hartley's two men. As for Hartley himself, he's a sick man, bedridden. Forde, his doctor, will vouch for him, as far as the last few months are concerned, anyhow."

" Yes. You said that there was one small matter——"

" Bates's evidence of a big, clumsy, crouching figure skulking in the grounds of the Hall just before it was fired. Yes. That and the bandstand attendant's last view of Smith. There was, also, of course, Roy Hartley. These three were all last seen in the grounds of Denacre Hall, or making their way there."

" The servant girl. What about her ? "

" No. No one saw her anywhere, as far as we can find out, after she left her situation. That's really all the facts we have."

" There's the savaging. We can rule out an animal ? Yes, it was merely a passing thought. I've never seen such extraordinarily brutal mutilation of a body before. The children were also . . . Yes. H'm. Well, Greer, what do you make of it. Not much ? No. My opinion too. You'll want to get back to the Deanery, I expect. Yes. I think we'd better see the two men who found the children's bodies. We shall want to see Hartley, but that can wait. The morning, I think, will do for the men. By the bye, I'd like that gunning fellow who chased young Hartley to be here in the morning also. All right, Greer. I'll be along later, unless you're back. Well, Haynes, to-morrow morning at eight-thirty."

Constable Baxter, who should have reported off duty at six on the Monday morning, was discovered by his relief lying dead behind the bandstand. His helmet and baton were missing ; his head was battered into an unrecognizable mush ; his left thigh was broken and the ribs on his left were stove in. Before he had been killed his dentures had apparently been crammed down his throat.

And Welling perturbed, horrified, and most uncomforted, once more drew near to the haunted borderland of panic.

CHAPTER XX

WELLING IS NEWS

I

In seven days Welling had jumped from a six-line news item to at least a column 'special' in all the national newspapers.

Late on Monday afternoon the star-reporters and the camera-men began to arrive by rail and road; and by noon on Tuesday few, if any, of the big dailies were not represented on the spot by men whose names were common currency in Fleet Street. *The Yorkshire News* indeed jerked that voluble war-knight correspondent, Sir Henry Shore-Williams, out of his comfortable retirement to cover the story, while *The Manchester Warrior* persuaded Wallace Bernard, the eminent crime-novelist, to put his theories to the test to the tune of a column a day.

The Morning Clarion man button-holed Haynes on the steps of the Town Hall before that worried officer had digested his breakfast.

"I've nothing to say at all," snapped Haynes sharply, "nothing, nothing."

"There's no doubt, of course, that it's the work of one man," suggested the reporter.

"Possibly not. I can tell you nothing. This is not the time for guessing or for talking. Our hands are too full."

"Then you've——"

"No time to spare. Good-morning."

The Mayor, when interviewed by *The Wire* representative was equally reticent about the facts, although not unwilling to talk generalities. " Everything is being done, everything, but the matter is in the hands, the very capable hands, of our own police under Superintendent Haynes. With the assistance of Scotland Yard, which is now available, I think there is every hope that the criminal will shortly be apprehended. Very shortly, I may say."

" You think an arrest is imminent ? "

" I think, I am sure, that certain lines the police are following will bring good results."

" Those lines point in a certain direction ? "

" Undoubtedly."

" To a certain person ? "

" I cannot go as far as that. Naturally and rightly, the police keep their own counsel."

" There is considerable uneasiness in Welling ? "

" Naturally there is some—er—anxiety."

" But nothing in the nature of a panic ? The people don't fear further violence ? "

" The city is quite calm. The people have implicit faith in the police."

" Just as a personal view, sir, do you think the facts point to a native, or rather a resident, shall we say, of some years' standing, as the perpetrator ? Do you——"

" I'm afraid it is too early to answer that. You must really excuse me now."

Clarence George, as a friend of the literary editor of *The Daily Leader*, took charge of that paper's representative and invited him to lunch. " You've not the faintest hope of getting any official information," said George after a meal, " first, because there's none ; and second, because Haynes daren't, even if he wanted to, open his mouth, lest the big fellow from the Yard put his fist into it."

" Perhaps you yourself, Mr. George——"

" Well," judicially, " what little information there is I

have. We of the Press, you know. Yes, what little there is."

" You think——"

" I think, or rather, I'm sure. I'm prepared to wager the murderer will be found not a quarter of a mile from where we're now sitting."

" Found ? Do you mean his body ? You think——"

" I don't think anything. You must allow me a certain discretion. But your people should have the story covered from a new angle. Who's your news editor, Brampton, eh ? Brampton. No I don't know him. Cossor's the man I was thinking of ; he's the literary editor. Well he'll put it to Brampton that, say, a couple of wild-life articles on the district would rivet attention far more than the ordinary reporter's clap-trap. Saving your presence, you know. You might sound Brampton. I've the stuff ready—just a little linking-up to connect on with the outrages. I'll tell you a man to see for news : my neighbour, Colonel Bowers. He's a theory by the way that all the crimes were committed by a local recluse named ffoliot. He may wax eloquent and expansive on that topic, if you handle him skilfully. But come into the garden and see my dogs before you go, and Lillibulero. Lillibulero ? Simply marvellous. A toad, and as intelligent as Larry. That's Larry ; down, sir ! Wake up, Nell, you lazy old darling. Come out of it Larry ! Don't skulk in company. Say how de do, Lilli. You see that window ? That's my study ; the finest panoramic view of Welling possible. You'd better send your camera-man round. And don't forget about Brampton. You'll catch Bowers before he goes out if you're sharp."

" I never give interviews to the Press."

" I'm sorry, sir, but your neighbour, the distinguished writer——"

" Mr. George ? "

" Yes, sir. Mr. George sent me along."

" Oh, Mr. George sent you along, hey ! "

" I'll hardly presume to that extent, sir ; but he certainly suggested you might care to talk——"

" Did he make any further suggestions ? "

" Well, sir, he said you'd a theory that the crimes were committed by a local recluse."

" A *what* ? "

" A recluse."

" Oh. A recluse. Was Mr. George good enough to give the name of this retiring gentleman ? "

" Folyat was the name, sir, I think. Yes, Folyat."

" ffoliot ! " smiling a trifle grimly ; " so Mr. George said that, hey. H'm ! I suppose it often happens in your—er —profession. Well, never mind, nothing. You don't know Mr. George very well ? Of course not. He didn't suggest that another suspect was a Mr. Owen Jones, by any chance. No. He's doubtless keeping that for your next visit. Well, I'm sorry I can tell you nothing. You'll have a drink before you go ? "

2

The Morning Clarion on Wednesday gave a column to the interview between their special representative and Superintendent Haynes.

"The capable local Superintendent" (began the report), " despite sleepless nights and harassed days, very courteously granted me some precious minutes.

" He replied to my first question by stating emphatically that nothing was *known*. It was, however, obvious from his emphasis that a very great deal was suspected. He did not contradict my suggestion that the police were following a line of investigation that would shortly lead to an arrest.

An arrest, one may venture to say without stretching the facts, is imminent.

"The difficulties of the case have been immense, and it is no exaggeration to say that rarely has the Yard had so difficult a problem to solve."

The article then reviewed the main facts of the affair, adding a few biographical and topographical details, and concluding with the words : Pictures on back page.

These pictures included a panoramic view of Welling from Belton Bridge, a sheepish looking portrait of Maxton, the labourer who had found Donald Petit's body, and a back-view of Superintendent Haynes.

The Wire of Wednesday had a two-column spread : *Exclusive Interview with the Major of Welling.*

" Mr. Andrew Banks, the Mayor of Welling" (began the account) "readily acceded to my request for an interview.

"Mr. Banks, who in private life is the well-known inventor and manufacturer of the non-slip stud, emphasised the complete trust of Welling in its police, a force than which there is no more efficient body in the Kingdom. Welling was fortunate, he pointed out, to have the services of Superintendent Haynes, who was now working on the case in collaboration with Superintendent Allen and Detective-Sergeant Greer from Scotland Yard.

"His worship was of the opinion that an arrest is imminent.

" ' I have no doubt at all in my mind,' he said emphatic-ally, ' that the lines upon which the police are now working will bring things to a successful issue.'

" ' You think,' I asked, ' that these lines point in a certain very definite direction ? '

" ' Undoubtedly ; a *very* definite direction.'

" ' And toward a certain person ? '

" ' That would be indiscreet. It is for the police to say.'

"The reply, given with a whimsical twist of the lips, left

no doubt in my mind that a certain person was designated, and that the Mayor, were such frankness permissible and expedient, could have given the name that will, it is to be hoped, very shortly be common property."

The report ended with the words: See pictures on back page.

The photographs included a panoramic view of Welling taken from the cupola of the Town Hall, a view of the Teal estuary from Belton Bridge, a particularly inappropriate smiling portrait of Baxter the murdered constable, and a grotesquely unusual aspect of the Cathedral taken from the roof of *The Sentinel* office.

The Daily Leader had a triumphant three columns: From our Special Representative.

"We have been fortunate enough" (said an editorial note) "to obtain for our readers the exclusive views of the Welling horror from two of that city's most distinguished residents, Mr. Clarence George, the writer, whose name and fame and writings are not strangers to our columns, and Colonel Bowers, D.S.O., who commanded the 1st Batt. of the Meadshires in England during the war. He was awarded the D.S.O. at Spion Kop, and was twice mentioned in despatches by Sir Redvers Buller.

"Mr. Clarence George" (the report began) "who received me most courteously and genially, and entertained me to luncheon at his charming villa in the North Close, was emphatically of the opinion that an arrest was imminent. Mr. George further enunciated the startling view that the murderer would be found, and found shortly, within the Cathedral precincts, *or not far therefrom.*

" 'We, in Welling,' went on the distinguished writer, ' have the fullest confidence in our local police, and now that Scotland Yard has arrived to collaborate with our own men, we are convinced that confidence will shortly be justified.

" ' It is strange,' the great naturalist continued, ' that it needs a loathsome crime to focus the eyes of England upon one of her beauty spots, and one, I may say, whose flora and fauna are unsurpassed in charm and interest.'

" Returning, with obvious reluctance, to the question of the murderer, the famous author, his fine eyes sparkling with his reckless disregard of discretion, bluntly named to me the wanted man, and suggested that corroboration of his opinion might be obtained from his neighbour, Colonel Bowers.

" After a pleasurable, and all too brief, visit to the pets in the celebrated naturalist's garden (not forgetting Lily, the wonderful frog) I was compelled to hurry off for my appointment with the gallant Colonel.

" Our interview was as brief and as businesslike as one would expect in dealing with a soldier.

" ' A terrible affair,' agreed the Colonel, ' but we've every hope now of a—well—as you may—oh, decidedly.'

" ' You think an arrest is imminent ? '

" ' Undoubtedly. I expect an arrest shortly, very shortly.'

" Colonel Bowers then succinctly reviewed the happenings in Welling during the previous twelve months.

" Before leaving, I ventured to mention the name Mr. Clarence George had suggested as that of the murderer. While expressing no surprise or disagreement the distinguished soldier obviously had information pointing to an entirely different person."

The back page of *The Daily Leader* contained a panoramic view of Welling from Clarence George's study window ; a portrait of the naturalist with Larry and Nell at his feet, a squirrel on his shoulder and Lillibulero squatting on his palm ; and a dreary looking view of the hedge behind which was found the body of little Amy Robson.

CHAPTER XXI

BRASS-TACKS

I

The inquest on Dr. Perseval was held on Tuesday, and that of P.C. Baxter the next day. In both cases a verdict of wilful murder by some person or persons unknown was returned.

Giving evidence at Baxter's inquest, the police-surgeon, Dr. Rushton, ventured the opinion that the constable had been knocked out by a blow on the point of the jaw, and then battered with his own baton. "It is possible," said Dr. Rushton, "that the force of the blow broke the unfortunate man's dentures, and the shock caused him to swallow them. The further brutal treatment to which the victim was subjected was probably committed after his death."

Dr. Forde, replying to the coroner at the inquest on Dr. Perseval, said that death was probably caused by the injuries to the brain. It was, however, difficult to judge with precision, owing to the savage mutilations, most of which, especially those of the throat, were sufficient to cause death. He was, however, of the opinion that the savaging was done after death, with the possible exception of the injuries to the arm and shoulder socket. He inclined to the view that the head injuries were caused by a metal instrument, such as a burglar's jemmy, or an iron stancheon or railing.

"Or a flatiron?" asked the coroner.

Dr. Rushton looked surprised. "Well, yes, possibly; by the apex of the iron, or one of the corners."

Up

" A flatiron was found this morning by the gardener at the Deanery. It was lying under some bushes, and from its position might have been flung out of the open bedroom window. It was rather rusty, but not otherwise soiled or stained. There have, however, been many hours of rain since the night of the murder. You would not rule out such a weapon ? "

" No," doubtfully, " but it has obvious disadvantages for a surprise attack."

The police surgeon, while corroborating Dr. Forde's medical evidence, was of the opinion that the throat injuries were the cause of death. " I think that Dr. Perseval was savagely strangled before he was well awake, and that the other injuries were due to maniacal blood-lust. The bed," he added, " shewed signs of a struggle which one would not expect if death were due to a smashing blow on the head."

" You do not mean that Dr. Perseval was strangled while asleep ? "

" No. Strangling during normal sleep is, of course, impossible. There is bound to be awaking, and consequent struggling. Two minutes, at the least, would elapse before unconsciousness began."

The funeral of the Dean and the constable took place the next day, and Welling, a city of mourning, followed its two citizens to their graves.

In consequence of an hysterical article in Saturday's *Sentinel* headed *Is Anyone Safe ?* Superintendent Haynes called upon Owen Jones at his private house. The interview was brief but warm. Whether it would have borne fruit will never be known, for by the time the next issue went to Press there was nothing more to be said, unless it were in the nature of an apology.

2

On Sunday afternoon January 16th, Haynes, Allen, and Greer met in Haynes's small office to review the events of the week. That week had been a busy but a fruitless one.

"Let's get things clear," said Allen. "First, we'll tackle what we know. There's the matter of the footprints. It was rather lucky the frost broke and turned to rain over a week ago, but not so lucky that it's poured ever since. There were quite a dozen distinct footprints in the Dean's kitchen garden, and it seems pretty obvious that the man who murdered the Dean shinned up the water pipe, assisting himself by the tall trellis. As far as the children are concerned the snow obliterated all traces of footprints. However, we find that the trail of prints that made a beeline across the garden of Denacre Hall, was made, as far as can be judged, by the same man. But the impressions were so softened by rain that they might have been made by any dozens of boots of about the same size. It doesn't help us much. They were certainly big boots. Much bigger than those worn by Crowson or Bates. We'll return to these two gentlemen in a moment.

"Finger-prints : an embarrassment of riches, isn't it ? But unfortunately only in the Dean's room. And they're by no one of whom we've a record. That doesn't get us far for the moment. Now, Greer, your talk with Crowson and Bates. There was no difficulty about it ? No. Well we'll take Crowson first. A blank pretty nearly, wasn't it ? "

"Practically, sir. Crowson did say, however, that he'll be glad to clear out. The job's not to his liking, despite the unusual rate of pay."

"In what way, Greer ? "

"Well, he's been at a loose end apparently for weeks now. The car hasn't been out except to run the valet into

Welling for shopping. Crowson seems to be the sort of chap that can't content himself with idleness ; doesn't read and has no hobbies except his engine ; and I gather he's given so much time to that and the car that they'd not shame a battleship. Even then time has hung a lot on his hands."

" Any information about him. Does he drink? Go whoring ? Has he a girl locally, do you know ? "

" There's nothing known against him. He visits *The Crown* occasionally, but is very moderate. No, there's nothing."

" Except that he's in a hurry to quit ? "

" Well," hesitatingly, " I rather think he's scared."

" H'm, the whole city is scared, for that matter."

" More than that ; a little personal fright all to himself. He's scared of his employer."

" That's more promising. Just how ? "

" He won't be drawn, but there have been things happening at the Hall which have frightened him."

" Does he say when he's going ? "

" Yes. As soon as his boss is about again. He's been wanting to give in his notice he says for a long while, months in fact."

" Months ? "

" So he says. But he's not been able to see Hartley, and Bates has persuaded him against giving in his notice by writing."

" So he's been scared for months ? "

" He didn't actually say so, but I gathered as much."

" Yes. What do you make of that, Haynes ? "

" The murders have nothing to do with his funk ? Isn't that it ? "

" Or that he was expecting them, and wanted to get away beforehand. Perhaps we won't go as far as that : shall we say he feared something or other pretty bad was likely to happen, because—eh ? "

" Because he's already *seen* some queer things ? " ventured Haynes.

" Yes. Seen and heard probably. Now what or *who* was there for him to see and hear ? "

" No one, as far as I know. There was Roy Hartley, of course."

" Yes. He lived there some months, didn't he. Had visitors doubtless. Did Crowson say anything about Mr. Roy Hartley, Greer ? "

" No, sir. He didn't say much about anything."

" Well, now Bates. What did you get out of him ? "

" Nothing at all. He simply said he knew nothing, and had never seen anything, or heard anything unusual."

" That was a lie, of course. He's changed his tune, hasn't he, Haynes ? Didn't he tell you something about a hulking, crouching figure he saw over a year ago ? "

" Yes. He'd possibly forgotten."

" No. I rather think if we knew all Bates knows we'd not have far to go. Does he talk of leaving ? Is *he* scared ? "

" No ; just bad-tempered. He said he'd be there until Mr. Hartley was dead."

" Dead ? Is that what he said ? "

" Yes. He said the boss was dying ; mentioned it quite casually, as if it were common knowledge."

" Well, he's more or less right," said Haynes. " Dr. Forde is there every other day, often every day. Hartley is practically bedridden. He's been weakening now for months."

" Was he an invalid when he came ? "

" Not in the slightest. He looked a strong healthy man, not much over middle-age. Good for thirty years."

" What's his trouble ? "

" Heart."

" I'm afraid we shall have to see him. We'll consult Forde first. Let's see, it's four now. Ring up Forde, will you, Greer. Yes ; say we'll come round at once, or if he prefers it, you'll run him here in the car."

Greer was soon through, and after a short conversation he said, " Dr. Forde is coming round now, sir. He'll be here in a few minutes."

" Good. Let's have some tea, Haynes. As soon as we've had a talk with the doctor we'll go round to the Hall. I'd like to have a few words with Bates first, but perhaps that would be best left till afterward. I'm rather inclined to have Bates here."

" Not Crowson ? "

" I don't think so, Haynes. Crowson's scared, and obviously doesn't know much. He's merely guessing ; probably is doubtful if it's not all imagination ; thinks it's too queer to be true. No, if he were scared at something he really *knew* he'd have skedaddled long ago."

" But you think Bates knows, and is therefore *not* scared."

" Yes. That's the trouble. Bates knows something ; there's no doubt about that. What he knows is apparently not enough to scare him away. Or else—well, Haynes ? "

" You don't mean that Bates is our man ? "

" Well, I don't know. Why isn't Bates scared ? Frightening things have happened at the Hall, before and after the murders—— "

" He may be too much attached to Hartley to leave him ? "

" Yes. Or he may lack imagination, and not be able to foresee—hello, here's Forde. Come in, doctor ; it's exceedingly good of you. We haven't, I hope, robbed you of a much-needed nap. You'll have some tea. We'll talk while it's coming. You'll forgive our haste. Now we want to see

Mr. Hartley. Yes. At once ; this afternoon. Is he fit to answer questions ? "

" Fit ? He's weak, of course, but there is nothing to prevent him answering questions. He's not dying, you know."

" No ? But I understood that that was just what he *was* doing ? "

Forde shook his head. " No, no. But I must qualify that a little ; he's a sick man, his heart is in a pretty bad way, and he is therefore liable to a sudden death, which, of course, in a way, may be said to be dying."

" Apart from heart affection, doctor, what is his trouble ? "

Again Forde shook his head. " He knows a great deal more about his own case than I do. I think he called me in merely for company's sake. Beyond a first examination I have done nothing, and neither prescribe for him nor advise him."

" But just what is your personal opinion, doctor, if it's not trespassing——"

" Not at all. It's not a professional secret. It's as plain to his servants as it is to me. He is suffering from senile decay."

" At sixty, or thereabouts ? "

Forde nodded. " That is the impression I got when I examined him, and that is the impression that the most inattentive visitor would get now. He's an old man, whose vitality and strength have drained out of him."

" That loss of vitality is not due to his heart affection ? "

" On the contrary, the cause of it, apparently."

" H'm. Perhaps you would come along with us, doctor. Yes ? Hello ? Come in."

A constable, flushed and breathless, entered and stood at attention.

" What is it, Robinson ? " asked Haynes.

" There's been shooting at Denacre Hall, sir. Bates, the vally, is dead, and the chauffeur is badly hurt."

" Where is the chauffeur now ? How do you mean, badly hurt ? Is he dying ? "

" We took him into one of the downstairs rooms, sir. Sergeant Clarke is with him. Shot through the shoulder and groin, sir. He's not unconscious. Doesn't seem to be in much pain. Dr. Rushton has just gone up."

" H'm. What car have you outside ? "

" The big Daimler, sir."

" Come along then, Haynes, Greer, doctor, you'll come, will you. Have you seen Mr. Hartley, Robinson ? "

" No, sir. There was no sign of anyone about."

" You didn't go up to his study? Didn't try to find him?"

" No, sir."

" All right. You're sure it was shooting ? "

" Yes, sir. Crowson said so himself. It was his revolver."

" *His ?* Never mind. Come along. You're driving ? Good. Tell me as we go."

CHAPTER XXII

SILENCE OF DAVID HARTLEY

" Was the valet killed outright, Robinson ? "

" Yes, sir."

" Where was he shot ? Through the head ? "

" He wasn't shot, sir."

" Not shot ? "

" No, sir ; his head was battered in. With a large stone. A big flint the size of my two fists ; so Crowson told us."

" Us ? "

" Yes, sir. Sergeant Clarke and myself. I was making for the station to report off duty and met Sergeant Clarke by The Pines. We stood talking for a minute, and were just parting, when we heard two shots fired quickly. They came from the direction of the Hall, and we both started off at once. We thought we heard two more then, but they were very faint."

" You didn't think it was a shot-gun ? Someone rabbiting ? "

" No, sir ; they were too sharp for that. I thought it was a rifle."

" What was it ? An automatic ? "

" No, sir ; an army service revolver. Crowson——"

" All right, thank you, Robinson. Here we are. You say Sergeant Clarke's there. Right. Remain here with the car. Are you ready, doctor ? "

Three minutes later Doctor Rushton met the party as it trooped quietly into the corridor leading from the east to the west wing.

" How's Crowson ? " asked Allen.

" Pretty fair. I'm waiting for the ambulance. Clarke is with him."

" You think he'll recover ? "

" He's a chance, but not a very big one. The bullet that entered at the left groin, has, I fancy, smashed the haunch-bone of the pelvis ; it has not emerged. There is rather severe intestinal hæmorrhage."

" Is he in much pain ? Can he stand questioning ? "

" He's a bit drowsy. I've given him a quarter grain injection. No ; he's in no pain just at present. You can question him."

" Stopped one, eh, Crowson ? " said Allen, as he, Haynes and Dr. Forde seated themselves by the lounge on which the chauffeur had been laid. " All right, Clarke ; you'll find Greer outside. You might see if you can get a word with Mr. Hartley."

" Not that I think he will," he said to Haynes, as the Sergeant left the room. " I fancy the bird has flown."

" Two," said Crowson weakly, but smiling.

" *Two ?* "

" Yes. I stopped two."

" Yes ! of course. Do you feel you can tell us something about it."

" I'm all right. I'll tell you what I know."

" That's fine. Go ahead."

" I'd got the car outside the garage. The engine had been running badly. Not that I'd been out in her, but I'd been running her in the garage. I'd just been altering the timing. I'd got the bonnet raised and was stooping down talking to Bates, who was on the other side sitting on the rear mud-guard."

" You couldn't see him ? Was the engine running ? "

" No, I was stooping. No, the engine wasn't running. It had been and I was going to start up again in a moment."

" Good."

" We were talking about what everyone else is talking about just now—the horrible things that had been happening round about. Bates was saying something about being fed up with things, when he suddenly stopped. Just then the end of the wrench I was tightening up with slipped and jammed itself against the shaft, and in trying to release it I forgot about Bates. I noticed, in a way, that he'd stopped talking, and yet I *didn't* notice it, if you understand what I mean."

" Yes, quite."

" The wrench came loose with a jerk, and I barked my knuckles. I was swearing to myself when I heard a queer noise from the other side of the car. I think it 'd been going on for a good time before I really noticed it, before I *listened* to it, as you may say."

" Yes. What sort of noise was it ? "

" Like heavy breathing, sort of as if someone was trying to breathe under water."

" Yes."

" And then there was a bump as if something had dropped on to the car. It shook me and I called out, ' What the devil're you up to ? ' And then I stood up and looked over to where Bates had been. I didn't see him for a second, but I saw someone else. And I don't want to see anyone like it again."

" A man ? "

" Yes. A big hulking sort of slouching chap. Long arms hanging down his sides and a great stone in one of his hands. I could see blood on it and what I thought was bits of a mat."

" Just a moment. Was he like anyone you know ? "

" God, no ! I've seen things at the pictures like him. He'd a pasty sort of face and a big mouth too full of great teeth. He was staring at me and grinning. Just for half a moment I thought his eyes seemed like—but it was only fancy of course. I——"

" Never mind about it being fancy. His eyes seemed like whose ? "

" Well, a bit like the guv'nor's. It was the colour being the same, I suppose, and it being a queer colour, a sort of washed out blue."

" That's interesting. Yes."

" It's taking a long while to tell, but it all happened in a couple of seconds or so. I turned my head from looking at him, and then I saw poor Bates sprawling over the mudguard, his face and head all bashed in. I let out a shout and the devil with the stone made for me. I always carry my service revolver in a holster at the side of the car. It's a fad of mine. I thought he was going to let rip with the flint at me and I ducked and slipped round to the step, grabbed my revolver, and as he came round the bonnet I fired twice before he collared me."

" You missed ? "

" Must have done. Anyway, it didn't stop him, and before I knew what was happening he'd got his arms round me. Must have dropped the stone. But I don't know. It was like being smothered by a bear. And then the revolver went off and I felt a horrible wrenching burning sort of pain in the guts. And I think I fainted. I do seem to remember something like being lifted up in the air and chucked away ; but I'm not certain. The next thing I *do* remember is being here where I am now." His face was suddenly twisted by a spasm of pain.

" Hurting you ? Dr. Rushton will look after you. There was only one shot fired after he got hold of you ? "

" I only heard one, and only felt one. But I've a packet in the shoulder as well. I don't remember it. God !

My guts are hurting now. Could I have a drink? I feel sick."

At that moment Dr. Rushton entered, and rising to go the two officers left the wounded man in his charge. "The ambulance has arrived," said Rushton, as they were closing the door; "you've finished?"

"Thanks, doctor, yes. Send Clarke along with it to the hospital with instructions to wait there until he's relieved."

Allen closed the door softly, and then opened it again, and putting in his head said, "It's all right, doctor, here is Clarke. I'll see to it. Dr. Forde, perhaps you'll join us. We'll just take a look at Bates."

The body of the valet was lying upon a mackintosh sheet on the floor of a small sitting-room at the far end of the corridor. Another mackintosh sheet covered it, leaving the boots protruding.

Allen raised the sheet from the head and looked down at the smashed and battered face and skull. He turned his glance to Haynes, Greer, and Dr. Forde standing beside him. No one spoke. He lowered the sheet gently over the broken head and moving aside led the way into the corridor.

"And now for Mr. Hartley," he said, rather as one asking a question than making a statement. "Where is his bedroom, doctor?"

"He's quite likely to be in his study," rejoined Forde; "he's *not* bedridden, you know, despite all the talk to the contrary."

"When did you see him last, doctor?"

"Friday. It was before lunch, and he was then sitting in his study writing. Hardly the action of a bedridden man. His bedroom's on the next floor and his study the floor above, next to the library. So we'll take them as we go. Here we are." Dr. Forde stopped outside a door and knocked twice. As there was no response he knocked again loudly, without result.

" I think we may as well go in," said Allen, and turning the handle, pushed. The door opened, to his obvious surprise. He entered quickly, Forde by his side, and the other two following. A glance was sufficient. The bed was unoccupied and was made.

" We'll return presently," said Allen ; " there's nothing here for the moment. Will you lead the way, doctor ? "

Coming to Hartley's study door Forde repeated his performance with like result.

" We may as well enter." And turning the handle, Allen pushed, to find the door locked.

He knocked again loudly, and then beat on a panel with the side of his fist. He drew back, and taking a revolver from his pocket, he said, " Put your shoulder to it, Greer, and duck when it goes in. Keep to one side, doctor. Haynes, you'll follow me in."

The door went in with a crash, Greer ducked and fell prone. Allen cleared the fallen door with a jump, his revolver raised. And then he lowered his arm and cried out.

Supine, spread-eagled upon the floor, lay the body of David Hartley. The face was battered, but not beyond recognition. One leg was bent at the knee at an impossible angle. The throat was cut from ear to ear. A case of surgical knives, wrenched open, lay on the table, and lying about six feet away from one outflung hand of the dead man was a blood-stained lancet.

The four large windows were shut and the catches secured. On the table were two large red-bound manuscript books. The cover of one had been violently snatched off and hung by a ribbon over the edge of the table. The uncovered pages were rumpled and smeared with blood.

There was no sign of any other person living or dead in the room.

As Allen and Dr. Forde came out, leaving Haynes and Greer in the room, Allen pointed to a trail of dark spots that, in the light through the open doorway, now showed up plainly on the pale blue carpet of the passage. He stooped, touched one, and then stared at the moist red stain upon his finger-tip. He turned for a moment toward the room and again pointed. A trail of dark spots ran from under the smashed door across the floor to the overturned chair by the table.

CHAPTER XXIII

THE PANIC

Of the many emotional motives that may inspire and actuate a crowd the two most devastating in their effects, both momentary and lasting, are fear and cruelty—fear as portrayed by panic, and cruelty by the hue-and-cry. And cruelty is too often the child of fear.

A man or woman who joins in the orgy of a hue-and-cry returns from that primitive debauch a changed being, not marked and scarred superficially, but altered in essence, fundamentally different, the roots of life attacked, virtue gone out of them : there has been a spiritual breaking down, a decadence, a degradation.

A man or woman who has been caught up in the paralysing whirlwind of a panic has passed through an ordeal that can never be forgotten, has seen a breach made in the wall of human decencies, and through that breach has stared at unimaginable things ; has stepped forth from familiar common ground, and in one stride has come into an unknown territory, where the eye sees the incredible and the blind fingers touch the unnameable. One sees, shrinks in disgustful horror, and surrenders : panic is the unconditional capitulation of man to nature.

And Welling surrendered to panic upon the morning of Monday January 17. The shops remained closed and shuttered ; the schools opened to empty desks ; offices, warehouses and wharves, deserted by night-watchmen, waited in vain for the coming of the workers. Only the policemen, postmen, dustmen, and newsvendors went their rounds, as they will do on the eve of Judgment Day.

The morning papers did nothing to lay the evil spirit that had invaded the city ; rather did they increase the possession. No national daily gave the haunted city fewer than three columns, and by the afternoon Welling was news as far north as Spitzbergen and as far west as New York City.

At four o'clock that afternoon the police took the unprecedented action of issuing from *The Sentinel* office a single page sheet under the title of *The Welling Police Gazette*. It contained a brief statement, signed by Superintendents Allen and Haynes, to the effect that while in the present juncture no official statement could be made, yet a definite assurance could be authoritatively given that the acts of criminal violence were over. " Documents now in the possession of the police," ended the manifesto, " make it clear that with the death of David Hartley the menace has passed away. Welling citizens will show their loyalty, and best serve the interests of their city and of justice, by going about their business as usual." Twenty thousand copies were printed and distributed.

But the faith of the citizens in the efficiency and credibility of the police had been too undermined by the events of the past twelve months for this assurance to have any noticeable effect. In truth, in the eyes of many of the people, the very foundations of the earth were shaken, and the heavens seemed about to fall. About dusk, it is true, some hundreds of men and youths patrolled the streets in twos and threes and small groups, but the raising of a hue-and-cry at the expense of a burly tramp seen skulking round the bandstand, his subsequent pursuit through the city streets, and his sobbing screams as the pursuing mob overwhelmed him and trod him underfoot, more than outweighed the soothing verbiage of the Police Gazette.

Darkness fell, with Welling a frightened huddle of

WP

beleaguered fortresses, rather than a pleasant congeries of self-satisfied villas and philosophical cottages.

There were few dwelling-places that did not burn all available lights during the long hours of the night.

" Haven't *you* any information, Mason ? " asked Richard after dinner that evening. " O. J.'s now hand in glove with the peelers ; surely that's worth something in the way of a stable-tip."

" I've not gathered any. The only morsel I have is more or less common property : the peelers, as you persist in calling them, have possession of Hartley's journal."

" Which blows the whole gaff, eh ? "

" Perhaps," shrugging his shoulders. " Anyhow, we'll know to-morrow."

" The inquest ? "

" Yes. The crowd who's been subpœnaed will surprise you. I'd forgotten that scrap of information."

" Are you one ? "

" No, but I shall be there. I'll tell you a few. There's Mrs. Perseval, who was wired to on Sunday night, Forde, Bowers, George (heaven knows why), the Mayoress, our dear Letty and Ally (as Crowson's landladies, I suppose !) Thatcher Burnett and his wife, Robson at the garage, Mrs. Petit, Mrs. Baxter, the news-boy fellow Baines, Maxton and about a dozen more. It's being held at the Town Hall—one of the smaller rooms. Of course it *would* be. Accommodation for about forty people and at a moderate estimate five thousand will clamour to get in. I believe twenty-eight Press tickets have already been issued. Doors open to the public at ten-thirty and curtain goes up at eleven sharp. If you want to stand the ghost of a chance you'll have to be there by six. I'd wangle you a Press ticket if it were only a common or garden murder or rape, but this is in the prima donna class, and it can't be done. I may be squeezed out myself."

" Thanks, but I've no inclination at all in that direction. I've got the day off ; the schools will stay shut till Wednesday. What do you think will come out ? Hartley as the devil in the machine ? A sort of automatic murderer rather than a double-barrelled one. But you don't seriously think Hartley's the man ? "

" I'm damned if I know what to make of it. If Hartley's not the man who else is there that so fits the facts ? "

"But Hartley's been bedridden for weeks, months, isn't it?"

" He's not, as a matter of fact. I got that from O. J., who had it from Forde. But even that doesn't help much, for Forde is prepared to swear, will do at the inquest, I believe, that Hartley has been much too ill, too physically weak, to leave the Hall for quite six or eight weeks. He's apparently just pottered, tottered rather, from his bedroom to his study and back again. But of course, unless the journal discloses the whole affair there's not likely to be much learned about Hartley. If Crowson had pulled through it might have made all the difference."

" He didn't say anything before he died."

" No, he was rambling most of the time and doped. He thought he was back in the line. Several times Clarke and Greer (who sat by his bed eight hours without a break) thought he was talking about Hartley and began to jot it down when it dawned upon them that Crowson was praising or cussing his S.M., the colonel, or some brasshat."

" This journal, which appears to be the chief exhibit, seems to me to tell more in Hartley's favour than against him. Have you ever heard of a murderer keeping a diary of his crimes. A bit too risky altogether. I should say, speaking without the book in a double sense, that it's never been done."

Mason smiled. " I'm no expert criminologist, but it may be as well to keep in mind that Hartley's done several things in his life that haven't been done before. Isn't his whole career unprecedented ? "

" Perhaps. I'm not so sure. I fancy Hartley was only a man of very great talent. I mean he was a first-rate, super-first-rate if you like, *ordinary* man, everything of the best, you know, but built according to plan, like a millionaire's steam-yacht. Consequently in his actions and reactions he'd not differ from the normal man. Now, had Hartley been a genius——"

" Which he's generally reckoned to be," interrupted Mason.

" Bosh ! the very fact that he's ' generally reckoned ' to be by his contemporaries proves he's not. Where was I ? Why the devil do you interrupt my best moments. Just a minute. Yes. Had he been a genius I'd have agreed the journal might damn him, genius being among other things an infinite capacity for being daft. I can imagine say, da Vinci, keeping tot of his killings, but not Hartley."

" Which only gets us back again to the original question : if Hartley's not the man, who is ? "

" Hartley's journal is not necessarily connected at all with the murders. I'm prepared to believe, in fact, that Hartley's the man, but I'll not be a bit surprised if there's no word about his bloodthirsty hobby in his diary. It may only be a dull record of his little intimate personal affairs. The sort of thing we all keep for a short time at one period or other in life, usually in adolescence. You know the kind of drivel : Raining all day. Had a wretched headache. Think I shall give up smoking. No letter from Rose. N.B. Must send for that new ointment for pimples."

Mason shook his head. " There's more in it than that. I'd be prepared to wager a fair amount it'll prove a biggish thing—confession or not. I've been getting books for Hartley for the last year, and, judging from my ignoramus standpoint, he's been at work on queerish lines. Unluckily I can't read German and my Latin—well, you weren't at Winchester ? Winchester's Latin, Eton's English, and Harrow's Greek : never heard that story ? Never mind now. It's fifty per cent. libellous, like most of 'em. There's twenty minutes before *The Crown* shuts : shall we run over ? "

" Thanks, not to-night. I'm off drink altogether somehow. And I'm so sleepy I can hardly think."

" That's your gormandising plus the fire. You talk about my wolfing——"

" I know. We all eat too much. We'd be better on a quarter of the vittles we shovel down, but it's Auntie Robbins's fault, she'd demoralise a holy anchorite on a fast-day ; the man who could resist her grub's not yet born. Well, chin ! chin ! have one for me if you *will* go boozing."

CHAPTER XXIV

THE GREY GHOST AS COUNSELLOR

I

Despite his tiredness Richard could not sleep. He tried his favourite sleep-bringer, *The Life of Colonel Hutchinson* by Lucy Hutchinson, but for once it failed. He shut the book, switched off the lamp, and lay with closed eyes. And presently his imagination was staging a drama in which he fought and won a fierce verbal battle with the Lord Protector.

He switched on the light and tried Boswell, but in a short time found himself standing impudently up to Sam Johnson with figurative fingers at his nose, an attitude the great browbeater often provoked in him.

He tried a dozen volumes, one after the other, but each seemed to irritate him to more fretted wakefulness. Lamb for once lost his charm, and became no more than a child-man, pranking himself out with his latinisms and his artificial whimsies, and giving up tobacco and booze with the mannered simperings of a retiring prima donna. Byron seemed no more than a vain and pompous sensualist ; Hazlitt a bookish bore ; Dickens a weeping-willie ; Thackeray the unconscious monarch of his own snobs ; Wells a strident pedagogue ; Galsworthy a gentleman's gentleman ; Shaw an unimaginative ego-maniac ; and even William Canton a sentimentalising bletherer.

The untidy heap of books at the foot of his bed grew larger as he denuded the bookshelf at the head. The

Cathedral clock struck eleven, twelve, one and two, and still sleep eluded him.

At last, certain now that the grey ghost Insomnia, was to be his bedfellow for the night, he once more switched off the light, kicked the pile of books noisily on to the floor, and stretching out his legs, lay staring up at the shadowy blur of the ceiling.

He passed in mental review his year at Welling, and as the minutes ticked away he felt the menacing approach of that grey depression which now so often overwhelmed him.

He fought against it, striving to fill his mind with trivialities, with little foolish tags of rhyme, with memories of his childhood. He visualised numbers in chalk upon a vast blackboard, and tried to work out their square root to a dozen decimal places. He drew ingenious geometrical designs of miraculous intricacy, and pretended that he was squaring the circle.

He began upon that vast board to draw caricatures of his family, of his friends. He found himself drawing an indelicate and cruel cartoon of the dead Dean, and with a sweep of a gigantic duster wiped it off. He drew a careful portrait of Mason, and then he tried one of Rachel. And suddenly, staring at the white outline he saw that it was not Rachel but Ann. He swept the board into invisibility but from the blank darkness it left, the face of Ann looked out at him, not a mere outline of white chalk but with the vivid colours and soft shadows of life. And presently she stood there complete and whole in all her naked loveliness.

And once more the wheel began to turn, slowly breaking him.

Somewhere about five he fell into an exhausted and uneasy slumber, tormented by dreams and nightmares in all the motley of folly, grotesqueness, horror and lust.

He was woken at a quarter past seven by Rose's knock at the door with his early tea. His body was drained of vitality, his muscles ached and dragged, his mouth seemed unpleasantly full of his tongue. He sat up slowly, his head spinning. He caught sight of his face in the glass and stared disgustfully at its yellow pallor, seen so dimly in the half dawn.

" God ! I look like Methuselah," he shivered ; and padding gingerly to the door, opened it, and took in his tray. He poured himself out a cup quickly, stirred in three lumps of sugar, and drank it greedily. He lit a cigarette, and picking up his towel and shaving things, set off for the bathroom.

Half an hour later he came down to breakfast to find nothing ready. " All right, Rose," he said, " never mind bacon, I'm in a hurry. Just an egg and some coffee. Oh, well, tea then. And I shall be out all day. No. I shan't be back till late, midnight perhaps. Post in yet ? Never mind, bring them in when you bring my breakfast."

It was barely twenty minutes past eight when he came out of The Pines and set off briskly down the High Street. He had decided to do a day's tramping, and without any particular will or wish in the matter, had fixed on the same walk that he and Rachel had done together in October.

He wore an old shabby flannel suit, a tennis shirt, thick soled brown boots, was bare-headed, and carried a black-thorn he'd cut from a hedge during a walking tour some years previously.

It was a dull but mild morning, and a S.W. wind, which promised to freshen, was piling up banks of cumulus along the horizon behind him.

He passed the peeping ploughboy and the milk-maids shortly after nine, and reached Sapton warm and thirsty about ten. It wanted half an hour before opening-time, but finding he'd fewer cigarettes in his case than he thought he entered the bar of the Sapton Arms.

" Morning, zur," said the proprietor, with a nod of recognition, " warmish, zur, s'morning. Gin and ginger, zur, eh ? " smiling.

" *Are* you open yet ? "

" Oh, it's all right, zur, if you don' stan' too near the window. I'm right out of Players, zur ; on'y Woodbines and Weights. Ay, yez, not too bad. I don't smoke but a pipe myself. You'll have a Bass ? Well, thank you, zur, a cider. Thank *you*, zur. Here's my respects."

Richard dawdled on to Creyde, and thence, at a still slower pace, to Barton Olney. It was after one when he entered the little pub there and asked for something to eat.

" We've some cold mutton, to-day," said the landlord, " and hot baked potatoes and har'cot beans."

" You've not any sweet-cured bacon, by any chance," smiled Richard.

The man looked at him closely. " Why, by gor, of course, zur. I didn't recognise you. I remember you and the young lady, why, last zummer, now, wasn't it ? "

" October."

" October, it was. Yes, we've some sweet cured."

" And eggs ? "

" And eggs."

" Marrow jam made with honey by——"

" The missis ! " laughing. " She shall open a fresh pot. Du I remember now ! Two Basses in one of them blue china mugs. 'Zat right, zur ? "

Richard nodded.

" And your young lady wanted a pot for four, eh ? " chuckling. " She's not with you ? "

" In London."

" Ah. I'll just tell the missis to put the bacon on. Thank you, zur, I will."

It was nearly five when Richard reached the tiny cottage opposite the church at Banbridge. The same plump little woman smilingly believed she could give him some tea, smilingly hoped he'd not mind her company, and smilingly ushered him into the cosy little kitchen where the same bright fire winked invitingly through the glossy black bars.

" One egg, sir, or two ? " she asked.

" Supposing I said three, and a big slice of your home-made cake, what then ? "

" I'd put out the black-currant jam, which is home-made too," she laughed.

" So you *do* remember me ? "

" We get few visitors here," nodding. " I'm not likely to forget one."

" Two," said Richard, as she busied herself at the cup-board.

She turned round presently, her hands full. " Of course I remember your sweetheart."

" She's in London."

" It's a long way. The eggs are ready, sir. I'll just wet the tea. Will you help yourself. It's a terrible long way. Her home there, maybe ? "

" She lives in a flat," replied Richard, scarcely conscious of his reply, his mind a torrent of sudden tumbling thoughts.

" Not alone, sir ? It's not good for a young maid to live alone. Nor for a man. God made them to live together. He made the one for the other. Is the tea to your taste ? "

" Splendid," replied Richard, who now was hardly listening to the old woman's chatter. " Have you a time-table ? "

" A what, sir ? "

" Time-table. For the trains."

" The guide, sir ? The 'bus guide. Now where did I see it last. I'd not be surprised——"

" Isn't that it ? "

" Well, now, if that—— "

" Don't bother ; I'll get it."

Richard turned the pages hurriedly and then looked at his watch. It was twenty minutes to six. Creston Halt was over a mile away and the Melcombe-Paddington express would leave Welling at 5.45. Dammit ! wasn't Creston Halt in ! Here it was. *Creston Halt dep.* 5.50. Could he do it ? He jumped up, pushed half-a-crown into the astonished old woman's palm, and was out of the cottage and running across the field path toward Creston before she had taken in the situation. " And he's only eaten one egg, the silly boy," she said softly. " I'll pop the other two back and hard-boil them. Tom will like them with a bit of cheese for his tea."

Richard stared furiously at what seemed to him the amused indifference upon the face of the porter-station-master at Creston Halt. " Gone ? " he said. He looked at his watch. " It's not five-fifty."

" Gone, zur ; it's paaars' the ten tu, zur."

" There's no other train to London."

" Not to-day, zur."

" To-morrow's no use." Damn the bovine idiot. He'd knock the grin off his chops for two pins. He turned away.

" There is a train—— "

" A train ? Dammit ! I thought you said there wasn't."

" A train, zur, an excursion train. Going up for the foot-ball replay. You know, zur, Salcaster and Cheltenham in London."

" Stopping here ? "

" No, zur ; it's not on this line, but it'll go through Marley Junction about 9.0, and get to London about five in th' morning."

" How far's Marley Junction ? "

" Seventeen mile, zur."

" Good God ! d'you think I can walk seventeen miles in something under three hours."

" No hurry, zur ; I'm closing down here now. I'm going in to Marley after I've had a bit of tea, and tidied up a bit, and put my lad to bed, and seen after the rabbits."

" Aren't you doing any gardening ? " ironically.

" No, zur ; not to-night. The missis is in Marley hospital with a cancer. They've took her breast away. They do say she'll do well now. I'm going in to see her, and I'll take you on behind. If you don't mind waiting in my little place. Perhaps you'll have a drop of tea with the little lad."

" Fine. I'd like nothing better. How do we go ? Horse-back ? "

" No, zur," laughing, " 'orse-*power*, a little two-stroke I've got, but she'll pull us comfortable. Well, I'll just lock up, zur."

At seven o'clock Richard, having done more than justice to a second tea, sat by the fire with little six-year-old Tom Collins on his knee. The youngster, with a shawl over his night-shirt, was heavy with sleep, but he would not sur-render to his desire while this pleasant-voiced stranger continued to tell him wonderful tales. But finally sleep conquered, and while his father clumped noisily overhead, Richard stared down at the flushed face, rumpled hair, and slightly parted lips, of the small sleeper on his lap.

Was that what he would do some day ? he thought. To beget. Was that the meaning of life ? Nothing matters if the race goes on, the line endures, the chain is not broken : was that the beginning and end of truth ? Of love ? Was this all Rachel meant ? All Ann might have meant. Would all his talents, his ambitions, his hurts and his joys come at last to something like this—a small new thing, urgent with life, restless, eager, curious, such as he was only thirty years ago. From generation to generation : was that the riddle of the universe ? Or the key rather. There was no riddle. The boy stirred in his arms, and in sleep tightened the clasp of one arm about Richard's neck.

He stared into the boy's plain little face. Despite himself, distrusting, despising the emotion, he felt strangely drawn to the youngster. He thought of the scriptural phrase : *his bowels yearned over the child*. Good God ! was he to sentimentalise over a pasty faced little brat, who was just as futile and wearying a little jackanapes as all the other pasty faced little brats he had taught during the last twenty years.

He suddenly remembered the letter from his agent, Jackson, that had arrived by the morning's post. He smiled as he thought of the vistas it opened to him. He heard the clumping feet overhead begin to descend the stairs. With a half-sheepish grin he bent his head and kissed the child's forehead.

2

The excursion train with its freight of squeezed, fusty, stiff-jointed, good-humoured, patient sportsmen coughed its way into Paddington at five o'clock.

Rachel's flat was in Maida Vale, less than a mile away. Richard set off to walk. As he passed under one of the station lamps a policeman looked him up and down. Conscious of his old flannels, his crumpled tennis shirt, his tousled hair and unshaven cheeks Richard did not return that appraising stare, but hurried on, half-feeling

in himself the placating abasement of the destitute out-
cast.

A church-clock chimed the quarter as he ran up the
steps of Rachel's flat. He rang and waited. After a few
moments he rang again, a long drawn peal. Presently he
jabbed the button savagely, and kept his finger pressed
against it. He saw a light switch on, heard a door open, the
faint soft pattering of feet, the jarring grind of the bolt.
And then the door was flung wide, and Rachel stood looking
at him, the light behind her shining full on his face.

He put out his hands. " Let me in. Don't say anything.
Don't ask me anything, Rachel." He stumbled into the hall.

" You're earlier than I expected," said Rachel amazingly.

But he was not listening. He was sitting on the small hall-
settee, staring at his rumpled trousers and muddy boots.
His shoulders were drooped and his hands hung down
between his knees.

Rachel closed the door softly and turned to him.
" Wouldn't you like a hot bath ? And some breakfast ? "

Richard looked up. " I should. No breakfast. But I'd
like some tea. I'm sorry I've dragged you out of bed. God !
I'm miserable."

" Don't be silly, Dick. You're tired and dirty. Where on
earth have you been ? Now do go up and bath, and then
come down into the sitting-room and we'll have some
tea. You look half-frozen, too. I'll have the room warm
before you're down. Of course you're miserable at this hour
of the morning wandering about London."

Half an hour later, clean and brushed and warm,
Richard came into the cosy little sitting-room and found
an arm-chair drawn up to the electric radiator, and tea and
cigarettes on a small table beside it. Rachel had drawn up
a couch to the other side of the radiator, and half lay among
the cushions with her feet tucked under her. With her

honey-coloured hair and flushed face thrown into relief by the black satin cushions, and the graceful lines of her body faintly suggested by the dainty wrap she had thrown over her night-clothes, she made a picture that most men would have been quick to appreciate.

Richard did not even look toward her. He sat down, poured himself out a cup of tea, drank it quickly, and lighting a cigarette, leaned back in his chair and stared into the red glow of the radiator.

" Aren't you going to kiss me ? "

He leaned over and switched off the light.

" You needn't turn out the lights to kiss me. There's no one to see."

" I'm not going to kiss you."

" No. Not after that nice hot bath, and the tea *and* the cigarette ? "

" You'd hate it if I did—presently."

" Indeed. And where have you been all the day, Billy boy ? "

" Tramping."

" I thought as much. Have you seen the evening——"

" I couldn't sleep last night. I often can't sleep now. I've come here to tell you why. I——"

" Have you by any chance seen the evening——"

" I've come to ask you to forgive me. I've cheated you, lied to you, deceived you. I've pretended I love you——"

" And you don't ? "

" I do. Rachel, I do love you. I want you. I can't get on without you."

" Is that what you came to say ? It's not new. I thought we were getting married——"

" Rachel, you must listen to me. I'm desperately unhappy. I don't know how to begin, where to begin."

" Let me begin for you. You're in love with Ann Brown."

" Rachel ! " He sat up, putting out one hand toward her. In the dim red light from the radiator she saw his face only as a shadowy blur, but that sudden cry was more revealing than the brightest glare.

" You were one of her lovers. I might have known it. I do know it. I think I always knew it. You poor Dick."

" Rachel, don't. How did you know ? " He came over to her and knelt down by the side of the couch. He put his face beside her on one of the cushions. " I was her lover, Rachel," he said miserably. " I am her lover," desperately, his voice breaking, " I want her——"

" 'Sh Dick. You needn't tell me any more. Not another word till you've answered my question."

" Yes."

" Have you seen last night's evening papers ? "

" What evening papers ? Why ? No, I've seen nothing."

" I thought not. You must be the only man in England who hasn't. You've an incredible half-hour in front of you. Sit still. I'll get you *The Evening Times*."

CHAPTER XXV

. . . the elements
So mixed in him that nature might stand up
And say to all the world : This was a man.

I

Rachel rose from the couch, switched on the light, and left the room. She returned presently with a copy of *The Evening Times* to find that Richard had ensconced himself in her place, and was lying back stretching his legs luxuriously.

" I'm so tired," he said, " I could sleep a week."

" This will wake you up," smiling. " And now I'll leave you to yourself. It's a wretchedly foggy morning, or will be when it *is* morning, and I shall follow your example and have a hot bath. By the time I'm down again you should have finished, and then we'll make tea again and talk it over. Is there anything you want ? Grub ? There's biscuits and cheese and fruit in the sideboard. No. You're all right. Cheerio then."

As the door closed behind her Richard picked up *The Evening Times*. Across the top of the front page ran the heading *The Astounding Hartley Case*. That page was devoted entirely to the evidence given at the inquest, and at the bottom an editorial note said, " Extracts from David Hartley's journal will be found on pages 8, 9 and 10. The leading article, which deals with Hartley's amazing revelations, will be found on page 8."

Richard rapidly scanned the front page, his eye seeking the verdict. When he read that stupefying sentence of fourteen words he sought with a wild haste among the evidence for some explanation. He ran over the evidence of Doctors Rushton and Forde, noting that the wound in Hartley's throat had been responsible for his death, and that the battering of the face had been done with a large flint, which was discovered under the table. His eyes went from the medical evidence to a cross heading on the page which read *Superintendent Allen's evidence*. His glance dropped quickly from line to line in the column and stopped abruptly at the words :

" Superintendent Allen then produced the journal, a two-volume manuscript in red cloth covers, one of which had been torn off and was held together by tape."

There was at this point an editorial parenthesis stating that the text of the journal was on pages 8, 9, and 10.

Without more ado Richard opened the paper at page 8, and began to read that unbelievable revelation.

2

The Journal of David Hartley.—At the request of the coroner Superintendent Allen then read the following extracts and entries.

" It was toward the close of last century [read Allen] that I first became really interested in the many well-authenticated cases of multiple personality. There was Marie Vogler, the French peasant girl, normally a dull, semi-illiterate, and very modest girl, with all the limitations of her class, station and time. Under hypnosis, and at times apparently by her own will, she became at one period a viciously uncontrollable wanton with a spate of rich and fiery speech, at another a grave and ascetic philosopher with an amazing grasp of metaphysics, and again a brilliantly witty woman with extraordinary powers of fascination. There was also the equally interesting case of the Russian boy, Michael Ofstein, who after periods of prolonged sleep acquired entirely new personalities, widely differentiated in mental, moral, and even physical characteristics. There were also a number of Hindu cases, more marvellous, but not too well authenticated.

" It was possibly a second casual reading of Stevenson's *Jekyll and Hyde* while I was staying with Bramson the novelist, at St. Merryn in Cornwall, that really gave me the impetus to begin my investigations. Stevenson merely touched the fringe of the matter. It was obvious that it was not a case of a black and a white, but of an almost infinite gradation of greys between the two absolutes, if one could in fact postulate an absolute black or white.

" While conducting operations upon the brain, and especially in connection with the very interesting case of young Olwen, I had observed that slight injury to the Pons Varolii was followed, far more than in the case of equal injury to either cerebellum or cerebrum, not excluding even the delicate median fissure——" Allen paused here and looked over to the coroner. " The whole of the next three paragraphs, sir, are extraordinarily technical. It would be better if Dr. Rushton——"

" Perhaps Dr. Rushton, who, I understand, has had an opportunity of reading the journal, will give us the gist of that part," suggested the coroner.

" I am afraid," said Dr. Rushton, " I found it a little difficult to follow. There were many marginal emendations. But roughly Mr. Hartley suggested, to put it in plain words, that any change in the actual stuff of the brain completely altered the subject's personality. That is of course common knowledge. But Hartley went on to state that changes in the brain material, either ephemeral or permanent, could make, create indeed, what I can only call an entirely, a fundamentally new person, although actually being but another self of the creator. Further, Hartley claimed that this new person or personality could have a separate existence *physically* from the original person, and that the two separate persons could exist and function separately. Finally he ventures, in this part of the journal, the hypothesis that such changes in the material of the brain might be made by the exercise of the will, with the assistance of drugs to obtain a suitable condition. He emphasises, however, the probable ephemeral quality of these new personalities. I think that covers all the ground in the paragraphs to which Superintendent Allen refers."

Allen then resumed his reading.

"But it was not [the journal went on] until the war, when I had special opportunities for study and experiment, that I made any definite progress. That progress, however, was limited, bridled, shackled indeed, by a foolishly sentimental, but, I fear, ineradicable disinclination to perform upon others the necessary major experiments to prove my varying hypotheses. I am a congenital sentimentalist, and despite years of operating and vivisecting I time and again withheld my hand when, with perfect safety to my subject, I might have achieved success. I was, then eventually driven to use my own body.

"My early successes, however, did nothing to support my main contention that creations, or projections, as I came to call them, could enjoy a separate existence apart from the parent body. I found it a simple matter to change myself, while remaining shut up in my own body.

"But it is necessary now to make abundantly clear what I was aiming at. Briefly, I assumed, as I have already stated, that an infinite gradation of differing personalities dwelt within each human being. These personalities might be given a separate, if brief, existence without any very marked effect upon the parent body.

"But this matter of an infinite gradation was of course unworkable and for convenience I assumed that a normal male—as I have said I had only my own body for experiment—might, without too grave difficulty, be split up into some seven or eight very definite new persons. It was then a matter of choice what these new persons were to be. The fact that I was restricted to a single male is not so grave a handicap as it may appear. It would undoubtedly have added to the interest of the experiments had I had also a normal female to work upon, but a normal male, deriving as he does from male and female, possesses sufficient female characteristics for the purpose.

"It was needful then to make a definite decision as to the number and the characteristics of the projections. Early experiment had assured me that only one projection could exist at a time and must return, be drawn back, before another could be separated.

"For the sake of simplicity I then mapped, as it were, my being into seven separate and distinct personalities, projections, creations. Some of these were male and some female. I used the old standard of good and evil, dividing, in the first instance, my map into two halves, the one good, the other evil. These two halves were each subdivided into male and female. It will therefore be clear that I proposed to project from myself a personality entirely consisting of (using the quaint old standard) male goodness and one entirely consisting of female goodness. There would also be a projection entirely consisting of male evil (badness) and its female counterpart. Further, apart from good and evil, there exists a queer, unreasoning mischievous ape-like personality in all of us. It has no special male or female characteristics ; it is merely a sub-human survival. I proposed to project this. Again, it seemed to me that the whole masculinity, the complete maleness, of myself was a part of me that could be clothed with flesh and projected ; and likewise the whole femininity, the complete femaleness of myself, could also be projected.

"It may be noted here that many of the incidents of my public career were due to experiments upon myself— notably the now notorious sermon which I preached from the pulpit of Cheyne Street Church on Christmas morning 1923.

"It was, however, not until the summer of 1924, which I spent in the south of France, that I evolved the best technique for these projections. It would occupy too much space here even to summarise the varying methods I adopted from time to time and discarded. I reserve all these matters for detailed treatment in book form. Briefly, then, I found that this ordeal (for ordeal it was, a veritable ordeal of creation) was best borne, and gave the best results, if I abstained from meat and fermented drinks for a period of at least three weeks. At the end of the third week I took an ounce of castor oil and fasted completely for forty-eight hours, but drank freely of boiled water. Immediately before the attempted act of projection I took twenty drops of laudanum on a lump of sugar. I then lay down, composing my body, emptying my mind as far as possible, and exerting the whole of my will-power. For, in the last analysis it is a matter of will-power—the rest being mere method, technique.

" In order that I might proceed with my experiments undisturbed I had instructed my agents to find me a fairly large, detached, and isolated house in a quiet part of England. Early in October 1924 they wrote saying that

Denacre Hall, near the Cathedral city of Welling, was in the market, and seemed suitable in every way. They enclosed particulars, and I wired them to purchase immediately. I returned to England at the end of October and took up my quarters at Denacre Hall on December the third. The smallest possible staff was a matter of importance. I should have preferred only one servant, but finally compromised with a manservant, Bates, and a chauffeur, Crowson.

" I had long decided that my first projection should be one of complete male goodness, and during November and December I cut out meat and alcohol and reduced my smoking to a couple of cigarettes a day.

"On December the twenty-first I began a forty-eight hour fast, and at nine on the evening of the twenty-third I lay down on the lounge in my study, took the laudanum and composed myself.

" I lay still, exerting the whole of my will to create, to loosen, to project this personality from myself. The three following hours I can only liken to the experience of child-labour. But these birth-pangs I then suffered were not intermittent. I was racked and wrenched unceasingly until nearly midnight. And then, when under those terrible rending pangs which seemed to me as the worst agonies of dissolution, my resolution was surrendering, the pain ceased, and was followed by a drowsy languorousness indescribably delightful. I lay with my eyes closed. Abruptly my heart began a violent beating, and opening my eyes, I watched emerging from my body, at a point about an inch below the navel, a grey-white substance of much the same appearance as the ectoplasm produced by mediums.

" And presently there stood before me a self of mine, all the good in me incarnate, a living breathing person, a separate entity, a creation. It is almost impossible to describe my sensations at this incredible success. This self of mine was not, in strict truth, a separate and new being, for I found that our thoughts were mutual, and I could follow the interplay of all his emotions and feelings as if I actually experienced them in person. This sharing of thought and feeling, if not perhaps entirely perfect when the projection was parted from me by a considerable distance, always existed to a considerable degree, and enabled me to live in a way a double life—a much more than double life.

" It must not be supposed that I was astounded or stupefied. It must be remembered that here before me in flesh was merely a part of myself. It seemed, in a swift revealing flash, as natural and as commonplace as regarding one's image in a mirror.

"We conversed together. I found clothes and a name for this self of mine. He chose the name himself—Alfred Smith. Without egotism I may say that I found him at first a singularly delightful being. We talked the rest of the night away and made plans for his going out into the world. Physically I felt rather weak, my heart had not slowed down again to normal, and a queer sense of lightness made me slightly dizzy. While my other self was actually moving about I found that the most I could do was to walk slowly. Even this caused palpitation of the heart. Then and afterward I found, especially during the absence of my projections, that from bedroom to study was as much as it was wise to attempt. Otherwise I felt no effects from my ordeal, and mentally was alert and fresh ; and *hungry* seems the best word to describe the desire, the *ache*, for new experience.

" Alfred Smith bore no likeness to me ; he was shorter, frailer, and of different colouring. All the persons that I projected later were similarly unlike me and one another. Only in one or two instances were the eyes alike, and in one instance the eyes were identical with my own."

The coroner here interrupted the reading, requesting Allen to confine himself for the remainder of the reading to actual entries under dates.

"Very well, sir. The dates begin at the top of the next page. The first is December 24, 1924."

"Go on, then, Superintendent."

An editorial parenthesis here stated that lack of space prohibited giving all the dates, but that the most important ones, with Hartley's comments now followed.

"*December* 24, 1924. Alfred Smith left the Hall about dark.

"*December* 25. The brawling in the Cathedral.

"*December* 29. The unpleasant affair at *The Crown*. I then learned that I was vulnerable in my own person to assaults upon the body of my projections, and that I felt, but I am convinced to a lesser degree, pain inflicted upon them. I was not unprepared for this, but I confess that its actual occurrence came as an unpleasant corroboration.

"*December* 30. I decide to recall Smith. This, I feared, was to be an even worse ordeal than his projection and there was of course always the chance that it would be impossible. However, I was agreeably surprised. About midnight, without any of the preparations that preceded the ordeal of his projection, I lay down on the lounge in my study, composed myself, and concentrated my will upon his return. His entrance followed so swiftly upon the heels of endeavour that I was unprepared. Indeed the return was so simple, so painless, so unexpected in its ease and rapidity, that he had re-entered my body ere I was well aware that he was present in the room. He dissolved into me, diffused into me, at the point from which he had issued, without a sound, with no word or gesture of greeting. Only the heap of clothing, mired and wet, upon the carpet remained as evidence of his existence. A flood of strength seemed to pour into me. I felt invigorated in both mind and body, younger, fresher, more alert.

" An extraordinary sense of satisfaction and triumph pervaded me at this swift obedience to my will. It was as well that I could not foresee the bitter experiences that the future held.

" It was, however, curious that I now felt myself less enchanted with the personality of Alfred Smith. To put it bluntly, there had seemed about him a certain priggishness which made me doubt if some small base alloy had not crept into the crucible of his making. But with that, and with like matters in connection with the other of my projections, I must deal in my book.

" *December* 31, 9 p.m. Released the ape—for that is the only term by which I can describe the wanton, mischievous, unruly being I now projected. I clothed, fed and released him. He spoke little, but wandered about my study with destructive curiosity. He was an ugly, crouching, big fellow, and I was glad to see the back of him. He left just before midnight, and I, feeling very debilitated and weak, went to bed, and stayed there for the next three days.

" *January* 1, 1925. The ape's sacrilege in the Cathedral.

" *January* 2, 3, *and* 4. The ape lives up to my name for him. On the evening of the second, I had my first inkling that all was not likely to be well in dealing with such customers. I thought it time to recall him, but at my first attempt I failed completely, and felt so sick and unwell that I was forced to abandon the attempt. The following night I was at last successful, but the fellow set light to the Hall on his return.

" *January* 12. I projected femaleness in the form of an extraordinarily lovely girl. I named her Ann Brown and sent her forth, I must confess, with reluctance. I have rarely——"

Richard put the paper suddenly from him and half rose to his feet. The door opened and Rachel entered. She looked at him, strangely, diffidently. " You've not finished ? "

" Finished ? Good God no ! it's preposterous drivel ! it's——"

" But is it ? Finish it while I make tea. Would you like some toast ? We'll have an early breakfast. It will be light in half an hour."

" I can't finish it, Rachel. You tell me. My head's splitting. I simply can't wade through all those chunks of diary. But," sitting up and staring wildly, " Rachel, you don't seriously mean——"

She held up a hand. " Dick, you're becoming hysterical. It's no use asking me if it's true. It seems that it must be true. If you can't stand reading it I'll tell you the rest. But you, having lived in Welling, know it already. You must guess."

" I suppose I do. So Ann Brown was Hartley. Christ, how disgusting !

" Don't be absurd, Dick. She was a projection from Hartley, a——"

" You seem to have the jargon off pat," bitterly. " And all the story. I suppose this rag omits no spicy detail. I'm sorry, Rachel. God ! " desperately, " what lies it must be. I——"

" Do you want me to go on, Dick ? "

" Why not. Yes. But, as you say, there's not much I can't guess. Please go on. Don't take any notice of my outbursts. I suppose Roy Hartley followed Ann. But there was a real Roy Hartley, for Mason looked his name up."

" Yes. Hartley explains it later in his journal. He says that when Dean Perseval came to lunch that day, and spoke of his children, and their needing a firm hand, he suddenly decided to project a being who should be his complete maleness, and on the spur of the moment he offered him to the Dean, giving the name of Roy Hartley, who actually is his flesh and blood nephew, and is away in Mesopotamia excavating. Hartley trusted to his continued absence to avoid complications."

" H'm. But how did he come to give the rascal so much rope. On his own showing he knew what was happening."

" Yes, but, as you would have seen if you'd had the patience to read on, he found that the Roy Hartley projection struggled against his recall, and for a while struggled successfully. Moreover, Hartley reveals, with increasing clearness as the journal proceeds, that he himself is not the man he was physically, morally, and mentally, but especially morally ; he is a little soiled, a little bedraggled, broken down. He is not altogether unaware of this process of decadence, but apparently thrusts it away, and refuses to face it. Even the May Morrissey fiasco which should have been a danger-signal, he treats with indifference."

" May Morrissey ? She's new to me."

" She only existed for a few moments. Hartley decided, after conquering Roy and forcing him to return (Hartley of course suffered from the wounds in the leg that Roy received from the man Burnett)—where was I ? May Morrissey. Well, she was to be the projection of female goodness. Hartley wrestled for seven hours in pain and sweat to give her being, and then only succeeded in projecting a pale wraith, weak and frail and barely living, which almost immediately returned to him. He had intended to send her as a nurse-companion to the Deanery,

Mrs. Perseval being unwell. Hartley's sense of humour was evidently not at that time entirely destroyed."

" The dove in the eyrie ! Go on."

" Well, Hartley now confesses that he was being irresistibly drawn to the creation of a projection of male evil—he uses the word tiger. It is plain that he was beginning to be afraid that he was finding the control of himself passing away from him. It became at last a struggle between himself—his whole self, and the evil of him. And the evil won, and on the afternoon of last New Year's Eve he released, or it escaped from him, a projection of evil, of male evil—he again refers to it as the tiger."

" So that was the murderer. Do you really——"

" Let me finish, Dick. What that dreadful creature did, you know. The horrible part of it, though, is that once free from Hartley's body, it defied his control. That part of the journal is just heartrending. There's no other word for it."

" But it did return."

" Fear apparently drove it back, or a fellow feeling."

" A fellow feeling ! "

" Well, what else ? Hartley confesses that he ceased to regard its deeds with repugnance. In fact he was beginning to experience a loathsome sense of voluptuous pleasure. The tiger returned to his creator, and struggled with him, battered him, cut his throat, and, of course, died and disappeared with the death of his victim."

" You mean Hartley killed himself."

" I mean just what I've said."

" But, Rachel, do you mean that a coroner's jury of normal everyday Englishmen accepted that farrago of incredibilities."

" You saw their verdict."

" I did. *We find that David Hartley died by the hand of his own evil self.* God ! Rachel ; has the world gone mad ? Are we back again in the dark ages of possession. It simply can't be true."

" What other explanation can you offer for the happenings at Welling ? "

" There *must* be another. If that were possible, why *anything* is possible."

" Yes."

" Even God."

" God was always possible."

" Rachel."

" Yes, Dick."

" Come and sit by me. No, never mind tea. I don't want anything. Switch off the light. It will be daylight soon. I want to talk."

3

" That's right. Sit there. Put your arms round me. I'm tired."

" Are you going to sleep ? I thought you wanted——"

" I know. I can't think. I don't want to think about it. Rachel, don't let me think about it." He turned his face from her, and laid his head on her shoulder. Her arms tightened about him.

" Rachel, will you marry me ? "

" Of course. Wasn't that settled long ago ? "

" But this—it—it makes no difference ? "

" Nothing makes any difference."

He was silent.

She looked over to the window where the pale wintry dawn was beginning to uncover the shapes of the dark cloud-banks heaped above the distant roofs. Her mind went back to her father, so queerly like, so queerly unlike, Dick he seemed in retrospect. She remembered his rages, his boastings, his triumphant posings, his littlenesses, his lovableness. She saw him now clearly, and he seemed to her no more than a small, fickle, wayward boy showing off, bragging, declaiming, pugnacious and truculent. One moment all this, and the next running to a mother for protection, sobbing, crying her name, seeking the shelter of her arms. Was Dick any different ? Was any man different ? And her mother had loved her foolishly posturing father, dying in his arms, and he had come to her, a child of twelve, for comfort. She loved Dick. Women loved men. Her thoughts drifted into a confused catechism of life. Did men understand what women gave them ; forgave them. Did men understand women at all. Or women men. Is every human being a closed book. Are we all, in Kipling's phrase, solitary islands shouting to one another across seas of mis-understanding. Dick loved her, in a way, after his fashion. Was it the fashion of all men. Would there be other Ann Browns in his life. Could any man resist. Did any man want to. Were women, in this as in all other things, much dif-ferent. *Any* different. Were not all human beings alike. Wasn't that what this amazing business of Hartley proved. Capable of anything : the heights and the depths. How could we be closed books then. Except wilfully. Or solitary islands with their seas of misunderstanding.

She turned her glance from the window where the light was broadening fast. She looked down at Dick and sighed. Presently she gave a low laugh and began to run her fingers gently through his hair. He did not move.

" Dick," she said, " I think we're going to be happy. . . . If we don't expect too much."

She bent her head to kiss him and found that he was fast asleep.

THE END

27/20